GHOST VARIATIONS

GHOST VARIATIONS

THE STRANGEST DETECTIVE STORY IN MUSIC

JESSICA DUCHEN

Unbound

This edition first published in 2016

Unbound

6th Floor Mutual House, 70 Conduit Street, London W1S 2GF

www.unbound.com

ISBN (Ebook): 9781783529834

ISBN (Paperback): 9781783529827

Design by Mecob

Cover photographs:

© Malgorzata Maj / Arcangel Images

© Shutterstock.com

A CIP record for this book is available from the British Library

Printed and bound in Great Britain by Clays Ltd, St Ives plc

*For Michael, Laura, Hannah, Ben, Luca, Toby and Tom,
with all my love*

With grateful thanks to my brother, Michael Duchen, through whom I first learned to love the violin

Contents

Jessica Duchen writes for the *Independent* on classical music, opera and ballet, and during the past 25 years has interviewed many of the world's finest musicians. Her first four novels (published by Hodder) have gathered a loyal fan-base and wide acclaim. 'Duchen has a rare talent which is increasingly being recognised,' Gavin Esler, the *Glasgow Herald*.

Jessica grew up in London, read music at Cambridge, also studying piano, and felt torn at first between the prospects of a musical career and a literary one. Having decided to be 'sensible' – perhaps a debatable point – and choose the latter, she held editorial posts on several music magazines before going freelance to concentrate on writing.

Her interest in cross-genre arts finds music playing a vital role in her novels as well as her journalism, and she frequently narrates concert versions of two of them, *Alicia's Gift* and *Hungarian Dances*. She is currently writing an opera libretto for the composer Roxanna Panufnik, a commission from Garsington Opera for 2017.

Her output also includes two plays, biographies of the composers Erich Wolfgang Korngold and Gabriel Fauré (both published by Phaidon) and her popular classical music blog, *JDCMB*.

Jessica lives in London with her violinist husband and their two cats. She enjoys playing the piano, preferably when nobody can hear her, as well as cookery, long walks and plundering second-hand bookshops for out-of-print musical gems.

The following people helped to make this book possible by sponsoring a character.

Jelly d'Arányi is kindly sponsored by Irmina Trynkos

Donald Francis Tovey is kindly sponsored by Steven Isserlis

Myra Hess is kindly sponsored by the Jersey Liberation International Music Festival

Dear Reader,

The book you are holding came about in a rather different way to most others. It was funded directly by readers through a new website: Unbound.

Unbound is the creation of three writers. We started the company because we believed there had to be a better deal for both writers and readers. On the Unbound website, authors share the ideas for the books they want to write directly with readers. If enough of you support the book by pledging for it in advance, we produce a beautifully bound special subscribers' edition and distribute a regular edition and e-book wherever books are sold, in shops and online.

This new way of publishing is actually a very old idea (Samuel Johnson funded his dictionary this way). We're just using the internet to build each writer a network of patrons. Here, at the front and back of this book, you'll find the names of all the people who made it happen.

If you're not yet a subscriber, we hope that you'll want to join our publishing revolution and have your name listed in one of our books in the future. To get you started, here is a £5 discount on your first pledge. Just visit unbound.com, make your pledge and type ghostvaria in the promo code box when you check out.

Thank you for your support,

Dan, Justin and John
Founders, Unbound

Harold Gray
Anthony Hacking
Kulvinder Hambleton-Grey
Mary Hamer
Nigel Hamway
Laszlo Harkanyi
Julian Haylock
Rustem Hayroudinoff
Anthony Hewitt
Amanda Hurton
Steven Isserlis
Nani Jansen
Guy Johnston
Dan Kieran
Judith Knott
Horst Kolodziej
Piers Lane
Jane and George Little
Harriet Mackenzie
Roxanna Macklow-Smith
Samuel Magill
Ben Mandelson
Dr. Marion Gedney
Paul Maskell
Hugh Mather
Murray McLachlan
Viv McLean
Alice McVeigh
Zamira Menuhin Benthall
James Mews
John Mitchinson
Francis Norton
Nadia Ostacchini
Lewis Owens
Lev Parikian
Norman Perryman

Sarah Playfair
Justin Pollard
Catherine Rogers
Andrew Rose
Tomoyuki Sawado
Seb Scotney
Margaret Semple
Sue Shorter
Mary Sigmond
Steven Spooner
Eleanor Stanier
Gillian Stern
Clare Stevens
Tot Taylor
Madelyn Travis
Irmina Trynkos
Robin Tyson
Liubov Ulybysheva
Angelo Villani
Marion von Hofacker
Jo W
Ricki Wagner
Helen Wallace

Prologue

16 February 1938

She stood at the side of the stage, invisible to the audience; violin in one hand, bow in the other, her eyes half closed against the brightness above. A thrum of expectation was reaching her from the gathered listeners in the auditorium. Outside, in Regent Street, snow had been falling when she arrived; now it felt like a benediction. Her dress was white and silver, bright and pure, as if she were taking her first communion.

This concert would be unlike any other she had given. During one concerto by a composer of genius, a piece nobody here had heard before, she must prove that every note she had played, every letter she had written, every pain she had battled, was worthwhile for its sake. Half an hour to learn whether she was still herself, still strong after the past years' turmoil; still there to command the concert platform that used to be her true home. Alone, inward, she summoned one spirit, and prayed for his blessing. 'In art alone,' she remembered, 'we find salvation.'

'Ready, Jelly?' Adrian was beside her, calm on the outside but, who knows, perhaps as tumult-ridden within as she felt.

'Ready.'

He stood aside to let her walk on stage first. She crossed herself, then stepped forward into the light.

Part I

1933–1934

Part I

Chapter 1

Jelly d'Arányi's assistant, Anna Robertson, seemed to enjoy keeping her employer's feet attached in some small way to the earth. By the time their Eastbourne hosts called them downstairs for drinks, a frost was forming on Anna's bedroom window; Jelly, though, had dressed for dinner in a crimson evening gown with a fashionable, deep-scooped back that exposed her shoulder blades. She had spent enough of her childhood in the 19th century to cherish a lingering nostalgia for its flamboyance and poetry.

'Jelly, you'll catch your death,' Anna protested. She preferred a plain skirt, court shoes and cardigan; tonight it was buttoned up to her chin. Suffering from a chronic cough and a slight fever, she had been asleep for two hours while Jelly was practising. Last night Jelly had performed the Brahms Violin Concerto in nearby Hastings; today she could not rest. Another concert ahead meant more music to prepare.Jelly was pleased to see Anna looking a little brighter. 'Darling, don't worry about me. I just want you to feel better.'

The dining room was warm, the fire smouldering in its grate beneath the mantelpiece. There a silver frame held a photograph of the Southerns' two sons, who had both fought at Mons in 1914. One body was never returned; the other boy came back with an uncontrollable twitch of the head and neck, unable to speak. After two months in a nursing home, he disappeared one night. Trawling a nearby lake for evidence, they discovered he had found peace at last in its waters.

The windowpanes multiplied Jelly's slender image skimming across the lamplit hallway, the gleam catching her necklace – a gift from a long-ago admirer. Ten or fifteen years previously, scarcely a day would pass without a delivery boy on a bicycle bringing flowers, a parcel or an invitation to a dance – and Jelly

loved dancing. Many weeks, what with concerts, salons and dinner parties, she'd seen in the dawn three or four times. This year
at the end of May she would be 40. Part of her still felt no older
than she was in 1916, on the day before she heard that Frederick
Septimus Kelly was dead.

'Jelly d'Arányi!' Charles welcomed her with a mock-
ceremonial bow as she swept in. 'There she is. Muse to Bartók,
Ravel and Elgar, angel to Vaughan Williams and Holst, and no
wonder. You look positively scrumptious.'

'And I'm a deeply grateful guest, as ever. I don't know how
many years I've been staying with you after concerts now.'

'I've lost count, and the more it is, the happier we shall be.'

She gave him a kiss. He returned it, twice – then turned to
Anna and pressed her hand to his lips, perhaps so that she would
not feel left out.

'Charlie, dear, are you flirting again?' His wife, Mary, gave
a tut that Jelly judged only semi-serious. 'Why don't you pour
Jelly and Anna a nice glass of sherry? Goodness knows they've
earned one.'

After they had eaten and the maid had cleared the plates, Charles
sat back, a crystal decanter in front of him. 'So, ladies, what's after
port? Cards? Charades?'

'We could have a good session, as there are four of us,' Mary
suggested. 'It's always better with more people.'

Anna and Jelly exchanged glances. 'Mary likes to play the
glass game,' Jelly explained.

'Load of rubbish, but if Mary gets a kick out of it I don't
mind,' Charles declared. 'Who knows, these supposed spirits
might even tell us something useful this time. What shares we
ought to buy, or how the economy is ever going to get out of
this damnable hole.'

'Don't swear, dear,' said Mary. 'Jelly, Anna, will you play?'

They both hesitated, Jelly fidgeting with the cross at her throat. 'I've always felt it's just... not quite right,' she said.

'I find it too scary,' Anna admitted. 'Adila sometimes wants me to join in, but I don't dare.'

'But what harm can it do?' Mary cajoled. 'It's only the glass game, not a séance. We're not spiritualists – anything but – and there's no ectoplasm or ghosts appearing to worry about. Why not join us, just this once?'

'Do humour her, dear Jelly,' said Charles. 'Otherwise I'll be in for a double session tomorrow.'

Jelly looked from Charles to Mary, and at Anna, who gave an almost imperceptible shrug. 'Just a few minutes, perhaps,' she said. It seemed the polite solution.

'We can stop whenever you like,' said Mary. She beamed at Jelly, then drew the curtains, closing out the world. Opening a drawer in her bureau she brought out a well-used Ouija board, its black print fading towards sepia. The letters of the alphabet were marked on it in a wide semi-circle of two rows, the numbers up to nine – plus zero – in one row beneath, as well as the words 'Yes' on one side, 'No' on the other and 'Goodbye' at the bottom. This she placed in the centre of the table, with a small planchette pointer on top. Finally she extinguished the lamp and lit one candle; dim lighting would aid concentration. In the glow of its flame, Jelly saw the faces of her companions turned to gold, while their surroundings melted into the darkness.

They took their seats, two on each side of the table.

'Very gently,' Mary instructed. 'Everyone rest one finger on the pointer. Whatever happens, don't push. Let *them* move it as they wish. I'll ask the questions.'

For a while the pointer stayed immobile. Then beneath their fingers it gave the slightest shudder.

'Is there anybody of friendly intent who would like to talk to us?' Mary intoned. And as they watched, the pointer began to slide over the board towards the letter N.

'Are you doing that?' Jelly mouthed at Anna.

'No! It's just… moving on its own. How on earth… ?'

'Mary, it's you!' Charles accused.

'No, it is *not*. Hush, please.' Mary was officious, noting down the letters 'N-O-T-Q-I-T-E'.

'That's ridiculous,' Charles said. 'If there's nobody there, how can there be someone to say "Not quite"?'

'Sometimes I am not quite here either,' Jelly tried to joke.

'They're having fun with us, so let's have some fun with them, or whoever is moving the pointer this time. Let's ask some real questions. The stock markets. Volatile as hell. So will the Dow Jones move up or down tomorrow?'

The pointer spun from letter to letter: F-T-S-C-V. 'Gibberish,' said Mary. 'Let's keep on.'

Jelly was indeed not quite there. A wall of tiredness had come upon her – the inevitable delayed reaction after the post-concert euphoria. She half followed the pointer beneath their fingers, with scant concern for the outcome.

The arrow glided to the letter A, then in succession to D-I-L-A. Jelly's stomach gave a flip. '*Adila?*' she said.

Jelly's sister Adila was, according to her friend, Baron Erik Palmstierna, a psychic 'sensitive'. For her, messages would come through unusually clearly and at considerable length, often whirling the glass along at high speed, in English, French, German or even perfect, grammatical Hungarian. News of Adila's gift spread rapidly through those circles that interested themselves in 'psychical research'. She would interpret the incoming messages while a minute-taker – sometimes her husband, but more usually Erik, who was the Swedish minister to London – transcribed them, one letter at a time. Jelly, living with Adila and her family, usually managed to avoid these sessions, finding them most uncomfortable when the messages made sense. Ill at ease with Erik, she would have preferred her sister's talent to be restricted to the violin.

'What's Adila got to do with the stock market?' Charles demanded.

The pointer chuntered on, letter by tortuous letter.

'It seems to say something along the lines of "Adila is playing beautifully at this moment",' Mary declared, reading back her transcript. 'Jelly, is she?'

'No, no, *no*,' Jelly insisted. 'She has a concert today, but it was this afternoon, not this evening. You see? This is just a silly game!'

'Don't call them names,' Mary said. 'They don't like it.'

The pointer bowled off again, faster. The letters spelled 'Gad you'.

'Glad? Who is it you are glad to see?' said Mary. 'Is it Jelly?'

The arrow meandered towards 'Yes'.

Jelly pulled her hand away as if from spilled acid. 'I'm sorry, I'm not happy doing this. I'll go to bed now, if you will please forgive me.'

'I will, too, if that's all right,' Anna said quickly.

'But – ' Mary hesitated. Jelly seized the opportunity to throw her arms around the Southerns in turn, to bid them goodnight and to thank them profusely for taking such good care of her and her ailing assistant.

'Now the mystery will remain,' Charles said, as she made for the stairs. 'Who knows what message might be waiting in heaven for Jelly d'Arányi?'

Anna paused on the landing.

'Do you really believe in that glass game, Jelly?' she asked.

Under her discomfort, Jelly pondered. 'To be perfectly honest, no. And you?'

'It's not that I don't believe in God. But I don't think I believe in this as well.'

'Good. Let's get some sleep.' Jelly kissed her assistant on both cheeks, then retreated to her guest room and welcome solitude. Was it not simply wrong to disrupt the heaven-set boundaries of our living dimension, and wrong to disturb the dead, even if they sometimes seemed willing to be disturbed? Supposing the spirits were not who they claimed to be, but demons waiting to misguide or destroy you? And if a spirit was communicating – in truth – how was she supposed to accept such a notion? How was anyone?

She had grown extra-resistant to the glass game since a message arrived purporting to be for her from Sep Kelly. If Sep wanted to speak to her from beyond the grave, she didn't want to know. It would not bring him back. Besides, she couldn't bear to imagine his bullish and uncompromising Australian spirit buzzing around someone's dining table like an invisible mosquito. Sep had been blown up in the Battle of the Somme. If he were still present, if he loved her after all, precious little good it could do them now.

At first, in the aftermath of the war, she added her tears to the outpourings of grief among her equally bereaved friends; for a time, they yearned to attempt reunion through any means there might be, glass or otherwise. With the passing years, the futility of it began to creep up on them; life grew harder and bodies older, but nothing would bring back the departed. Now, trying in vain to sleep, Jelly was wishing she had gone straight home.

Jelly, Adila, Adila's American-Greek husband Alec Fachiri, their little girl Adrienne and their yappy fox terrier named Caesar lived on a Chelsea cul-de-sac – off the Fulham Road by St Stephen's Hospital and what used to be the workhouse – in a graceful Victorian villa with a fake Italian bell-tower and tripartite windows. From within, the sky appeared to divide into three like a Renaissance altarpiece. Their friends dubbed the place Hurricane House: you'd understand why as soon as you went in and faced the piles of books, magazines and sheet music, along with the ornaments spilling off the shelves – vases, tea sets, photographs, Hungarian dolls, Dresden china figurines, musical boxes that no longer worked. And the sound of instruments being practised simultaneously in different rooms would blend now and then with the chime of clocks that never struck together. Here, Jelly felt as much at home as she could anywhere, now that their parents were dead.

The three sisters and their mother, Antoinette, arrived in Britain when Jelly was 16, bringing with them little more than talent, charm, the good name of their great-uncle Joseph Joachim, and a handful of concert dates in Haslemere. Jelly still remembered Wesselényi Street in Budapest where she spent her childhood: a dark chimney of a road, snaking into town just behind the Great Synagogue of Dohány Street. How precarious life there must have been, and with what care their mother had concealed this; Jelly had been aware that times were growing tougher, with no idea why, and if Antoinette had had her own reasons for wanting to leave her husband behind, she kept them to herself. These days Jelly sometimes wondered what had passed between them, how much her mother had had in the bank, if anything, and whether the concerts that she and Adila gave with their pianist sister Hortense had been out of volition or out of necessity. It was too late to ask.

She could not pass the former workhouse without imagining how it must have felt to be its inmate. Though she earned well, relatively speaking, for her performances and recordings, she knew she would have commanded still higher fees had she been a man and that her imminent 40th birthday, had she been a man, would be seen as the start of her prime, not the end of it. Once she had dreamed about having her own house, but those earnings were not what they were ten years ago, before the Depression, and Adila and Alec would not hear of her leaving them in any case. Still, she was well aware that she remained an unpaying guest in their home – in her darker moments, perhaps a 'maiden aunt'. Joking about her nomadic concert life, declaring, 'I'm a Gypsy,' she could never quite escape the sensation of glassy surfaces under her feet: slippery to walk on, easy to shatter.

It was nearly lunchtime when Jelly arrived home from Eastbourne via Victoria Station. On the steps in her old mink coat, juggling suitcase, violin case, handbag and keys, and listening with delight to Caesar's piercing welcome-home bark, she caught a glimpse of Mrs Garrett next door, slipping away from an upstairs window. The Garretts did not consider the foreigners at No. 10 entirely suitable people, especially not Jelly, whom they knew was unwed, went on the stage, sponged off her brother-in-law and kept peculiar hours. Jelly smiled and waved. Then came the skittering of Adrienne's feet on the hall floor and her little niece hurtled out into her arms. 'Auntie Jeje!'

'Hush, sweetheart, you'll scare the neighbours,' Jelly laughed, dropping everything and lifting her to cover her face with kisses. 'Oof, what a big girl you are.' Adrienne gave a giggle, smoothing her cheek against the fur of her aunt's coat. Caesar charged through the doorway a second later, slobbering with joy all over Jelly's stockings.

'Ach, *Sai* darling, you're home. Today, I know, there will be a miracle!' Adila stumped out in her house slippers, calling Jelly by her family nickname – pronounced 'shy'. Her hair stood out in intense curls around her head. To judge from her look, she had surfaced within the hour.

Jelly put down Adrienne and the sisters swamped each other with hugs and greetings, Adila's preternaturally dusky. She insisted that when she'd had diphtheria, aged nine, it had affected her voice, pushing it down to the tenor register. 'Tenor?' Alec would joke. '*Baritone*, my dear.' He always insisted he'd fallen in love first with her voice – it resembled his chosen instrument, the cello.

'You've obviously been up for hours,' Jelly teased her.

'We had a late dinner after the concert.' Adila pushed the door open to usher everyone inside. 'I made *boeuf bourguignon*. Apron over concert dress, musician to mama in moments, and we danced until two. We missed you, darling – the dancing is never so good without you.'

'Last night? But Adi... What time was your concert?'

'So, everyone arrived about 7 for drinks, we began at 7.30, the singer and the pianist did the first half, I did second half with... Sai, have you seen a ghost?'

Jelly's guts were twisting into a knot out of all proportion to yesterday evening's minuscule significance. 'It wasn't in the afternoon?'

Adila raised an eyebrow. 'Why?'

'Nothing, nothing... ' She changed the subject, fast. 'Did you hear what happened to me in Hastings? The local conductor had appendicitis, so guess who conducted instead? Adrian Boult!' She gave a gurgle of laughter. 'I know it's not funny really, but I was *so* pleased to see him.'

'He is the best of them all.' Adila scooped Adrienne up into her arms. 'Adri, darling poppet, come along. Auntie Jeje has to unpack. Let's take Caesar to the park.'

In Jelly's room, above the studio extension, a music stand perched between a silver-gilded writing table in the corner and antique wardrobes crammed with concert gowns, cloaks, coats, hats and a rickety tower of Chinese silk boxes containing ostrich-feather fans – mostly broken now – that she and Adila had collected as girls. While Jelly emptied the suitcase in her usual post-tour routine and chattered with Maria, Adila's new maid, she fought to regain her equilibrium.

It was a normal weekday, normal as can be. Adila's husband Alec was at his chambers in the Inner Temple. The house's sounds were pattering about in their usual sequences of cleaning and, as far as possible, tidying; a piano tuner had arrived to attend to the Bechstein in the music room; and from the window she spotted her sister and niece in their hats and coats making their way up the road, Caesar on his leash padding beside them. Everything was normal. Soon she'd forget about Eastbourne, the Southerns and that smallest yet most uncomfortable of coincidences.

Chapter 2

Even if Jelly did not forget, she allowed her incoming tide of concerts, practising and travel on slow trains and wave-buffeted ferries to submerge the incident. Until, that is, she and Adila found themselves at odds over a party that Baron Erik Palmstierna was holding at his Swedish ambassadorial residence on Portland Place. There'd be dignitaries galore and members of the Society for Psychical Research, too – occasionally one and the same.

'I don't think I can go,' Jelly told Adila. 'I have too much work to do.'

'I may have to stay home and work as well,' said Alec. The women of the house sometimes forgot how demanding his job was, so discreet was he about it.

'Fine,' said Adila, 'then don't go. But I shall be there to support Erik.'

'I hope he hasn't asked you to *play*, Adi?'

'Darling, he has not, but of course I shall play if they want me to. A little Bach, perhaps.' Nothing would deflect her. 'It would be quite wrong not to go.'

'Yes, given the amount of time you spend with him,' said Jelly. The comment was as barbed as she was capable of being.

'It will be worthwhile soon, even to you,' Adila growled.

'But these drives... what are you *doing*?' Jelly said, then regretted it, lest her sister misinterpret this as a different kind of suspicion. Perhaps part of it was. At the notion that Adila might ever part company with Alec, Jelly's slippery surfaces began to tip under her feet.

'We talk about the questions we should ask,' said Adila. 'Then we go back to the glass and we ask them. You're welcome to join us. But no, you don't believe in it... so don't be a Caesar in the manger.'

On any quietish Sunday when they were at home, after they had been to Mass and enjoyed a family lunch, the stocky and dapper figure of Erik Palmstierna would materialise outside in his car. If the day were fine, he and Adila would go for a drive – Erik loved driving, the faster the better; she would trot out to meet him in a flurry of hat, fur and bead necklaces, as eager as a young girl on a first date. Later they would have a session with the glass, for which Alec might or might not join them. Jelly was always relieved when Adila's musical commitments interfered with the baron's plans, for her sister's career as violinist remained almost as busy as her own.

Adila refused to accept Jelly's resistance to their 'psychical research', eager to point out that concern with the esoteric was part and parcel of artistic life, whether in the form of spiritualism, Theosophy or both. Jelly knew by heart the decades-long list of Theosophically inclined artists: Alexander Scriabin, Paul Gauguin, Charles Rennie Mackintosh, D.H. Lawrence, Khalil Gibran, Gustav Holst, for a start. 'And I need hardly mention the Yeatses,' Adila added. 'But it's so simple. It's the heart of religion, without the mumbo-jumbo.'

Jelly did not see why, just because it was fashionable, just because Willy Yeats was involved along with his wife 'George' – one of her dearest friends – that meant she should be too. She had read, many times, pamphlets declaring that Theosophy, or Ageless Wisdom, represented the unifying thread behind all the world's religions: the same truth illuminating the various beliefs, rituals, symbols and myths. That was already quite enough mumbo-jumbo for her. She hated arguments, and she knew Adila would never budge. Therefore she would kiss her sister and let her win.

Feeling mortified, she began a hunt in her room: somewhere she was sure she had a photograph of herself and George in their twenties, glowing with joy at the top of Garsington's sloping lawn, Jelly with hair plaited and coiled around her ears, George with a long dress and a cascade of loosened tresses.

Together, post war, they had made up their minds: in art alone one finds salvation. Her cupboards held box upon box of old letters, postcards, concert programmes and photos, but the one she wanted now was eluding her.

She felt a tug of loneliness; George, Willy and their children had moved away to Dublin. 'Without you,' she said to an imagined George, 'none of this would be happening. Why did you have to introduce us to Erik?' George used to participate enthusiastically in the esoteric practices of salons like Eva Fowler's, those regular gatherings at which the literary met the musical, the artists met the patrons, the curious met those who intrigued them, and the glass game and table-tapping were as likely pastimes as listening to a poetry recitation or a performance by Jelly, Adila and their friends. Jelly remembered George explaining the 'automatic writing' from 'messengers' that she insisted she'd learned to channel in order to fuel her husband's creativity. No wonder she and Erik became friends when he arrived in London as envoy. Jelly could still hear George's voice across party chatter – 'Sai! Adi! Come and meet this wonderful man… ' Moments later Erik's bright gaze was locked with Adila's, and Jelly, to whom most men gravitated, turned away to find another drink, sensing her own superfluity. Perhaps because George was her friend, Erik's implantation in their life seemed her own fault.

A blackbird was singing on the window ledge. Jelly slid open the casement and, making birdish noises, reached out a finger. The creature stared at her, head tilted, before springing away into the air. Jelly decided to escape the house by walking Caesar in Battersea Park, where she could look at a new sonata. She enjoyed learning music by reading the score in the sunlight, under the trees. Once a piece was in her head, it was easier to transfer it later to the violin.

She was fastening Caesar's lead when the telephone rang. Anna answered it in the study. 'Jelly, come quick – it's Tom Spring Rice, he's in Dublin.'

Jelly experienced a brief rip in the fabric of time, along with an immediate awareness that something was wrong. She flew up the stairs; Anna tactfully left her to talk alone.

'Tom? Darling! How are you? What are you doing phoning all the way from Ireland? When can we see you?'

'Ah, Jelly, you never change. Still the warmest welcome in all of England.' Tom's voice sounded different – not that she had spoken to him for several weeks, but she knew his tone almost as well as she had once known Sep Kelly's.

Tom could have become a professional pianist, had he tried, or so Jelly thought. Like Sep, he won a music scholarship at Balliol College, Oxford; like Sep, too, he had lessons with Donald Francis Tovey, the d'Arányis' oldest friend in Britain. Still, it wasn't easy to be a musician if you also had to please your family. Tom neither expected nor wanted to inherit the baronetcy in Ireland, but when it happened he went obediently into the diplomatic corps. There, he'd been as lucky as a tomcat, landing on his paws: when the Twenties were about to start roaring, he was posted to Paris.

Jelly remembered his apartment in the rue de Seine: sunshine on the glass, the smell of fresh baking from the patisserie across the street, and waiting for her on Tom's piano, her black tango shoes with red heels. Her circle had vested interests in living as hard as they could, trying to swamp with fresh sensations the involuntary flashbacks to roaring guns or the arrival home of loved ones' books from the trenches, their torn pages splattered with mud or worse.

This time, though, Tom sounded distant: a reed of a voice, echoing from another world.

'I've got some news, Jelly – '

'– and what are you doing in Ireland?'

'Sai, do please listen.'

Tom began to explain. He had been very ill in hospital. Now he had decided to resign his post and return to County Kerry. Sometime, he didn't know when, he would probably have to go into a nursing home. And that would be the end.

'I'm sorry.' Tom's dear, warm tenor cracked slightly. 'There was so much I wanted to say to you... things I wanted to tell you and ask you... but now there doesn't seem to be very much point.'

Jelly couldn't get her breath. If only she could rewind time to five minutes earlier when there was no phone call, when she thought Tom was perfectly well. 'But there must be something someone can do? Have you been to Harley Street? You must see the *best* specialists.'

'I've seen them, my darling.'

'A second opinion. A third. A fourth! You must try everything. I'll help you, I won't rest until we find someone who can make you better.'

'It's too late, Jelly. An operation or two might give me longer, but ultimately there's nothing to stop it.'

'But what is "it"?' Something secret, silent, of which nobody dared speak? If this were the same 'it' that had destroyed her mother, eating away at her until only morphine could ease the pain and only death could end it –

'It is what you probably think it is,' he said, sounding perfectly good-humoured.

'But you are too young to die!' Jelly cried out.

'I'm 50 – hardly your average spring chicken. Besides, nobody is *ever* too young to die... Look, I've been lucky. I've had a wonderful life, wonderful friends – and wonderful you – and on balance I prefer the idea of a short life, but a fine one. Who wants a life that's long but horrible?'

Jelly was weeping onto a pile of unopened post. 'How... how long did they... ?'

'I may be all right for a while, especially if I go for the surgery. I may see this Christmas, but as for the one after, who can say... '

His equanimity astounded her. 'When can I see you?'

'If there's any time you could come to Ireland... I'm afraid

I'm unlikely to be up to the crossing. And if you do... well, I can't promise to be the best company.'

Jelly grabbed the diary out of Anna's top drawer. Her spring was chock-full of concerts, all over the country – Torquay, Oxford, Bournemouth, the Wigmore Hall – and in a horrible irony she had to go to Belfast, but needed to come straight home the next day. Some musicians, Jelly knew, would cancel concerts with impunity. She never had. People invest time and effort in going to listen to you; you can't let them down. 'There *has* to be a time.'

'Jelly... it's all right, you know.'

A pause. She knew what he was trying to tell her: if she went, she would be going to say goodbye.

She'd never said goodbye to Sep. He vanished back to France when his leave was over, and that was that.

'Listen... ' he said. 'Please don't feel you have any obligation towards me. I've never wanted to hold you back. Certainly not now. You understand?'

She could scarcely say that perhaps he could have tried harder to hold her back. That it wasn't fair that she should have to endure him dying as well as Sep and her parents and too many friends, and that he was not only too young to die, but too good, too kind. And that to break off now what little there was between them would compound the unendurable with the inexplicable. 'Isn't there something I can do?' she pleaded, skirting the issue. 'Anything I can send you, anything that will help, even just a little bit?'

'Yes,' he said, after a moment's thought. 'Jelly, dearest girl, will you promise me one thing? Whatever happens – don't change. Stay true to yourself, no matter what it takes. You are the best, brightest star in my firmament, you know that.'

'And you in mine... ' Their relationship was not really a relationship; it was a friendship blended with a might-have-been. Yet now that it must end, the lack of fulfilment hit home.

'You couldn't belong to me,' he said. 'You belong to your

music. You have so much to give, so much love and joy for everyone who hears you. Don't be distracted. It's your true purpose and it will make you immortal. And then I can die happy, knowing you will, in a manner of speaking, live for ever. That's all I want, my dear.'

Anna looked round the door, but stopped short, seeing Jelly in tears.

Jelly put down the phone. 'Tom's dying,' she said.

Jelly knew that without Adila, Alec and little Adrienne, and Anna too, she'd be adrift in a hostile ocean, holding on to one tiny plank of violin to stay afloat. It was ten years since her mother had died; her father, left behind in Budapest decades ago, was a more recent, still seismic loss. The friends to whom she could turn in difficult times were at some distance. Donald Tovey lived partly in Norfolk, partly in Edinburgh; Myra Hess, her pianist duo partner, was in St John's Wood, but spent months every year on tour in America; George was, of course, in Dublin.

The grief assailing Jelly now was not something she would choose to inflict on any of them.

'You should have married him while you could,' said Adila unhelpfully, clasping Jelly to her jewel-clad bosom. 'Shall I not go to the party? You shouldn't be alone tonight.'

'No, you must go. Please, Adi. He's still alive, so there's still hope. There *has* to be hope.'

'I'm here,' Alec said, attentive and concerned. He would be busy, of course; his legal paperwork was interminable now there was anxiety that Japan might leave the League of Nations. He told his family little about his work, especially that for the League – partly because he was not supposed to talk about it. If Adila or Jelly pressed him for news, he would keep it brief, for instance explaining only that the new government in Germany was not well liked.

'I'll look after her,' Anna promised. 'Jelly, why don't we go out to eat, just the two of us?'

Around 8, they drove to Soho for dinner at Kettner's, Jelly's favourite restaurant; the oak panelling and slender staircases reassured her with their very familiarity. They picked a table by a generous window that gave them a vantage point overlooking Romilly Street, then ordered cocktails as a treat. Jelly distracted herself by telling Anna about dining here with Maurice Ravel, chattering in French, enjoying champagne and feeling somewhat underdressed, so elegantly attired was he; and about the night, after a concert and the ensuing party, when she'd ended up playing Ravel all the Gypsy music she remembered from Budapest. Soon afterwards, he'd told her he was writing her a new piece, provisionally called *Tzigane*.

'So, I say I'll play his piece,' Jelly said, gulping her White Lady, 'and he says "*wohn*derful, you must give the premiere at the Wigmore Hall!" And the premiere is booked, and the seats are sold. But where's my piece? You know when he sends it to me? Three days before the concert. *Three days*, can you imagine?'

'Yes, Jelly.' Anna had heard the story at least 20 times, possibly 200.

Tzigane sounded desperately difficult. Ravel had been far from sure it was playable, despite giving Jelly only 72 hours to perfect it. 'It's not so hard once you know it,' Jelly said. 'But I *didn't*!'

Normally at this point she would laugh. Yet tonight the fragility of that experience seemed not silly, but alarming. Supposing she hadn't succeeded? Supposing she had messed up the world premiere of *Tzigane*? Ravel wouldn't have been blamed; she would. The critics might not know what to make of the piece, but they'd have recognised second-rate violin playing. What a precipice she had lived on without even noticing. How much she took for granted – had she learned nothing from losing Sep?

'Jelly, why didn't you marry Tom?' asked Anna. 'I think you love him – or you did once?'

'Darling, of course I love him. I love *everyone*.' The tears in Jelly's eyes made a fairground mirror distortion of Anna's face. 'There's no point thinking about it, not now.'

Supposing she'd married him after all, ten, fifteen years ago, and they'd had a little Adrienne of their own, or several? She'd have had to stop playing professionally. She'd have been Lady Monteagle, wife of a diplomat, an aristocrat. She'd be seen as a strange person with bizarre Hungarian origins, the daughter of a policeman, a woman who once upon a time used to be a famous musician – how shocking in those circles. Everything she had worked for would have been worthless. And after he was gone their children would have spent the rest of their lives missing him…

'Jelly!' Anna passed her a handkerchief. 'Hush now! Your imagination's running wild.'

'But you know I'm right. It's not possible to be a female musician and be married. It simply *is not*. Except for Adi, of course, but she's an exception, and Alec's an exceptional husband, letting her keep playing.'

'But… ' Anna was holding a forkful of baked fish and gratin dauphinois poised between plate and mouth. 'Don't you *want* to be married someday, Jelly?'

'Why, darling? You do, don't you?'

'Well… I think it's natural to want a home, children, security… '

Jelly paused. With Anna in the mood for domestic yearning, which was fair enough for any girl her age, she didn't want to reveal the image that the word 'marriage' usually conjured for her: a goose-down pillow pressed over the nose and mouth. But to lose Tom… She could still see, too, the possibility she had sacrificed.

'Since Sep, I just… have had other things I wanted to do,' she said aloud. 'And you see, I *have* a home, and a child – she's my niece, but I couldn't love her more if she were my own daughter.'

Walking back to the car, Jelly felt weighed down, more by anxiety than by good food. 'You know, I never ate much when we were young,' she confessed, to entertain Anna. 'My father used to tell me I was the ugly one of the three of us. Perhaps I was afraid I'd be even uglier if I put on weight.'

'Oh Jelly, that's awful. You're so gorgeous!'

'Maybe I was at your age… ' Jelly smiled, keeping at bay the awareness of her looming big birthday. 'It's very funny, really. He used to say I was the ugliest and the best of his daughters. And I always thought that if I believed one part of that, I had to believe the other as well.'

Over central London a crescent moon dangled, seeping out silver. The theatres had not yet finished, so the pavements of Soho were quiet except for a few dark-coated figures walking dogs under the street lamps, which were dimmer than those in surrounding areas because the wattage here was three times lower. Inside the little restaurants, lively with the staff's Italian and Greek banter, diners were finishing meals and enjoying a smoke over coffee or brandy. Jelly caught snippets of conversation, plus the tip-tip of high heels and walking sticks against the paving stones.

Tables stood empty, though. Shops she remembered had gone out of business, several nightclubs too, since the Depression had hit the capital; wooden boards, nailed at random angles, barred windows and doors. In the shadows, along the side streets, another type of woman still waited and hoped. 'There's still a demand for *that* in a depression,' Anna remarked as they passed, trying not to stare at exposed shoulders, lacy stockings or the excessive make-up designed to hide the ravages life left on these women's faces. Jelly felt sorry for them. Some of her friends had no patience for that sympathy, but she was convinced nobody would take such a path except out of dire need. Few women had the mix of education, determination and good fortune that could lead them into careers. If their families lacked money, or gambled or drank it away, if they had no job, if they were not fortunate enough to marry, what alternative was there? And there would be children they could not afford... what then? Death at the hands of a back-street abortionist? Unless you were born into the right strand of society, you had scant hope of a decent life in this peculiarly brutal country.

That meant many things, as Jelly had learned long ago. She still sometimes had nightmares about the moment shortly before the war when she was performing in a salon concert and spotted surreptitious sneers cross the faces of two Lady Somebodies, one making a small yet unmistakeable gesture involving her nose. Jelly had expected that it was one's musicianship that counted, not one's racial or religious background. Her innocence burned dry. Unlike Hungary, where viciousness was virtually paraded, England tried to keep its own two-faced brand of cruelty hidden.

Yet even being born into the uppermost strand of everything could not protect Tom, the kindest and dearest of men, from the slow-motion illness that was defeating him.

The house in Netherton Grove lay quiet, the daffodils in the front garden glimmering in the moonlight. 'Come in and have some coffee?' Jelly suggested.

'It's quite late – are you sure?' Anna glanced at her watch.

'Of course, and I'll send you home in a cab later, whenever you like.'

'Maybe a quick cup.' Anna smiled and followed Jelly inside.

Upstairs, Adrienne was asleep, and from the big bedroom, Jelly could hear the soft snoring of her brother-in-law.

Jelly and Anna settled in the drawing room with a pot of coffee and some delicate porcelain cups that had belonged to Jelly's mother. The piano was closed, and on a side table stood a bouquet of tiger lilies, a trophy from Adila's latest concert, spicing the wooden floor with crimson pollen.

'I miss my mother so much.' Jelly filled Anna's cup. 'She always knew the best thing to say and do. They say only the good die young... Do you sometimes feel that everyone has *gone?*'

'I can see how you would,' Anna admitted. 'Your mother and father, and Sep, and... '

The prospect of Tom joining this list cut through Jelly. She could cancel everything and go to him now; perhaps marry him, even though it was too late to build a life together. Or she could accept his exhortations to stay away and concentrate on her music. If only there were wise words to be found. If only she had known where she really stood with Sep before he had been killed.

'You know – I was thinking... '

'What, Jelly?'

'Don't laugh, but we could try the glass game.'

Anna recoiled a little. 'You want to do that? Are you sure?'

'Perhaps there'd be advice. Even – my mother?' She tried to smile, to hide the pain she experienced at the notion of her beloved mama trying to reach her through a moving tumbler – or Sep doing so. Tom's words expanded in her mind: be true to yourself, true to your vocation. Glass games were not true to anything Jelly held dear; but Adila made it look so easy...

'I didn't think you believed in it,' said Anna.

'I don't.' Jelly gave a laugh. 'It's just a distraction. Perhaps we'll ask questions only for you. About the nice young man you mentioned the other day?'

Anna nodded, her expression unreadable.

Jelly fetched from Adila's bureau a set of small letter cards, which they used for word games, and laid them out alphabetically in a circle on the dining room table. In the centre she set in place an upended tumbler. A scratch and whine at the door revealed Caesar, who should have been in his basket by the back door, but had begun to hanker for company on hearing their voices. She let him in; he lay across her feet and thumped his tail before going to sleep, nose on paws.

Next she scrawled 'Yes', 'No' and 'Goodbye' on pieces of paper ripped from a notebook, barely legible in her strange, wide-lettered writing. As a child in Hungary she had gone to school for only eight days; each time she'd cried so much that eventually her mother could stand it no longer and kept her home. After that, Jelly played her violin to her heart's content.

They lit a sole candle; the rest of the room disappeared into the night, while an island of creamy gold highlighted the whorls in the wooden surface. Now this seemed a cavern fit for other-worldly activities. The two women sat opposite one another, exchanging smiles to conceal their nerves.

'Ready, darling?' Jelly said, to reassure herself as much as Anna. 'So, let's sit quietly and clear our minds… '

They waited, each with one finger on the glass, silent, focusing. The candle flame flickered in Jelly's exhalations.

'Do we need to invoke something?' Anna whispered.

Jelly thought of Mary Southern's opening invitation. 'Hello, is there anyone of friendly intent who would like to talk to us?'

Twenty seconds more went by in stillness. Perhaps it wasn't going to work? Then, beneath her fingertip, Jelly felt a slip of energy, like the prickle of an electric current.

The glass gave an unmistakable shift. Jelly and Anna breathed and waited. It moved, first left, then right – and was still.

Anna took a deep breath. 'Is Mrs Antoinette d'Arányi there, please?'

'Darling, don't ask for my mama. It's not a telephone… '

Jelly was becoming aware of heat gathering in the centre of her palms – a concentration of some intensity, first a superficial tingling, then gradually digging deeper and deeper. Soon her hands seemed to be pierced through with a thousand pins, and around the central spots, numbness began to spread through her fingers and the muscles at the side of her palms. Before she could say anything, let alone make a break for safety, the glass started to glide along the table.

It circled the letters once, twice, and yet again; then swerved towards G and on to its next choice, apparently galvanised by a propulsive force that Jelly knew was not hers and, to judge from Anna's frightened eyes, could scarcely belong to her, either. Anna, left forefinger on the tumbler, noted down letter after letter. Jelly, transfixed, was wondering what was happening to her hands. Wasn't this what occurred when someone received stigmata? Yet there was no sign of blood – only the bizarre impression that someone had plugged electrodes into her palms.

In due course they derived from the glass one simple phrase: 'Glad to see you' – which was almost the same as the Eastbourne incident.

'Is that Jelly's mother?'

The glass slid towards 'no'. Then, before either of them could ask a question, it plunged onwards, letter by agonising letter, forcing their concentration.

Anna noted down the sequence. 'This is a little strange.'

The glass slowed and ceased its motion, leaving them to read back the transcript – once, twice… five times.

'No?' Jelly stared into Anna's eyes, feeling winded.

'I'm not seeing things,' Anna said. 'Are you reading this the same way?'

'Does it say what it seems to?' The closest approximation to the letters appeared to be: 'A composer seeks your aid'.

Anna was moistening her lips; Jelly reached out to give her hand a reassuring press and found it chilly with fright. Part of her wanted to switch on the light and declare all of this, in best Donald Tovey fashion, nuff and stonsense. Could the composer perhaps be Sep Kelly? The pressure in her palms was becoming almost painful. She thought she could make out, in the candle-light, a pink spot in the centre of her free hand, as if she had held it over a flame for a moment too long.

She heard herself speaking, doing the one thing she had intended not to do: asking questions that were not for Anna, 'Please, in what way does this composer seek my aid?'

The glass began to move even faster, as it might for Adila. It was many long minutes before it finally came to rest.

'He left the earth before you were born,' Anna read out. 'He would like you to find a piece and play it. It has not been played for many years.'

They looked at each other in fear and wonder.

'This is crazy,' said Jelly. 'It talks in sentences?'

'I want to stop,' said Anna. 'It's too strange. Please, Jelly, can't we put on the light now?'

'Just one minute more? I've got to know who this is,' Jelly pleaded. Clearly it was not Sep; she didn't know whether to be sorry or thankful. 'Perhaps it's Onkel Jo.'

Adila was one of the last pupils of their great-uncle, Joseph Joachim, whom they and many others called 'Onkel Jo': the vio-linist who had been a close friend of Johannes Brahms, and of Robert and Clara Schumann. Joachim's playing and teaching had shaped generations of musicians; he was a celebrated per-former and strict, demanding instructor who had died when Jelly was 14. 'And if it is... who could the composer be? For Onkel Jo – surely Brahms?'

They waited, fingertips poised on the glass. After a lengthy pause, it drifted through a golden patch of light towards the R.

The name built slowly, letter by letter.

In front of their eyes two words were forming: ROBERT SCHUMANN.

Jelly felt as if she had fallen head first into the sea and was trying to pull herself out, feet and hands slipping in all directions. This couldn't be real.

'Concerto,' spelled the glass, a step at a time. 'D minor.'

'Jelly,' Anna said, 'you're playing a practical joke on me.'

'But no, *you* are playing one on *me*.'

The motion under their fingers continued. 'May be museum,' the transcript read.

'I'm scared,' Anna pleaded. 'Aren't you?'

Jelly was experiencing an inner clash of titans: a thick-skulled ogre of scepticism, aided by a Himalayan Yeti of fear, was wrestling against her musical self – which, at the notion of an unknown violin concerto by Schumann, had sparked into a burgeoning inferno of curiosity. This couldn't be real – but what if it were? What would the piece be like? She had to know more.

'Hello?' she burst out. 'Are you still there? Is it – this concerto – is it any good?'

What a question to ask a spirit messenger. It wouldn't reply to such insolence. But that inexorable motion was beginning again. The letters kept flowing, as if pouring out of the glass, as if the visiting spirit, now that it had acquired this peculiar access to life, was determined not to relinquish it.

'"It is not my best work",' Anna read out the transcript. '"But it is better than much music being written today"… ' She shoved back her chair, clattered to her feet and plunged for the nearest lamp. 'Jelly, no! Help! That was *Schumann*! That was Schumann himself! I can't do this! We have to stop. I've never been so terrified in all my life.'

'It's all right.' Jelly's whole body felt icy except for the heat in her palms, as if all her blood had rushed to them and formed whirlpools there. Electric light swamped the candle; the spell cracked and fell away.

In the brightness they blinked, steadied their breathing and clasped hands. Jelly's head had begun to throb with exhaustion. They sat without speaking, trying to absorb at least some small measure of what had just happened to them.

'Why Schumann?' Anna ventured. 'Why would it be him?'

Jelly racked her reeling mind for any possible explanation. 'He was a great friend of Onkel Jo. Actually I think it was Onkel Jo who introduced him to Brahms.'

'Schumann was much older, wasn't he?'

'Yes, Schumann would have been in his forties, Jo and Brahms were both in their early twenties, and they both adored him. Don't you love his music?'

'I remember Myra Hess playing the Piano Concerto – my hands hurt from clapping, it was so wonderful... So if there *is* a violin concerto, that would be really important, wouldn't it?'

'I suppose it depends on the piece, but if it's as beautiful as the Piano Concerto – it's almost unimaginable! You know how often I play the Brahms and Mendelssohn concertos? It could be as significant as those. It could transform the whole violin concerto repertoire; it could transform concert life. Or certainly... it could transform mine,' she reflected, 'if I found it.'

'Wasn't there some appalling tragedy around Schumann? I can't remember what happened.'

'He became very ill – perhaps with manic depression – and eventually he lost his mind and he died in a mental asylum. Donald Tovey still winces when he talks about it.'

'He went mad? Did that affect his music at all?'

'That,' said Jelly, 'is a good question. I'm not sure anyone really knows the answer.'

Many questions hung in the air, most of them unasked. After Anna had gone home in a cab, Jelly sat at the table staring at the letters, the tumbler and the transcript lying where they'd left them. Her hands had cooled, her head cleared. What idiocy was this? She hadn't pushed the glass. Anna was so frightened that she couldn't have done so either. There had to be a rational explanation.

If this piece of insanity was to be believed, she had received a message from the spirit of Robert Schumann, or his... representative. Telling her that a violin concerto he had written was lying unplayed somewhere and he wanted her to save it. Astonishing – an extraordinary demand, an overwhelming responsibility – that Schumann should choose *her*. But supposing it was a trick of some kind, a deception, or worse? If something truly supernatural had taken place, how could she be sure this communication was benevolent and not demonic?

She could wait for Adila to come home, then tell her everything. Or she could clear away the evidence and pretend nothing had ever happened. It had to be nonsense. The very idea of a concerto by Schumann having lain untouched all these years was ridiculous; if such a thing existed, assuredly every violinist in the world would want to play it. Besides, she'd lose face if she admitted that she had been indulging in the glass game, since she habitually poured scorn on Adila and Erik for it.

Jelly read back the transcript one last time – then took it upstairs to stow at the bottom of a drawer in Anna's desk, in case it might someday come in handy. She'd leave it there, forget about it and tell her sister nothing now, nothing ever.

But while the clock ticked, while Alec and Adrienne slumbered, oblivious, in their bedrooms and Caesar downstairs gave canine snores in his basket, and while around 3am the engine and brakes of a cab signalled that Adila was home, Jelly lay awake, still electrified. If Onkel Jo and his friend Robert Schumann could be there, communicating, then so could Bach and Beethoven, so could Shakespeare, Plato, Aristophanes, so could Napoleon and the Duke of Wellington, so could her mother and Sep and...

Supposing she ignored the messages, dismissing them as the product of her own wishful thinking – and then the work turned up after all? Supposing she were to find it and perform it? Supposing she could free it, save it from oblivion and infuse it with renewed life?

She heard Adila moving about in the bathroom, humming

to herself as she shed her evening dress and jewels. The tune was from Schumann's Violin Sonata in D minor. Still wondering, Jelly let herself fall into an uneasy sleep.

Chapter 3

When Jelly tried to set off with Anna for Norman Hartnell's salon one morning a couple of weeks later, the Fachiri family car refused to start. Anna, whose duties extended to occasional chauffeuse, sat in the driver's seat, turning and returning the key. The car's coughs reminded Jelly of Anna's own.

'It's not going to work.' Anna climbed out. 'We'll have to take a bus or taxi.' Their part of Chelsea wasn't well served by trams.

'I can go on my own,' said Jelly. 'You should keep warm, with that cough.'

'I'm fine,' Anna insisted, 'and I'd so love to come along... '

The pair set off together along Netherton Grove towards Fulham Road, Jelly carrying her Bergonzi violin in its case. She always took it to dress fittings to make certain she'd be comfortable playing in the gown. Her shoes, though, were designed for style, not motion, which made it difficult to walk fast enough. Punctuality was ingrained in her; nobody would book a performer who was never on time.

At the corner, she spotted a large black car approaching. 'Look, there's a taxi!' She put up a hand, but it showed no sign of stopping.

'That's not a cab,' Anna laughed, 'it's a hearse!'

The coffin-shaped back section was empty. 'Not for you just yet, ladies!' the driver called, with a wave.

Anna snorted. 'What a nerve!'

A bus was pulling in; they stepped onto its rear platform. Jelly stared after the hearse. The incident had left a peculiar chill upon her.

Anna wanted to sit on the top deck, in the open air, which afforded the best panorama of Chelsea and the river.

'Aren't you cold?' Jelly worried. 'There's such a wind – we should go downstairs.'

Anna obeyed reluctantly. 'I love it up there.'

'Darling, I'm worried about you. You need to take care of yourself better... '

'Jelly, tell me... ' Anna changed the subject. 'Have you looked into – you know – whether there really is a Schumann concerto?'

'I haven't really had time.' She tried to sound nonchalant. She didn't want to admit that she was far too scared of their glass messages to follow it up.

The sunlit river came into view; Jelly, enjoying the sight, remarked that her mother used to say the glitter on the water was mermaids putting on their diamonds. Perhaps the Thames was home to some English counterparts of Wagner's Rhinemaidens, she added – though the Thamesmaidens would probably be drinking tea and listening to a recital of gramophone records on the wireless...

'Jelly?' said Anna. 'We shouldn't be going south.'

Silently cursing herself for still not knowing which was the right bus into town, even after six years in Netherton Grove, Jelly nearly lost her balance hurrying towards the back, hanging on to the railing with one hand and her violin case and handbag with the other while the bus plunged over uneven tarmac.

'Please, could you tell us the best way to Bruton Street?' she asked the conductor against the noise of the traffic.

'Where, luv? That's a grand foreign accent you've got, but I can't understand a word you're saying. Hooton Street, was it?'

'*Brrr*uton Street.'

'Ah – I'd say you need to get off me bus and go to Wandsworth Town station, just round that corner there. Change at Clapham Junction for Victoria.' He looked Anna up and down. 'You all right, miss?'

'Fine, thank you.'

Flustered on the pavement, Jelly spotted a road sign pointing to the train station. But this was a part of London, though not far from her home, that she wasn't convinced she'd seen before.

All around, disused shops sat black-windowed and deserted. A patina of soot clung to glass, walls and doorways; men, work-less, though of working age, stood smoking in clusters; a group of passing women, faces pale and pinched – with hunger, per-haps – were hauling along grubby and recalcitrant children, and Jelly winced as one mother lost her calm and cuffed a squalling lad across the ear, which only made him cry even more. Sweat-ing with alarm in her clean coat, tailored blouse and tulip skirt, plus those wretched heels, she felt overdressed and seriously anx-ious about the time. She imagined hostile eyes following their every step across the road. A symbol caught her eye, scrawled on the filthy wall under the railway bridge: the crooked flash logo of the British Union of Fascists. Beside it, in ill-formed white-painted letters, were the words JEWS OUT.

Wandsworth Town station was set back from the parade of what used to be shops and it was busy; people who had jobs were still on their way to work. They joined the stream on the stairs to the platforms, hemmed in on all sides, closer and closer, by an army of clambering feet and swinging, pointed umbrellas. Jelly felt the inadvertent thump of a heavy leather briefcase against her leg. Anna, just in front of her, was clutching the banister hard. Her chest was moving up and down, and Jelly, glancing at her hands, was struck by them: were they really so skeletal? Why hadn't she noticed before? Above them, a train clattered in across the bridge and she was wondering how to reach its doors despite the crowding when Anna stood still, swayed, then crumpled.

Jelly let out a cry in Hungarian, so shocked was she.

Anna was struggling to get up, racked with uncontrollable coughs, gasping out, 'Oh, sweet Jesus… ' Her face was the colour of the clouds.

'Darling!' Jelly put her arm around her to lift and guide her to the side of the landing halfway up the stairs, where she keeled over to the ground. 'Speak to me!'

Why was everyone walking by without even looking? Anna had bent double like a piece of cardboard, trying to muffle her desperate spasms in the folds of her clothes. When she paused, heaving for breath, her coat had acquired a soot stain from the station floor. Along the grimy mark were bright red blotches of blood.

'Someone, please help us!' Jelly shouted. Looking at the blood, she was beginning to feel faint herself.

By now they had attracted the stationmaster, who took one glance at Anna with Jelly cradling her prostrate form, and ran for a telephone.

'Don't be frightened, there's help coming. You'll be all right.' Jelly despaired of her own distraction. How could she have been so stupid as not to notice how ill Anna looked? Had she been working her too hard? Had she grown unwell so slowly that one small strain too much had tipped her over the edge? And never a complaint, never a word... Coughing blood – that was why the commuting crowd had rushed away from them.

'Hartnell,' mumbled Anna.

'As if I'd leave you now!'

Anna's eyes, huge in her too-thin face, gazed up into Jelly's at last. 'You're so kind, Jelly,' she said. 'You're such a good, sweet, real sort of person, and we never tell you... '

The sound of a siren cut through the stairwell's echoes, and a minute later two ambulance men were pounding up the steps towards them. Anna's pulse was taken, her condition assessed and a stretcher brought. Jelly could hear the tension in their barked instructions.

'She's my secretary and my friend,' she told them. 'I'd like to go with her, please.'

Jelly perched on a fold-out seat in the back of the ambulance, holding Anna's hand, searching her face for any sign of awareness. She had either drifted into a light sleep or started to lose consciousness. It had to be what Jelly feared: the dreaded tuberculosis, which nobody dared talk about, even though it was everywhere. Less usual, though, in Chelsea, where they had assumed it was a disease of the slums and the dosshouses.

'That's an infectious disease, Miss, and it can infect anyone,' said the ambulance man who was monitoring Anna's weak pulse.

If only she had bothered to see a doctor sooner. 'Don't let her die,' Jelly prayed.

'It's all right, she's not at death's door,' he reassured her. 'But she should've been with us a long time ago.'

'I envy your job. I should have liked to be a doctor.'

'What's the accent, Miss? Can't say it's one I know.'

Jelly recognised the tone of voice: suspicion. She used to hear it more often before, during and just after the war: the English loathing of anything foreign. Since the recent upheavals in Germany, the doubt had begun to creep back. 'I'm Hungarian,' she said, fighting back her alarm.

'Hungarian? That's a rum one... ' She could hear his relief that she wasn't German. 'When are you going back?'

'I've lived here more than 20 years.'

'Oh yes? Don't you miss it? A country of your own?'

'This *is* my country now,' she said, still quailing a little.

'Can't be easy, being foreign, things as they are. What's in the box, then?'

'Violin. I'm a musician.'

'Oh, a Hungarian Gypsy violinist?' The ambulance man laughed aloud – he had no idea why she might not laugh with him.

'Gypsy girls aren't allowed to play the violin,' Jelly said, conversational, keeping her calm. She registered that they were driving uphill. 'Where are we going?'

'The Savoy.' He gave her a wink. 'Nah, Miss – closest hospital there is. Putney. There in no time.'

They unloaded the barely conscious Anna on the stretcher; Jelly followed, her nostrils assaulted by a stench of disinfectant and blocked drains. Blinking, she took in the surrounding anxious muddle, the officious nurses, the pallid relatives of patients sitting on wooden benches in the lobby: hollow-cheeked faces, blank eyes. She had no doubt now that what she was seeing was hunger. This was the look of people who would give their children what food there was, but go hungry themselves. It seemed impossible that they could afford their treatment; the papers were full of the way costs had been rising of late. Thinking of her own life, she wanted to hide somewhere for the shame of her shelteredness. How alien her world would seem to these people; yet, were it not for her music, she might have been one of them. The sea of greyness in front of her was punctuated only by the crimson flowering of bloodstains on Anna's clothes, quickly concealed with a sheet.

'Give us a tune, love?' One of the men caught her eye and winked. She smiled back.

'I would, but… ' She gestured at the ailing Anna on the stretcher.

'Never mind,' he rasped – he had the voice of a heavy smoker. 'Probably only play for rich people anyway, don't you?'

Jelly was trying to keep hold of Anna's hand. 'Miss, we have to take her in to see the doctor… ' an apologetic nurse intervened.

'Jelly.' Anna opened her eyes with effort. 'Don't worry. Please go home. If you come back tomorrow, they'll have cured me.'

'Please take good care of her,' Jelly said to the nurse. 'And please send the bills to me. My Anna is "more precious than rubies".'

Back at home, Jelly telephoned the salon to rearrange her fitting.

Only hours ago, it had been imperative not to be late for Queen Mary's preferred designer. Images galloped through her mind like speeded-up film – Anna, the ambulance man, the smoker's accusation – along with an imagined portrait of Tom, confined to a hospital bed, emaciated and fading, telling her to be true to her vocation. She longed to take a jug from Adila's kitchen and mix in it a spiritual punch: one part Hungarian energy, two parts empathy, five parts music. Then she'd pour out the magic potion for them all.

Adila and Alec were going out that night with the Palmstiernas; Erik had taken a box at the New Theatre on St Martin's Lane to see *Richard of Bordeaux*. A young actor in the leading role, John Gielgud, was the talk of the town, Adila said. 'Come with us, Jelly,' she pressed. 'It'll cheer you up.' Jelly didn't want to be cheered up; she preferred to stay home and get on with some work.

She had been asked to perform a peculiar piece that had only just been issued. The score had arrived fresh off the press from the music publishing firm of Schott's in Mainz: a concerto supposedly written by Mozart aged ten, dedicated to Madame Adelaide de France, daughter of King Louis XV. It seemed, to Jelly, too good for Mozart at ten, but not good enough for Mozart any older. Perhaps it was by someone else, passing it off as the child genius's work. She loved it anyway; just because something wasn't perfect, that didn't mean it wasn't worth hearing. Now she had to memorise it.

Adila had a systematic way to learn music by heart; Jelly simply… remembered. Adila, who had studied for years with Professor Jenö Hubay back in Budapest, and later with Onkel Jo, was organised and analytical. Jelly, seven years younger, also went to Hubay, but never had another proper lesson after they moved to England. Her instinct seemed to carry her in the right direction. When little Madge Harvey-Webb, Adila's pupil and Adrienne's friend, said to her, 'But Jelly, how do you do it?' all she could offer was, 'I don't know, darling – I just do.'

Several hours vanished into the Mozart. By 10pm, her stomach was empty and grumbling. Wondering what Anna would eat in hospital, if she were well enough to eat at all, Jelly closed her violin case and went down to the kitchen. Adila and Alec would go back to Portland Place with the Palmstiernas for supper after the theatre; Maria the maid had the day off. Sometimes, when Jelly was home on her own – which was rare – she would go to a small restaurant on Fulham Road, but tonight she felt too tired and despondent to contemplate that.

In the pantry she found a basket of potatoes, onions, mushrooms and a cauliflower, plus some home-baked cake in a tin, made with what Adila called 'desecrated coconut', and on one shelf stood half a loaf of bread and a box of a dozen eggs. From the food saver – a silverish box that squatted by the pantry sink with a tray of ice and water at the bottom – she took out the butter and spread a little across two pieces of bread, which she cut meticulously into soldiers. She found a small pan on the shelf next to the stove, filled it with water and popped an egg into it. When everything was working, she stood watching the egg bobbing up and down in the bubbles.

Jelly wasn't sure how long an egg needed to boil – about four minutes, she thought. Did it start to cook before the water was actually boiling? You couldn't open an egg to see how it was doing, then put it back for longer. Her wristwatch had no second hand, so she ran upstairs to the hall to time it by the one on the painted face of Alec's family's grandfather clock. It was wrong too, of course. Every clock in the house told a different time.

Downstairs, the water was dancing in the pan and the egg's shell had split, letting out some of the white. Jelly, resigned, fished it out and settled at the table to enjoy the messy yet welcome result of her endeavour.

The morning dawned foggy and Jelly found it difficult to wake up, having been more exhausted by Anna's collapse than she'd realised. Between sleeping and waking, though, she found an idea coming into focus. She wondered why such things so often took shape in the morning, out of dreams. She did not, after all, 'only play for rich people'.

Adila was downing coffee. Jelly pulled on her raincoat, tied a light scarf over her hair and fetched her violin case. 'I'm going to see Anna in hospital.'

'With your violin?' said Adila.

'Definitely with my violin.'

In the smog, London had sunk into slow motion. This stinking murk would surely be enough to give anyone consumption; it was like breathing in days-old porridge. After deciding to walk the last stretch, Jelly, looking down, could see only a suggestion of her own feet. When she rounded a corner and spotted the red-brick blocks of the hospital, she slowed further, wondering if they would allow her to carry out her plan.

The sister at the entrance desk stared at her and her violin case. 'Miss d'Arányi?' she echoed when Jelly gave her name. 'I saw you play at the Winter Proms. You did the Bach Double Concerto, with Adila Fachiri. It was amazing! Please come with me, I'll take you up to Miss Robertson.' She scrambled to her feet. Jelly was happy to see that she had already brightened someone's day, and she hadn't yet played a note.

Here, the day needed brightening. In these labyrinths, your footsteps resonated back through your head, and people passing kept their voices low, as if at a funeral. Though the windows were plentiful, the smog seemed to press in against the glass. She followed the nurse along a corridor, passing several wards where long rows of beds stood in ranks.

At last they turned a corner into another ward and stopped beside a partially curtained booth. Anna lay on the bed within, curled into a foetal position under a starched white sheet, her light hair wispy on the pillow. Jelly, her heart cracking, hesitated, remembering how infectious consumption was. Still, it was a little late to worry; Anna had been working in their house for several years.

She crouched beside Anna and spoke her name softly. The girl, who looked almost too weak to move, visibly brightened at her voice.

'Jelly? You came to see me?'

'The fog is foggy, but it doesn't stop me.' She sat on the edge of Anna's bed. 'I thought I'd play you something.'

'Here?'

Jelly followed Anna's gaze around the ward. Some patients lay asleep or listless, others were coughing and shivering visibly despite the lack of air, while screens of buff-coloured curtains shielded the most serious cases from sight, though not always from sound. She could feel many gazes upon her as she unpacked her violin. 'Yes,' she said, 'here.'

'Oh, Miss – Miss d'Arányi… ' The ward matron spotted her and marched over. 'You can't play the violin in here. This is a hospital.'

'All the more reason to do so,' Jelly smiled.

'But it's forbidden.'

'Really? Just a little music to cheer people up?'

'Let her play to us?' came a voice across the ward.

'Please – we would love it,' Anna said. A chorus of further pleas around them seemed to take the matron by surprise.

'Hmm.' She cast a sceptical eye around her charges. 'All right. Just a few minutes.'

Standing near Anna's bed, Jelly played Bach for her friend, for all the patients and, inwardly, for Tom, as if it were the song of a deity. Around the beds, curtains moved aside. Submerged in her task, Jelly was half aware, yet never allowed her concentration to waver. Anna's eyes began to shine, vivid against her fever-dimmed skin; while the music progressed, tears rose within them. An elderly woman in a corner bed, coughing convulsing her, gathered the bedclothes against her mouth to stifle the sound. Several people who had been lying flat managed to lift themselves upright against the pillows; their blank expressions had gone, replaced by a light of wonder. One young girl slumbered, motionless, throughout – but in her sleep, she began to smile.

At the end Jelly lowered her violin and looked into the silence. The love she'd wanted to give them was gleaming back at her from the patients, some tearful, some uncomprehending, a few lost in dreams; from two nurses and the matron, who had opened her mouth and failed to close it; and from a distracted-looking doctor who had hurried in to see what was going on and stopped short, apparently as dumbfounded as if he'd discovered Johann Sebastian Bach himself waiting for treatment.

'Brava, Jelly!' Anna exclaimed, finding the strength to start clapping. Gradually, as Jelly smiled, amazement dissolved into applause.

She considered: these people, some unable to sit up, all too ill to attend a concert – and many who wouldn't have done so even if they were well – deserved the spiritual comfort of music as much as any healthy person did, probably more. If they can't come to the music, the music must go to them. Whoever decreed that it should only be performed in a formal venue, where people pay for tickets and aren't allowed to speak to the musicians? If you wanted meaning in music, this was where you'd find it: in a place of suffering, where Bach's humanity could strike home.

'Miss d'Arányi… ' The doctor came up to shake her hand.

'I do hope I'm not a disruptive influence, Doctor?' Jelly said.

'Well, I'd never imagined someone could simply walk in here and start playing a violin. You need to get past matron first! But,' he added, when they'd both stopped laughing, 'this is extraordinary. Just look at them. You've done more good for these poor souls than we can manage in a month of Sundays.'

'I wouldn't go as far as that, Doctor. But I'm grateful you didn't throw me out.'

'You know, if you'd ever like to come back and do it again, we'd be overjoyed.'

'I'd love to,' Jelly promised.

'Music and medicine are close, but sometimes not allowed to be close enough,' he remarked. 'We only treat the physical, whereas you can bring consolation – and that's a rarity in this place. I don't know how some of them find the will to get well again.'

'Jelly?'

She dived back to Anna's bedside.

Anna seemed to be struggling for words. 'Thank you, Jelly,' she managed. 'I'll never forget what you did for us all today.'

At home, the thought of the patients, their response, the doctor's reaction, Anna's face transfigured as she listened – none of it would leave Jelly alone. She'd once played in a children's hospital, which nearly skinned her heart alive, but every note there seemed to mean ten times more than one anywhere else. At Exeter Cathedral recently, she had seen the evening light reflected in the eyes of her audience while she played, amid a silence more intimate than that of a salon, despite the gaping space – or perhaps because of it. Music as human goodness incarnate: that was what Tom saw in her. He knew that was the best she could give. Now she felt she had a doctor's blessing as well. For that vision, defiant, she resolved her direction. She would set herself against the supposed spirits of the dead, towards healing the proven ones of the living.

She hunted through Anna's desk for her concert diary. There, at the bottom of the last drawer, lay the paper on which she had written down the message from Schumann, if Schumann it were. Her hand hovered above it, vacillating, as if to touch it would be to accept its content. Why was she keeping it if she could not do that? Why couldn't she forget? The image of the concerto, if concerto there were, troubled her; she pictured it shut away somewhere similar to that hospital, stricken and mute. She couldn't save Tom; she could help Anna, without being able to make her well again; but if there really were a piece of music to rescue... Jelly pushed the thought away, slammed the drawer shut and tried another.

At last, diary retrieved, she licked her fingertips and began to turn the pages. The winter, six or eight months away, was relatively quiet and most of her concerts were in Britain. There had to be moments in which she and the largest venues she could find would be free on the same evening. She could go any time to play her violin in hospitals, in ordinary schools as well as Eton, working men's clubs besides the Wigmore Hall. But the idea that had grasped her demanded somewhere to seat 1,000 or more. An audience of the unemployed, admitted free, plus bene-factors who would pay only a donation for charity at the end – it had to be possible. In her mind one image came into focus: Westminster Abbey.

But – only one concert in one venue? Why not several? And why wait? Why not do it now?

Chapter 4

Not that arranging anything at all would be easy without the best-organised person Jelly knew.

'I can't come back.' Anna's voice on the telephone was tearful. 'They say I have to get away from London and out to the country, because of the air. I don't know how I'll live without you all.'

Anna elected to go back to Scotland, to a sanatorium close to her family. The levels of irritability rose in Netherton Grove as the sisters tried to take charge of their own affairs. 'It's not the same without poor little darling Anni,' Jelly lamented. Whenever she opened the bottom drawer, there was that piece of paper, reminding her. R-o-b-e-r-t-S-c-h-u-...

Putting together at short notice a major tour involving some of the country's greatest cathedrals was not technically impossible. But Jelly had not anticipated how much work it would take, often requiring quick responses and a good memory.

'We ought to have a manager,' Adila grunted, hunting for a lost note on the back of a receipt.

'They'd take over and make us do things we don't want to do,' Jelly protested.

But she enlisted the help of a well-connected friend: Katharine Tennant, Margot Asquith's half-sister, who was fundraising for 'alternative employment options'. Now, whenever Katharine called her, she needed answers. How much time did she want between concerts? Would she work with the resident organist? Which pieces would they perform? Jelly muddled up her programmes and confused her dates. Her fingers itched for her violin while other concerts loomed – she ought to be practising, not spending so much time on administration.

She took a train, alone – dismal without Anna for company – to Devon and back, to give a recital; then a train and boat to Belfast and back for a concerto. She lay awake at night, still feeling the motion of wheels and waves beneath her, exhausted beyond the point of sleep. Myra Hess always used to say that the reason there were not more female musicians was that most women are too sensible to want to spend their lives on trains. Jelly agreed, but it would have been much more fun if Myra were there too. Next, she had to play, of all places for an apolitical Hungarian, at 10 Downing Street, for Ramsay MacDonald – even though Alec had told her, in careful terms, that foreigners were starting to be excluded from British concert platforms. 'I can't bear it,' she said. 'It's like 1913 all over again.'

Jelly had never applied for naturalisation – she felt it would be dishonest to claim to be British when she was not. The scorn she'd experienced on arrival at some venues in the provinces before the war, as a young girl still learning English, had alarmed her: finding the right words, aged 20, to answer a stranger's tirade – 'Why do we have to listen to you when we've plenty of fine musicians of our own?' – had not proved easy. It was around then, too, that her mother gently suggested changing their name from the Germanic 'von' Arányi to the French-style equivalent – and her favourite concert hall, the Bechstein Hall, soon had to change its name to the Wigmore Hall, since even German pianos were publicly loathed. Once the war struck and musicians from abroad were banned, she'd been fortunate that most concert promoters loved her so much that they somehow neglected to check her nationality. No guarantees, though, that this would be the case if it all happened again. Alec worried about Oswald Mosley's popularity and had started to call the *Daily Mail* the 'Daily Rail', since it regularly roused its readers to decry the number of Jewish immigrants who were arriving to escape the new regime in Germany.

After one small organisational cyclone too many in Hurricane House, Alec – perhaps guarding what remained of his peace of mind – decided to defuse the situation, encouraged by the diplomatic Erik. He suggested that they should treat themselves to a short holiday: a long weekend together in Dorset. 'It'll do you good, Sai,' he insisted. 'We need to look after you, because you're not looking after yourself.'

'You always do look after me,' Jelly said. The last thing she wanted was a break.

'Are you sure?'

Jelly knew he could see through her attempts at pretence. 'If you and Adi want me there, then of course I'll come along.'

'And with Erik?'

'It's fine,' said Jelly. 'Really, it's fine.'

She tried to defer to Alec, who respected the baron for his books on Swedish history and his passion for democratic politics, over which detractors used to call him 'red outside and white beneath'. Erik in return never missed a chance to compliment Alec on his own book about the Permanent Court of International Justice. Alec's legal work for the League of Nations and Erik's involvement with the organisation – a priority for his government – meant the pair's discussions were cordial at least, or, at best, of possible international significance. Now Japan had announced it would withdraw from the League, Alec feared Germany would follow suit. 'If the League can't even make all those countries agree on a single symbol to represent it,' Jelly asked him, 'and if one country can just walk out and leave if it wants to, how is it supposed to achieve world peace?'

Squeezed into the back of Erik's open-topped car beside Adrienne and the long-suffering Alec, Jelly clasped her niece's hand so hard that the little girl cried, 'Ouch, Auntie Jeje!' Jelly scolded herself: she should be grateful for a trip to a hotel at Studland Bay. She offered up a silent prayer, lest Erik's obsession with speed should send them all to the spirit world to which he was so devoted.

Erik's wife, Ebba, had stayed behind, spending a few days with their daughter, Margareta, and the latter's French husband. Ebba's health, Erik said, would make it difficult for her to enjoy a break that involved brisk walks over sand dunes. And she would probably not approve of Studland Bay's naturist beach.

At the top of a long climb, the sea spread before them, Old Harry jutting up from the water like a snowman on blue satin. Erik stopped the car; Adila sprang out and made for the cliff edge, Adrienne and Caesar cantering behind. 'Adri,' shouted Alec, 'be careful!' All around rose the sweetness of incipient honey in the heather and the contented rumble of bees. 'Oh, what *air!*' Adila boomed.

'Adi, they can hear you in Poole,' Alec teased her.

'There's something of eternity and consolation about the sea,' said Erik, who had started his career in the Swedish navy.

'Didn't you find it dull?' Alec asked.

'I read a lot of spiritual philosophy.' Erik gave a grin. 'Unless it was night in the crow's nest, when you could only watch the stars and feel the swell of the ocean. You sense your own insignificance within that immensity.'

The hotel, in a hollow sheltered from the coastal winds, soon slid the newcomers into place. Adila disappeared into the bathroom for a while, as her stomach sometimes insisted she must, then took a nap. Adrienne and Caesar made for the bottom of the garden; a scattering of other guests smiled to see the little girl in lilac playing with her dog. Relaxing on the terrace, the baron offered Alec his finest tobacco.

'I'm not supposed to smoke,' Alec admitted, twirling his pipe in one hand. 'My doctor says it's bad for my lungs. But this smells amazing.'

'First class,' said Erik. 'Riff cut, blended with whisky and made in Sweden. Come on, Alec, live a little. It's tosh about tobacco damaging the lungs. On the contrary, it helps to aerate them and soothes away any possible infection.'

Jelly, outside to keep half an eye on Adrienne and the dog,

watched the men from a safe distance. Erik was more Mediterranean in appearance than any other Scandinavian she knew;
the intensity of his heavy-lidded eyes, she thought, could make
him virtually glow in the dark. Beside his aristocratic Swedish
drawl, Alec's still-detectable American twists and pointed vowels
sounded less subtle than usual, but the baron had built much of
his career through his skill at public speaking, while Alec's was
founded upon quietness and concentration. The most obvious
thing the two had in common was sizeable moustaches.

The second most obvious thing was Adila. Her vitality
seemed to rub off on Erik; her energy fed him like an addictive
substance.

'There you are!' came her dark voice, and she strode out
onto the terrace – her figure as lavish as her cooking, her peri-
winkle gaze direct between strong, level brows, giving a smile
that would be visible from the back of the largest concert hall
– and Erik's face shone like a Christmas tree set with a hundred
candles.

'I'm all right here, Auntie Jeje,' Adrienne called. 'I don't
need watching.'

Jelly blew her a kiss, then wandered upstairs to take out her
violin: if in doubt, practise.

The inevitable began soon after dinner.

They'd enjoyed roast chicken and a fine Bordeaux; now a
long marine twilight set in that seemed to concentrate the scents
of mown grass, heather and Swedish pipe tobacco. Adila coaxed
Adrienne upstairs for a bedtime story; and while the men took
cognac in the smoking room, Jelly settled at a table in the lounge
to write to Tom. She summoned a cheery tone for her letter
that concealed her disquiet at the idea that she should, and could,
have been there to look after him herself.

She was on a sixth page, telling him about the dunes, the
baron's fast car and the fact that there was a naturist beach a five-

minute drive away, when Erik came in: 'Jelly, do join us – we have a private salon for our research.'

In a quiet parlour draped with brocade curtains and lit by one lamp, Erik had set up a round table with his own set of letters and a tumbler borrowed from the kitchen. Jelly paused in the doorway. This was the last thing she wanted to do; the dinner had been good, the wine even more so and after that tiring drive she'd have preferred to go to sleep. She'd managed to avoid such sessions since her secret effort with Anna. 'Where's Adi?'

'She's upstairs with Adri – we wait for her.' Erik's face softened. 'She galvanises our friends beyond.'

'She galvanises real people too,' Jelly said pointedly.

'Reality has many facets.' The baron did not flinch. 'Eventually, I hope, there will be a book, thanks to Adila – it will change the way mankind regards the world of spirits. It may change world consciousness for ever. Look at all this.' He picked up his notebook from the table and rustled through the pages; Jelly glimpsed paragraph after paragraph in his curled, thick-inked writing, the words close yet clear.

'Can I see?'

The baron, smiling, handed it to her. She read: '*Progress advances from the lower towards the higher, until perfection is reached, evil being the lowest stage.*'

'Don't we have enough trouble in this world without worrying about the next?' she remarked.

'But the messengers can help us – they can give us guidance in troubled times. People are confused, Jelly. We're so insecure, we're so lost.' Erik, arms behind his back, started to pace up and down; she couldn't help wishing he'd keep still. 'Everything we knew, everything we took for granted, it's all turning into fairy dust. We need the advice of those who know better. Can you imagine what problems we could solve with their wisdom? Read this, received by your sister, letter for letter, word for word: these are teachings for daily life, answering the questions we all want to ask… '

Jelly ran her gaze over lines and more lines: about the importance of individuality and the ridiculous tendency of human beings to wish to be alike. The spirits, it seemed, had the impression they were watching a world of dummies, growing dumber by the day because of their fear of being different, killing off the very essence of what each of them could otherwise have offered to life and art. It was pompously expressed – as it might well be, coming from Erik's pen – while the sentiments were worthy of Adila at her most extreme. This was the perfect book-child of its creative parents: one eloquent Swedish ex-MP and one determined, impassioned Hungarian artist who adored being different. Jelly smiled, more to herself than Erik; strange that he and Adila should need prompting from spirits in the beyond to pen something so evidently in keeping with their own beliefs.

'But Erik, isn't that human nature, wanting to fit in?' she ventured. 'It doesn't necessarily mean people are "dummies". Especially now, don't you have the feeling that people don't want to… stand out? The way things are?' She knew too well how it felt to be thought different, therefore a threat – for matters as innocuous as a foreign accent, a darkish complexion, Slavic cheekbones, an artistic profession.

'That's the whole point.' Erik sounded too patient. 'It shows us that this is nothing but illusion. Fear, doubt and insecurity spawn unnecessary problems, and can stop us from finding solutions to them… Come and join us now?'

'Please excuse me, Erik, but I must finish writing to Tom. He's having an operation next week and we hope it may save him, at least for a while… I'm so worried about him, but all I can really do is write to him and pray.'

He let her go; she retreated to the lounge while the team set to work. Each minute that went by she thanked Providence that she was still there, still writing; nothing untoward had taken place and an hour had passed...

It was as if part of her knew what was going to happen.

Adila was in the doorway. 'Jelly! Come here, quick!'

In the parlour, Erik and Adila had taken the glass while Alec was transcribing the incoming messages. Jelly looked over his shoulder. He had written down: 'Tell Jelly remember concerto.'

'What concerto?' said Alec.

'Wait, there's more coming – I can feel it.' Adila, with a dramatic shiver, pressed her finger to the base of the glass. Erik rushed to join her; heads bowed in concentration, they watched it glide. Did the centre of Adila's palms grow hot? Jelly didn't want to ask.

Powerless, she hovered in the shadows beyond the lamplight so that nobody could see her face while the apparently spirit-loaded glass pounced upon letter after letter.

'Schumann. Museum Weimar. Tell Tovey,' Adila interpreted. 'What on earth does that mean? Why Weimar? What's it got to do with Tovey?'

Three pairs of astonished eyes turned towards Jelly. 'Sai, what in the name of Beelzebub is going on?'

'It's nothing.'

'Stop pretending! A concerto? Schumann? *Nothing*?'

'I didn't take it seriously. I mean – Adi, I'm no good at this, you know I'm not.'

'*What* didn't you take seriously? Out with it! I won't stop asking until you say, so you might as well tell us now.'

Jelly, trapped, moistened her lips. Two minutes later Adila, Alec and the baron knew everything she had been trying to forget while she plotted her cathedral tour.

'Adi, did Onkel Jo ever say anything to you about a Schumann violin concerto?' she finished, pleading.

'Not that I remember. I am certain, no. A hundred per cent, definitely, certain he did not.'

'If anyone knew about it, it would have been him,' Alec agreed. 'It might have been written *for* him.'

'This is crrrazy,' Adila growled. 'Oh, Sai! How could you hide such a thing? A missing Schumann concerto! Imagine if you found it and played it. It would be yours, all over the world. You'd go down in history as the woman who rediscovered it.'

'Why me?' said Jelly. 'Why not *you*? You were Onkel Jo's pupil, not me. And whatever does Schumann know about Tovey?'

'Schumann didn't know him, but Onkel Jo did, very well,' Adila pointed out. 'And Jo loved you, you know. He tells me, on his *deathbed* he tells me, "Make sure little Jelly's doing her bowing properly, as I showed her… "'

'It's incredible!' Erik was ecstatic. 'Jelly, you are chosen by the angels. How can you refuse their summons?'

'I do wonder what the music would be like,' she admitted. 'If there is some… '

'Jelly, these messages do not come from nowhere. There will be a concerto, and you will play it. You will bring an unknown Schumann work to the world, at the composer's own request. We will all help you. Try and stop us!'

'Supposing it *isn't* real?' Jelly felt outnumbered, shouted down by people stronger – or at least louder – than she was. Nobody was present to back her up; Alec, inscrutable behind his moustache while his wife and her friend assailed Jelly, took no sides. 'Supposing these spirits are not who they say they are, and they're misleading us, giving us information that's false?' she said. 'And then we ask everywhere and it's not true. Imagine how silly we'll look.'

'Not nearly as silly as we will if someone else finds it first,' Erik pointed out. 'Supposing we had the chance, but we didn't take it? That's the one thing that people truly come to regret: losing an opportunity for no reason other than self-doubt and fear. Don't be afraid, Jelly. Grasp this with both hands – you won't regret it. We must make enquiries. Promise me you will start writing to people who might be able to help.'

'But if it is real – surely we wouldn't tell people how we heard about it? We wouldn't tell them about... this?' The glass sat motionless amid the letters.

'Of course we would,' Adila countered. 'An amazing story, and evidence that the spirits are real.'

'Wouldn't it be... rather dangerous? Not many people believe in this kind of thing, not any longer.'

'They will *have* to then. And we would be so proud... Sai, you must investigate. And if you find it soon, you can play it for your cathedral tour – imagine the impact! Wouldn't that be amazing?'

As the youngest of three siblings, Jelly had spent much of her life feeling that other people were bigger than she was. Her habitual response was simple: she let them have their way so that she could get back to her violin.

She concealed her sense of defeat behind her brightest smile, her warmest goodnights, and a silent recognition that on the final point – the cathedral concerts – Adila was right. Now it would only be possible if she could find the piece fast.

After many sleepless hours despite the countryside tranquillity, Jelly got up early and took Caesar for a walk. He had spent the night in a strange kennel and deserved a treat. She wandered with him up the hill to the headland and there perched on a rock close to the edge, listening to the waves below.

Jelly could rarely hear the sea without imagining Sep Kelly crossing it – whether in life, towards the killing fields of northern France, or perhaps equally, in death. She had dreamed, that night in 1916, of a ship setting out into the ocean with no destination. She thought nothing of it; someone had written to her, telling her that Sep was fine and that he was writing her a new piece. He was already dead, as she heard ten days later when his sister, Maisie, came to the house to tell her, weeping and incoherent. Jelly wept with her, then scarcely stopped crying for a month.

Nobody knew what to say to her. Sep had never spoken one word of love, let alone proposed marriage, yet everyone thought them virtually engaged. They'd spent much time together, but as duo partners, never lovers; when they met, out came her violin, up went the piano lid and off they went to work. They communicated better through music than most couples do through touch. She would signal a nuance with a breath, an inclination of her head or a slowing of her bow arm and he, despite looking straight ahead at the music on the stand, would sense her need and meet it at once. They never played anything the same way twice; if conversation was fun, musical dialogue was even more so, transforming a Mozart sonata into mutual teasing, or Brahms into a shared moment of emotional eloquence that they never tried to replicate in real life. At least, Sep did not, however much Jelly wished he would.

He was still at the piano: on the Bechstein at Netherton Grove stood the John Singer Sargent sketch showing the broad forehead and forthright gaze of a scholar, plus the thickset neck of a rowing champion. She wasn't sure what had happened to Sep's gold medal from the 1908 London Olympic Games; perhaps Maisie had kept it, or sent it home to their parents in Sydney.

She'd had admirers, suitors, lovers, though never Sep; he'd never even tried to touch her. Perhaps he didn't want to; Adila thought he preferred men, but Jelly tried to stop her ears to that notion. Instead, she'd had to deal with Tovey, who once uttered a painful declaration, awkward and red-faced, making her squirm, much as she adored him; anyway, she was sure he spent longer pursuing Maisie. There was Bartók, who first fell for Adila and later for Jelly and came to their Budapest house almost every day for five years, which mightily embarrassed them; the cruel young girls they were then thought only that he had no sense of humour. Elgar, who termed her his 'tenth muse', tried to kiss her after taking her to the British Museum, which she was too young and innocent to know was a popular den for assignations – and he was 35 years her senior, and an Order of Merit, too! In one stroke he'd wrecked any chance that she would ever play his interminable violin concerto. And poor, dear, Tom – the best of them, if she could have felt as strongly for him as she had for Sep.

She could still hear the first sound of Sep's arrival in her life: his fancy car pulling up outside Donald Tovey's home in Surrey, one glorious May morning full of shouting birds and lilac blossom. Cars were uncommon in those days, so the arrival of a noisy engine on a sleek machine meant that every schoolboy in Englefield Green came running out to stare and point.

You know at once when you meet someone who will change your life, even if you have no idea how it will happen. Jelly knew at one glance that Sep would, but the first thing he did was to laugh at her. People did, then, before she was famous enough to be more than one of 'those darling Hungarian sisters'. Hortense, sweating with nerves at her piano, was the fragile beauty; Adila, the eldest, was the powerhouse violinist, pupil of the great Joachim; but Jelly was the baby, the one with the Gypsy looks and the silly name.

'Where did you get that name, then?' Sep challenged her, sipping Tovey's tea. Most English people were too polite to ask outright, but Sep, for all his Eton schooling and Oxford scholarship, was an outsider, as Jelly was herself. His Australian accent clung to him like bathing trunks – despite, or perhaps because of, the English high society into which he'd tumbled, by design of his father's money, but distinctly by accident where his own nature was concerned.

'I was named after an African princess.' Jelly raised her chin, trying to look taller. 'Someone my father met when a group from Dahomey came to Budapest.'

'There was an African princess called *Jelly*? That's a *trifle* unlikely, isn't it?' Sep teased her, those 50-carat blue eyes sparkling into her teenaged face.

'I've heard *all* the jokes before, you know. Jelly, trifle, ice cream, getting my just desserts. It is very tedious.'

'Then I shall just have to be more original, shan't I? Tell me more about this African princess.'

'I think it was originally spelled J-E-L-I, but our father wanted to make it look English. I don't think he had the first idea what it meant. And it's "Yelly", not "Gelly". Though I must say I am not in the habit of yelling very much.' She saw the corners of Sep's eyes crinkle and his teeth glimmer as she battled with the Hungarian twists of her vocal cords. They seemed to be stronger than she was.

'You could change it, you know. You could choose any name you like.'

'But I *do* like it! I have a name nobody else in this country has ever had. Why would I want one that belonged to someone else first? It would be – how do you say in English? Second-hand!'

Sep laughed, a deep, raucous, Australian laugh, his head on one side; he evidently thought she was a poppet, as everyone seemed to. Jelly was furious that she wasn't even two years older, which could have made all the difference. He was nearly 30 and awfully venerable.

'Tell me about yourself, then,' he said. 'Start with your name and tell me something I can't guess about what you think and feel.'

Jelly pondered. 'My name is Jelly von Arányi. And... '

'Go on,' he prompted. '"And I know that... "?'

'My name is Jelly von Arányi and I know that nobody has ever had my name before.' She was emboldened. 'Nobody else has ever had my name. Nobody else has ever lived my life.'

'And live it you do and you shall!' he laughed. 'I can see that in the way you set your jaw.'

'That's probably from the violin... '

GHOST VARIATIONS

'Of course, you play the violin, don't you?' He stopped laughing. 'The Tove's been *yelling* Jelly's praises. Come on, let's see what you can do. What shall we play?'

'Brahms.'

'Brahms? *You* play *Brahms*? That's no music for little girls.'

Jelly fumed. 'Try me.'

'All right, then.' He suggested the second sonata – the most concentrated and supposedly straightforward of Brahms's three. Jelly refused. She plumped for the third, in D minor, the last, loudest and most violent. Best of all, it had a pig of a piano part. Jelly flung herself into the melodies and gave Sep, at the keyboard, a run she hoped he would never forget.

'Wait for me!' he shouted as she galloped into the finale. He was an Olympic champion; he should be able to keep up. She flew on, gaze unbendable, challenging him. By the end he was sweating more than she was. A crash of applause surprised them: getting their breath, they found Tovey, Hortense, Adila and their mother, all watching with widened eyes and mouths. Jelly laughed; Sep joined her. She'd made him follow her lead, thus far.

'Come on, Sep, take a breath,' Tovey advised, clapping a hand onto his shoulder. 'Let me have a go.'

'Game of chess?' Sep suggested.

'Absolutely.' Tovey sat down at the piano and began to play the first prelude and fugue from Bach's *Well-Tempered Clavier*. Sep grabbed the chess set from the bookcase – an inlaid board full of mother-of-pearl and contrasting bright woods – and set out the pieces. He flipped a coin. 'Heads!' shouted Tovey from the piano without missing a note.

Jelly stared, amazed. 'You can't play the piano and chess at the same time!' she exclaimed.

'Nuff and stonsense,' said Tovey. 'Watch me.'

'It's tails. I'll take white,' said Sep. Tovey started on the C minor Prelude and Fugue as Sep made his first move and called it out to the professor, who considered deeply, Bach rattling out under his fingers, before responding: 'Pawn, G–four!'

'They might do this for hours,' Adila whispered to the startled Jelly. 'Let's go outside.' Jelly could have stayed and watched the slope of Sep's neck and shoulders, muscular from rowing, and his beautiful hands while he controlled both ends of the game, shouting his moves to Tovey and receiving decisions back while the professor played, from memory, through the entire first book of the Bach 48 Preludes and Fugues, then started on the second.

Since Sep, she had never felt the same about anybody else, and she saw no reason to compromise. Probably Tom had never married because he was waiting for her; and she had waited, too, waited for her emotions to fasten upon him for sure and for all time. They both kept waiting and waiting – when, if it were going to happen, it would probably have done so the first day they met.

About a week after she heard that Sep had been killed at the Somme, Jelly, who had sunk into an arid subterranean world of mourning, woke around 2am. Suspended in a state of semi-dream, as if she were hovering as a spirit over her own body, curled alone in her bed, she thought she heard... What? She knew it. What was it? The opening melody of Sep's violin sonata? He'd written it for her in his head, in between digging trenches and dodging Ottoman ammunition; then he'd written it down on the boat, leaving Gallipoli after the horrors of battle. It began with a strong theme, full of nobility and poise. But what she heard in her mind's ear now seemed to reach her from the other side of a distant sea, as if in the scraping of a beginner violinist, as Sep, a pianist, would have been: the sort of valiant *try* that goes straight for the nerves under your teeth.

Sep had not said goodbye to her before he left for France.

Was that his farewell? Jelly came to, the sounds scratching away inside her head. She felt exhausted even before she could stand.

Back at the hotel, after breakfast, Jelly resumed her place at the desk overlooking the lawn to begin writing to people who might help her start hunting for the Schumann manuscript, notably Tovey. Taking time to ensure that language and hand-writing were logical and legible, and would not frighten away her targets, she scarcely noticed the hours pass. It was only when a bark reached her – high-pitched, officious, unquestionably Caesar's – that she realised her companions were nowhere to be seen. Beyond the window she glimpsed the flash of Adrienne's lilac dress and the gleam of her mahogany hair, while the dog galloped by, chasing a ball.

'Adri?' Jelly went onto the terrace. 'Where are Mummy and Daddy and Uncle Erik?'

Adrienne shielded her eyes from the sun with one hand. 'They went to the beach.'

'Without you?'

'Mummy said it's a beach that children and dogs can't go to, so we should stay here and you'd look after us. Not that we need looking after, you know, but that's what she said. She didn't want to disturb you, because you were busy.'

'Oh,' said Jelly. 'I see… '

So Adila, Erik and Alec had gone together, à trois, to… *that* beach, leaving her to babysit. And without telling her, because they thought she was too busy to listen – or perhaps because they didn't want to explain. Jelly felt briefly floored, but this was not something to tell the blissfully innocent and dog-focused Adri. She placed her outgoing letters on the hotel's post pile, then went into the sunshine to play with her niece.

Chapter 5

Myra Hess, cigarette smoke curling around her, listened long and well after Jelly burst into tears in the middle of the Brahms Sonata in G major.

In the pianist's Carlton Hill studio, lined with gold-hued hessian and gleaming with sunlight that slanted in from the garden, they were rehearsing for a Wigmore Hall Brahms centenary concert at which they would play all three of his sonatas. Jelly had been fighting back a longing to tell her duo partner about the visitations through the glass. Many years of working together had taught her that of everyone she knew who understood Schumann and how to play his music, Myra was by far the best; but that of everyone who would ridicule the notion of messages from beyond the grave, she would laugh longest and loudest.

Dotted around the studio stood photographs of her family – her parents and siblings, that is. No husband or children for her, any more than for Jelly. She turned down her first love, a violinist named Aldo Antonietti – Italian, yet hailing from Kingston-upon-Thames – because she intended to devote her life to music. Nothing should interfere with that. 'You can't be earnest about more than one thing in life,' Myra insisted, 'and I'd need to be earnest about marriage as well as music, and I can't do that.' Aldo wanted her to marry him and stop playing the piano. 'Balderdash,' said Myra. Neither she nor Jelly could understand why a man would fall for a woman with a vocation, only to insist she must give it up; music was, after all, a sizeable part of who they were. Yet if rejecting Aldo had caused Myra pain, Jelly accepted that she'd never know about it; her friend, sociable though she was, kept such feelings under strict lock and key. Later, Benno Moiseiwitsch proposed – but they'd have been two pianists together in the same home. 'God help us, never mind the neighbours!' Myra joked.

Here in St John's Wood, Myra shared a house with two sisters, friends who didn't mind her practising, and she identified in silence with the great rip in the fabric of their lives, having lived through all of it with them. They were the only survivors of five siblings. Their brother was killed in the war; afterwards their two younger sisters, grief-stricken, died together of a joint overdose. Nobody knew for certain whether it was accidental or deliberate; perhaps nobody wanted to know. Myra eventually adopted as her bedroom the one in which the girls' bodies had been discovered. Jelly wondered how she could stand it, but the pianist, throwing open all the windows and applying paint, curtains and music of her own, wasn't one for hauntings. Jelly could scarcely bear to set foot in there, so Myra confined their meetings to her studio.

A critic once commented, in the nicest possible way, that Myra resembled a solid, modern, reliable wristwatch fashioned to the latest design, while Jelly was a golden antique pocket watch, 'the best that money can buy'. The pair derived much hilarity from that. 'There we go, ticking away like time bombs!' Myra said.

They looked, nonetheless, as different as those imaginary watches would be. Myra was the shorter and rounder of figure, her dark hair draping like angel's wings from a centre parting above a direct gaze that missed no detail. Jelly was taller, indeed taller and darker than her own sisters, bony and flexible – Sep used to tease her about being double-jointed; her posture was open, her movements generous and impulsive, and her laughter as ready as her tears.

This time the tears were sparked by her increasing awareness of another difference between her and Myra: for the pianist, life was a photo, not a drawing, and she could manage it with commensurate clarity. She was tougher than Jelly, more practical and astute; a woman of this century, not the last. Was Jelly what the critic had said: an antique, admired for her old-fashioned beauty, but created in the past and for the past, useless beyond it? The Brahms sonata's slow movement seemed filled with mourning, chiming so strongly with hers that it felt almost too painful to play.

'You have to go to Tom,' Myra said, when Jelly had explained everything that was going on – except, of course, for the mysterious concerto. 'You mustn't think you're being disloyal to Sep. He's in another world, perhaps, and he won't care. He'd mind if you didn't, I think.' She, too, saw Sep as Jelly's unofficial fiancé.

'Tom keeps telling me to concentrate on work and not worry about him,' Jelly said, 'and I just… don't know how I… '

'… would say goodbye?' suggested Myra gently. 'That I can understand very well.'

'What would you do, if you were me?'

'I don't know. It seems to me that you want to be with him, but the prospect of that pain is stopping you, and no wonder. In the end perhaps you have to trust your instinct… '

Sep had died without her being able to tell him that she loved him; now Tom might, too; and she could save neither of them. Her instinct was telling her something different: that she might instead save, even resurrect, another entity. A Schumann concerto.

Myra's fingers moved softly across the keyboard, tracing a chorale-like theme that Jelly didn't recognise. 'What's that?' she asked. 'It sounds like Schubert.'

'Funny you should say that. Actually it's a little theme by Schumann that nobody knows, used for some variations by Brahms.'

Jelly tried not to show the shockwave.

'It's for four hands. I've been looking at it with Irene Scharrer.' Irene was Myra's oldest friend, a fellow former piano pupil of Tobias Matthay. 'Rumour has it, according to Uncle Tobs, that Schumann thought this theme was being dictated to him by the spirits of Schubert and Mendelssohn. Of course, the poor man was losing his mind at the time. Brahms wrote these variations after Schumann died. Isn't it lovely?'

The music stood open on the piano beside the violin sonata; Jelly peered over Myra's shoulder at the notes. Extraordinary to think that Schumann himself had believed in such things. If she told Myra her own Schumann story, Myra might think that she, too, was losing her mind. Yet Jelly had seen the words forming, with her own eyes, and she knew she hadn't pressed on the glass, and she knew she had never heard before of a violin concerto by Schumann.

'It's beautiful,' she said. 'Do you think it really was dictated by spirits?'

Myra burst out laughing, then twirled into a jokey cadence that neither Schumann nor Brahms would ever have written.

Jelly's letters from Dorset began to bring her some returns around the time of her birthday in late May – though not all were happy. Armed with her best hat, a sleek black suit and several layers of necklaces, she took up invitations to coffee, tea and sherry. The first of the latter was with the friendliest critic from *The Times*. He owned a copy of the first edition of *The New Grove Dictionary of Music and Musicians* and looked up Schumann for her. 'No mention of a violin concerto,' he said. 'None at all. Admittedly, this edition may be out of date. Don't you think, though, that if there was a concerto, I'd know about it?'

Jelly thanked him and went to morning coffee with another critic – James Gambrell, whom she respected yet feared a little; in his study he adopted the stance of a tutor interviewing a student across a college desk.

'My dear Jelly, how nice to see you... but why the devil are you looking for a missing violin concerto by Schumann? Or, indeed, any missing work by Schumann? You are surely aware of the situation vis-à-vis his suppressed compositions?'

Jelly blinked. Suppressed compositions, plural? 'Actually, I wasn't,' she said, keeping her eyes wide and innocent, trying to let charm make up for her pitiful ignorance. 'Please tell me?'

Gambrell took a long inhalation from his pipe. A number of Schumann's late works, he explained, were unpublished, assumed 'missing'. The truth was more awkward.

Schumann, he related, spent his last two years in a mental asylum at Endenich, near Bonn, the culmination of his long illness. All his life he had worked in a ferment of intensity, his highs bringing flurries of inspiration in which he might compose obsessively in one medium for weeks, months or more, turning out masterpiece after masterpiece; as for the lows, these lay beyond agonising and often rendered him unable to write at all. He fell in love with Clara Wieck when she was still in her teens; her father tried to separate them, on the grounds that the unstable Schumann would make a thoroughly disreputable husband for his Clara – a prodigy whom he had raised to be a great pianist, not housewife to a manic-depressive composer whose music was too interesting ever to make much money. The young couple took him to court and won the right to marry, which they duly did, the day before Clara's 21st birthday. The passing years brought them many children, musical glories, great friendships, but then – Gambrell lowered his voice – calamity.

'Schumann was quite, quite mad, possibly because he had a malady of, er, unfortunate origin that resulted in this, namely syphilis, or possibly because he had an inherent instability – or, I suspect, both. Whatever the truth, he went stark, raving *nuts*. People do say, of course, that a tendency towards these dual extremes is very common among our great artists and can fuel their output, which may well be the case here. But if that was what caught up with him in the end, it was tragic. He himself asked to be sent from his home in Düsseldorf to the asylum, because he was afraid he might harm Clara or the little ones. Poor Clara was left with seven children to bring up on her own.'

'My great-uncle adored Clara,' Jelly remarked. 'We always revered her memory.'

'Of course you would, as your great-uncle Joachim was one of Clara's inner circle of confidants, together with his close friend Johannes Brahms – who was himself in love with Clara, or so we believe. They were a true triumvirate, a triangle of power over the legacy of the unfortunate Schumann. All three of them went to Endenich when he was dying. Imagine, Miss d'Arányi, they stood by his body together, mourning, after his soul departed. Thereafter they kept together and closed ranks. It is perfectly possible that Clara discussed with Joachim, and with Brahms too, whether to suppress some of Schumann's more dubious late compositions: those they considered might betray the fact that his mind was no longer entirely coherent.'

'But surely Onkel Jo wouldn't have… ?'

'Well, put yourself in Frau Clara's shoes. One does not want one's husband's memory sullied by a work that doesn't do him justice.'

'But why do you think these pieces *wouldn't* have done him justice?' Jelly protested. 'How can we know, if nobody's ever heard them?'

'The chances of there even being a violin concerto are exceedingly slim. Look, he only met Joachim in the early 1850s – as you know, Joachim and Brahms were respectively only about 22 and 20 when they got to know Schumann, so any concerto he wrote for your Onkel Jo would indeed be a late work. It is eminently possible that Clara would have burned it. And if it does exist, it will have been hidden for a reason – namely, that it is probably not very good. Best let sleeping dogs lie.'

Jelly thanked the critic and drank the rest of her coffee, hoping its strength was the only reason she felt so tense. Fancy saying a work must be no good when there was no proof it even existed! Supposing it did exist, and it was a treasure, and she might find and play it and prove its worth, whether or not 'spirits' had any part in it? Going home in a cab, she closed her eyes and pictured ecstatic audiences, a new recording contract, a best-selling set of 78s, an American tour, some of which had been elusive of late... but above all, a resurrection, the only one that she could accomplish.

At home, she was battling frustration – an increased chance of the piece being real, but no indication of how to follow its trail – when the telephone rang, bringing to her the one person in the world who might know something concrete. Tovey had been off work for a year with health problems, so in her letter she had intimated merely that she wanted to consult him, should he be well enough.

'*Jelly!*' came the high trumpet tones of Tovey himself. 'What a plate greasure! How *are* ye?'

'Donald, how wonderful to hear you! Something astonishing has happened... ' Unlike the two critics she had spoken to, Tovey had been close to Onkel Jo in person. 'It's so peculiar I need to talk to you about it properly,' she said. 'Please can I come up and see you?'

Settling into a train compartment alone with her violin, Jelly experienced a naughty if good-humoured guilt at enjoying her solitude. Sharing a home with Adila and her family was adorable, and she felt grateful to them every day; but the holiday with Erik had not felt holidayesque.

It seemed to her that Erik and Adila had fastened on to one another's spirits and she could not decide which of them was clinging harder. Alec seemed neither worried nor jealous, but Jelly could not forget the jolt of discomfort that went through her upon learning that they had gone to the beach without her and Adrienne. Yet as a guest in her sister's household – however much Adila and Alec insisted that it was her home too – she could scarcely afford to express any objection.

The view from the train window was freckled with soot, now and then obliterated by clouds of steam; the song of the wheels made a tempting accompaniment. She had a compartment to herself, so to use the time productively she took out her violin and spent the rest of the journey practising.

At Edinburgh's Waverley station, iron girders overhead clashed with the bright northern sky. Jelly packed up the Bergonzi and swung down her old leather suitcase – she'd travelled light, for once. She could not see Tovey at first in the cluster of people waiting to meet the train – then out of the steam-misted station depths there emerged a familiar tall figure, wearing a pale hat and a light suit, perfect for a spring evening. Under bushy eyebrows, his eyes, wide-set and capable of what she regarded as inspired ferocity, glowed at her across the concourse as he strode forward to help her with her case.

The morning after a joyous musical dinner party in her honour at Tovey and his wife Clara's house, the professor took Jelly to work with him. Edinburgh University's music library was well populated with students cramming for their exams, though Tovey remarked as they passed that its catalogue system desperately needed updating. On his study door, a plaque declared him the Reid Professor of Music: inside, floor-to-ceiling bookshelves were stuffed with volumes accumulated during his two decades in the post. Running her fingertips along their cracked spines and embossed titles, Jelly thought the books smelled of all the lost worlds within their pages. She imagined sentences fluttering out like moths, dusted with the scents of coffee, chocolate, cigar smoke, a hint of whisky.

'The coffee and chocolates are real.' Tovey settled behind his desk. 'Have some.' He pushed a box towards her; Jelly pounced on a walnut praline that reminded her of the *palacsinta* she had loved in Hungary. Tovey sipped coffee. 'Now, tell me what's going on. Something is eating you up.'

Jelly took a breath, then began to explain in full her search for Schumann's Violin Concerto.

He heard her out. '*Gott in Himmel*,' he breathed when she'd finished. 'Jelly, are you sure about this? You must realise it sounds perfectly preposterous.'

'But think, Donald, please – you see, it doesn't matter *how* we know, if the concerto is real... '

'Adila has never heard of it?'

'She insists Onkel Jo never said a word, and she'd remember, wouldn't she?'

'Perhaps. But Adila is a busy lady. She gives a great deal, to her career, her family, her students and the best parties in Chelsea. And this spiritualist stuff – she regards it as central to her life, doesn't she? Personally I can't help being a scornful sceptic... ' He took another chocolate and a sip of coffee, mingling the two in his mouth. 'We need written evidence. I have some books that may tell us, so let's go hunting.'

First he extracted a fat volume entitled *Life of Joachim*, by Andreas Moser. He turned to the index; as Jelly watched, he fell still and his eyes brightened.

'Ha! Jelly, look! First time lucky.'

Under the index heading SCHUMANN was an entry that said, clear as Scottish sunlight, VIOLIN CONCERTO IN D MINOR.

'Schumann wrote to Joachim about it,' Tovey said, reading rapidly. 'So... yes, Jelly. It's real. You're very pale – are you all right?'

Jelly was silent. There, in print, was the confirmation she needed. She had been inwardly prepared for Tovey to continue declaring the whole story bunkum. Perhaps she'd hoped he would – because whatever was she to do about it now?

Tovey was following the trail. 'It seems... yes, it was written for Joachim, naturally, and he gave a performance... Ah. Look, Jelly. A Schumann letter, written from the asylum at Endenich. It's to Onkel Jo, saying he wishes he could have heard his performance of the D minor Concerto, quotes "which Clara speaks to me about so enthusiastically".'

Jelly tried to summon her voice. 'It wasn't... quite real... before.'

'Good. Now it is. Let's see... '

He spent a few minutes jotting notes, checking pages and staring thereafter into space. Jelly kept motionless for fear of disturbing him.

'So, it's from 1853,' he said at last. 'That does make it, as your critic friend suggested, a late work... Completed that October. Which, my dear, is exactly when he met Brahms for the first time. That gave him a boost – he was enchanted by this brilliant young man and his music.'

'When was it that Schumann had his nervous breakdown?'

'Five months later. He ran out of the house in his nightclothes one evening during carnival, threw his wedding ring into the Rhine and leapt in after it, apparently intending to drown himself. He was saved, but after that, he asked to be sent to the asylum.'

'And the Violin Concerto?'

'From the look of these,' Tovey said, tapping the volumes in front of him, 'our elusive concerto may have been the last big orchestral work he ever wrote.'

'So – perhaps a flood of inspiration, and then a crash?'

'Here's something else.' Tovey pored over a page, translating from the German. 'There's a letter here from Joachim to Moser, about the concerto... and – hmm. He doesn't like it very much. He says it shows, and I quote, "a certain exhaustion, which attempts to wring out the last resources of spiritual energy", though "certain individual passages bear witness to the deep feelings of the creative soul... "'

'But how can we know unless we can hear it?'

'Precisely. It is only fair to Schumann that the work should be heard and assessed anew.'

'Surely if Clara was "enthusiastic", it can't be one of those pieces she wanted to suppress, like that critic said.'

'Think of the situation. Schumann is ill in an asylum; Clara is forbidden to see him, so she's writing to him. Now, supposing Tom were a composer, he had produced a piece of questionable quality and you had to write to him in his current unfortunate condition to tell him you had heard it? You would be "enthusiastic" too, I think.'

'Where do you think we should start?' Jelly asked, deflecting the topic away from the painful thought of Tom – who had once been Tovey's pupil and remained his friend.

'I suggest you contact two people,' Tovey said. 'First, Onkel Jo's daughter, your cousin Elisabeth Joachim, in Oxford; and next, Eugenie Schumann, the daughter of Robert and Clara, who lives somewhere in Switzerland. She is the last of their children to survive with body and mind entirely intact.'

'Really? What happened to the others?'

'Several died young from tuberculosis. One, Ludwig, went mad like his father, but much younger, and spent the rest of his life – decades of it – in an asylum. Marie, the eldest, died just a few years ago, having mainly devoted herself to caring for her mother. Clara was very good at inspiring people to care for her, Brahms included.'

'You never met Brahms, did you?' Jelly was not quite four years old when the composer died.

'Alas, no. Onkel Jo always said he would introduce me, but we were never in the same country at the same time. And then it was too late...'

An image of Tom lingered in Jelly's mind.

'The glass said the concerto was in Weimar. Perhaps I should go to Germany to look for it.'

Tovey's smile vanished. 'Jelly, I wouldn't do that if I were you.'

'Whyever not?'

Tovey wandered to the window and stared out at the quiet

morning, the townsfolk going about their business, bicycles and a few cars and trucks rattling up and down the hills. 'You wouldn't believe it possible from here. Jelly, listen: apparently there are disappearances, beatings, bricks through windows, notices in shops and restaurants forbidding Jews… There was an official boycott, so I'm told, of Jewish businesses in Berlin a month or so ago and now, I think in Frankfurt, they have forced the dismissal of all Jewish actors and musicians from their companies. It looks as if they are trying to negate Jewish influences wherever they can. I think you shouldn't go.'

Jelly tried to absorb this information. 'But I'm not Jewish, at least not entirely, and surely they can't hurt me if I'm foreign?'

'Onkel Jo was Jewish, so effectively that makes you part of his family and probably, therefore, Jewish as well – at least to the mind of a Nazi.'

'But he converted. He became a Catholic, quite young… '

'I know, but is Jewishness a matter of race or religion? For Jo, it was religion. To the Nazis, it's something quite different.'

Images of Berlin ten years previously swirled in Jelly's memory – nightclubs, jazz, the most outlandishly dressed people she'd ever set eyes on, actors and authors and incredible conductors and singers. It used to be so free, so open.

'No longer,' said Tovey. 'Don't go, I beg you.'

'But if I can convince… '

'Jelly,' he interrupted, 'will you please listen to me? I didn't want to tell you this… but they have just destroyed all the busts and statues of Onkel Jo, and renamed Joachimstrasse.'

Jelly recoiled. 'But he was their greatest violinist… '

'Yet not an "Aryan". That is their chief concern.'

'But it's *stupid!* People are the same, they have the same needs and the same duties and – '

'I don't pretend my analytical skills extend anywhere beyond music, let alone to politics. Still, it strikes me that there's a tipping point in any ideology when facts and sense start to matter less than the imposition of that ideology for its own sake.

And then people may decide it's in their interests to pretend to believe in it, even if they don't. It's fascism, Jelly. And even if you yourself might be safe, I personally forbid you to visit a country that's foisting this upon its people.'

The vandalism against her great-uncle's legacy stung Jelly as if she'd swallowed a hornet. Everyone would know about her Jewish roots via Joachim. But how could one quarter of one's inheritance make such a difference?

'My father was chief of the Budapest police,' she protested. 'He was part of the establishment, he was known and respected… '

'That won't hold any sway with the Nazis. Don't underestimate them. They are pigs rooting for the truffle that is power, and when they smell it there's no stopping them.'

'Donald – you don't think it'll happen here too, do you?'

'Heaven willing, the majority of the British are too set in their ways to adopt anything so crudely alien,' Tovey remarked. 'But there are elements, especially in the upper crust of society and also among the disaffected unemployed, who are taken with Oswald Mosley, and we cannot deny they would like it to do so.'

'Whatever would happen to me and Adila?'

Tovey gave her a quick and penetrating glance. 'Try not to worry about it, Jelly. Keep vigilant and stay away from trouble. Meanwhile, our concern is that concerto… '

Jelly, unsettled, took stock. 'So the concerto is in Germany; Germany is ruled by the Nazis; and I can't go.'

'Brava.'

She drummed her heels in frustration. 'If we'd had this message a year ago, or two, there'd have been no problem. Instead, the "messengers" had to appear just after Hitler took over! *Why?*'

Tovey sipped coffee, cold in its cup. 'I wonder that as well.'

'What we need, then,' said Jelly, 'is someone who is already *in* Germany and who has the contacts to go and look on our behalf. Do you know anyone? An academic? A composer?'

A broad smile unfolded across Tovey's face. 'You know something? I believe I know the very person.'

Chapter 6

Ulrich Schultheiss, assistant editor at the music publishers B. Schott und Söhne in Mainz, had not slept for five nights. Possibly ten. Sometimes, switching on the wireless to hear the news, which was often no longer news but whitewashing, he suspected he might never sleep again. The Chancellor had declared his political party the only one in Germany, effectively banning all others; that seemed to confirm Ulli's worst suspicions that Hitler was not only dangerous, but medically insane.

Mainz, Ulli thought, should have been a small enough town not to feel the shifting tectonic plates of world politics. All that changed when the director of the local conservatoire, Hans Gál – a fine composer and even finer man, in Ulli's view – was evicted from his post one month after the college had renewed his contract.

'It contravenes the law, surely?' said Ulli to his boss, Ludwig Strecker – the joint proprietor of the firm with his brother, Willy. Two tall men in their fifties blessed with imposing Roman profiles and a steely charisma fed by the endurance tests of the 1914–18 war, the Strecker brothers were on first-name terms with the entire music world of central Europe and beyond.

'Law? What law?' Ludwig said. 'These madmen can do whatever they want. Gál is Jewish and he's out. It's nothing to do with his music or his teaching, let alone the law.'

'But why does nobody do or say anything? Why aren't there protests?' Visiting the conservatoire to see a friend, Ulli had found its stone staircases and dark wooden doorways echoing with the usual wails, scales and studies, the corridors dotted with students smoking after class, while professors lunched in the café opposite. Business as usual – but without Hans Gál.

'You can't be surprised if people are afraid to speak out.'

'But if they can force this, what next? If people just let things happen... '

'Oh, Ulli.' Ludwig was shaking his head. Ulli knew he had experienced the trenches and still had nightmares about them, though he rarely spoke of it. 'You're very young,' was all he said.

The Gáls made a furtive visit to Willy Strecker's family to say farewell, one night when Ulli happened to be there for dinner. They were leaving, they said, so that their friends would no longer be compromised by seeing them; the Third Reich officials were observing and noting every move of the town's Jewish citizens. 'Don't those busybodies have anything better to do with their time?' Ulli grumbled.

The Gáls walked away across the square with their two sons, avoiding the streetlights, heads down, dark hats and scarves all but concealing their faces; with a fearful lurch he wondered when he might ever see them again. He shut himself inside the cloakroom for a few minutes so that his boss would not witness his emotions getting the better of him.

He had seen it approaching, yet he didn't want to believe it. It had been baking at the back of the Depression's oven for years. The new recipe of this nationalist cake – thick textured and full of nuts, Ulli thought – lured disaffected young people who couldn't find jobs, since there were none to be had; it seemed aromatic, too, for older folk who'd blame anyone but the government and world finances for what was going on: immigrants, Jews, Gypsies, sodomites, and anybody who dared to ask too many questions.

Ulli could easily have been part of that. His father never came back from Ypres, and he still recalled the anguish of mortification when he arrived at school during the war in a blazer three sizes too small, lightheaded and nauseous because there was no breakfast to eat, nor any lunch to look forward to. He thanked God, and his mother, for his music; in contact with the piano keys and the spirits of Beethoven, Bach or Schumann, he felt the world's madness give way to beauty, inspiration and order, while the music lasted. He wished to serve that beauty, inspiration and order; now working for Schott gave him the chance to do so. And so the Streckers, and Ulli with them, watched, waited and fought what corners were theirs to fight; namely, those of the composers whose works they published.

Each morning Ulli bicycled to the office from his flat on the outskirts of Mainz – a small apartment with a living room occupied mainly by his Bechstein piano. He would ride along by the river Rhine, past the dusky pink stone of the ancient cathedral and into the medieval streets of the town centre, cobbles under his wheels, oak-beamed façades around him – as pretty as a set for Humperdinck's *Hänsel und Gretel*, which Schott published, and as German as one for Wagner's *Die Meistersinger von Nürnberg*, which Schott also published. On the Weihergarten he left his bike outside the building, then unlocked the heavy wooden door that led to the main staircase between the street and the courtyard. There in the hall he found himself face to face with Richard Wagner.

'Good morning, Herr Richard,' Ulli said silently to Wagner's bust. It had a noble mien – much idealised – and Ulli never failed to bid it good morning. Wagner's operas brought the company coffers quantities of income: they owed the old codger a dreadful debt of thanks. And whatever you thought of the man, his unspeakable arrogance and the suspicion that every time he looked in a mirror he saw Nietzsche's Superman, there was no getting away from the glory of his music. He had unveiled the libretto of *Die Meistersinger* to Willy and Ludwig's grandfather downstairs in the same offices some 70 years earlier. The Strecker brothers, having inherited the family business, insisted that nothing in that historic space must be changed, so the Wagner Room kept its character: the fine-limbed wooden furniture, the graceful cornicing, and a very elderly piano – nobody dared to touch it now – on which Liszt and Wagner had both played. While other firms moved to Berlin to be at the centre of German cultural life, Schott's stayed put, their location and history prime assets. Here in Mainz, Johannes Gutenberg had invented the modern process of printing: now the Streckers kept their products rolling off the presses not a mile away from that first machine. And Ulli, as general, all-round, right-hand editorial man, would make certain that everything was progressing smoothly and on time. Beauty, inspiration and order. Strange ideals, perhaps, at a time of fire – of the Reichstag, of books, of democracy itself – but ones only to be found in art.

'Tough day ahead, Ulli,' Wagner's bust seemed to warn him this morning. 'Hold on and keep your strength. You're going to need it.'

Fräulein Kammerling tapped on his office door minutes later. 'Dr Schultheiss, I have a call from Herr Doktor Professor Donald Tovey at Edinburgh University. He wanted Dr Strecker, but please could you speak to him?' Willy was away in Munich, meeting another composer, Carl Orff.

'*Tovey?* On the phone? Of course – please put him through.'

While he was Schott's representative in London, before the Great War lobbed him into the indignity of the Alexandra Palace internment camp – which was not palatial at all – Willy Strecker served as Tovey's unofficial concert agent and business manager, as well as his publisher. Schott still published his compositions.

Ulli listened as Tovey explained the developments at the d'Arányi and Fachiri family home, his incredulity growing with every word. A Schumann violin concerto? Messages from a glass game? The whole thing had to be a joke.

'A Schumann concerto turning up would be astonishing, but who in the name of heaven is going to believe this? And from Joachim's great-nieces? Professor Tovey, these ladies may be amazing musicians – I remember hearing Jelly play when I was a boy – but they are having you on.'

He'd been barely eleven, visiting family friends in Surrey a year or so before the war broke out; he retained a faint image of a slender, scarlet-clad, flame-like presence whirling through Beethoven, Brahms and something very Hungarian. He'd thought her beautiful, but a little weird, as if she had landed on the earth from a distant world; perhaps a bird changed into a woman via some inverted Ovidian metamorphosis.

'I'd love to tell you this is one big jest,' said Tovey. 'But… Jelly and her sister are not like that. In a funny kind of way, they're innocents. They don't know *how* to be dishonest. They grew up with a ferocious father – can you imagine, head of the police in Budapest… '

'So, you're convinced they are not making it up and they haven't just stumbled upon something Onkel Jo once said over the *palinka*?'

'There *is* a concerto, and its existence is noted in at least one very good book. And no matter how it has come to our attention, it's time to find it. Here is my question: do you think the doctors Strecker might consider helping to track it down, on the premise that they may then publish it?'

Ulli thought fast. It would be an amazing stroke of fortune to lay hands on such a work, especially if it turned out to be as good as Schumann's Piano Concerto. 'Perhaps Willy could write to Joachim's son. I'm sure he mentioned he was interned together with him in England during the war… ' Odd, he reflected, that bonds forged in deprived communal conditions, over scant meals, or at unthinkable toilet facilities, could be stronger by far than those made over champagne cocktails at the Hotel Adlon. He had never had friends as close as those he made in childhood, stealing apples and pears from the orchards and gorging on them by the brook through the meadows. They were all hungry, they all had nothing to lose, and they would never forget one another's parlous state in those days, no matter how well subsequent fortune might treat them.

'Ulli, I'd be most grateful if you could run this by him, or at least the existence of the piece – there's no need to mention the, er, spirit aspect. I've had to almost physically restrain Jelly from jumping on the first boat to go and look for the manuscript herself.'

'Perhaps she should.'

'Awkward and potentially dangerous. Joachim… '

'Oh, God.'

'At least they're in Britain,' said Tovey. 'At least they're safe.'

A circuit connected in Ulli's mind: Tovey's tone was tremulous enough to tell him that the d'Arányi sisters' safety meant the light of the sun and moon to this revered academic.

'Jelly is playing the supposedly Mozart "Adelaide" Concerto in November. I believe you've published it, so why don't you come over for the concert? Then you could meet her and see for yourself.'

'Thank you, Professor Tovey,' said Ulli. 'I might just do that.'

Katharine Tennant, who was organising Jelly's charity tour, had lined up more than the three or four cathedrals Jelly had envisaged. The project grew like an orchid in a hothouse; now it had blossomed into nine events. If anyone tried to say no, Katharine, her determination and tenacity veneered with charm and her Asquith accent, simply wouldn't listen, and her targets would find sooner or later that they had said yes, even if they hadn't meant to.

'Darling, you're a miracle worker,' Jelly beamed at her over tea. 'I dreamed this up at the end of March, and you've made it all happen by June!'

'It's been easy,' Katharine smiled. 'People are only ever reluctant to take on a great musician if they actually have to *pay* them, which in this case is not a concern.'

'You're much too modest.' Jelly gave her a hug.

She was convinced that the rapid take-up must reflect a genuine appetite for the concerts. At each, she would play for free, welcoming all comers, with a collection afterwards. Every dean leapt at the chance of a charity performance by Jelly d'Arányi. They recognised the longing for order and beauty in this pea-souper of a depression; music was the quickest way to achieve it – and though local music societies could offer live concerts to those in the know, provision of them in large venues at no cost seemed a godsend. Jelly might be delighted, but now she had to work, work and work. And as if York Minster were not an intimidating enough place to begin, in a magnificent coup Katharine had managed to book her and Adila to play together on 10 July at the venue Jelly most wanted, Westminster Abbey. The one thing they could not do was to find the Schumann Violin Concerto in time for the tour; Jelly had no choice but to watch that part of the dream evaporate. She simply had no time to pursue it.

To say the cathedral tour was the most demanding thing she had ever attempted would do it an injustice. The cycle of exhilaration and exhaustion swelled around her, as if she'd swallowed Alice in Wonderland's potion and found herself dwarfed by her own dream. At York she began to understand the scale of her task. A place's essence, she knew, can seep into your body as if by osmosis and coerce a response more physical than rational. Still, she wasn't prepared for the malevolence in the air. Tom had told her often that she was too sensitive for her own good, sometimes too imaginative as well; but Jelly remained convinced that places carry the energy of lives that are played out there, and that atmospheres can change irrevocably when they house intense suffering. So it was in York.

She had thought unemployment severe in London; here it was worse still. 'For those of us who are fortunate to have gainful work, things are perfectly all right,' the driver from the Minster's Deanery remarked, collecting her from the station and watching her casting about as they drove, taking in the surroundings. 'There are picture houses springing up absolutely everywhere.

But you do have to be, so to speak, from the right side of the tracks.'

'What happened?'

'Industry – or lack of it. Everything has collapsed in these parts. This county was the powerhouse for textiles and coal mining, but no longer. You might see some truly appalling slums, which we hope will be demolished. One wouldn't wish to house one's animals in such squalor. Ahh, here we are – this is the Deanery. Let me take your bags... '

The house was tranquil and pleasant, clambered upon by roses in full bloom; it would have been easy to stay in, enjoy chatting with the dean and his wife, practise, and ignore everything beyond her room and the Minster. Once she might have done so, but no longer. She wanted to see beneath the surface.

'I might go for a little walk,' she told her hosts. 'I need to stretch my legs... ' And she gently dissuaded them from their well-intentioned offers to go with her.

It did not take long to find what she was looking for. Beyond the glories of the Minster and the generous streets close by, the atmosphere sank still further. The foggy air reeked of lingering smoke and coal dust; her stockings were turning black. She wandered down a side road and found herself in a warren of unkempt terraces, which summer seemed to have left untouched. Passing a dark stone building that looked like a hostel – a dosshouse, mental asylum, or combination of both – she heard moans and muffled shrieks through an open window, and a group of four children ran out and surrounded her, pointing at her suit and hat and pleading for money. One of the girls, muddy-legged, her dress little more than stitched-together rags, was the same height as Adrienne.

'Where are your mummy and daddy?' Jelly asked them.

'Our father's dead in the mines and Mam's got a cough and she's on the drink,' said the smallest boy, who couldn't have been more than five. His shins, beneath the end of his short trousers, were covered in purple bruises and red, scabby scrapes, unwashed and untended. He wore no shoes – and Jelly was horrified to see shards of broken glass scattered around the street, as if someone had thrown a bottle out of the nearest window.

'Where do you live?'

The eldest girl pointed at the house where Jelly had heard the screaming. 'There since last week, but Mam can't pay t'rent, so we have to get out before t'collector comes.'

'But where do you go to school?' she asked. They laughed in her face. The older boy had just today found some work pushing a barrow. The two girls went out begging. They'd come from Darlington, they told her, walking all the way, looking for some uncle or cousin to help them, but he wasn't here after all.

Jelly couldn't bear it. She emptied her whole purse into their upturned hands.

'Come to my concert in the Minster,' she said. 'It doesn't cost anything.'

'What? In there?' They couldn't believe her. One of them noticed her accent and scowled. 'Are you German, Miss?'

'No, Hungarian.' She brushed it aside. 'Really, come to the concert, and bring your mam. I'd love it if you did.'

Surprised and a little subdued – whether by the cash or the concert idea – the children mumbled thanks and ran away through the murk towards the dosshouse. Jelly turned to go back, wondering whether music really could do anything for people in such desperate circumstances.

The Minster glowered out of the fog; when she went in to explore, the lighting was dim and the place so gigantic that the tops of the pillars vanished into sepia shadows. She'd been here several times: previously, in the pre-Depression days, it seemed to embrace her, its transepts spreading like affectionate arms. Now it sat still, impassive, while Jelly's playful heart seemed paralysed. 'There's no need to worry,' the dean assured her. 'You are undertaking a pilgrimage of compassion, so everything will go well.' After the interval, he told her, he would make an appeal for the Northern Industries Workrooms and centres for the unemployed in the Cleveland district.

She tried to turn her attention back to her playing. She'd chosen the programme with care; almost an hour and a quarter of music, most of it slow, since rapid pieces full of twirls would be swallowed like plankton in the whale-belly cavern of a cathedral. The result: the slow movements of the Mozart D major, the Beethoven and the Mendelssohn concertos; a complete Handel sonata; and the immense solo Chaconne by Bach, from his Partita No. 2 in D minor.

After scant sleep, she spent the morning rehearsing with the organist, Dr Edward Bairstow; everyone encouraged her, praised her and brought her cups of tea, Dr Bairstow exclaimed in delight at the contrast she was bringing them from what he called the 'poisonous materialism' of their times, and Mrs Bairstow came bustling in to press upon her the loan of a jersey, since it was so chilly inside, even though it was the middle of June. Jelly's mouth felt dry while her hands were damp with sweat. She had begun to doubt that anyone would have the slightest inclination to listen to violin music in any case, free or otherwise. By the time the bells had struck 7 and she was in the vestry preparing, she was wondering why this escapade had ever seemed a good idea.

She fastened her simplest brown and white concert dress and dabbed on just a little lipstick and face powder; she did not want to emphasise the embarrassing gulf of privilege between herself and the audience she sought. She wanted to be as close to them as she'd been to those patients in the hospital. All she could do was play her best and hope it was good enough. If nobody turned up, then nobody turned up and there'd be nothing she could do about it.

And then the doors of the Minster were opened with a great creak that echoed up to the roof; and peering round the vestry door, she could see them arriving, people streaming into the Minster, row upon row; the volume of talk, swirling around the arcs of the building, rose moment by moment. She watched, incredulous. Was the whole of York here?

Side by side with Dr Bairstow, hearing her own heart thudding and the ringing rush of blood behind her ears, she stepped out into the vast space. Applause surged towards them. She glanced around the pews; to one side, some well-heeled listeners: a silk scarf, a glimmer of jewellery. These people would contribute to the collection. At the back, those who would benefit: people who could pay nothing, yet would enjoy the performance in just the same way, possibly more. Music has no respect for bank accounts. Jelly thought of the children she'd met the day before, and prayed that they, too, might be there, somewhere at the back, though she'd prefer them to sit at the front. The crowd was so large that she could scarcely take in the faces; families huddled in the distant pews, elderly couples came in with walking sticks, and at the end of one row she spotted a tall man, one of whose legs was missing below the knee – an ex-serviceman, she was sure. A makeshift wooden crutch was propped beside him.

Once silence fell, Dr Bairstow started the Mozart *Andante cantabile* from the D major Concerto; Jelly was staring down at the stone under her feet, trying to absorb herself in the music's tranquil atmosphere. Drawing out her first phrases, reaching up to a high note that seemed to last for ever, suspended in ecstasy above the shifting harmonies, a welcome sense of security took her, the knowledge that nothing could go wrong tonight after all. The acoustic nourished her sound, letting it sail out to the rapt audience; and between the pieces the clapping pounded and pleaded: more, more, give us more... Lowering her violin after the Mendelssohn Concerto slow movement, she spotted the one-legged veteran wiping his eyes with his sleeve.

At the end she greeted well-wishers in a daze of hope and a certainty that what she had decided to do was, after all, necessary beyond doubt, even if it might provide only a drop of comfort compared to the amount needed. But there, in the throng making for the door past the collectors, wasn't that the little girl who was Adrienne's age? Jelly tried to catch her eye and wave. The child gave her a lopsided grin, then took a coin out of her threadbare pocket – it must have been from the money Jelly gave them yesterday – and to Jelly's astonishment, deposited it with a flourish in the collection bucket.

Time to move on; the next day it was Hexham, and after that, Durham, which to Jelly was the most beautiful of all, yet which brought even more pain than York. You can perform the Bach Chaconne at sunset by the altar of a holy site more than ten centuries old, while a thousand people drink music through golden dusky light; but when they come to you afterwards and tell you their stories, the reality begins to hit home.

Two women came up to Jelly to thank her, each with several children in tow. She asked them a few gentle questions and their stories came tumbling out. Nearby Newcastle, once thriving with shipyards and coal mines, lay with its wheels stilled and its furnaces cold. Their husbands had not worked for two years. She looked down at the little boys, who were pulling on their mothers' hands, itching to get away from this dull grown-ups' conversation. Their toes were popping out at the ends of their cracked shoes.

What prospect was there for the children, the women demanded, watching their fathers losing the dignity work gave them? All they had left was dole; and everyone looking over their shoulders to see who was worse off than themselves; and the Means Test men who would march into the house and force them to sell their chairs before allowing them a farthing of government support. The mothers talked, sentences falling over one another. Nobody was hiring, but the government, in faraway London, still blamed the unemployed for not wanting to work. Of course they wanted to work. No one would choose to raise a family on a handout of a few shillings a week. 'But us, we can't change the world,' said the younger woman. 'We can't change anything.' Jelly, clasping the neck of her violin, listened and didn't know what to say.

She wanted to understand why; so did they. Was this the paying-off of debts incurred by the war that finished 15 years ago? The knock-on effect of the stock-market crash – the poor forced to fund the greed of the rich? Or something even worse: a loss of faith? And in the middle of that – an angel, a violin, the music of Bach.

'Thank you, Miss d'Arányi. We'll never forget you. We'll never forget what you did for us tonight.'

Jelly could barely answer; she was in tears. 'I am so moved. I am speechless... I had no idea it would be like this.'

A headline in *The Times* seized on the York Minster dean's remark about 'a pilgrimage of compassion'. That wasn't her idea. She wanted to play for nothing to people who had nothing, because she had something to give. Their response was more precious to her than any financial return. This should be commonplace for a musician, she told Adila – but apparently it was extraordinary.

Her confidence grew. After Durham, she had four days to get her breath before Lincoln; then time to go home briefly before starting the southern route to Winchester, Salisbury, Chichester, the big day at Westminster Abbey, and finally Gloucester. She began to experiment. In Chichester she started by playing in the organ loft, then came downstairs for the Bach and only then noticed that the audience wasn't packed only through the nave, but through every side-chapel and outside in the cloisters. The south was less harrowing, the concentration of poverty less intense; from Winchester, 75 per cent of the takings would go to the Northern Industries Workroom Council, where it was most needed, and the remainder to the unemployed of Hampshire.

English summers, though, were English summers, and cathedrals were difficult to keep warm when it rained – as it did, copiously. Before the concerts, while she paced about in the vestry, sometimes Jelly's hands were so cold that the knuckles hurt as if she'd rammed nails into them. Her gowns might be simple, but the backs usually involved the fashionable plunge, exposing her shoulder blades to the chilly church air. Waking in hotels or deaneries the morning after, she would feel pain colonising her spine, arms and sacroiliacs as if injected while she slept. Everywhere her audience came up to thank her for giving them so much of her spirit. She fixed her smile, looked them in the eye and thanked them in return, while in truth she wanted to crawl away and howl. The spirit wasn't the problem. It was her body that was wearing out.

July arrived. Jelly, aching and exhausted, was home at last with just two more concerts to go, sitting in a Chinese silk dressing gown on her bedroom floor surrounded by mounds of unopened correspondence. She felt she had scarcely enough energy to slit the envelopes, until she found one she really wanted. *How I wish I could be with you for the Westminster Abbey concert,* Tom wrote. *Please don't waste your time worrying about me. Go there and play wonderfully. That's all I ask.*

Jelly hunted for a handkerchief. There was one by her bed. She sat down to mop up, but a cricket bat of exhaustion seemed to swing into her face. Surely she could take just 15 minutes for a nap. Caesar found her there and jumped up to lick her face before settling by the crook of her knee.

Four hours later, Adila, who was joining her to perform in the Abbey, was less easy-going.

'Sai! What's going on? I'll call the doctor.'

'No, Adi, I just need to rest. Let me sleep.' Jelly smiled at her sister, who leaned over and hugged her as if trying to transfer her overwhelming energy into Jelly's delicate frame. She was in such pain that she could scarcely turn over.

The evening before Westminster, Erik arrived with a bouquet

for the sisters almost the size of the sofa. Jelly hauled herself upright and put on a white blouse and light skirt. She'd been in bed for three days. Claws of pain dug into her back when she tried to bend over her chest of drawers to find some stockings. The impact of each step rebounded through her right hip.

'Jelly's hurt her back and she's tired out,' Alec was telling Erik when Jelly, after clunky progress down the stairs, arrived in the music room. Adila was arranging the flowers in a porcelain vase that bore only one tiny chip. The evening was warm and she had flung open the doors to the garden, letting in the scent of roses and rays of light giddy with spiralling sunbeams. Madge had come for a lesson, but now she was out on the lawn playing with Adrienne, a tennis ball and the dog. Alec and Erik were both relaxed and smiling in their shirtsleeves.

Jelly made an effort to put on her public self, trying to ignore what was happening to her joints. She saw a flash of concern in the baron's perceptive eyes.

'It's all right,' she said. 'I'll be fine tomorrow.'

'She won't let us call the doctor,' Adila growled. 'Three thousand people we expect in Westminster Abbey and my sister cannot move!'

'I won't make you play on your own, if that's what worries you,' Jelly teased.

'You will have good company,' Erik said. 'We have had a session this afternoon with our friends, who tell me they will all be there to hear you.'

For a moment Jelly thought he meant living people. She wondered how much Adila truly believed in the presence of these spirits – and how much she might herself. Adila, as far as she knew, had never questioned her belief in the messages any more than she had questioned her belief in God. But Jelly, seeing the consumptive patients around Anna, the begging children in Yorkshire and the shipyard wives in Durham, now found herself inwardly interrogating any deity's actions on a regular basis.

'Don't worry, Sai,' said Alec. 'The reality is only what we

can do for others, human to human. Believe me, you're doing more than most.'

A commotion from the garden and the little girls bounced in, flushed, happy and ready for cake and ice cream.

'Darlings! Something wonderful has happened: we have been speaking to Schumann and Joachim,' Adila cried, slicing giant pieces of plum cake. 'Just think, when you are there tomorrow listening to us, so are they!'

Madge's astute blue eyes cast a sphinx-like stare at her violin teacher. 'I was going to ask, please can I telephone Jane to pick me up?' Jane, Madge's stepsister ten years her senior, was an excellent cellist who often came round to play chamber music.

'Of course, darling – tell her come now and have tea – and tomorrow you will both come to the concert?'

'Isn't it only for unemployed people?'

'No, no, it is for everyone, free, and then there is a collection at the door for the unemployed. That is the point.'

'A collection to which all those spirit friends are not well placed to contribute,' Alec remarked, while Madge slunk towards the telephone. 'I hope her mother won't change her mind about the lessons.'

'She's so gifted! She's making such progress! Whyever would she change?'

'Well, don't you think we should perhaps be more discreet about these little visitations? Not everyone approves, you know. People find it a bit odd. You know attitudes aren't exactly as receptive to these things as they used to be.'

'But, sweetheart, it's true, it's happening *to us*. How can one argue with that?'

'People only believe what they want to believe – and if they don't want to believe something, nothing you say will change that. They'll always find a way round it. It's human nature. Besides, there are too many frauds... '

'*You're* sure it's real, aren't you?'

'I'm ready to be convinced,' he smiled.

Adila glowered. 'This is still *incontrovertible evidence* – there *is* an afterlife and the spirits of the departed are communicating with us. What are they going to do about that? One day our research will show it all... '

'I love the way it's called "research",' said Alec. 'Who's for another cup of tea?'

Big Ben was striking four when Jelly and Adila walked together into Westminster Abbey. Inside, they paused at the Tomb of the Unknown Warrior. *For the unknown war dead, wherever they fell.* They both remembered the unveiling in 1920 and the crowds that flocked to pay tribute to the dead soldier. Over 1.25 million in the week after the burial, Alec reported. Queues as far as parliament. Everyone in the country seemed to have someone to mourn – a husband, a father, a son, a brother, a fiancé, or several of these. Jelly had shed tears in Westminster Abbey for Sep, though at home she rarely spoke of her pain. Everyone might tease her about being overemotional, but she was quite capable of keeping her deepest feelings to herself and her violin when she wished. Seventeen years after Sep's death, the tombstone still tore at her.

Adila understood; she slid her arm through her sister's and squeezed. She read out the inscription at the side: '"Unknown and yet well known, dying and behold we live... " Do you think it's Sep, down there?'

'It doesn't seem fair that we only mark this one because we think he was British,' said Jelly. 'They all fought for us.'

She stood absorbing herself into her surroundings: the Gothic arches, the dark wood of the screed, the tombs of Chaucer, Purcell, King Henry V. Stained glass scattered flecks of royal blue, tangerine and scarlet onto the ancient stone.

Supposing the spirits of those composers and her great-uncle really were there, watching her? And if they were, what of Sep? What of her parents? She had to stop thinking about it.

They decided to play from the organ loft, where it would be easiest to coordinate with their accompanist. Shortly before it was time to start, after he had gone out to make his preparations, Jelly lay down on a rug on the floor, stretching out her aching back. Above her, soot-stained vaulting reached towards infinity.

'Sai, we should go and get dressed.' Adila held out her hands to pull her up.

'I'm floating. Come and try it.' Jelly patted the floor beside her.

Adila lumbered down and lay back. The sisters stayed there in silence, gazing up into the arches. 'You could take leave of earth like this,' Jelly said.

'Listen, everyone's arriving… '

The hum of voices in the air reminded Jelly of bees in the Dorset heather. Staring only upward, while different protrusions of carved stone tossed sounds between them, she couldn't identify the directions of the myriad noises. They could have been the spirits murmuring, winging around in search of a good spot on which to perch and listen. Proof of spirits meant proof of an afterlife – and was that not the real problem with her Schumann concerto?

'I feel better. Let's go and change.' As Jelly stood up, the blanket of pain seemed to rise and carry on rising, leaving her body clear, her breath controlled and her hands warm, supple and ready for anything.

'Nervous?' Adila was moistening her own lips.

'Not remotely.' With her violin and bow in her hands, her sister beside her and, who knows, invisible spirits giving their support, Jelly felt the freedom of the stage taking hold. Tonight would be one of their best concerts. She needed no more reassurance.

Chapter 7

'Sai! Come here, *quick*!' Adila was in the hall, hair wild, eyes aflame, a telegram from Erik in her hand. 'We have found the Schumann Violin Concerto!'

Jelly flew down the stairs, narrowly avoiding an overexcited Caesar underfoot. It was late August; they had just returned from a holiday in Scotland, staying with the convalescent Anna by a Highland loch. Erik and Ebba had spent the summer in Sweden – but returning to London, Erik engineered a diplomat's circuitous route.

'He has managed to go to Berlin, and he has found the manuscript himself, in person.' Adila shoved the paper towards Jelly. 'It was in the Prussian State Library. In the wrong file.'

Jelly read the impersonal typewritten words over and over again, wondering why she didn't share her sister's joy.

'We are to go to their dinner party the day he's back and he'll tell us everything!' Adila grabbed her by the waist and whirled her round the hall in a manic waltz. 'Today, I knew, there would be a miracle. It is found! Found!'

'Found? If only it were that simple.'

In Portland Place Erik presided at the head of the table, with Adila to his right, Jelly to his left, Ebba at the far end with Alec beside her; the Palmstiernas' daughter Margareta and her husband François were visiting from France and sat in the centre, one on each side; and, in between, more dinner party guests were arrayed in alternation of the sexes – men in black tie, women in sleek evening gowns, their jewels grabbing light from the chandelier above and the tall candles in the middle. Jelly, wearing crimson silk, and Adila, in lilac satin, both leaned towards the baron as he described his unlikely ambassadorial adventures in the music libraries of Berlin.

'But what's the concerto *like*?' Jelly begged.

'Unfortunately,' said the baron, 'it's one of my great regrets that I have never learned to read music. So I'm afraid… '

'And they wouldn't let you photograph it?' Adila pressed.

Indeed they had not. It was pure chance he had found it at all. He had gone first to the Musikhochschüle library, where nothing was in evidence, but overhearing him talking to the librarian, a passing academic glanced round and suggested he try the Staatsbibliothek – the Prussian State Library – instead. There, some official in uniform barred his way, accusing him of being Jewish, prodding him in the chest with a gun. Erik, who was stocky and dark, had to produce three rounds of diplomatic papers before he was believed. Once inside, he found nothing of interest in files marked SCHUMANN, but acting on a hunch, well aware of the possibility of misfiling alongside misidentification, he decided to check those marked JOACHIM as well. This revealed a modest sheaf of faded manuscript paper signed with the name 'Robert Schumann'.

Not that anybody at the library had been particularly aware of the treasure stashed away in their archive, but once they were – oh dear. That was just the start. For one thing, there were apparently several manuscripts of the same piece, in different formats; he had only found one of them. The archive's head, hunting through some records, told him that another, the first movement with piano score, had been used for a play-through at Zwickau, Schumann's birthplace, three years earlier, but was then laid to rest again. And last, but assuredly not least, a note accompanied the file, declaring that the concerto was 'not for publication'. It was not to be performed until 100 years after Schumann's death.

'But it's not lost at all, or even suppressed, if it's been played?' Ebba challenged her husband.

He shrugged. A private try-out with piano, no orchestra, precious little audience; that didn't really count.

'You're over-romanticising the entire situation. Someone already knew about it,' Ebba protested. 'A *lost* concerto? That, my dear, is not "lost" in the slightest.'

'But the concerto is strictly embargoed,' Erik explained. 'There is a clause, apparently placed there by – Adila and Jelly – your cousin Johannes Joachim, who apparently wrote this, according to his memory of his father's words. When did Schumann die?'

'In 1856… Oh *no*.' Jelly, calculating, took a long draught of wine. 'That means – it is not to be seen for another 23 years?'

'Willy Strecker at Schott's is bound to help,' Adila insisted. 'Jelly, didn't you say Tovey had been in touch with him, or his assistant, some nice young man there?'

'Embargoes are extremely awkward in legal terms,' Alec said. 'Often you're dealing with someone's last wishes, people's wills, that type of thing…'

'But what is this note? Some silly, unreadable squiggle from Johannes?' Adila was tapping her heel hard against the wooden floor, which fortunately was protected by an oriental rug.

'But why?' said Jelly. 'How can we ever see the piece?'

'We'll have to wait until 1956,' Adila growled. 'You will be 63. I will be 67.'

'Seventy,' Alec mouthed at Jelly, with a wink. Adila sometimes took executive decisions to reduce her own age.

Adila ignored him. 'There has to be another way.'

While the men went into the wood-panelled library for post-dinner drinks and cigars, Jelly and Adila adjourned with the other women to Ebba's parlour. Adila gazed with delight, as she usually did, at the sweep of staircase and down at the pillared entrance hall, tiled in black and white. 'Wouldn't you *love* to live in this house?' she said.

'Perhaps you should move in,' Jelly remarked, with equanimity. She wondered how Adila could possibly be happily married and still entertain such closeness to another man; she was sure that in her sister's place, she could never have done so. Nor did she share Adila's passion for the Swedish Residence. She could be happy living anywhere, provided it had heart – which was precisely what she found lacking *chez* Palmstierna. If everything looked too perfect, you couldn't tell what was going on beneath. She regarded perfection as a graceful variety of hiding place, possibly a form of dishonesty.

The baroness, tall, grey-haired and charismatic despite her disability, walked stiffly, supported by her maid, who held one elbow and kept patiently in step with her. Neither the magnificence of her home, nor her evening dress – ivory silk with fabulous pearl beading – could protect her from spending much of her life in pain. Nobody talked about its causes, although the general consensus was that it was either a form of rheumatism, or perhaps a neurological issue, which Jelly did not understand. How it affected her daily existence, and her married life with Erik, was something nobody would dare discuss. Jelly, who was trying to hide her anxiety about her own painful joints, watched her, warm with sympathy, cold with dread.

The women settled in window seats or armchairs, taking turns to go into the bathroom to refresh their powder and make-up, meanwhile chatting about children and grandchildren, husbands and servants – for most of this gathering still employed staff. Jelly had little to add to any of those topics; as ever, when her friends discussed the illnesses, foibles and growing pains of children, she felt herself excluded. She went over to Ebba's chair and crouched beside her. 'How are you feeling, Ebba? I hope we're not being too much of a strain on you.'

'As if you could be, my dear.' The baroness patted Jelly's hand. Few of the guests felt it tactful to mention their hostess's state of health, but Jelly knew how to show that her concern was for the person, not the problem. 'I'm pleased to be taken out of myself for an evening,' Ebba remarked. 'And you know, dear, we enjoy your company – and Adila's – *so* much. There are no accents in London to match yours!'

'Oh, but baroness, darling, your accent is beautiful.' The Swedish inflections could easily be mistaken for aristocratic English ones, with a drawn-out roundness that Jelly preferred to the delicate little vowels of Princess Alexandra or the Asquith family, including Katharine; they always sounded as if they were trying not to bite into a bee.

'My accent should be more English by now.' Ebba smiled. 'But of course, it is not the accent that matters in one's friends.'

'Of course not. It's the spirit, the soul!'

Ebba glanced up at a tall woman who had sailed across to stand beside them; she wore a misty blue gown, her gold-grey hair wound into a smooth chignon, her smile as toothy as any Jelly could remember encountering. 'My dear, I don't believe you and Lady Chiltington have had a chance to talk yet. Julia, do sit with us. We were just discussing what matters most in one's friends and suggesting it is vitality of spirit.'

'Ahh, it's all about breeding,' Lady Chiltington enthused, settling herself into the chair next to Jelly's with back straight and hands clasped. 'You must realise how important that is. Now, you and your wonderful sister are descended from a Hungarian count, are you not? This is clear to me, in the grace and graciousness about you.'

Surprised, Jelly waited for her to continue.

'Please have a look in my bureau, dear.' Ebba pointed to an inlaid wooden desk and cabinet in the corner. 'You will find an interesting pamphlet, something I think Julia would like to show everyone.'

There Jelly discovered, in the centre drawer, a printed booklet. *Journal of the British Eugenics Society.*

'I've spoken for them several times.' The baroness patted sweat from her own forehead with a handkerchief. 'Julia, though, is the real expert… '

'Do you know about eugenics, Miss d'Arányi?' said Lady Chiltington. 'The ideas are perfectly feasible, you see, and *so* important. Ebba's campaign is that Sweden should become more active in promoting this area of research. Sweden has the most wonderful man, a Dr Herman Lundborg. He is a race biologist and he has devoted most of his career to the subject. He became head of a Swedish institute for the study of this field and I am eager that Ebba should encourage her country to build further on his work. They are excellently placed for it.'

'But… why race biology? I mean, we're all the same, we're all human beings… ' Jelly interrupted – and as she spoke she sensed the chatter quieten as the eyes of four strange women, plus the baroness, her daughter Margareta and Adila all turned towards her.

'Oh, Miss d'Arányi, you are a true innocent.' With one hand, adorned with glitter-laden rings, Lady Chiltington took the pamphlet from Jelly, who seemed to have lost her strength. 'Yes, naturally, we are all people. This is the whole point. You see, future generations can all be better people than we are, provided that breeding is controlled.'

'Like pedigree dogs, then?'

'Quite possibly.' Lady Chiltington did not flinch. 'Scientists agree, today, that all manner of things are determined by heredity. It's vital to the human race's welfare that we learn more about it. For instance, some diseases are inherited, yet need not be. There are qualities of the human soul, too, which are inherited, yet need not be. Imagine, first, a world free of terrible illnesses. I, for example, have survived an operation for – a certain condition.' A look from Ebba told Jelly that Lady Chiltington meant unmentionable cancer. 'How can we be certain that this disease does not pass through the bloodline? How can we be certain that my condition is not to be inherited? How can I be sure that my daughter will not suffer, at my age, as I have? And my grandchildren too?'

'But are you saying that you would be willing not to have

had your daughter for the sake of ridding humanity of this – whatever this condition is caused by?'

'It would be painful to decide, of course, but if I had had that knowledge, if I had had that opportunity, I might well have made that choice. I would not wish to breed children for suffering. Who would?'

Jelly noticed Margareta, a stunning Scandinavian beauty, cast an anxious look at her own partially incapacitated mother. How strange, and sad, that Ebba seemed to give her support to this bizarre notion when in the past she had been so down to earth – indeed, a great feminist campaigner in the days of the suffragettes. 'Awful things can happen to anybody,' Jelly said. 'Any of us could catch pneumonia, or fall and break something... '

'Imagine, Miss d'Arányi,' said Lady Chiltington, her front teeth protuberant, 'that perhaps, generations from now, with the appropriate practices, we can breed a human race with bones strong enough *not to break* when someone falls. Do you see? We must focus on what is best for humanity as a whole, don't you think?'

Jelly thought of the Durham shipyard families, the ragged York children; bound up simply with surviving, nobody there would give such ideas a moment's thought. As for what was best for humanity as a whole, no similar magnanimity was being offered to help them.

'In a way,' Adila cut in, '*we* are the product of an early form of such thinking.'

'*Ja-ha* –?' said Ebba.

'Our grandfather married our grandmother partly *because* she was Jewish,' Adila announced, loud and clear. 'He thought the best way to stop discrimination against the Jews was for them to integrate, convert and marry non-Jews. So, here we are!'

Jelly cast around for her shawl. Her instinct was to take herself far away from this conversation – preferably home. She doubted that that story was true, for one thing; for another, she privately doubted the origin of their own 'title', wonderful though it sounded, and as all their relations now were dead or distant, it was impossible to check. Moreover she was far from confident that shouting about Jewish relatives in this company was wise. During her tour, attending dinners and receptions galore between journeys, she had been hearing remarks about how ridiculous it was to consider intervening with Germany 'just to defend a bunch of Jews', and once a reference to a distinguished scientist as a 'Jewboy'. Einstein, discoverer of the Theory of Relativity, no less. Why should anyone care what his race was, what he looked like, where he came from? It was his mind that counted and if people couldn't appreciate that, it said more about them than it did about him.

On the other hand, she didn't want to assign the topic too much importance. If she walked out now, she'd never hear the end of it from Adila. Were she to bide her time, the matter might be quietly buried. She distracted herself by going to close Ebba's bureau.

'How fascinating, dear,' Ebba was saying to Adila; her smile had turned somewhat fixed. 'So what exactly is your, er, background?'

'Our father was half Hungarian aristocracy and half Jewish, and our mother was Polish with Italian and Danish roots. And she spoke beautiful French.'

Jelly knew that her sister – as ever, tougher than she was – responded to fight-or-flight situations by blazing into battle with a full arsenal of verbal grenades, while Jelly simply fell silent, let her talk, or fled. 'And by the way,' Adila declared in her most vibrant baritone, 'our Jewish grandmother was the sister of the great violinist Joseph Joachim, who was a friend of Brahms and Schumann and was my own marvellous teacher. He taught me everything I know! *Zo...* '

Jelly, fiddling with the bureau lock, felt the key slip out of her hand; it clunked onto the floor and caused a distraction, which she hadn't intended while Adila was fighting the good fight. Why wouldn't her fingers obey her?

The baron had hired a dance band for the evening, and from the drawing room the cheerful rhythm of a foxtrot on saxophone, piano and bass breezed out to the parlour. Dancing would solve everything. Dancing always did. Saved again by music, Jelly led the way.

The other women quickly dispersed to find their partners, or new partners. She, for the moment, lingered on the landing. Watching the dancing, she had the odd sensation of looking back at a world that might at any moment slip through her fingers like the bureau key. In front of her passed her sister and the baron, perfectly in step, Adila's arm relaxed across Erik's; they seemed able to maintain a conversation and dance in serenity at the same time. As the quickstep ended, the baron and his psychic sensitive embraced at what seemed to Jelly inordinate length.

'Jelly!' Erik called out to her, one arm still around Adila. 'Please may I have the pleasure of the tango?' Jelly's tango was legendary. Adila let him go, laughing, and crossed the room to join Alec, who was waiting a safe distance away, in conversation with Lord Chiltington.

Erik's touch on her back was firm, yet his hands slightly too warm, his demeanour a little too intent, his laugh never as ready as those of her favourite easy-going, high-spirited dancing partners, Sep and Tom. Jelly concentrated on the music. The band's pianist was playing with his eyes half closed: an old tune that pulled Jelly back into her memories – the rue de Seine, the apartment, Tom's bright gaze and laughter all around, all night long; and back then, if her feet hurt, she was happy because it meant she was loving her life. Now her joints seemed to have been stabbed with needles and each step took concentration, so as not to betray the problem. Nothing had felt quite right since her bout of exhaustion after the cathedral tour. If this went on, she would have to see a doctor, which she dreaded lest it should turn out that the pain would not disappear of its own accord.

'Jelly, don't worry so,' Erik said, holding her. 'Everything will be all right, sooner or later.'

She still could not relax. Why did he and Adila take off for those Sunday drives? Adila loved Alec – anyone could see that – didn't she worry about upsetting him? Adila was so open, so transparent, that Jelly was certain she couldn't have hidden it if she were really having an affair. Perhaps this was all her own anxiety, when in fact it was none of her business. Even so, Erik had found the Schumann concerto, *her* Schumann concerto – was she to be indebted to him for ever?

'Thank you, Jelly.'

'Thank you, Erik.'

The pianist slowly opened his eyes, as if sliding back from an astral voyage to the seedier districts of Buenos Aires. He sported a bushy moustache and round spectacles; he wouldn't have been out of place as a maths professor or, perhaps, a cartographer. She wondered of what, or who, he had been dreaming. For a minute she felt that part of her matched his spirit, time-travelling in parallel. As the band began 'Sophisticated Lady', his gaze met hers for an instant. She couldn't tell whether he recognised her; musicians often did, if less frequently now than ten years ago.

When they took a break from dancing, the baron himself brought in beer for the band, and Jelly went up to the pianist to tell him how much she was enjoying his playing. He answered with a strong German accent. His English wasn't good, but good enough, and she drew him easily into conversation.

He was Jewish, from Charlottenburg, west of the Berlin city centre, he said. There, the harassment started with a beautiful rocking horse, a present from his mother to his three children. The Nazi thugs raided their flat and took it away, along with anything they could find of value, sentimental as much as financial. His wife had a fur coat, which he had given her after saving for months for it; they took that too. His children were picked on in school, first moved to the back of the class, then shunted to a different classroom, then expelled because a tiny quota had been brought in for Jewish pupils, which the school exceeded. And it went on, step by malicious step; low-level sadism, then more, then worse, whittling away at their life and livelihood chip by chip.

'Where are they now – your wife and children?'

'At home still. I came first to look for somewhere to live, and some work. God willing, they join me.'

'When?'

'As soon as I can give them a life. I am living in one room in a hostel and it's no good for children. I am here three months.'

'And are they… all right?'

'My wife writes to me saying yes, they are fine. But you know, post can be intercepted and censored, so I do not know if she tells me the truth. You heard they have been burning books by Jewish authors?'

Jelly felt herself chilling from fingertips to ribcage. 'Surely not?' she pleaded.

'I'm sorry,' said the pianist – as if it were his fault. 'But it's true. In general, few people want to hear the truth. And really, nobody outside is interested. They think it is nothing to do with them, it's just a problem for the Jews of Germany… '

'How will you get them out?'

'I don't know. I must find a job, perhaps playing in a hotel or restaurant, then send some money. I trust in God we will find a way.'

The musician's eyes had a depth that reminded Jelly of Myra, her closest Jewish friend. She asked his name.

He gave a slight, stiff bow. 'Bernhard Rabinovich, Miss d'Arányi.'

'Ah, you've unmasked me.'

'Madame, I have played all the piano works of Ravel and many of Bartók, and I would know you anywhere.'

'Jelly! Do come and join us.' Margareta was beside her in a bedazzlement of blonde curls and peach silk. 'I still haven't seen you properly and I need you to tell me *everything*.' Margareta adored Jelly, as young people often did – she was one of them in all but actual years – and Jelly saw Bernhard's eyes linger on the girl's slender figure, her regular, wide-set features and golden Scandinavian skin: an ideal 'Aryan' blonde, as Ebba must have been at her age. His expression was infinitely sad. Jelly wondered if or when he might see his family again.

She excused herself and wandered away with Margareta, asking her about her small children. A portion of her mind stayed with the refugee musician.

It wasn't long before Erik appeared beside them with a gentle cough. 'Papa!' Margareta gave him a kiss; Erik, returning it, lit up with pride and love. Jelly tried to deflect a brief stab of longing that her own severe-natured father might ever have taken such pride in her.

'Jelly, I have to tell you something. It was too noisy earlier.' He drew her by the elbow into the hallway. 'Listen, we have been talking again to Schumann.'

This man had held the missing manuscript in his hands, yet he couldn't sing her one melody from it. Jelly waited.

'He begs us to tell you not to forget. So we absolutely must write to Eugenie Schumann. If anyone can have it released to us, it is the composer's own daughter. She lives in Interlaken in Switzerland and I have her address. But, Jelly, the letter must come from you. You are the musician, you are the one she will respect. I know it's been a difficult and hectic summer for you, but now we know where the manuscript is, it's time to try… '

'She must be very elderly now. Isn't there someone who can be a go-between? Does she have children? Or a husband?'

'Neither.' The baron smiled into his moustache. 'She is a lady who prefers to stay with her own kind.'

'How do you mean?'

Erik whispered in Jelly's ear: 'Eugenie Schumann is a daughter of Lesbos.'

Jelly tried not to shriek aloud in delight. This was, after

all, the daughter of Robert Schumann himself and the eminent Clara; a woman who had been dandled, as a toddler, on the knee of the youthful Brahms. She loved to hear about individuals who went their own way, regardless of convention or censure, people like Ethel Smyth, the composer who was once jailed for throwing a rock through the window of a patronising cabinet minister, and who had written her a concerto for violin and French horn just five years ago.

'In that case,' she declared, 'I shall write to her *tomorrow*.'

Schumann's daughter! Jelly wished she could summon the important-sounding tone of a diplomat like Erik or a wise academic like Tovey. After she had used up ten sheets of paper scrawling words that she suspected were illegible, she asked Alec for help. The letter was finished within an hour.

What disturbed her was that Erik seemed to be annexing the concerto, making it his project rather than hers, when the spirits – if spirits they were – had asked specifically for *her* attention. That a London-based musician with a Jewish heritage should be selected to recover this concerto from Nazi Berlin seemed irrational at best, on the spirits' part, and ridiculous at worst. Still, the idea that Erik could not even read the notes on the page infuriated her, revolving in her head like a gramophone record trapped under an insistent needle.

'Sai, he wants to *help you*,' Adila insisted. 'People do want to help, you know. They are not all such bad souls as you seem to think.'

'I don't think he's a bad soul. I just wonder… what he stands to gain.'

'Proof,' said Adila. 'About the spirits. It validates everything we've been working for.'

That, Jelly reflected, was exactly what worried her. No matter how convinced Adila might be, few outsiders could believe in such a thing unless they saw it for themselves – and even then it would be hard to accept. Were Adila and Erik not setting themselves up for a serious dose of disappointment? Her concerto – or Schumann's – was only a small concern for the baron within a much larger quest.

There was one concerto-hunting avenue that she could pursue alone: her cousin Elisabeth Joachim in Oxford. But by the time Jelly finally telephoned her to ask if she might visit, she had received a reply from Switzerland, its contents far indeed from what she had hoped.

Elisabeth, Onkel Jo's daughter, had settled in Oxford with her husband, Harold Joachim, who was also her cousin. He, a philosopher, had spent most of his career at the university, where he had now been Wykeham Professor of Logic at Merton College for some 14 years. To visit them was not only easy, but a joy: it gave Jelly the perfect excuse to wander again through Balliol, imagining Tovey strolling by with Sep and Tom. She loved to picture how life might have been if she'd studied at Oxford herself, immersed in writing, discussing and arguing, playing her violin only for fun. If she'd had the right education to attend St Hilda's College for ladies, perhaps she could have read Greats, the Greek literature and philosophy she loved... though of course her handwriting was so awful that they would probably never have let her in. And in those days, when she was young enough to be a student, they would not have given her a degree, whatever her handwriting was like, since she was a girl. What nonsense: the same work, the same achievement, yet no recognition or reward if you happened to be female. Oxford had only agreed to confer degrees on its women students in 1920, when it seemed the natural step following the introduction of voting rights for women over 30 who met a property qualification. Cambridge took great pride in not following suit.

The new term had just begun and the freshers were easy to spot, timid and goggle-eyed, clutching books, tethering bicycles, so desperately young. Thinking of her male friends who had been just like these boys at one time – Sep, dead at the Somme, and George Mallory, lost beyond the clouds on Everest, and Tom, sick and fading in Ireland, and Aldous Huxley, working on his latest book in Italy, one that he hoped might cause a bit of a splash – Jelly stared at the boys with their short back and sides, their blazers, spectacles and tweeds, and wondered what would become of them all.

The Joachims lived on a tree-lined street off Banbury Road in Summertown, north of the city centre, but south of the suburban sprawl that had attached itself to Oxford in the past decade. They kept their substantial house simply furnished and open-hearted; Jelly remembered several teas there at which she found them entertaining Harold's students with plentiful cakes, plus string quartets in the lounge. Harold, a quiet man with beautiful hands, was a good violinist in his spare time and in the quartets had often taken second violin to Onkel Jo's first.

It was several years since Jelly had last seen Elisabeth; approaching the villa she had a brief attack of nerves. The inhabitants of Hurricane House, fond though they were of their cousin, couldn't help wondering whether she entirely approved of them, for here in the heart of establishment academia, where Harold was admired for his writings on idealism and the 'coherence of truth', Elisabeth had developed a hint of her father's piercing gaze.

Her welcome, though, was warm as can be, complete with scones, jam and clotted cream. Soon Jelly, sipping from the family china, was happily filling her in on the gossip from London and the way that Adila's teaching, modelled on Joachim's, was making such a difference to young Madge. They chatted about Tovey, the music societies, the students, the Proms, until finally Elisabeth said, 'Jelly, it's very unlike you to turn up needing to talk about something and then not talk about it. What's happened? Is there news of the concerto?' Jelly had told her the basics when she telephoned to arrange the visit and Elisabeth professed herself amazed.

'Read this.' From her handbag Jelly drew a small envelope containing two thin sheets of paper, sent from Interlaken.

Perusing them, Elisabeth grew very still. '*Never?*'

'That's what she says. Never. It should never, *ever* be played. Lisa, this is horrible. Can you believe that there is a concerto by Schumann, but his daughter insists we are never, ever to be allowed to play and hear it? I can understand a hundred-year ban, perhaps, but… '

Eugenie Schumann had other ideas. Although she could have been no more than 5 years old when her father died, and was now 82, she declared her memory vivid. The decision to put the concerto aside, she wrote, was her mother's alone, not Joachim's. Clara, she insisted, had taken years to determine what to do about it, discussed it at length with Brahms and Joachim and had even asked the latter to create a new finale for the work, as she considered Schumann's defective. She had made it clear to her children that the concerto contained traces of his final illness.

'I shall never forget the instant in our home at Frankfurt-on-Main,' Eugenie wrote, 'when my mother came in to us and said, with deep but suppressed feelings visible in her face: "I have just agreed with Joachim and Brahms that the concerto shall not be published, not now nor at any time. We are entirely in accord on the matter."' She went on to speculate on the anguish, responsibility and courage that must have been entailed in making that decision, inspired, she insisted, by the triumvirate's love for, and faithfulness to, Schumann's memory and their desire to show him only at his best.

'They were high-minded people.' Elisabeth refilled the cups. 'Vati always said that Clara's standards were unutterably lofty, and that most remarkably of all, she could keep to them. Why would she not marry Brahms? Schumann was dead; why must she devote herself solely to his memory? Brahms loved her and he adored the children. Eugenie once wrote about how he used to perform acrobatics on the banisters to make them laugh.'

It struck Jelly that the spirit messages had given no indication that Schumann's own family might raise objections. And though there was an expression of regret supposedly from Onkel Jo himself, suggesting that perhaps his original judgement of the concerto had been too harsh, not a single letter in the glass game, not so much as a 'yes' or 'no', came in purporting to be from either Brahms or Clara.

'You don't remember anything about the concerto? Nothing your father might have said to you, or to Harold? If there's anything at all that could counter her... '

'Not that I can think of,' said the mystified Elisabeth.

Jelly had written to Eugenie in great hope and in a spirit rich with wit and enthusiasm, imagining her as a freethinking and enlightened woman. Not as someone who might send her *this*.

'She's certainly free-thinking,' Elisabeth confirmed. 'She had a relationship with another woman for over 50 years. That takes courage.'

'Who was she? The – friend?'

'A singer. Marie Fillunger, apparently an excellent musician, a friend of Brahms and devoted to Eugenie. Clara was remarkably accepting. She of all people knew true love when she saw it.'

Jelly stared at Eugenie's handwriting. 'I know we're talking about some of the finest musicians who ever lived... but how can we be sure they were right?'

'Harold would have ways to look at that,' Elisabeth remarked. 'He would probably say that until we can be sure we have every single fact in place, nothing is demonstrably true. Until *all* the components are assembled, every suggestion can only be partially right and partially wrong.'

'That's exactly it,' Jelly said, eager. 'We don't have all the components for the truth, and we can't have them until we have the concerto itself! I can't bear it that Erik has seen the manu-script, but he can't read it. He can't tell me the first thing about the music.'

Elisabeth cast a shrewd eye over her het-up guest. 'You're quite flushed, Jelly. I hope this business isn't coming to mean more to you than is strictly necessary?'

'What gets to me is that the only person I know who's seen it is *him*. And I don't understand how these spirit messages are showing us one thing, but what happens is something else. I even think I am going a little mad.'

'Presumably you haven't told Eugenie that you first heard of this work through messages from *her father* in the beyond?'

'No, no, but... '

Elisabeth surveyed her, head on one side. 'What is it you're trying to do? Why is this concerto so important to you? Forgive me, but it seems to be coming to obsess you a little bit.'

'It's there,' Jelly hedged, 'and they chose me to find it.'

'Other than that.'

'I don't know... I'm perhaps – trying to save something. The only thing that I might ever be able to save.'

'Like a kitten from a lake?'

'Not exactly. More a matter of... salvaging something good, something worthwhile out of my life, while I can.' Jelly fought the tears that often accompanied her mental images of Sep, Tom, Anna, the hospital patients, the Yorkshire children. 'Do you think your brother Johannes would be able to help? Could you convince him?'

'Oh, Jelly... ' Elisabeth hesitated, avoiding Jelly's watery gaze. 'It's very difficult. I can't quite contemplate asking him to do that, having seen how Eugenie feels about it. And as for what he'd say about your spirit messages... well, I'm not sure that I can feel it would be the right thing.'

Jelly despaired. The spirits must advise, then. She would prefer wise words from live human beings. But if not that, what else?

Chapter 8

Ulli Schultheiss thought the Queen's Hall one of the finer venues he had had the pleasure of attending, at least in terms of acoustics. The place had scarcely changed in the 20-odd years since he first walked through its doors as a star-struck schoolboy, visiting from pre-war Germany. He wondered if it had even been repainted.

The best of British, Tovey remarked, escorting him up Regent Street from his hotel near Piccadilly Circus, but the hall still seemed to Ulli the embodiment of British understatement, or underestimation, possibly, of its contents' worth. It stood on the corner of Langham Place, beside a small church that now was dwarfed on its other side by the pale stone of the recently completed BBC Broadcasting House. The interior was a delicate taupe. 'Supposedly the colour matches the belly of a London house mouse,' Tovey declared, while they queued to leave their winter coats and hats in the cloakroom.

Ulli felt fortunate to be here at all. He'd persuaded Willy Strecker to delegate the trip to him, on the grounds that any discussions concerning the Schumann Violin Concerto could be merely speculative at this stage. Strecker responded to his cautious mention of 'spirit messages' with remarkable equanimity. What really mattered was the concerto's commercial potential. Fighting the embargo would require a considerable input of time and effort; they should not get involved unless there was a convincing case for it. The piece had to be good enough, and if Clara and Joachim had chosen not to publish it, perhaps it really was questionable. 'But go, Ulli,' said Strecker, after some consideration. 'See what you can find out. Then see what you can do.'

He kept to himself the impression that this hall looked a little miserable. Taking his seat beside Tovey, he surveyed the ceiling mural, where there sailed some desultory cupids. Over several centuries of composition, Britain had produced nothing better than Elgar and Vaughan Williams. Music simply did not hold the same status here as it did in Germany or Austria; the latter coddled the world's finest composers with the architectural equivalent of fine gateaux and *schlagobers*.

'Are you writing music at the moment?' he asked Tovey. He was under strict instructions from Mainz not to mention the professor's recent heart trouble.

'I am, if a little slowly.' Tovey seemed pleasantly surprised to be asked. 'My opera's going to be done, finally.' He was shifting his spidery legs about in the cramped seat. 'How is life in Germany?'

'Difficult,' Ulli admitted, lowering his voice. 'You know they have made a Reichsmusikkammer, an official section for music within the state's cultural department. One of their jobs is to look at the planned concert programmes and decide which they can sanction, and which not.'

Tovey nodded, glum. 'I've read something to that effect. Who makes the decisions?'

'Artists. Some of our finest artists. Wilhelm Backhaus, Wilhelm Furtwängler – '

'Oh, not Furtwängler? The best conductor I've ever had the pleasure of hearing... '

'And Georg Kulenkampff, the violinist. Not that I rate him quite as much as the other two, but still... '

'But these are great, great musicians – surely they're not in sympathy with the regime?'

'As I said, it's difficult... I think they have no choice.'

'Which violinists do you admire?' Tovey changed the subject.

'A few years ago I heard little Yehudi Menuhin. In Berlin, wearing knickerbockers. That was some kind of miracle. He has such intensity in his sound, something almost prophet-like. I've heard child prodigies before, but never one like that. I fear he may have ruined me for all other violinists.'

'Well, I hope Miss d'Arányi will change your mind,' Tovey smiled.

Where Jelly d'Arányi was concerned, Ulli had a tickling in the nose – an instinct he usually trusted – that the investment of time, money and effort in travelling to London would be repaid. If this missing concerto could be secured, and succeeded, and he was the person who helped to recover it, that could bode well for his own future. He had heard from colleagues that the Streckers spoke of him as likely heir for a senior post. Perhaps in sending him to see her they were giving him a chance to prove himself.

'What is the latest about the Schumann story?' he asked.

'Stalemate. Jelly needs you, Ulli. She needs you to help her with this. Schott's are probably the only people who can.'

The orchestra was in place; the audience quietened and applause greeted the entry of the conductor, Adrian Boult. After an opening overture and commensurate clapping, a dark-haired, slender figure in a red dress made her way onto the stage with him. While the concerto's first bars sounded, Ulli sought a closer look at Jelly d'Arányi. He'd retained, from years ago, a faint impression of a light shimmering through the throng like a will o' the wisp.

Her image filled two rounds as he peered through his opera glasses: just as he remembered, all scarlet gown, dark hair and rather dusky skin, her eyes kindling the flame he recalled. And when she began to play she seemed more spirit than body. She moved not like a normal musician, but like a dancer, with her entire being. He imagined that when she spoke to him eventually, he might hear not her human voice but the Bergonzi's emanating from her delicate throat. So this was what had captivated all those composers. This solitary woman had sparked into existence a whole new repertoire of violin pieces. Something exceptional had to lie behind that.

The concerto didn't sound much like genuine Mozart. The harmonies were in no way radical or sensual enough; the melodies were unmemorable. And though Jelly d'Arányi was giving it all the energy she would have devoted to Ravel's *Tzi-gane*, somehow it was not... well, *what* wasn't it? What was the matter? Perhaps she was having an off night. Not that her devoted audience would know – but to a trained ear that heard music every day, year round, the fact that not all was well could not go entirely unnoticed.

'She sounds a little tired?' he ventured at the end, while Jelly took curtain call after curtain call; her public, no doubt, still saw the lithe, Gypsyish girl they had always loved.

'She's had a difficult year,' was all Tovey said. 'Let's go and see her.'

In the corridor outside Jelly's dressing room – a dingy spot that in Vienna or Berlin would have been assigned to a broom rather than a soloist – Ulli watched Tovey watching Jelly, who was fluttering about like a scarlet-clad sparrow, embracing her family. Two little girls: who were they? Not hers? They couldn't be; they adored her far too much for her to be their mother. Everyone received the same wild embrace from her, whether they were her close friends or unknown fans waiting for autographs. Great paprika-strong hugs, intense lingering handshakes, a smile that put the London Power Company to shame. And Tovey... Tovey was long married and settled, Ulli knew, but it was obvious to anyone with a sensitive eye – from his softened gaze, the gentleness with which he stooped towards her, the way he reached out to brush her wrist – that the professor might once have been head over heels in love with this woman. Time goes, passion with it, but the traces never quite vanish and sometimes the full feeling floods back as if to trick you. Tovey's hands shook slightly when he returned Jelly's hug, as if she were still the youthful violinist he had known in the century's first decade. Her face powder left a pale streak along his dark lapel.

'This is Ulrich Schultheiss, from Schott's Music Publishers in Mainz,' said Tovey to Jelly. 'He is a grand fan of yours.' And the whirlwind was upon him, Jelly grabbing his hand, and the current that coursed from her nearly jolted him off balance. He looked down into her face, stricken with vertigo. It was a very, very long time since this had last happened to him.

'Darling, darling, you came all this way to hear me?' she beamed. Did she preserve that accent deliberately, for its charm? If so, it worked.

He'd had a long day of travelling: the boat, the train, a taxi. Perhaps the giddiness was really from that... As if from a distance, he heard Tovey's voice introducing him to someone else – Adila Fachiri, Jelly's sister, and Adila's husband, Alec; and one of the little girls was theirs, the other was Adila's pupil, and an older girl, Jane, was the pupil's sister, and a poised and strong-faced woman beside them was... good heavens, the pianist Myra Hess, who cast him an inscrutable stare; and they were inviting him back to their house for a party, a fair distance from his hotel, but he'd go, because now he couldn't not.

'I'm so glad,' Jelly said. 'I very much want to talk to you about something rather special.'

'Ah, yes.' Ulli was smiling like an idiot; he couldn't help himself. 'Tovey mentioned you have a... project... '

It took a minute for the cab containing Ulli, Tovey and the Harvey-Webb sisters to turn in to Netherton Grove, because another car was backing out of it. The street was a cul-de-sac, but easy to mistake for a thoroughfare between the Fulham Road and the King's Road. When they pulled up outside No. 10, Ulli could see this was the ideal house for these extraordinary beings. It was an outlandish terracotta colour, and it sported a fake Renaissance citadel effect, a bit like a bell tower. Hungarians trying to be Italian in Chelsea!

Inside, the party gobbled him up into a stew of languages and accents, together with the dog barking and a gramophone working its way through a stack of dance-band records. 'It has its place,' Adila told him. Her bluebell eyes clear and direct, she was as striking as her sister, in a wholly different way: fairy god-mother rather than elfin pixie. And a nurturing fairy godmother, at that: she was holding out towards him a huge silver bowl of sausages. Ulli tasted one; it was surprisingly good. 'Germanic food in honour of you and Mozart,' Tovey joked, behind him. Ulli couldn't work out whether or not he meant it. English irony sometimes eluded him.

The table was heaped with delights: the best potato salad he had tasted since his mother's, a big pot of Hungarian goulash rippled with dark red paprika; rice to go with it; a cold ham for those who preferred to avoid such exotic flavours.

'I don't know where in the world she manages to get that Hungarian paprika,' remarked Myra Hess, smiling politely at Ulli over her plate.

'It really is amazing,' Ulli agreed. 'Madame Hess, I am a great admirer of yours. I'm Ulrich Schultheiss from Schott's in Mainz…'

'So I gathered.' Myra paused, munching goulash. 'Well, there it is, there it is,' she said eventually. 'I understand I can no longer go to Germany. Isn't that strange, when here people often assume I am German myself? It seems such a shame that music and musicians must be caught up in political matters. But shall we simply hope the situation over there comes to a swift close?'

'I hope so.' Ulli cringed with embarrassment about his home country, especially since its evils could be met with such ele-gance; the pianist's manner was as polished as the British royal family's. 'Madame Hess, I can't tell you how… how much I love your playing.' He wanted to say, 'How sorry I am about what's happening in Germany,' yet did not dare to. At home, in a party like this – not that there were many parties exactly like this – you wouldn't know who might overhear, or how dangerous it would be if they did. With distance, understanding struck him of how deeply this state of affairs had seeped into him.

'Thank you, Dr Schultheiss. Don't worry, Germany now is

not your fault. None of us can help the accident of where and to whom we are born. Now, do please excuse me, I must say hello to Professor Tovey.' As dignified and upright as the queen mother, Myra smiled and slipped away, out of sight.

Still feeling the stab of mortification under his sternum, he distracted himself by listening to different voices. He identified the Swedish accent of a glamorous yet, he thought, semicrippled baroness with a walking stick, whose husband seemed to be an ambassador; but he was defeated by his host, Alec Fachiri, whose elegant tone was tinged, as it turned out, with a mixture of Greek roots and American upbringing. What a strange milieu: famous musicians on the one hand, and the most serious, high-ranking diplomats and lawyers on the other. Like a zoo in which the tropical night creatures and the penguins had all been housed in the same enclosure. What could have brought them together?

Adila laughed long and loud when Ulli asked how she and Alec met. It was a mystical story, she declared. She'd been sauntering past Harrods one day when she was overwhelmed by a premonition: she was about to meet her future husband. 'So surprised I was,' she confided, pressing his elbow with one hand and balancing the dish of sausages in the other, 'that I looked around to see who on earth it might be!' She had spotted a swarthy, serious-faced young man with a big moustache – and he was so unlike the type she would ever take a fancy to that she decided she'd been grievously misled.

'Did you speak to him?'

'No, nooo! But several weeks later we have a chamber music rehearsal and our cellist is ill. He doesn't want us to cancel because of him, so he asks a friend, a fine amateur, to take his place. And into the room walks the same gentleman with the moustache! I tell you, Doktor Schultheiss, I could not *believe* it!'

'Please, call me Ulli. Everyone does.'

'He wrote me a letter afterwards,' Adila said in a deep purr, 'telling me he liked my voice. And you know, my voice is a little difficult, so at once I fell, *crazy*, in love! Then there was a *won*derful fancy dress party in the roof gardens of Selfridges, and we meet and we admire the view and we walk under the pergola holding hands and we dance all night together... and Hortense, who we call Titi, our other sister, the prettiest one, danced with a beootiful man and fell in love too – ah, what magic... We both marry our beloveds that year. And *presto*! We are here!'

Ulli laughed. The sheer energy about Adila was scary and warming and enchanting, all at the same time. And the voice... was quite a voice.

'Fancy dress?' he said. 'What did you go as?'

'I was a Gypsy.' Adila gleamed like Gypsy fire itself. 'Titi was a shepherdess.'

'And Jelly?'

'A savage.'

'Wearing... what, exactly?'

Adila's laugh rang out like a trombone. 'Wearing not very much at all!'

'Herr Doktor Professor Schultheiss, *darling*.' Jelly herself was at his elbow, beaming high voltage up into his face. 'What is this about my savage costume?'

Ulli hoped she couldn't sense him picturing her in what little there was of it. 'I've been hearing the story of how your sisters met their husbands.'

Jelly's skin glowed in the lamplight; he could see crow's feet beside her eyes, and shadows beneath them, but that added complexity to her face rather than dimming its radiance. 'Please, my dear.' She pressed his arm with slender yet powerful fingers, like a tropical bird's talons. 'Let me get you something more to drink, and we must sit and talk.'

'I would *love* something more to drink – thank you, Miss d'Arányi.'

'Jelly, darling, Jelly as in yelling.' She darted to the table and poured him the biggest glass of red wine he had seen since the stock-market crash. 'Come with me to the Green Room? It's quiet there.'

Ulli followed this luminous avian creature away from the crowded dining room, up some stairs and round some corners; here the sound of the party faded to quiet. The Green Room, he saw, was a type of library; on one side its shelves spilled over with classic literature, including several volumes that sat face forward, ready to be dipped into – Yeats, Tagore, Huxley. On the other side dwelt books on law, Italian art and architecture, and a number of faded, cloth-bound tomes that turned out to be Hungarian, mainly from the last century. A sizeable Chinese antique picture, with muted gold background and black brushwork, loomed out of one book-free space. The wall coverings were grass-green silk, the curtains too, and Jelly, arraying herself and her scarlet dress on a green chaise longue, seemed to him a flame that hovered over a lawn lightly enough to leave it unscorched. She patted the velvet beside her, smiling up at him. Ulli hesitated, for the merest quarter of a second wondering exactly what sort of invitation this was.

The answer struck him at the same moment: perhaps Jelly d'Arányi had no idea that her gesture could possibly be misconstrued by a healthy young man from a culture other than her innocent world of openness and warmth. It seemed to throw his reactions back into his face, where they demanded analysis, and told him that they'd been inspired by his own absolute, sinful, wishful thinking.

He sat down beside her and said, 'Tell me about the Schumann.'

The story was bizarre, but the evidence was firm. Ulli stayed silent for a minute once Jelly had finished explaining. Tovey had mentioned the 'spirit messages', but he hadn't realised how certain, how unquestioning of them the d'Arányi sisters would be. Of course, he knew people at home who would also have believed this tale without a moment's hesitation; unfortunately some of those same people had been quick to sign up to National

Socialism, filled as it was with esoteric symbols – an inverted Indian emblem, for goodness' sake – and a system of mythology about 'Aryans' that, however fictional, was inducing otherwise intelligent beings to swallow its excesses. Ulli had spent summer evenings downing lager under the linden tree in the local *Biergarten* and listening, from a safe distance, to some of his neighbours talking in ways that made the idea of concerto-seeking messages from the souls of Schumann and Joachim seem refreshingly benevolent. But whatever implausible circumstances had brought it to light, the concerto was real and it needed someone to reach it and retrieve it, beyond the keepers of Clara's flame.

'I don't understand how hiding it away can do any good,' Jelly pointed out. 'It's as if they said: this is how it is, *fin*, and everybody accepts it. But it does not have to be this way. It's their choice. If it turns out the piece is not good, that's one matter. But they don't know the truth! Not to look at it, not even to see what the reality is... '

'I couldn't agree more. People wear blinkers – sometimes it makes life easier. And we all want to imagine Frau Clara as a musical saint who must have been infallible.'

A whiff of Jelly's scent reached Ulli's nostrils. His former fiancée had refused to wear any at all, saying that perfume made her sneeze. Jelly's smelled like freshly cut grass in midsummer.

'What would you like me to do?' he said.

'Ideally, fetch it from this library and publish it. Then I can be the first to play it. Ulli, there is so much pain and death and loss in this world, but here is one good thing we can do, one beautiful thing we could save. And we can save it together. We can bring it back to life! Wouldn't that be wonderful?'

Ulli felt embarrassed: only that afternoon – which felt a century ago – he had been thinking about matters as selfish and idiotic as the concerto's lucrative potential and his own possible promotion. He leaned towards Jelly, whose expression resembled that of a pleading child, and said, 'You know, I believe I can help. My employer, Willy Strecker, told me that he met your great-uncle's son, Johannes Joachim, in an English internment camp and they became good friends. The concerto must have been in Johannes's possession, so it must be his responsibility. And you know how it is with old friends, especially from difficult times. Perhaps, should he give permission to publish the concerto, it would naturally be to us. As for me, I will do everything I can, both for Schumann and for you.'

A thunder of steps on the stairs and Adila was in the doorway. 'Sai, quick! We are dancing. We need you!'

Jelly sprang to her feet. 'Ulli, will you dance?'

In the drawing room the Fachiris had moved aside the furniture and rolled up the rugs; now Alec was busy stacking up some fresh records. Ulli, walking downstairs with Jelly, noticed a strange ritual taking place: nobody was quite ready to begin. Instead, they were turning expectant gazes towards the stairs, even though Alec's first record was spinning and crackling and a familiar melody – a tango – was ready to seduce them all. He felt his face grow hotter as the eyes of 50 guests all fastened on to him.

'What's happening?' he mumbled to Jelly.

'It's the tango. We have a little tradition! Come on, Ulli – we must be the first.'

Of course, the person everyone was waiting for was the violinist whose arm, at that very moment, was tucked through his own. He had little choice but to escort her to the centre of the floor and become her dancing partner. Not that he'd have wanted to be anywhere else.

Thanks heavens he had learned the tango in some… well, interesting places in Berlin, when he was a student at the Musikhochschüle ten years ago, and the steps came back to him, for Jelly was easy to dance with. She trusted him. She followed where he led, yet she led him, too, signalling what she wanted to do with the intensifying of one finger's touch on his back or the slightest insistent pressure of her palm against his. He thought up a combination of twirls and pivots and encouraged her into them; she spun and swirled as he wanted her to, head inclined over one shoulder, and watching the balletic tilt of her neck, he laughed with delight. It was almost a shock when the music finished, much too soon.

'Ulli, you are a glorious dancer!' Jelly, getting her breath, led him to a deep-cushioned sofa. Sitting beside him, legs extended forward, she changed the subject with the alacrity of a tennis player swinging into a rally. 'So, tell me. Do you like reading?'

'I love books better than anything except music,' he assured her.

She loosened her shoes – red satin – and shook them off her feet. 'And who are your favourite writers?'

'I greatly admire the works of Thomas Mann and Herman Hesse, in particular Hesse. Do you know *Narziß und Goldmund*?'

'I don't, because my German is not so good, but I would love to read it.'

'It's a beautiful book, a masterpiece... about seeking, about extremity of experience, about beauty in all its forms. It came out about three years ago and I loved every word of it. If there's a translation I will get one for you. What about you? Who are your favourites?'

'I love the ancient Greeks. Plato, Aristophanes... '

'Really?' Ulli didn't want to tell her he was not used to women being well versed in the classics, in case it offended her, but he was fascinated all the same.

'And I love poetry.' She was leaning back on the cushions, watching him. Her toes, divested of restrictions, were wiggling beneath her stockings. 'I can recite you a good chunk of the *Rubaiyat of Omar Khayyam* if you wish. Who do you most like among the German poets?'

'Oh... ' He was wondering if Jelly had ever taken lessons

from a hypnotist, the way she was looking at him. 'Well, I suppose my great favourite would be Heinrich Heine… '

'Recite me some. A love poem?'

Recite poetry? She wanted him to recite a love poem to her? 'I'll see what I can remember,' he said, sensing his face grow warm yet again. This woman made him blush so often that she was turning him back into a stupid schoolboy. 'It'll be in German… '

'The original language is always the best,' she encouraged. 'Keep it soft, and it will be fine.'

Ulli cleared his throat, then began.

'Im wunderschönen Monat Mai,
Als alle Knospen sprangen,
Da ist in meinem Herzen,
die Liebe aufgegangen… '

'What does it mean?' asked Jelly.

'It's the first poem in Schumann's *Dichterliebe*.' He suspected she knew perfectly well what it meant. '"In the wondrous month of May, when all the buds are springing, there is in my heart, love that is bursting forth".'

'So beautiful.' Jelly gave him the most tender, open-hearted smile he had ever seen from any woman. He returned it: sweating, terrified, doomed.

Around them, nothing in this house ever stopped moving and whirling and ringing. Tango gave way to rumba, sausages to bowls of trifle, and at some point recorded music to live. Garlands of laughter reached them from the music room along with a thread of sound from the piano.

'Let's see what's happening.' Jelly bent to fasten her shoes.

And at the back of the house, if Ulli had thought nothing more could surprise him tonight, he found he was wrong. An image faced him that he would never forget: Myra Hess in her black lace gown, lying flat on her back across the top of the Bechstein piano, reaching down to the keys beyond her shoul-

ders and playing, from this unimaginable angle, utterly perfect
Bach.

When the second-last guests left, around 3am, the Fachiris and
Jelly, still chattering and singing to each other, set about tidying
up. Only the Palmstiernas remained. Ebba had fallen asleep in
an armchair; Erik shut the drawing room door softly so that she
would not be disturbed.

'How did you get along with that charming boy from
Mainz?' Adila asked Jelly. 'I hear he's working for Richard
Strauss's publisher.'

'He's *very* nice... '

'Jelly! Naughty girl, what have you been doing?' Adila
demanded in Hungarian.

'Oh, just the usual,' smiled Jelly. 'And I think I won... '

'I beg your pardon?' said Erik. 'That language of yours... '

'Never mind, never mind.' Adila caught her sister's eye and
the pair stifled private laughter.

'More seriously, yes, he's working for the Streckers,' Jelly
said, 'and he thinks perhaps he can help us with the Schumann.'
A shadow of anxiety crossed her with the simultaneous brightening in the eyes of her sister and the Swedish ambassador. 'He
thinks Willy Strecker knows Johannes Joachim well enough to
have an influence.'

'What about Elisabeth? Doesn't she? Johannes is her
brother, for God's sake.'

'She's not a publisher,' Jelly pointed out. 'And after all, we
are his *cousins* and there is nothing we have been able to do.'

She smiled again, this time to herself, thinking of her new
friend. Ulli Schultheiss inspired confidence: a tall man, fair and
open from tip to toe – face, attitude and mind all matched.
Bright, direct gaze, the type she liked best. She had adored Sep's
forthright Australian nature, and Tom's bright and breezy Irish
equivalent; Ulli's directness was far removed from that evasive,

slippery Englishness that often annoyed her. She'd noticed him relaxing as the evening went on; in the Green Room he'd been so tense, goodness knows why – was it the language barrier? 'He did well at the love poetry,' she told Adila in Hungarian, 'and he's a wonderful tango dancer, too.'

'Didn't you think he was devastatingly handsome? He really likes you, I can tell.'

'I'm too old for him. If only darling Anna were here – he'd be ideal for her… '

'For goodness sake! He's a lovely boy, with a nice behind! Very round and firm. They do not grow on trees. And his job is very responsible, so he can't be under 30. If I were you, I'd – '

'Oh Adi, do stop it… '

In his hotel, Ulli was still awake, experiencing a form of turmoil that he'd prided himself on having avoided for a long while.

His former fiancée, Lotte, led him on for four years – now the engagement was on, now it was off. Now she was after someone else, usually richer than he was; then she arrived back at his doorstep, hair in her eyes, wanting to weep on his shoulder; and each time she put him down only to pick him up again, he loved her still more.

He visited her one evening and found her running a fever, but walking her dog. The next day he arrived at the same time to find the house plunged into mourning. Lotte – with whom he'd fully intended to spend the rest of his life, even if she was impossible – had been carried to a better world by a lethal strain of pneumonia.

The shock floored him for months; after that it lingered. His mother needled him to tell her how he was coping, but he never spoke of it. If he felt lonely, he played the piano: the necessary concentration let him think of nothing else. The rest of the time he worked hard, keeping his mind occupied. His colleagues valued his devotion to the firm; he loved the company and the composers he couldn't help considering 'his', even if they were really Ludwig and Willy's. Taking calls from Richard Strauss or Igor Stravinsky, proofreading their new works, often becoming one of the first to play their pieces through, in private at his piano, he could still flourish in his natural habitat. He dined with Willy and his family once every week, and with Ludwig in the *Biergarten* once every other week. Every two Sundays he took a train out to the village to see his mother. Life was good. Yes, the Nazis held power and the Depression held sway, but he was employed, in his dream job, and he gave thanks for that every day in his prayers. Things must change if he could only hold on long enough…

Ulli turned over, shunting one arm out from its trapped spot under his chest. His ears took in the detail of late-night London: motors growling in the street, the claws of some creature scuttling over a dustbin lid, the glass xylophone of something that could only be a milk van, for dawn was approaching. He was a responsible man, a respectable man, a person of judgement. His work depended on the soundness of that judgement. He was not, at the vital age of 31, about to lose his head to a crazy Hungarian violinist, world famous and much older than he was. Many others had fallen for Jelly before him; that didn't mean he must follow suit. But through his mind there flickered the idea that he didn't have to leave London straight away. If the Streckers were willing, he could stay an extra day. He could perhaps invite her to coffee, or lunch, or tea, or cocktails, or dinner, or all five. But he'd need some daring and he wasn't sure he had any. He dozed, then woke with the sound of his own snore as a sunny morning lightened his windowpanes in time for breakfast.

Jelly rose late. Her dreams had reverberated with the tango to which she and Ulli had danced; now she had to clear all that away and prepare for her next recital.

'Adi, I'm going to the park,' she said, glancing into the dining room, where Adila was working her way through a large pot of coffee.

'Today, I know, there will be a miracle,' she mumbled in return, 'and I need one for my head… '

Caesar's leash in one hand, a book of music in the other, Jelly made brisk progress down the road, along Cheyne Walk and over Battersea Bridge to the park, where her ancient but serviceable fur coat and a brown hat over her ears protected her from the autumn chill. Caesar snuffled around the tree trunks, as far as his leash would let him, while Jelly settled on a favourite bench to focus on Bach.

The tango didn't want to leave her. Nor did the image of her lovely friend, who looked so open and danced so well. It was the sort of evening your brain wants to hug. Caesar trotted over and put his snout on her knee.

An hour and a half later, she was about to let herself in, giving the ever-vigilant Mrs Garrett her habitual smile and wave. No doubt the Garretts hadn't approved of their long, late party. It wasn't as if they weren't invited, because they always were, but they never turned up.

Adila, eyes gleaming, flung the door open before she could turn her key. 'Darling, come quick! Your lovely Deutsch Doktor with the delectable *derrière* is here, waiting for you.'

Jelly could hear the piano. She made a clattery dive for the music-room stairs, and glimpsed, through the door's rectangular glass panes, the gleam of Ulli's fair hair; he was trying out the Bechstein. He sounded good. Very good. He was playing something she knew. A surging-waves accompaniment, a singing, faraway melody – it was from Schumann's *Carnaval,* the number that was supposed to be a portrait of Chopin. Jelly watched, breathed, and prepared herself.

'You like Bechsteins, Ulli?' She strolled over as if she had left him where he was only minutes earlier.

'I have one myself, rather like this.' He stopped playing and his gaze met hers, every bit as bright as before. 'It has a lovely woody, tenory tone. You can really sink your teeth into it.'

'And you like Schumann? That was so beautiful.'

'I love Schumann. He's my favourite, especially to play. Jelly, please forgive me for just *arriving*, but I... '

'Darling, I'm thrilled you're here! Now, what can I give you? You want some coffee, or something to eat, or perhaps we go for a walk, except I've just been for one with our doggie, and – '

'No, no, Jelly: what can *I* give *you*?' Ulli smiled over the piano at her, and for a second he reminded her so much of Sep that she wanted to weep. 'May I take you out to lunch?' he was saying, and she, eyes watering, gave a mute smile and nod.

The closest restaurant to the house was the family-run place on the Fulham Road, opposite the Forum Theatre cinema. Here Jelly often used to have lunch or an early supper, with Anna or sometimes on her own; it offered fare such as toad-in-the-hole, roast chicken and Ravel's favourite steak and kidney pudding. 'I was actually thinking of the Savoy, or the Regent's Palace Hotel,' Ulli suggested.

'I don't mind where we go, unless you are especially eager to try them,' she said, carefree. 'But I often eat here. It's very nice. Friendly.' On the door, Ulli spotted a handwritten notice in smudged ink declaring: 'No shellfish, no tinned food, no foreign produce.'

'Most soloists would think it is not smart enough for them.'

'If it's not smart enough for *you* then we take a cab to the Savoy!' Jelly gave a grin. Like a little girl, she was teasing him, laughing, with the assumption he would laugh with her.

He cursed his own tactlessness. 'That wasn't at all what I meant. For you, the best should be obligatory.'

'Aha, but we are here together,' Jelly declared, 'so wherever we are, that is already the best.' She pushed open the swing door and Ulli noticed the warmth of the waitress's greeting, and the way Jelly chattered to her as she led them to a favourite table in the window. The décor was plain, the typical English oak and beige, but the tablecloths were clean and white and the whiff from the kitchen seemed appetising.

'Jelly, there is so much I'd like to ask you, I don't know where to start,' he said, once they were settled. Opposite him, Jelly's face was bowed over the menu, her bobbed dark hair swinging across her cheekbones.

'Start by choosing some food,' she smiled. 'The lamb chops are extremely good. With mint sauce.'

'Mint sauce?' English food. Sweet mint with meat that was bound to be overcooked. 'Fine, I'll try it. Did you never think of staying in Hungary, or moving somewhere a little less far from home? Why London? Why not Vienna or Berlin?'

'Fortunately we did not choose Berlin,' Jelly remarked. 'We like it here. Adila liked it best from the beginning – I think because Onkel Jo was here often and spoke of it to her – and it just… worked. I'm not sure why we came or why we stayed… but now it is home, absolutely. But Ulli, tell me things. Where do you come from? Why do you play the piano so well?'

'I was born in a little village not far from Mainz. My father was killed in the war, so then it was just me and my mother. Later I went to Berlin to study the piano.'

'And who was your teacher there?'

'Professor Schnabel.'

Jelly gave such a cry that heads turned at the next table. 'How amazing! Artur Schnabel, he is a genius, the best, the very best!'

'That's what I thought too. I still see his face every time I play a Beethoven sonata. Now I play only for my own enjoyment. I really wasn't good enough.'

'But Schnabel, he doesn't take just anybody. You must be good. And you sound good, extremely good.'

'The fact is, I didn't like performing, all the nerves. And

then… ' Lotte and her parents wanted him to get a proper job. By the time she died, he had one.

'Something happened? Something difficult, I can see.'

How sensitive she was. She reminded him of a fine piece of gold leaf conducting an electric current, shimmering with its own receptivity. He told her the sorry history, and watched her face soften and her eyes brim with sympathy.

'I know what it is to lose someone,' she said. 'I lost my mother so long ago, but each day it's as if she is still here with me, somewhere. And I have lost many others, too… I feel, sometimes, I am surrounded by ghosts. And it is not only the glass game that brings them.'

'That portrait on the piano? It is very impressive. I think, perhaps, he was your fiancé?'

'Not exactly, but I did hope to marry him. He was Australian, a wonderful composer. He died at the Somme.'

'You must have been very young.'

'Twenty-three.' Her voice held all the pain of being at your most hopeful and lovely, ready for affection, passion and plans, only to see your friends and potential lovers slaughtered one by one. And losing one great love…

Ulli thought of Ludwig in the trenches and Willy interned at Alexandra Palace, and himself at school, doing his mathematics, practising the piano, battling the great rent in life caused by his father's death. 'So my father on the German side was perhaps fighting your Australian fiancé on the British side. They both died. I am German and you, I assume – if you'll forgive me – may be Jewish if you are Joachim's great-niece. And now here we are having lunch together in London. Is this not insane, Jelly?'

'That's war. That's the world. What can we do?' Jelly's face darkened, then brightened. 'I am partly Jewish, partly not, and Adi, Alec and I are Catholics – but why should that matter? We must make up for these crazy people. We must live to our fullest in the present, no?'

'Definitely.' Any last shred of sense was leaving Ulli. He wanted to lift her out of her plain wooden chair, tuck her under one arm and carry her off somewhere safe and warm where he could feed her the finest cakes, brush her hair, run a bubble bath for her, wrap her in satin, take care of her in every way there was. 'And since your tragedy, Jelly, there's no one else in your life? Do you mind that I am asking?'

Jelly seemed to hesitate, tracing a pattern on the tablecloth with one fingertip. 'Sometimes I have the feeling that everyone I love then dies.'

Ulli absorbed this statement, waiting for her to continue.

'There was someone, almost. Not quite. Not now. Someone I've known for a long time, and we are – well, friends, but close, if at a distance. I hardly ever see him. But now he is very ill. He calls me and tells me he will die sometime quite soon... '

'You care very much for him, don't you?' Ulli's appetite had begun to fade, just as the waitress brought roast chicken and bread sauce for Jelly, and the chops for him. They were indeed overcooked. The fibres caught between his teeth: possibly mutton rather than lamb. Even if it wasn't 'foreign'.

'But this is perhaps normal.' Jelly was folding her handkerchief back into her bag. 'Love is simple, Ulli, but nothing around it ever is.'

'I know.' He reached for her hand, raised it and kissed her knuckles. Her smile was gracious; perhaps kind, perhaps more, yet – now he understood – infinitely sad behind all that sparkle and charisma. What had this woman seen? What did she know of music and life, of this world and the world beyond? Far, far more than he did, that was certain.

He had to make a decision; he had to draw back, however magnetised she had made him, and he sensed she had enjoyed doing that, Heinrich Heine and all. Would he have accepted being third best to the dead composer and the dying baronet? Or fourth, given that her first husband was really her gorgeous Bergonzi violin? Besides, she had suffered enough; he would not risk adding to that. Tomorrow he must go home to Mainz. God alone knew when he'd come to London again; and Hitler would make sure Jelly never came to Germany.

'I wish the world could be a different place,' he said.

'And then?'

'Then we would play music together, when nobody was listening, and I'd walk the dog with you. And sometimes you'd come to Mainz and we'd go to Berlin and visit Professor Schnabel, who wouldn't have left the country if the world were this different place. And we'd walk by the Rhine and go to Bayreuth to hear Wagner, and we'd travel around Bavaria and see Neuschwanstein, King Ludwig the Second's castle on the mountain. You'd love Neuschwanstein, it's a crazy place. A little bit like your house.'

Jelly began to laugh, but suppressed the volume into a gentle, upward gurgle, just as Ulli sometimes did himself. Their way of laughing was so similar – and the matters, too, that made them laugh – that once they'd started they couldn't stop.

'Even Neuschwanstein Castle couldn't look stranger in Chelsea than my sister's house!' Jelly managed to say. 'Ulli, I tell you, we will do it all.'

'You think so?'

'Of course. Sometime your government will change and everything will become more reasonable again. Then I'll come and visit.'

'I shall insist.' Ulli dared to reach out and twist one dark strand of Jelly's bob around his forefinger. And with that ballerina-like tilt of her head and neck, she leaned her cheek towards his hand and rested it in his palm for a second, eyes closed, lashes lavish and dark against her skin. Relishing it. As if it might not happen again.

Outside Hurricane House they paused by the drive.

'I should go,' said Ulli. 'I have to pack.'

He half hoped she would invite him in, half waited for her to do so, but he could hear the squeal of children playing inside the house, the strains of two violins – Adila was teaching – and there, peering out of an upstairs window next door, was a nosy neighbour. This was no time, even if it were the only time.

'And so… goodbye, then.'

'Only *auf Wiedersehen*. That's the only German I know!'

'*Auf Wiedersehen*, my dearest Jelly.' Ulli clicked his heels and kissed her hand. 'Promise me we stay in touch.'

'Of course we stay in touch. And the Schumann. Please don't forget about the Schumann?'

'I promise you, Jelly, that even if it is years before we meet again, even if the world goes to hell around us, I will get hold of that Schumann concerto and you will play it. I swear to you on everything I hold sacred.'

Jelly laughed. 'You sound like a Wagner opera!'

'Perhaps, but it's true. We will do this together.'

'Our shared endeavour… ' Jelly smiled as if a window had opened in her mind.

'We will write, and sometimes we can even telephone. So, *auf Wiedersehen*, dear Jelly.'

'See you then, Ulli.' She stood on tiptoe and kissed his cheek.

Chapter 9

As the year slid towards its end, Jelly wrote letters. To Anna in Scotland, telling her how much she missed her, and about Ulli and how no day went by without her wondering if she would meet him again. To Ulli, too; and in Mainz, once he had learned to decipher her bizarre handwriting, he wrote back. He told her he'd prompted Willy Strecker to contact his old friend Johannes Joachim, Elisabeth Joachim's brother.

'What's the matter with Elisabeth?' said Adila. 'Why can't *she* persuade her brother?'

'She doesn't want a fight with Eugenie Schumann,' Jelly pointed out. 'It's not in her interests. But it is in Ulli's, or at least in Schott's. They'd sell masses of copies of the piano score and solo part; and they'd hire out the orchestral parts for performances and that would be worth a fair bit.'

The financial practicalities of the concerto's existence had clearly never occurred to Adila, paling for her beside the significance of the spirit messages; yet to Ulli, the latter were clearly of no concern whatever. Jelly, caught in the middle, mulled it over while she practised.

The stamps on Ulli's letters bore a chunky image of a shield-bearer, while the postmark showed the eagle of the Third Reich: it looked like an Egyptian hieroglyph balancing atop a swastika, an inside-out symbol from Sanskrit, as if the Reich couldn't make up its mind which mystical tradition it most wished to ape. But the address would be written by the flowing, cultivated hand she now knew well. 'Look, Adi!' shouted Jelly. 'Ulli says Willy says Johannes says yes!'

'Johannes says yes to what?' Adila whirled across the hall to read the letter over Jelly's shoulder.

'He has agreed to let Willy Strecker see the manuscript and assess the concerto! And then they will decide whether to publish it.'

'Oh, Sai, *you* should have said yes to Ulli! You have this chance with this lovely young man, and what do you do? You *ask him to look for something in a library?* Listen. Make him come back here and take you out dancing. Then I will make sure Alec and Adri and I are away and you have the house to yourselves and... '

Jelly screwed the envelope into a ball and threw it at her sister, who batted it straight back. Soon they were making so much noise that Caesar started to bark and Alec came down to see what was going on.

Their joy was short-lived. After a week had passed, Ulli's next letter contained something considerably stranger.

My dear Jelly,

The most peculiar piece of news has come to us from the library.

Johannes Joachim, as you know, was the depositor of the Schumann manuscript. The library's director, Dr Altmann, knows this. But he insists that because the concerto was left there with instructions not to release it for 100 years, that condition must be kept, even though the depositor himself, who first placed that embargo upon it, says that he would like to change the condition!

I'm afraid we are up against a form of bureaucracy that is so rigid – and so exultant, if you like, in the exercising of its authority – that it is unlikely much more can be done at present.

I remember, however, that I made you a promise. I will do everything in my power to keep that promise.

I remain yours, etc.,

Ulli

Jelly re-read it three times to make sure she had understood. The depositor wished to change the conditions of his library deposit. And the library would not implement the change because it went against his original request. This made no sense. Something more had to be behind it. It should have been so simple for Ulli, sanctioned by his respected publishing house, to enter that library, find the manuscript and photograph it. He could only be stopped if someone *wanted* to stop him. Who could that be? And why?

'I have every confidence in you, dear Ulli,' Jelly wrote.

'I will find a way to come to London again soon,' he wrote back. But months went by; letters flowed; progress did not.

The Fachiris saw in 1934 with champagne and trepidation. Jelly and Adila gave concerts and lessons, Erik worked on his book and Alec sweated over the intricate legal paperwork entailed by the upheavals at the League of Nations. Germany had indeed given its notice to leave, as he had feared; the rest of the League wished to talk about limiting armaments, but Hitler seemed hell-bent on doing the exact opposite. Expansionism was on the German cards, and while the League argued, Hitler used the time to his own advantage. If Germany and Japan could simply walk out of an organisation – one that was set up after the Great War to ensure it never happened again – once it no longer suited their purposes, then the whole ethos of its existence came into question; it could be fatally weakened, which might prove catastrophic for everyone else. 'The League has been too nice,' Alec, exhausted, remarked one evening to Adila and Jelly, over a whisky. 'Far too lenient. Trying to be sensitive instead of calling a spade a spade.'

'Can't you do anything about it?' Adila challenged.

'Me? All I can do is deal with the legal fallout afterwards. Anyway, did you see this?' Alec fetched a newspaper from his briefcase and placed it on his wife's lap. It was the *Daily Mail*. 'Hurrah for the Blackshirts' read the headline above a front-page article by Viscount Rothermere, which asserted that the notion of a 'permanent reign of terror' in countries under 'Blackshirt' control had evolved solely from the 'morbid imaginations' of their opponents. 'This paper's feeding us nothing but lies, lies, lies,' Alec said, 'yet people gulp it down without questioning it, while there's real suffering, real danger out there – and we could help, but we won't because of these mendacious, self-serving... It makes me sick.' He downed the rest of his drink in one. Adila and Jelly stared at him, unused to such outbursts.

Jelly shunned the glass game, infuriated by the stalemate over the manuscript and terrified at the thought of the marching Blackshirts. Anybody could be drawn to them, Alec said, from the unemployed to Eton lads, some believing they had the answer to keeping out the communists, others determined to restore the glory of British imperialism, or some such guff, which meant reasserting their superiority over filthy foreigners. Beside this, Erik and Adila's glass game sessions seemed oddly disconnected from ordinary life. Don't forget the concerto, the glass pleaded. Jelly hadn't forgotten. She simply didn't know what to do next. The spirits might be positive, but the humans were not.

Erik had yet another idea. 'Perhaps we should ask Ulli to look more closely at the embargo – there might be a legal loophole,' he said. 'And also we might consider asking the British Ambassador in Berlin to raise the matter with Herr Hitler himself. I hear he is fond of music.'

When time allowed, reading offered the single best escape Jelly knew. Aldous Huxley sent her a copy of *Brave New World*. She took it up to the Green Room to begin.

What horror emanated from her old friend's prose: the portrait of a society that denied family, destroyed love, grew babies in bell jars and made certain that anyone different – raised with the old values of ineluctable ties between mother and child or man and woman – would probably face execution or suicide. How and why had he conceived such a vision?

'You saw *Metropolis*, didn't you?' Adila remarked. 'It's in vogue to be clever like that, to conjure up nasty futures for fun.'

'That was years ago... ' This is more than fashion, Jelly wanted to protest. Something in Aldous must have prompted him to envisage that Hatchery and Conditioning Centre that had 'only' 34 storeys.

Myra sent a postcard from New York, addressed to Jelly as 'Darling Gut-Scraper', signed 'Hyra Mess', and showing the tallest building in the world, which had many more storeys than that; it was a little over three years since Herbert Hoover had pressed a button to switch its lights on for the first time. The New York Jelly used to love would lie in the Empire State Building's shadow from now on.

Myra's increasing celebrity in New York had turned into a long, intense love affair with the city. Jelly wasn't certain why her own fortunes in the US had not expanded too; she had not been invited back after touring there with Myra two years previously. Perhaps she needed to engage a manager to make such things possible. She and Adila preferred to employ a PA, preferably the much-missed Anna; but besides having an assistant of her own, Myra swore by her managers. Jelly had none, and her administrative skills had never extended to making calls on her own behalf to concert promoters, orchestras and music clubs. That – as she knew from the cathedral tour – would take time away from working on the music. And so the dates in her diary were starting to seem sparser than of late. Each week she promised herself that next week she would do something about it. But recently she'd noticed that when she and Myra went out together, admirers often approached them, wanting an autograph. Myra's autograph.

'It's because of *Jesu, Joy of Man's Desiring*,' Adila insisted. 'Everyone's crazy for it.' Myra's piano transcription of the Bach piece was selling by the lorry-load. 'You need something like that to help you out of this – this – '

'I need the Schumann Violin Concerto,' said Jelly. 'And the word you want is "rut". Oh, if only Anna were here… '

She thought of writing to Myra in America for advice, but before she could, a letter arrived from Myra's assistant, Anita, reporting that the pianist was in hospital in Boston. Major surgery was required, with a long recuperation time; she would not be well enough to return to England for some while. Practising on automatic pilot, Jelly smarted with loneliness, terrified for her friend.

It was October 1934, with the leaves dropping from the trees and the whiff of early northern snow on the wind, when the telegram from Ireland that Jelly had been dreading finally arrived.

'Go, darling,' said Adila. 'Don't worry about us. Go to him.'

Jelly, numb, called the operator to book a call to the nursing home to which Tom was now confined. She must go to Dublin.

The house stood on a side street, set back from the road and overshadowed by plane trees. It seemed peaceful enough, more so than any London hospital, with those rows upon rows of orderly beds; but when Jelly was shown into the hall and up a wide staircase towards the room that had become Tom's final home, she understood that he might never see the outside world again – he who had travelled so widely and so well.

When the nurse opened his door, though, an unexpected sound reached her. Laughter. And a familiar voice, strong, musical and slightly Scottish. There, sitting by the bed in an armchair, drinking coffee and telling jokes to his ex-pupil, was Donald Tovey.

'They told me you were on your way.' Tovey bumbled to his feet and wrapped her in his tweedy wingspan.

'Hello, Jelly.' There came a depleted voice behind her.

She bent to kiss Tom. His face was skeletal; his eyes, huge in that surround, seemed to pop out from his shrunken cheeks and brow; what remained of his hair, which had been tousled and light, had turned straggly and grey. She could see the ridge of his skull beneath his skin, yellowed against the white pillowcase. His glasses lay abandoned on the bedside table beside a dog-eared copy of one of his favourite Thomas Hardy novels, *Tess of the d'Urbervilles*.

He took her hand; she felt for the strength in it she used to know, but this mix of bone, tendon and skin did not really amount to flesh; the only energy belonged to her. She closed her fingers around his. 'Bit off colour,' he mumbled. 'Dosed up. Sorry.'

Tovey caught Jelly's eye: 'Morphine.'

'You're not in pain, darling?'

'No. Happy to see you. Jelly. So happy.' The words were an outline, no more. Jelly cursed her own cowardice: she should have come sooner. She hesitated to ask Tovey to leave them alone together, since he had travelled all the way from Edinburgh to be here.

'We were going over old times.' Tovey, his gaze full of empathy, glanced from one to the other. 'The Wigmore concerts. Do you remember, Jelly, Sep was there?'

'Of course. And we brought Ravel over.'

'And Elgar tried to kiss you.' Tovey smiled, but Jelly did not. Elgar, too, had died this year.

'Now Elgar's gone, everything's different. As if he was the last of it all.'

'I'll say hello,' Tom tried to joke. 'Perhaps I'll meet them. I'll greet them for you, Jelly, yes? Schumann, Brahms, Onkel Jo… '

'Don't talk like that. We'll get you well.'

'Sweet Sai.' Tom tried to prop himself up on his pillow, but to no avail; soon he had slipped into deep-drugged sleep. Jelly and Tovey sat silent while his breathing became intermittent – a long pause followed by a deep, rapid lungful, then a barrage of short, gasping intakes, as if each could be his last. His hand lay chilly and grey within both of hers.

'This happens,' Tovey said. 'Don't be alarmed. He is peaceful and has no pain, which is all we can hope for.'

Jelly picked up the Thomas Hardy book. It fell open in her hand. '"Experience is as to intensity",' she read, '"not as to duration".'

She felt tears welling up. 'Darling Donald,' she said, to distract herself. 'How are you? How's Edinburgh? How's Clara?'

'Edinburgh is enduringly exuberant,' Tovey smiled, 'and Clara is charismatically cherishable. As for me – I'm all right, I think, but my hands hurt. I fear I'm not playing as well as I'd like.'

'Nor am I. My hands hurt too, and my elbow.'

'We should all emigrate. We should follow Sep's memory back to Australia, where it's warm and dry. Our bones wouldn't suffer as they do here.'

Jelly lifted the unconscious Tom's fingers to her lips and felt the icy ridges of his knuckles against her face. His breath was immobile. All she could hear was the staccato of raindrops on the window and the legato of Tovey humming as if to comfort them all. In Tom's vanishing frame: nothing. For a moment she thought he was gone. She was about to call out in alarm when his torso gave another effortful shudder. The body clings to life, sometimes even after the spirit wants to let go.

Death, Erik said, should be something beautiful, according to the messengers. That did little to help Jelly, watching him, choking back the agony of it from her throat.

His eyes opened a slit. 'Sai, dear,' he whispered, 'play to me?'

She kissed him. Nothing but Bach would do. She stood by

the window, letting the D minor Partita speak the thoughts she could not voice. Outside, rain spattered through the trees and the clouds breathed above them; a normal day on which someone would be born and someone else would die, someone would conceive and another would divorce, someone would win some triumph and another would lose a lover, all in one fragment of time, yet Bach lived on to talk of eternity through four strings, a bow and a strange-shaped wooden box with curled orifices to let the music out.

She finished the Partita and its Chaconne. Even that didn't feel enough, so she played the E major Partita as well. Perhaps it would cheer everyone up. It was only after an hour had passed, in which the sun broke through and made the damp windowpanes shine, that a nurse tapped on the door.

'I'm sorry to disturb you, but I have to give him a check, so would you please excuse us for a few minutes?'

'Of course.' She put her violin back in its case; Tovey draped her coat over her shoulders. His hand rested briefly on her elbow. His joints appeared more gnarled than she remembered, and the skin rougher – the hand of a man moving too rapidly onwards from middle age.

Downstairs, a lounge was designed for visitors, a space draped with autumn-hued curtains, each wall set with brown armchairs and sofas and, dominating everything, a grandfather clock with an overwhelming tick. Jelly wished it would keep quiet. An upright piano stood in one corner, lid closed.

Tovey, gazing about the room, clapped his hands to test its acoustic, singing out loud the while. 'It could be better if they took out the curtains and some of those rugs. Then we could have a house concert for everybody.' He clapped and hooted again. A puzzled staff member looked in to remind him, tactfully, that it was afternoon and the patients might be sleeping.

'But you want Jelly's music here,' Tovey said. 'This lady's violin playing has healing properties.'

The nurse looked embarrassed. 'Perhaps at teatime, sir.'

Jelly chose a soft armchair and curled up in it. Silence, but for that interminable clock with its pendulum: swing and clonk, swing and clonk, on and on. If she gave a concert in here, they would have to stop the clock. You can't stop a clock in a place where people have come to die. She closed her eyes and at once images assaulted her, showing her yesterday and today, this century and the last; Tom, Sep and her mother; Bartók, Ravel and her father; Hungary, England, Paris; George Yeats, at whose house she was staying in Rathfarnham, last night sipping red wine and showing her 4,000 pages of old mystery automatic writing; and –

'Jelly?' Tovey was crouching by her chair. 'You've been asleep for an hour.'

'What happened?' She heard the infernal ticking again.

'The nice nurse, the little one with the blue eyes, came in to say that our Tom is not in a very good condition at the moment. She thinks we should go now and have a nice cup of tea, and she will telephone me at my hotel and you at George's house when he's stable enough for us to come back. How does that sound?'

Jelly nodded an assent, sick at heart.

She spent all evening at the Yeatses' with one ear attuned for the telephone, which stayed mute. Willy Yeats was away in London. George, who was overjoyed to see her, though horrified by the circumstances, cooked a comforting stew; her son Michael chattered away about school, and her daughter Anne, perhaps hoping to distract Jelly, brought out a book of sketches she had made on an academy trip to County Cork. Anne, though only 15, was at art college. Jelly examined page after page, praising the deft curve of a hillside, the balance of perspective and structure in the whole. This young girl had the eye and hand of a woman. Jelly remembered, as if it had all happened to somebody else, that at Anne's age she herself was on the point of leaving Hungary and stopping her official studies altogether.

'What does "Sai" mean?' asked Anne.

'It's a little nickname that my family and some close friends use. It's "shy", spelled phonetically in Hungarian.'

'*Sai* is also a Sanskrit word,' George told her. 'It's hard to explain, but it means something like the divine mother and father rolled into one. So it's a divine presence. Someone who seems to have – well, something extra.'

'You've gone purple, Auntie Jelly,' Michael declared, with satisfaction.

'Well, I'm hardly a divine presence, am I! Anne, Michael, darlings, have you noticed we never choose our own nicknames?'

'But perhaps that's how your sisters saw you? How fascinating,' said George.

'Nicknames stick,' Jelly said. 'It doesn't matter. Really, it doesn't mean anything at all.'

The telephone screamed, waking Jelly in the spare room, catching George stirring porridge for the children's breakfast. Jelly heard her answer and utter a few monosyllables. She knew what it meant. Part of her spirit wanted to split off from her body and fly out after Tom's departing soul to embrace him one last time.

The rest of Jelly pulled a jersey over her nightgown and hurried downstairs. George was leaning on the banister, waiting to tell her that Tom had passed away at the break of dawn.

George went with Jelly and Tovey this time. Together they walked under the trees into the house where yesterday Tom was alive, yet today he was not.

'I'd like to be alone with him for a moment, please.' Jelly asked for the favour she should have sought when he was actually there.

Now that he was laid out under the sheet, the silent room seemed frozen, as if dead itself. He lay face up, eyes closed, arms straight by his sides, his features unchanged and now unchangeable.

Yesterday he was speaking to her, listening to her play, asking her for music. Today: a shell, its pearl gone for ever.

And there was the rub. Adila and Erik would declare that the soul lives on – it's still here somewhere, and can be contacted, and can speak through the glass or automatic writing. It is one with the universe; perhaps it waits to be reborn. Jelly, try as she might, couldn't feel that supposed truth. She listened and listened, yet could hear no comforting whisper in her inner ear and feel no caress of a ghost bidding her farewell. Only silence and stillness. The rain was back; through the window she could see the sheen of dampness on nearby roofs. What if, after all, there were nothing? No spirits moving the glass, no advice from messengers in the beyond; only a delusion at best, a fraud at worst. What price then Erik's certainty, Adila's devotion, the strange word of 'Schumann'?

Part of her had wanted to be there when the moment came and life turned to afterlife: to hold him as he faced the ultimate mystery. Now she was glad she had arrived too late. Despite everything, was this the reality? Stillness – silence – peace?

When Tovey came in, Jelly was kneeling by the bed, her cheek resting on the folded blanket. For once, she was not crying.

'Come along, my dear. Come on out now. There's coffee for you downstairs.' He helped her to her feet.

'I feel as if I've looked over a cliff,' Jelly whispered – she couldn't get her voice to work. 'And seen something... something empty and... *blank*.'

'Hush, Jelly. His suffering is over now. There's nothing more we can do.'

George was waiting with the coffee in the lounge; she held out motherly arms and embraced Jelly. Beside her, the clock's pendulum continued to swing.

Part II

1935–38

Chapter 10

After his visit to Britain in 1933 to hear Jelly play the not-really-Mozart concerto, Ulli went back to Mainz with his mind out of kilter. He slipped back into routine. He corrected proofs, wrote letters and sometimes, in the hall of the Schott's building, paused to gaze at Wagner's bust. Wagner, composer of *Tristan und Isolde*, should have known a thing or two about loving someone you shouldn't.

Ulli tried always to think first of his duties, not of his rights, and to be a man of honour, for the sake of Schott's. With his feet firmly on the office floor, it took him no more than two seconds to imagine the outcome were he to have an affair with Jelly d'Arányi and be found out. A scandal: an older woman, at least partly Jewish, a starry soloist with a past that people rumoured was dubious – when he began to mention her name he soon discovered that some in the music business thought she'd been Bartók's mistress, others that she was a man-eating femme fatale, still more that she would never even touch a man in preference to her violin. Besides, she had a vested interest in a work that she wanted his company to publish. Worse still, with relations between their countries plunging into the Channel, he had no idea how he might ever manage to see her again.

Even when her image flickered before his eyelids, delectable as *palacsinta*, even when he noticed, at Sunday lunch with his mother, that he hadn't heard one word she had been saying because his inner ear was full of violin music, even when he went about his usual business in Mainz, cycling past the cathedral and the sleepy river, and wondered what had happened to the part of himself that was still in London, dancing the tango and reciting Heinrich Heine, there was no choice at all. Once he stopped at the cathedral and, most uncharacteristically, went inside to say a prayer for peace of mind. Yet something about the altarpiece paintings there of the Madonna, perhaps the tilt of her head, reminded him of Jelly. Ulli made a rapid retreat.

Their correspondence continued – yet whenever he picked up his fountain pen to write to her, he found himself chewing the end of its barrel with anxiety. Her friend had died; mourning him, she wrote, she had been careless on tour, fell and broke her finger; soon afterwards, she was laid low by a septic throat that affected her ears; and recovering from that, she fell again and hurt her back. She was having to cancel concerts, much to her own horror, and planning ahead was difficult with nobody to help. At any other point in history except for 1914–18, he reflected, this time would have been free and she could have come to visit him, or he could have begged for some leave from the office and gone to her.

Instead, there came two further blows. The government reintroduced conscription. It applied in the first instance to men of 18 to 25, who all had to spend six months in military training; but should matters deteriorate, should there be war, and everyone thought Hitler intended this, Ulli knew he might find himself drafted. Then, with the announcement of the Nuremberg Laws in September 1935, he understood – with horrified incredulity – that for a German to marry or even have intimate relations with a Jewish or partly Jewish woman had just been made a criminal offence. He had dithered first for reasons of caution or 'honour', but now, if he pursued her, it could cost him both his job and his liberty.

'I'm living in some kind of nightmare, some dystopian film,' he said silently to Wagner's bust one blustery November morning.

'You had better get used to it,' came the answer within.

'Ah, Ulli… ' Willy Strecker blew in through the outer door, shaking dry an umbrella. 'Just the man. Pop in for a minute, will you?'

Upstairs, Ulli hung up his coat, then followed Strecker into the biggest office, festooned with framed composer portraits and pages of historic autograph manuscripts.

Strecker settled behind the desk. 'Ulli, we'd like you to go to Paris next month and make sure the music shops are still stocking our material. If they're not, try to charm them. And while you're there... it would be nice if you could drop in on a certain recording session and mention to the soloist the shadowy existence of a Schumann violin concerto.'

Ulli listened in incredulity. 'The Schumann? But what about Jel – Miss d'Arányi?'

'There's no reason she wouldn't play it. But this concerto is a bigger concern than one violinist. We need as much ammunition as we can amass. As our Führer might put it,' he added, with a certain sarcasm, 'we need to re-arm.'

'Who is the violinist?'

Strecker lowered his voice. 'Yehudi Menuhin.'

'Menuhin?' Ulli tried not to squawk with amazement. 'But he is a...'

'He is, isn't he?' Strecker sat back in his chair, smiling, circling his thumbs around each other. 'Ulli, there's a world out there that doesn't have race laws, and Yehudi lives in it.'

Ulli rose, clicked his heels softly together and went, dazed, to ask Fräulein Kammerling to book him a room at the Hôtel Lutetia, Paris.

'Strawberry ice cream!'

Yehudi Menuhin's face shimmered, pink, white and sweaty, in the candlelight. At the Brasserie Flo in Paris a waiter was carrying towards the party a tray on which stood an outsized glass piled with pink stuff, one extra-long silver spoon at the ready. As he set it in front of the young violinist, the entire gathering gave a cheer.

'Always.' The man seated beside Ulli gave his elbow a

nudge. 'His favourite. If a boy can't eat strawberry ice cream after finishing such a session, then when can he?'

'Naturally,' Ulli said. His neighbour was the boy wonder's father, Moshe Menuhin.

'When I first came to America, the first thing I did was to have a strawberry ice-cream soda. Now it's *his* favourite. There's a heritage for you!' Moshe – sharp, lively, slightly pugnacious, Ulli thought, with a high-domed forehead and receding hairline – raised what was left of his glass of champagne.

The entourage, which Ulli observed against the glow of the brasserie's wood panelling and stained-glass insets, consisted of the recording team: George Enescu – who'd conducted that day for Menuhin, his ex-pupil; an assortment of young girls vying for attention; and Yehudi's parents, plus his two sisters, one of whom, apparently a fine pianist and inseparable from him, had draped herself over his right shoulder. They were all clinking and cheering for the pleasure of the handsome young star in their midst. One of the girls had grabbed a piece of tinsel from the restaurant's Christmas decorations and placed it around Yehudi's collar, so that it cast up minuscule points of light around his face.

Moshe paid for dinner for everyone. 'Please, let Schott's help,' Ulli offered.

Menuhin senior paused in amazement before giving way to laughter that turned heads across the sizeable restaurant. 'Don't worry, Dr Schultheiss. You know what my boy earns per year? My friend, when this tour's over, he's going to take a sabbatical until his 21st birthday. And while he's away, this is time in which he could have earned 2 million dollars! So it's my pleasure that this dinner should be on *us*.'

Ulli made impressed noises. The generosity was admirable, yet he didn't entirely approve of the freedom with which such quantities of money were openly revealed these days – a trend, of course, of the new world. Ulli, though only 33, was a man of the old one; he would have been happier, perhaps, in the 19th rather than the 20th century. He wasn't sure, moreover, that it was sensible for any musician to earn as much as that; if everyone were to demand the same, the concert world would go bankrupt in no time. Think of Jelly, playing in those freezing cathedrals to help the unemployed, without taking one penny for herself!

It was nearly midnight, after a recording session that had lasted all day and well into the evening; the pressure on young Yehudi had scarcely let up. Compared to the world tour he was completing, it was probably easy. He'd been to South America, South Africa, India, Singapore and all the way to Australia. But not Germany. Back in 1933, before anyone had had time to ban Jewish musicians, he had taken the initiative and declared he would not play there as long as Hitler held power.

Ulli had come to the studio for most of the afternoon, capitalising on the chance to see Menuhin at work, close to, from the control room. What a face he had: fine brows, almond-shaped eyes, a patrician nose. His skin hadn't yet lost the glow of boyhood, and his smooth hair shone gold in the studio lights. His violin not only sang, but spoke. This marvel might not help them to winkle the Schumann concerto out of the library, but if they managed to winkle it and he were then to champion it, he could make the piece as famous as he was himself, anywhere in the world beyond Germany – most particularly in America – along with any of Schott's other violin concertos that he happened to like.

Since the head of the Reichsmusikkammer had changed – it used to be Richard Strauss – a blacklist had been brought in that banned the music of Jewish composers. This hit their publishers squarely in the pocket: in Germany no sheet music could be sold, no orchestral parts hired out for concerts. Schott had relatively few Jewish composers on their roster: Ernst Toch, Erich Wolfgang Korngold from Vienna and Mátyás Seiber from Hungary, but not many others. It seemed, though, that the biggest worry was not the immediate effect, but how much worse the future might be. 'Once people start banning things, it can be difficult to know when to stop,' Willy warned. Therefore they had to shore up their resources. There was, after all, an outside world, as he had said; and Yehudi was the young musical king of it.

Poor boy: fancy having to be known these days by the very name from which the term 'Jew' was derived. Moshe explained to the gathering that when he and his wife, Marutha, were looking for lodgings in New York they were welcomed by a landlady who misidentified Marutha by her blue eyes and declared she'd rent them the room because she did not want Jewish tenants. Marching away, Yehudi's mother-to-be chose the name of her unborn son in fury. At least, she vowed, nobody could ever take Yehudi to be something or someone he was not.

Ulli was aware that some of the party had been keeping their distance from him, or casting sideways looks when they thought he wouldn't notice. Whoever he was, whatever he thought, to them he was simply… German. Paris was nationalistic, opposed to political refugees from further east, yet also left wing; on the train he'd been reading a newspaper article about an alliance called the Popular Front which had created rare unity among the left only months ago, resulting in marches, riots and a strong presence for communism. A visiting German, however opposed he might be to his own government, was bound to sense the effects of that. He measured every word he spoke, changing the subject if a conversation sidled towards politics, for he was on edge with fear – rational or otherwise – that he might be overheard, then reported to the German authorities for fraternising with Jews. This would have been a fearsome concern in Mainz; and if Paris's walls lacked such ears, his nerves could not quite believe it. No call-up papers had come; he should not be an immediate target, but it was not impossible, and one mistake on his part might result in just such an eventuality. He couldn't help wondering if he had been sent here because he, rather than a company director, would then be the cannon fodder if something went wrong. Surely not? He trusted his employers not to put him in danger.

'Relax, Dr Schultheiss.' Moshe spotted his unease. 'We know it's not *your* fault. But I'd be telling a lie if I pretended we're not anxious to get home to California before everything blows sky-high. This city feels like a volcano.'

'I'm surprised you are here at all,' George Enescu told Ulli.

Ulli nodded. He much admired Enescu as a composer, performer and conductor, and longed to tell him the truth: that despite his fears he appreciated his employers' mercurial games and rather enjoyed engaging, together with them, in a type of passive resistance that entailed pushing as far as one could contrary to the authorities, but without shouting about it. If it were good for business, Schott's would find a way to do it. Sometimes he wondered how close to the sun his employers were prepared to soar without singeing their wings, or his. Unless he was indeed being followed, hopefully the authorities would not know he was in Paris to meet an important Jewish musician, hoping to persuade him to play a special and newsworthy German work. But if they found out... He pushed the idea away. He was here now.

Outside, he made sure he gained permission from Moshe and Marutha to travel alone with Yehudi in the first of several cabs that were to take the family and their friends back to the hotel through pre-Christmas Paris.

'There's something interesting I'd like to run by you, Yehudi,' he said.

'Oh yes?' The violinist turned his bright, girl-preoccupied eyes towards him.

Ulli prepared to unleash Willy Strecker's idea. 'Now,' he began, 'what would you say if I were to tell you that there is a violin concerto by Schumann that is never played?'

'Schumann?' said Yehudi, his face alight as if a magic strawberry ice cream had materialised before him. 'And... *is* there?'

'There is.'

'*Really*? Where? Why? What's it like? Why isn't it played? Can I see it?'

'It's in the Prussian State Library in Berlin. We have been attempting to acquire the rights to publish it, but the family is very resistant and at first they made it impossible.'

'And now they've relented?'

'Not exactly, but we're working on it,' said Ulli. 'There's a new director at the library's music collection – his name is Dr Georg Schünemann, and he used to be director of the Berlin Hochschüle für Musik, which is where I studied. We're hoping he will be a little less intractable than the gentleman who has, er, gone.'

There was, unfortunately, reason to believe that Schünemann had already been tractable – as Ulli had discovered that very morning.

With several free hours in Paris before joining Menuhin's recording session, Ulli had taken the Métro to the Rome stop, intending to spend some time visiting music shops near the conservatoire to meet and charm the proprietors, as Willy had requested. Music transcends politics, he said to them; they hastened to agree. He wondered if they really believed it. He scarcely did so himself; it was, as always, a useful excuse for deflecting more important issues. One store was displaying the latest issue of the magazine *La Revue musicale*. He picked up a copy and leafed through it. Then he stopped, blinked, stared.

He had not imagined it. He was gazing at an article about the Schumann Violin Concerto, written by a German musicologist named Hermann Springer. There, on the bright new paper of the December 1935 edition, was a facsimile of the first page of the piece's slow movement, in manuscript. Ulli hurried into a spot where the light was better. The bulb cast its glow onto the staves of Schumann's handwriting. He saw a suggestion of syncopation, some offbeat counterpoint, a simple melody written in an odd, complex way. For several minutes, focused on the very thing he'd been trying in vain to unearth, Ulli lost all sense of time and place.

Once the shock wore off, he forced the cogs of his brain into action, trying to visualise how this could have happened. Clearly, the Nazis were letting their own people in on the secret concerto. Perhaps there was more to that official 'embargo' than he had been led to believe.

'Here's an article about it,' he said to Yehudi now, taking one of several copies of the journal out of his briefcase. 'This fell into my hands earlier today, quite by chance.'

'Incredible. It must be fate!' Yehudi, in the dim pulse of the passing streetlights, bent his head towards the page that bore the photo of the manuscript. Ulli heard him humming a rough outline of the solo. 'Dr Schultheiss, this looks extraordinary. I have to see the whole thing. I *have* to.'

Back in Mainz, Willy Strecker sat poring over *La Revue musicale* while Ulli stood nearby, shifting his weight from foot to foot. 'They're up to something,' said Strecker.

'Who do you think… ?'

'At a guess, probably the Reichsmusikkammer, the culture bureau.'

'This piece says Breitkopf will publish it. First I've heard of that.'

'They can't. It's to *us* that Johannes Joachim gave his permission. At least, I believe that's the case. We need to stand up to this. We should have a sound plan for bringing it out and having it performed, sooner rather than later.'

Ulli nodded slowly. Every cool-headed argument now must go in favour of Menuhin as the sensible destination for the Schumann concerto if it were to be saved, long-term, from official meddling. Menuhin was the superstar of the moment, the one who drew the crowds and the reporters.

'We can't leave it only up to Miss d'Arányi,' Strecker

insisted. 'Twenty years ago, yes, but I can't see much evidence in her favour now.'

'She filled nine cathedrals in a row,' Ulli pointed out. 'Everyone adored her when I saw her play at the Queen's Hall.'

'That was then. But she's had injuries, she's been cancelling performances, she doesn't seem to have any coherent long-term planning beyond her regular circuits. We need more than that to put this concerto on the map. Yehudi only has to play a scale to land his picture on the front pages.'

Ulli went back to his desk and sat with his head in his hands. He had told Jelly nothing of his visit to Menuhin in Paris; he was afraid of upsetting her at a time when she was already suffering a litany of health problems. Even so, she had insisted on resuming her cathedral concerts for charity. What other artist would do such a thing? He longed to defend her more robustly to Strecker, yet hesitated to reveal their long-distance quasi-intimacy. Blank paper stared up at him while he chewed the end of his pen. 'My dear Jelly,' he wrote. He stopped, then pushed the paper aside and on a fresh sheet wrote to Tovey instead, asking if he could please send Jelly some flowers on his behalf.

He decided not to tell her about either the article or Menuhin until the true nature of the situation became clearer, for better or for worse. He had made her a solemn promise that she should perform the concerto – and he could not bear the notion of letting down someone about whom he cared so much, even in if in a ridiculously distant way. She must play the Schumann. Menuhin must play it too. He must find a way to keep his promise to her while also doing his best for Schott's. And all of this was, of course, to assume that Willy's plan of action could hold its own against whatever the culture bureau had been cooking up in Berlin.

Jelly was indeed having a difficult winter. She had struggled bravely through some concerts and recording sessions with

Myra and the cellist Gaspar Cassadó, and played at the Wigmore Hall; but her right elbow had seized up, and the impact of Tom's death still seemed to be draining her spirit, month after month. Frightened by the newspapers, thrown by reports that the Musicians' Union was vetoing visits by foreign performers, she applied for, and was granted, British naturalisation. Cinema orchestras were closing down at an alarming rate; many dismissed musicians were desperate for employment, which meant that foreigners would be an easy target for their anger.

'Sai, that policy is targeting American dance bands, not people like you,' Alec tried to reassure her, but she had no intention of turning back. Naturalisation was, after all, a gesture of gratitude to the country that had been her home for nearly a quarter of a century – and protection, of course, should foreign performers be banned.

As for her arm, nobody seemed to know what was really the matter. One doctor suggested she might have a form of rheumatoid arthritis, which could flare up, then subside, just as hers seemed to. Another insisted it was plain osteoarthritis. A third said that the problem was probably with her tendons, and time alone would be the solution. Yet another declared that it was all in the mind. 'You seem very tense, Miss d'Arányi. Perhaps a consultation with a psychoanalyst… '

'I don't need psychoanalysis,' Jelly assured him. 'I just have a sore arm.'

She felt guilty about having any problem at all after Myra related what had happened to her in the States the previous year. Suspected breast cancer. Thank heavens it had turned out to be a false alarm, but only after she had had radical surgery. 'I'm fine,' she assured Jelly, 'though it was rather boring to sit around recovering.' Jelly could scarcely bear to think what must be going through her mind underneath that stoic façade.

'It's not life-threatening and I'm sure I don't need an operation,' Jelly told the latest Harley Street specialist.

'I wonder, Miss d'Arányi, did you perhaps suffer malnutrition during the Great War?' the doctor asked.

'You were very thin as a girl,' Adila reminded her. She insisted on going with Jelly to all her appointments.

'But not malnourished,' Jelly insisted. 'Why do you ask?'

'That kind of thing can affect the strength of a lady's bones later in life,' the specialist explained, kindly enough.

'That's interesting – nobody ever told me that before. But I'm 42. Is that really "later in life"? And, forgive me, but each doctor I see tells me something different... '

He gave a wry smile. 'I find it inspiring, but also alarming, to think how much we in medicine simply don't know. I'd love to see how the profession will look a hundred years from now.'

Jelly put her blouse back on; she had to fumble with the buttons. 'I hear there's a cure being developed for TB. Is that true?'

'At the moment it's very expensive. But one day, I hope, the sooner the better, we'll have medical treatment available to all, no matter the cost. Don't you agree, Miss d'Arányi, that no human life should be valued less highly than another?'

'Then we must stop the wars, too.'

The doctor gave her an astute glance; he knew her generation well, those women whose loved ones never came back from the trenches.

'Jelly, my dear,' came Tovey's voice on the telephone, 'I have in my hand a copy of a French journal that contains an analysis of the Schumann Violin Concerto. It came out in December, but it has only reached me now.'

Jelly tried to speak, and couldn't.

'It would seem that under this regime, access to the concerto isn't forbidden any longer. It's just forbidden to *us*.'

'But Eugenie Schumann – ?'

'I hear she is even more outraged than we are. It looks as if

Goebbels and his Ministry of Propaganda have decided there's a use for this piece, so they're annexing it themselves.'

'But they can't. It's ours!'

'Unfortunately they can and they will. They can do anything they like. And remember, it is only you and I who consider that the Schumann concerto is "ours"... '

The article arrived the next day with the first post: a brown-paper parcel addressed in Tovey's writing. Jelly shut herself in her room with the package, counted to ten, then pulled off the string.

The words were real, printed: *Le Concerto pour violon et orchestre par Robert Schumann.* The article was in French; the author's name, Hermann Springer, German. And it said that the work was to be published by Breitkopf und Härtel in Germany – not Schott's.

Ulli had said not one word about this to her in any of his letters. He wrote to her often – not always about work, and many times inconsequentially, due, she assumed, to potential interception or censorship en route. He had not even mentioned the military shenanigans in the Rhineland; it was Alec who told her that the German troops had marched across the bridges, including the one at Mainz, to remilitarise the area, without France or the League of Nations being able to do anything to stop them. She wrote back to Ulli, aware that instead of letters to a mortally ill man in Ireland, she was penning missives to one who was perfectly well, but living in an enemy country that could clap him in jail if he had an affair with her. Several months ago an unexpected bouquet had arrived from him via Tovey, tumbling with roses and lilies; what it meant, she could only speculate.

She might adore Ulli, or the fantasy image of him that had lingered since their only meetings; but more importantly, she'd trusted him. He'd made her a promise. Perhaps it was her fault for placing too much faith in him.

Holding the lash of betrayal at bay by reading the article,

translating as much as she could, Jelly tried to keep her head; maybe she could pick up the feel of the music from what Springer had written. The first movement, stormy and intense: Schumann's turbulent, extrovert self. A slow movement that was the jewel of the work. And the finale: a big polonaise, rather slow. The desire to hear it, or better still to play it, took hold of her, so intense that it verged upon the physically painful.

Odd, though: a polonaise, a grand, traditional dance from Poland, seemed a strange way for a German composer to end a concerto. She could think of only one precedent: Beethoven's Triple Concerto, hardly an obvious model. Jelly considered this, swallowing coffee. Perhaps Myra, who knew Schumann's piano works inside out, could shed light on his inclinations.

Myra was home when Jelly phoned, though her voice betrayed the fact that she was busy practising. 'There's a polonaise in *Papillons*,' she remarked. 'It's a lovely thing, only his second official work, but it's deceptive – it's got some awfully fiddly bits in it.'

'But what does it *mean*?' Jelly pleaded.

Myra paused. 'I'm not sure it *means* anything – not the way a polonaise would for Chopin, being Polish… *Papillons* is supposed to depict a masked ball and I think the polonaise was traditionally the opening dance, wasn't it? Except that he puts it nearly at the end. Why do you ask?'

Jelly gave Myra a potted update on the Schumann concerto situation. 'And I'm also anxious about what people will think when I explain how I came across it,' she added.

At the end of the phone there was a stunned silence. 'Never mind how you found the concerto,' Myra said eventually, decisive. 'That's not important. The question is: what happens now that you have? And, it would seem, now that *they* have too?'

'Alec thinks the German government owns the rights, because it has been in the state library for such a long time – and I don't know what to do.'

'I don't think there's much you *can* do.'

'It ought to be mine to play first,' Jelly insisted. 'Nobody would have known it existed if I hadn't had that message.'

'Do you have anything official in writing from someone who holds rights in the piece, declaring that you must play it first? Beyond your sister's, er, transcripts?'

'If only... No, of course I don't. And I know that in the end it's...'

Jelly wanted to say, 'It's only a piece of music.' Not land, or an inflammatory political text, or a shipment of arms. Only a piece of music. And yet... It brought to mind other images of those she could not begin to rescue: first Sep, then Tom – and now, trapped in Nazi Germany, Ulli too. 'Honestly, Myra, if I lose it now... I don't know what I'll do.'

Chapter 11

'That's outrageous,' said Donald Tovey.

'You're telling me,' said Ulli. 'Did you see the footnote?'

'Georg Kulenkampff is to give the premiere in Berlin? And he wants a year of exclusivity? It's... outrageous.'

'And it is to be published by Breitkopf und Härtel. Nobody would ever have known where to find it if it wasn't for our efforts and yours.'

'Then it is in your interests as well as mine to put a stop to this,' said the professor, the lengthy telephone line crackling between Edinburgh and Mainz. 'Why have you let all these months go by, Ulli? Why did nobody send me this article sooner? I had no idea *whatsoever*. You can't have been entirely preoccupied with your Olympic Games?'

Ulli hesitated. People outside Germany had very little inkling, he realised, of the pressures that now faced him and his colleagues under the Third Reich. 'Herr Sir Doktor Professor,' he faltered, for Tovey, in that strange British system, had recently been knighted, 'we are up against some – well, *interesting* – situations here... '

'And is that a reason not to keep me informed?'

'Why is it in *your* interests to put a stop to it?' Ulli ventured. 'Because of our beautiful Hungarian?'

'"Our" beautiful Hungarian?'

Ulli stayed quiet.

'There is such a thing in life as fair play,' suggested Tovey. 'Nobody would have been alerted to this manuscript if "our beautiful Hungarian's" friend, the Swedish minister, had not gone to tremendous lengths to unearth it, using his intelligence and intuition to discover that it had been sitting all along in the wrong box. And he, and Adila, absolutely insist that Schumann's own spirit selected Jelly as its representative.'

Ulli let out a swear word in German.

'You could say "fiddlesticks",' remarked Tovey. 'It's not inappropriate. Nevertheless, Ulli, as you know, *they* believe it with all their hearts – and even I'm beginning to think there is some truth in it, one way or another. By the way, isn't it worth remembering that if Breitkopf publishes that concerto, they stand to make a small fortune out of it? That should belong to Schott's.'

The conversation at an end, Ulli sat, as was becoming his habit, with his hands over his eyes, breathing deeply. Of course the concerto should be Schott's; of course he wanted Jelly to be the first violinist to play it. But Strecker's enquiries had been making it increasingly clear that to assure either of these scenarios was going to require a gigantic fight, and the idea of having to do battle with representatives of this regime scarcely bore consideration... How had music become so entangled with politics anyway?

He had planned to spend the day on correspondence. It would have to wait. He called his secretary.

'Fräulein Kammerling, please try and get Dr Strauss on the telephone for me.'

Richard Strauss, whom Ulli considered Germany's greatest living composer, had for a short while run the regime's music department, the Reichsmusikkammer: the committee that also decided which composers and performers should be officially sanctioned by the Nazi party. Ulli had been horrified, but it was not his place to object, merely to make sure that Strauss's compositions were published on time. Strauss's appointment nevertheless came to a swift end when officials intercepted a supportive letter from the composer to his Jewish librettist, the writer Stefan Zweig. Strauss was out on his tail and his name was mud. Word reached Ulli that Goebbels had demolished the unfortunate septuagenarian in a final meeting, screaming at him that he was a nobody and would never, ever write music as fine as Franz Lehár's, leaving him shaking and tearful on the stairs at the Ministry of Propaganda. Strauss insisted that they'd never *asked* him to take the post, merely *ordered* him, and the alacrity with which they'd thrown him out said more about the composer's true self, Ulli decided, than the fact that he had felt obliged to do the job at all.

'My dear Dr Schultheiss... ' Strauss's voice was starting to sound doddery, Ulli thought. He was 72; it should be time for him to retire to Garmisch-Partenkirchen to grow roses and enjoy his grandchildren. Chances were limited that a composer would produce any more important works at this stage of life.

Ulli explained the Schumann situation and met with an exclamation, then a silence, while Strauss took in the story and its implications.

'Kulenkampff is a fine violinist,' the composer volunteered eventually.

'It's not the violinist we mind so much,' said Ulli, though for him it was. 'It is Breitkopf. You see, we've been involved with the retrieval of this work from the start. This business of the government overriding everything... '

'I know, I know.' Strauss certainly did.

'Is there anything you can suggest?' Ulli pleaded. 'I should explain that Schott's has started to lose money from the official blacklisting of our Jewish composers by your Reichsmusikkammer successor, Peter Raabe. It's not that your works are not doing well – they're doing extremely well – but if the company can capitalise on a hitherto unknown work by Schumann, then we'll have more to invest in promoting today's great composers, such as yourself.'

'Yes, yes,' sighed Strauss. 'I appreciate that, Dr Schultheiss, and I wasn't born yesterday. But I have no influence now, nor do I wish to. Not after... *that.*'

'I'd value your opinion in any case. I know you understand

this environment,' Ulli admitted. 'I might try to persuade Dr Strecker to organise a meeting with some of the official party people.'

'Raabe?' Strauss grunted.

Ulli knew Raabe as a second-rate conductor, a former Weimar *Kapellmeister* with an unhealthy fondness for the music of Franz Liszt. Ulli liked publishing Liszt, but not playing it; too much bluster for his taste. He had no doubt that Raabe was appointed for political reasons, not artistic ones. 'Yes, Raabe – and perhaps Goebbels himself. Do you think that, in a case as strange and significant as this, it could be necessary?'

'That *upstart pipsqueak*?' said Strauss. 'Yes, Goebbels might well take an interest... '

Ulli was possessed by a sense of unreality. 'I can't help wondering what could be so important about *a violin concerto*. So crucial that it might even capture the time and energy of Hitler's minister of propaganda,' he remarked.

'All I can say,' Strauss growled, 'is that, well, you'd be surprised.'

All the more reason to hold on to it, not only for the company's sake, but for the music's. Hitler had annexed Wagner and Bruckner for his own ends; he must under no circumstances be able to take Ulli's beloved Schumann as well. This long-buried work must remain a great Romantic violin concerto, and nothing else.

Except that the concerto, apparently, was not that great after all.

'I've had a look at it, and so has Kulenkampff.' Peter Raabe was tapping the base of his pen against the table, an unconscious movement that signalled nerves. 'It needs work if it's going to be playable, because it is a very peculiar piece indeed.'

The assembled men sat along two sides of a vast table at the Ministry of Public Enlightenment and Propaganda, under a high ceiling and heavy chandelier. From beneath the trees on Berlin's

Wilhemplatz, the building, a palace once upon a time, had glared out at the Schott's team, complete with Grecian façade: a relic of the true age of Enlightenment, the concept inverted for the Reich's purposes.

Ulli had lived in Berlin 15 years ago; each stone had held, for him, an imprint of something he'd heard, someone he'd seen, plans he'd made, somebody he'd kissed. Yet today Berlin felt tense, squeezed by a tourniquet of conformity, crushed beneath monolithic modern architecture. Even this ridiculous table seemed a manifestation of the city's new and forbidding ambience. Forbidding? Not his Berlin. Not as he remembered it.

He'd contacted Tovey to inform him of the forthcoming meeting, but begged him to say nothing yet to Jelly. Not until he and the Streckers had the outcome they wanted, signed and sealed on Third Reich notepaper.

He was present officially as assistant to Ludwig and Willy, but kept quiet about his reason for wanting to go. If he were there himself, he could raise the issue of Jelly d'Arányi and her moral right to play the piece first, in case the Streckers could not or would not. During the long train journey to Berlin, the brothers had talked little and smoked a great deal. Ulli didn't like to smoke, but today, beset with nerves worse than any he had experienced since he last gave a concert, he accepted a cigarette from Ludwig.

'It's all right, Ulli,' said his boss. 'It will soon be over. Nothing to worry about.'

The most alarming moment so far had been just before they were shown up to the meeting room. At that point Ulli would have given several teeth for the good sense never to have involved himself in this crazy project.

It was a comfort, in some ways, to discover that Goebbels was considerably shorter than he was. He, too, had to visit the toilet and brush his teeth and probably woke up his wife snoring. He had a club foot, and one leg an inch or two longer than the other. His polished shoe squealed against the wooden floor as he made his way to the table, cutting a figure that was no pro-totype of the Aryan master race. Pure fiction, Ulli remembered. There was no such thing. How could anybody look at this man and believe there was?

The Schott's representatives were outnumbered, with four officials opposite the three of them: Goebbels, Raabe, a clerk to take minutes, and one extra backstop whose purpose was not clear to them – perhaps for numbers, perhaps to scrutinise the publishers' every word. While Willy Strecker made his initial presentation, Ulli took a swig of water from a glass that Goebbels's secretary had brought, but had to cough when some of it went down the wrong way.

'So, your artistic view is that this concerto is not actually good enough to perform in its current state?' Goebbels said, responding to Raabe's assessment. The assistant scribbled min-utes in black ink. Ulli took notes for their side.

'Schumann's state of mind when he wrote it was very uncertain,' Raabe said, glancing to the Streckers. 'That is why the work was hushed up for such a long time and why the old lesbian in Switzerland is in such a huff over its unearthing. The fact is, her mother had a point. It's not top-quality Schu-mann. This matters, gentlemen. Let me explain. The Jew Mendelssohn's Violin Concerto is no longer to be heard in our concert halls, but unfortunately it's the most popular violin con-certo in the country. Something needs to take its place and so, if there is to be a concerto we can be proud of and that will fulfil its purpose here, then elements of it need to be reworked.'

Ulli listened and kept very quiet. So *that* was the idea? Mendelssohn's parents had converted to Lutheranism and the composer had been a devout Christian, more so than Brahms and probably more than Schumann himself. Clearly that well-known fact cut no ice with this team.

'I believe my brother is the right man to nominate an appropriate composer for the job,' Ludwig said. 'I understand your projected choice of Breitkopf, Dr Raabe, since they publish the complete Schumann edition. But I would respectfully suggest that Schott's could add value that nobody else could match. We have an exceptional level of commitment to this work – not least because it is our firm, and not Breitkopf, that has received permission to put it into print, from its original custodian, who deposited it in the library. I believe that that permission is exclusive and cannot be extended to the other company.'

'I see... We will look into that.' Raabe made a note.

'And how would *you* propose to take the matter forward, given our colleague's view of the piece?' Goebbels, his eyes oddly opaque, was said to be irresistible to women. Ulli couldn't imagine why.

'For a start,' Ludwig said, 'I know of nobody whose musical judgement I trust as much as my brother's, family issues aside. We would be honoured if you were to decide to award the concerto to Schott's, on the basis of a reworking by an appropriate composer of my brother's choice – one who is able to imagine himself into the head of a bygone genius. It would be a task for the finest craftsman, and we have many under our auspices.'

'Professor Kulenkampff wishes to adapt the piece to make his own playing edition,' said Raabe, 'and desires it to remain exclusively his, hence unpublished.'

'Professor Kulenkampff must of course do as he wishes. As for the performing edition that we will print, I have some ideas,' said Willy Strecker.

Ulli noticed Ludwig kicking his brother's ankle under the table – perhaps a glimpse of family dinners, when they were boys together in another century.

'We have several excellent in-house editors who can begin the process,' Ludwig said, 'and there are fine musicians in Frankfurt we can consult, besides the composers of our catalogue. All we would ask is the freedom to do so at our discretion.'

'Dr Strecker, you are more transparent than you realise, to the practised eye. I wonder exactly who you are planning to book, with these slippery words? You have some good composers in your catalogue. Mainly dead ones. But also, how many Jews, how many degenerates? I suggest you stop any such idea before you begin.' Goebbels's pinched voice grated on Ulli's ears. Hitler's bullying tone had spread among his subsidiaries like fungus on a bathroom wall. They wouldn't argue. They would blunderbuss and pistol-whip. Their ideologies, Ulli considered, were so spurious that they could never win an honest argument, so they imposed their will by force; there was no other way to do it.

'Your audacity has a certain appeal,' Raabe remarked, sarcastic. 'You're a brave man, Dr Strecker.'

'Or a very stupid one,' added Goebbels. 'We're under no obligation to allow you to go home to beautiful Mainz, you realise.'

The publishers stayed silent, digesting what they had heard. None of them had uttered one name.

'Perhaps you have a nomination of your own for a suitable composer?' Ludwig said, keeping his head. 'Or we might ask Professor Kulenkampff for his suggestion?'

Ulli, taking notes, felt sweat oozing up through his collar. How could he raise the issue of Jelly and the premiere in such an atmosphere? He had promised himself he would not leave without doing so.

He listened as Raabe and Ludwig batted names about. The key issue was that the violin as soloist must sound triumphant, representing a great leader – not a point that appeared ever to have occurred to Schumann himself. Hans Pfitzner? He'd put too much of his own stamp on it. Carl Orff? He'd probably leap at it, but the deadline could be a problem. He was a busy man, currently writing a massive new choral piece called *Carmina Burana*. Ulli hoped nobody would draw attention to that; he'd seen the Latin text and feared it would prove too explicitly erotic for the regime. The last thing Schott's needed was yet another banning. Willy would have chosen Paul Hindemith, the finest craftsman they knew, a string player himself, and a 'real' German – but even he had fallen foul of Goebbels, having written an opera, *Mathis der Maler*, about a painter who turned against the idea of war. Mention of him was forbidden.

'Whoever you ask will have to work fast,' said Raabe eventually. 'The premiere must take place as soon as possible.'

Ulli jolted towards hope: Raabe had said 'will' rather than 'would'.

'Speaking of the premiere… ' Ulli recognised the moment to make his bid: now or never. 'This concerto would not have come to light were it not for our efforts, acting on information from the eminent musicologist Sir Donald Francis Tovey and the violinist Miss Jelly d'Arányi. Miss d'Arányi is the great-niece of the violinist for whom the concerto was originally written. It is only right that she, as its discoverer and his close relation, should be the one to give its first performance.'

'The great-uncle is Joseph Joachim, the Hungarian composer and famous violinist,' muttered the hitherto silent backstop to Goebbels. 'He was a Jew and we have taken down his statues. Miss d'Arányi is his great-niece, originally from Budapest, where she was born in the Jewish quarter. She is extremely celebrated and it's rumoured that she was once Bartók's lady friend.'

Ludwig and Willy both stared towards Ulli, stunned into silence. So did Goebbels, half rising from his chair as he turned that implacable gaze upon Ulli's eyebrows.

'Oh, my dear friends,' Goebbels began. 'You come into my headquarters, requesting my time to discuss a great German premiere for a great German concerto by a great German composer – and your employee sits in front of me saying that he, personally, wants a Jewess to play it? One more word, Dr Schultheiss, and I will pick up that telephone and call my friend in the Gestapo headquarters. I consider your views more naive than treasonous, but possibly he may not. In this case you wouldn't see the beautiful pink cathedral of Mainz again for a long, long time. What must your employers here think of your judgement? Well, that's for them to decide. Isn't that so, my friends?'

'The d'Arányis are not Jewish,' Raabe intervened, to Ulli's surprise. 'One quarter, perhaps, but that's all.'

'You know perfectly well that's enough,' snapped the supposed backstop.

'They are devout Christians and the descendants of Hungarian aristocracy,' Willy Strecker managed to add.

'And of a Jewish fiddler,' said Goebbels.

Ulli stewed. To think that a man who held such power was so pig-ignorant, so poisoned with state-approved madness, that he would dismiss Joachim, the greatest violinist of the 19th century, best friend of Brahms and Schumann, as 'a Jewish fiddler'? Worse, he could not stand up and punch the living daylights out of him. He'd be shot. He understood now that nothing he and the Streckers did or said could change one cog in the wheel of Goebbels's gravy train. At least Raabe had inadvertently saved Ulli's skin, for now.

'Enough.' Goebbels detached himself from the table and began to pace the length of the room. 'She can't do it in any case. Professor Kulenkampff wants exclusivity. A nice, long year of it.'

Ulli diverted his gaze to the wooden table. Better not risk staring at the minister and his club foot. This was a man whose party wanted to sterilise or euthanize those who were crippled. Imagine his inner landscape. How he must hate himself.

'As we all agree, Professor Kulenkampff is a fine violinist,' Willy said. 'Nevertheless, that's a long time for one musician alone to perform such an important work. After the premiere there'll be soloists, orchestras and conductors queuing up to programme it, coming to us for the parts. What are we to tell them? That we can't help them because of Professor Kulenkampff? It would cause a great deal of bad feeling and would ultimately risk rebounding against the concerto and Professor Kulenkampff himself. So it's hardly in his interests.'

'German artists overseas will want to play it as well. We can't exclude performances abroad,' Ludwig added.

'There's another point, too, if I may,' Ulli ventured, trying to keep his voice steady. 'If the concerto is to replace the Mendelssohn in concert life, it needs to become well known rapidly, and though that will certainly happen if Professor Kulenkampff plays it, still it must be performed more times in more places than one violinist can manage, to increase the public's familiarity. Professor Kulenkampff has a teaching post here in Berlin and is highly sought after. I was a student at his college myself, actually, while Professor Schünemann was its director.'

Raabe gave a brief nod. Goebbels paused in his tracks.

'My colleague means that Professor Kulenkampff isn't free to tour and perform constantly, or he'd be neglecting his students, the next generation of great German musicians,' Willy said. 'We could usefully steer him away from exclusivity for the greater good of German music. He could keep exclusivity, of course, on his private adaptation. Subsequent performers could then make their individual arrangements.'

'You mean, your Jewish woman friend can play it,' said Goebbels.

'If she does, it would be in England,' Ulli pointed out. 'At best, she will be spreading the supremacy of German art in the British capital. And at worst, it's just a piece of music... '

Goebbels sat down. He stayed still in his chair with his hands over his eyes, thinking hard – in exactly the pose Ulli had taken to adopting. Ulli made a mental note never to do that again.

'My friends, my friends,' Goebbels said, putting his hands flat against the table. 'Your callow youth here has a lot to learn. Dr Schultheiss, you work for a music publisher that is in charge of some of the Reich's finest composers – and you, of all people, dare to say that a newly rediscovered work by Robert Schumann is "just a piece of music"? Learn this, if you learn nothing else today: *nothing is ever "just" a piece of music*. And remember, we can close down your entire company at one stroke of a pen, whenever we like.'

'Ulli,' said Ludwig later, over much-needed schnapps in a *Bierkeller* a safe distance away, 'have you gone quite mad?'

'I apologise, Dr Strecker,' Ulli said. His hands were still shaking. 'I had no idea... I was just trying to do the right thing.'

'We should sack you, and not just on their say-so. You put us all in mortal danger. The whole company! And for what? Why this sudden propensity for playing poker with the devil?'

'We won, didn't we?' Ulli pointed out. At the very least, to 'win' meant getting out of the Ministry of Propaganda at all.

'If we didn't need you in the office so much... ' Ludwig kept his voice low; there was no knowing who could overhear them, though it was a noisy place. The team had planned to stay another night in Berlin. Now, by unspoken mutual consent, they would take the next train home.

'Are you going to dismiss me?' Ulli asked.

'We don't give in to bullies. But Ulli, I advise you to play by the rules. It won't hurt. One more false step... consider yourself duly warned.'

Ulli nodded, experiencing shuddery relief. He did not remark that as far as 'playing by the rules' went, he was not the person who had thought of approaching Yehudi Menuhin with the Schumann concerto. He downed his schnapps. Even if he did nothing else heroic, he had stood up to Goebbels and lived to tell the tale. Now, though, he had to find a way to explain to Jelly the hard-won yet unexpected outcome of this desperate adventure – and for that he was going to need courage of another kind altogether.

A letter from Mainz found its way to Netherton Grove for Jelly. First, the good news, Ulli wrote. Schott's had won the right to publish the concerto, and Jelly to play it. He would send a photostat to her as soon it was available. It was to be prepared and, in places, altered editorially, by a fine composer and string player whose music she would know and admire, although the finished edition would not bear his name. For a few blessed seconds Jelly offered up prayers of thanks to her benign spirits as if they had sent gold cascading down from the heavens.

Then she read on. The liquid gold began to evaporate. Her performance would be the UK premiere. Kulenkampff must give the modern *world* premiere first, in Germany, on a directive from the highest echelons of the Third Reich. Nothing Ulli or the Streckers could say would change this. He hoped Jelly would understand. Had it been up to him...

'Kulenkampff? That ghastly Nazi?' The thought sliced through Jelly like cheesewire.

'I'm sure that under any other circumstances, it would have been yours,' Tovey said to her on the phone; she knew he meant to mollify her. 'This situation is unprecedented. And remember, a UK premiere is not so bad, is it? Besides, I know for a fact that it will be broadcast on the BBC Home Service – I spoke to Adrian Boult about it the other day.' Boult was now the BBC's head of music. 'He wishes to conduct it himself.'

How strange to think she had been playing unexpectedly with Boult the day before all this began. Bizarre, too, that one mysterious violin concerto could become such an emblem of territory and ownership; to her, Kulenkampff's newly awarded supremacy felt like an invasion, a violation of her ground, though Alec would no doubt advise her to be less hypersensitive. On a more practical level, she hoped that Schott's unnamed composer–editor would finish his work quickly so that she could learn the piece – though it was far from clear why anybody should have to interfere with Schumann's score. The edition would take most of the year, Ulli wrote, possibly longer, depending. On exactly what, he didn't say.

Chapter 12

One fine April afternoon, Ulli returned from his lunch break to find a proof and two photostats in a brown-paper package on his desk. He had been walking by the Rhine, eating his sandwiches, feeding some of them to the ducks and swans, and enjoying the spring sunshine. He opened the parcel and ran a fingertip across the freshly printed staves. This was the culmination of a process so involved, so detailed, so potentially incendiary – should the fact of Hindemith's involvement be revealed, or should the piece's revision displease 'them' – that he could scarcely believe it had come to fruition at all. Strecker, though, knew what he was doing; he chose the best man for the job and had enough confidence to take the risk. He was also helping to support Hindemith, a dear friend and client for whom times were difficult and growing worse. At last, there it was: the piano reduction with violin part, spread out in front of Ulli, waiting for him to check, correct and place his tick of agreement before the Streckers gave the sign-off.

Hindemith – who had had to put his signature to a statement distancing himself from anything Jewish or left-wing – had done his job well enough, Ulli judged. The changes seemed reasonably respectful of Schumann. That pleased him, though the danger remained that it might not please Goebbels or the audience quite so much. Besides Hindemith, they had drafted in a local string quartet leader, Gustav Lenzewski, in nearby Frankfurt, to help with the violinistic editing. Kulenkampff was working separately on his own violin part.

The photostats were precious indeed, for the agreement with the ministry stipulated that the printed score must be embargoed until the day of the premiere. Now Willy Strecker had asked Ulli to write two letters to accompany them. One would go to Jelly in England; the other to California for Yehudi

Menuhin. Jelly could make a start. Menuhin could make a decision.

'I worry about Miss d'Arányi… ' Ulli faltered.

'She will have it for Britain.'

'We promised her.'

'And we are keeping our promise. But we are looking ahead as well, no? Jelly d'Arányi's best days are behind her. Yehudi's are still to come, and soon.'

That, Ulli acknowledged silently, was part of the problem. 'The thing is, Miss d'Arányi – '

Willy gave him a wink. 'I should never have let you go to London that time. You've not been the same since. I hope you realise that that woman is the most famous flirt in the music world. She has been bewitching every man who crosses her path for more than 20 years. Ah well, perhaps it'll do you good. Now, if you please, the letters… Then bring them to me.'

Ulli, puzzled, followed his boss's instructions. 'Don't you want me to post them?'

'No,' said Willy, taking the packages from him. 'A friend of mine happens to be going by train to Metz tomorrow.'

'France?'

'You see?'

Ulli saw. Interception in the post of a great German concerto heading out of its home country to some Jewish recipients could prove a risk too far, even for them.

Later, he took the third copy home on his bicycle. After a quick supper of soup, bread and cheese, he closed his windows and curtains and sat down at his Bechstein. If only he had a violinist – well, Jelly – to read the concerto with him. Some of his colleagues had attended a private run-through at Dr Lenzewski's house and came back raving about the piece's depth and beauty, insisting that Joachim must have been out of his mind to agree it should be put away. Ulli had been ill in bed and missed the evening. In his more morose moments, he felt he missed life's treats a little too often.

While he played, he tried to sing the violin part, or whistle it; the score was intense and full of counterpoint. He hadn't been practising enough. If he could accompany Jelly, he'd practise four hours a day. The concerto's substance was another matter. He had worked on the edition in such detail and for so long that he had lost perspective on it; playing through from start to finish might restore that, with luck. Deep, yes; beautiful, yes; but if Goebbels thought this would be a replacement for everyone's favourite Mendelssohn, he might need to think again.

Mendelssohn's concerto flowed naturally and felt effortless; Schumann's didn't state, but searched. Mendelssohn flew and dived and looped the loop for his audience; Schumann plunged off the forest path, lost in contemplation. Ulli sensed, through his long and deepening acquaintance with the piece, that it could burrow into your soul and steal it. But he could not help wondering how it would strike those encountering it for the very first time. What if Goebbels did not consider it strong enough? What would be the repercussions for those at Schott's who had thought it was?

With any luck, Goebbels, as propaganda man, was less interested in the music than in how he could manipulate its story. Assuming they could pass that hurdle, what mattered longer term for Schott's was the response of violinists and whether they would want to take it up. Jelly was a given; Menuhin was the real test. If he didn't like it, the Streckers might consider the exercise had been pointless. And from what he could hear, through his own unsatisfactory strumming, Ulli feared that violinists might not after all flock to play this piece; it was too complex, too flawed, too unsettling. If Menuhin were to play it and enthuse about it, his approbation would encourage anyone with reservations to rethink. Yet if he received all the credit that should have been Jelly's, then her heart would be broken – again – and Ulli would feel responsible. She couldn't compete with Menuhin any more than Kulenkampff could. He was in no position either to prevent or to cushion that blow.

The decisive letter came sooner than he expected. In California, Yehudi was officially on holiday. A 'sabbatical' at the family home outside Santa Cruz. Ulli imagined the youth practising in a studio flooded with sunlight. As he read Yehudi's words, he wondered why he had ever doubted the outcome. Menuhin understood the work straight away, as perhaps nobody else would; he saw its greater significance, too. He had played it through with his sister, Hephzibah, and found it romantic, mature, sorrowful, profound; he had no doubt that it was 'the missing link' in the violin concerto repertoire between Beethoven and Brahms. And of course he wanted to give the modern-day world premiere.

It was on the doormat with the third post. A flat parcel bearing, oddly, a set of French stamps. Jelly cradled it unopened, trying to preserve the final moment before she saw the Schumann Violin Concerto for the first time.

'Oh, for God's sake!' Adila grabbed the package and slashed at the wrapping with scissors. Out it slid: the notes on the pages shone like black pearls. 'What are you waiting for? Let's go and try it.'

'In a moment.' Jelly took a minute to collect herself, pressing the score to her heart.

Adila, though she was no expert pianist, went to the Bechstein and tried to play a skeleton of the reduced score. The first movement. A surge of energy at the opening: a taut-strung rhythm, a long, jagged theme over a tense accompaniment. 'TAA – DAA – ta-tii – ti-*daa*… ' Adila sang while her hands crashed around on the keyboard.

Jelly prepared to play her first notes, which entered before the orchestral paragraph was finished, commenting, echoing, then wandering into the discursive trails of a melody that arched like a hothouse creeper, climbing as if seeking the light. Tears oozed down her nose as her fingers and bow felt their way forward. Finally the longed-for concerto was in her hands, yet she found she was doubting her own capacity to play it. Her injuries, illness and arm problems had left her lacking her old assurance; she had cancelled concerts and lost others; her records, it seemed, were not selling so well now, while buyers flocked instead to grab those by Fritz Kreisler, Jascha Heifetz and, of course, Yehudi Menuhin. Ten or fifteen years ago, the world's greatest composers were queuing up to write new works for her. Four years ago the public had thronged to her cathedral concerts: young and elderly, wealthy and impoverished alike. Would they still? She had been reluctant to admit, even to herself, the degree of hope that she was investing in the Schumann Violin Concerto as the vehicle that could rescue her. She had thought she was saving it. Perhaps the truth was the other way around.

'Bloody hell!' Adila grumbled. 'I can't play this. You need a proper pianist.'

Jelly, notes somersaulting in front of her eyes, was trying to navigate the theme's progress through Schumann's twisting branches. It was dark in this woodland, she sensed; he, too, was trying to find his way. Ulli was a fine pianist. If only he'd brought it to her himself, they could have read it through together.

The curve of contrast came back, deep down: a contralto, as if singing words of good sense from Schumann's sane self, perhaps from Clara. How could someone supposedly losing his faculties write music of such raw tenderness?

'Slow movement,' suggested Adila. 'Easier.'

A few seconds in, though, Jelly understood that it wasn't. The melody was there, yet not there. It began after another theme in the orchestra, led by a solo cello, but then fragmented: hinted at, displaced. And it was as if she knew it already, as if she knew how it should go, yet it didn't, not quite. The violin line meandered, and that second theme of the first movement had seeded itself here too, twining through the music in the form of an innocuous, almost imperceptible link from lower register to upper.

'Sai, you are *hopeless*.' Adila yawned while Jelly flopped into a chair. 'How can you cry *now*?'

'Adi, how can you *not* cry now?'

'I'm not you. But, you know? It's just come back to me.'

'What has?'

'I think… perhaps Onkel Jo played me this. I feel as if I've heard it, and I have an image of him in my mind… let me concentrate… ' Adila put on her psychic 'sensitive' expression. 'I am sure he played me this, or something very like it.'

'I remember something too, somehow… '

The melody seemed familiar, as if she'd heard it somewhere before, long ago. No! It was Myra. That was it. Myra had played her a Schumann theme on which she said Brahms had written variations. It wasn't the same, but it was remarkably similar. There, it was defined, hymn-like, complete. Here, Schumann was hinting at it, trying to grasp it, yet it eluded him. 'Brahms,' Jelly declared. 'That's why we know it. It's nothing to do with Onkel Jo. Come on, let's try the last movement.'

She stood. A transition from the slow movement, and then the *Alla polacca* – the Polonaise – loomed on the page, the instruction printed above an ant-heap of notes. She knew about this Polonaise, theoretically. Its silhouette, too, looked oddly familiar; soon she knew why. It was that same melody from the first movement, the one that curled towards an invisible sun, and now, at last, it broke through the canopy of leaves into the blue heavens, transformed. The spirit, transmuted. The earth shaken away, the essence flying out.

'Slower,' said Adila. 'The metronome mark. Look.' She tapped the number on the page.

'That slow?' Jelly was amazed; it sounded odd, anything

but dance-like, at such a stately tempo. But so instructed Schumann...

They started again, Jelly laughing through her tears, Adila swearing in Hungarian. It was a triumphant end, this polonaise: a victory after a great struggle. The music grew more complicated, with virtuoso passagework that would have shown off Onkel Jo's abilities, the piano twittering and trilling beneath, yet it seemed as if love, the spirit, life itself, must win eventually.

Their last note was together, but soon their laughter was louder than the music had been, and at an optimistic guess, Adila had hit one right note in every ten. Jelly needed someone who could do better.

While she was wondering where to turn next, the phone in front of her rang and there, at the end of it, was –

'*Donald!* The very person! Darling, how did you know to call me now?'

'Hush, Jelly... What's going on?'

'Wherever you are, can I come and see you? And can I bring the Schumann? It just arrived. We read it, Adi and me, and it's – it's so beautiful – but Adi's not... I mean, I need a pianist. Will you play it with me?'

Tovey didn't flinch. 'Clara and I are off to Norfolk soon. When can you join us?'

'Oh, Donald,' Jelly was fighting tears. 'I can't stand the idea of it being captured by those terrible people in Germany... '

'There, there,' he soothed. 'It's not your child, you know. It's still a concerto and you can still play it. Come and play it with me. And I'll be curious to know what Hindemith has done to it. He's a fine composer, but do you like his changes?'

Jelly stalled. She had her doubts about the adaptations and needed time to explore them more closely. The edition made clear where, and what, the differences were, though without indicating who had made them or why. Kulenkampff was apparently making a private edition of his own; therefore so could she. She hankered for the glass, in case there were messages – from

Schumann, from Onkel Jo, maybe from Sep too – that could help her navigate through it.

'And don't obsess over those "spirits" of yours,' was Tovey's parting shot.

It was a little late for that advice. Jelly, at home more often since her injuries, was at Adila and Erik's side day after day, for the messages from the glass now began to go into a startling amount of detail about violinistic ways to improve on the original concerto. Schumann apparently was not happy with Hindemith's interference, one message declaring the results 'not his technique'.

'Don't touch the glass,' Adila ordered Jelly. 'There must be no suggestion you influenced what the messages say.'

Jelly, taking notes but leaving the interpretation strictly to Adila and Erik, watched in incredulity as her sister encouraged, questioned and received word after astonishing word. Her pen at the ready, she watched the glass moving through the shadows, and scribbled down the letters. 'Use your judgement about bowing and often broaden the tone… ' the glass instructed. 'Keep your outbursts as a complete surprise. Your uncle knew that secret.'

'We must stop now,' Adila sometimes exclaimed. 'I'm exhausted! You've no idea how tiring this is.'

'Just two more minutes?' Jelly would plead. When the pointer moved to 'Goodbye' and the light went on again, she felt bereft, desperate for the next instalment.

'Stop panicking, Sai,' Adila laughed. 'Just go and write it all into your fiddle part.'

If only the performance plans could be progressing as smoothly; instead, she felt trapped in an administrative nightmare. At first Kulenkampff's concert was set for September 1937. Jelly conferred with Adrian Boult and they fixed upon a date for her premiere at the Queen's Hall in late September – which coordinated beautifully with the likely release of Erik's book by Constable Press. Then came the startling news from Schott that the Germans had postponed Kulenkampff's performance. Now she and Boult were obliged to change their date because Kulenkampff had to be first. Everything was duly rescheduled for October, with Jelly's performance three days after the German concert. But there was worse: according to Boult, apparently Yehudi Menuhin had somehow heard about the concerto, wanted to play it too, and didn't like the idea that anybody else might come before *him*.

'He wants to play it everywhere,' Jelly told Tovey, fighting her own fury, trying to keep her voice calm. 'And I have absolutely *no idea* how he got hold of it!'

'It's called publishing. Schott's is a commercial company and they'll wish to ensure as many performances as possible, in as many territories as possible,' Tovey pointed out. 'They'll be eyeing America. You mustn't take it personally.'

It must have been Ulli. The same man who had gone to the Nazi top dogs with his bosses and overstepped the mark, nearly getting himself sacked, to fight her corner. But he'd have been under strict instructions. He was on her side. She had to believe that; it was all she had to hold on to.

She'd thought Menuhin a violin prophet, a miracle of an artist. Now her arteries threatened to rupture at the sound of his name. If she were not to be the first violinist outside Germany to play the concerto, any hope was gone that it might re-establish her in the glory days of Ravel's *Tzigane* and Bartók's sonatas. The wunderkind could simply snatch the piece from her, and there seemed no way to stop him. 'I could have gone to America myself,' she protested.

'Jelly, don't take on so,' Tovey advised. 'Come to Norfolk and bring the Schumann, as soon as you feel ready. We've waited long enough for it. Now let's spend a few minutes enjoying it.'

Chapter 13

Deep in the countryside, Tovey and his wife, Clara, had a house they regarded as their real home. Hedenham Lodge was in a secluded spot, difficult to access. This, Tovey admitted, was half the point. The sole good thing about his 'year off' in '32 recovering from his heart issues, he said, was that he could spend most of it there. It was a graceful place, early 18th century, set into a rich and soggy lawn and surrounded by brambleful hedgerows, shrubbish hawthorn and ancient trees bowing under the weight of their own leaves. Jelly liked to imagine Jane Austen characters flitting about the slender-framed drawing room, or leaning on the windowsills to enjoy the soft air that drifted in from the Broads.

Tovey was nearly 62. Jelly still thought of him as a perpetual thirtysomething, as he was when she first knew him: his intellect still flamed like a crêpe Suzette. But even she could not deny that his physical state was changing with the years. Either his spine was less straight, or his tall-person's stoop might have grown more pronounced.

'I don't mind being slightly closer in size to you,' he told her, when she pressed him about his health. 'What I do mind is what's happening to my hands.'

The swelling around his knuckles was pronounced, shockingly so. 'Does it hurt?'

'I wish I could be brave and say it doesn't. But it does. It hurts rather a lot. What hurts most is that it's becoming more difficult to play the piano. I shall have to follow the example of Clara and stick to late Brahms.'

'I didn't realise she played.'

'Schumann's Clara. When she was changing from guardian angel to glorious grandma, Brahms wrote intermezzos, rhapsodies and the like for her to play, which weren't technically complex, but could not be bettered in terms of profundity. I shall be very happy with them, assuming I can even manage that.'

'You are a wonderful pianist – you will be fine.'

'Dear Jelly.' Tovey leaned down and kissed her forehead.

Jelly wondered what could make the difference: perhaps just the growth of a microscopic sliver of bone. Could something indiscernible to the human eye become a tipping point, switching you from one state to another – Tovey from a day when he could play his piano, if with difficulty, to one on which he could not? It was so alarming that she tucked his arm through hers to banish the notion.

Clara had made a sponge cake, which Jelly enjoyed with gusto after her journey; at the kitchen table they chatted about family matters and life at Hurricane House. Jelly had to break the news to the Toveys that things at home were not what they had been. Soon the house would feel emptier than she had ever known it. Caesar, their beloved fox terrier, had passed away in his basket at a ripe old dog age of 15. And to her distress and Adila's, Alec had decided that in September Adrienne, who was nearly 12, must be sent away to school. They were dreading it, for much of the house's internal sunshine came from the lively, lovely girl who wasn't so little any more, yet was still small enough for them to spoil. The school was far away in Somerset.

'Alec won't hear a word against it,' Jelly said, confessing her misery. 'He wants to get her out of London, in case there's... trouble.' Alec was convinced there would be another war with Germany.

'That's sensible, you know – and besides, she has to grow up sooner or later,' Clara pointed out, cutting more cake. 'Before you know it she'll be writing you chirpy letters about lacrosse and sponge pudding.'

'Do you think there will really be a war?' Jelly asked.

The moment of silence before Clara said, 'Let's pray that there may not be,' spoke louder than her response.

While Jelly and Clara talked, Tovey sloped away into the

drawing room with the Schumann score. They could hear him humming and singing out loud to himself as he read through it at the piano.

'Go on, Jelly,' Clara said. 'You're itching to go and play it, I can see. Don't worry, I won't eat all the cake while you're gone.'

Tovey launched into the first movement at exactly the pace Jelly wanted. Despite the pain and stiffness in his fingers, the music took wing: she was hearing it at last as it should sound, full of energy and great generous sweeps of Schumannesque heroism. She hadn't told him that what he read of her violin part in the piano score might not be precisely what he heard; she and 'Schumann', together, via the glass game, had tweaked at some 200 bars, dotted about through the piece. Tovey kept going, lost in the music, his face ablaze with the thrill. Halfway through the slow movement, she noticed he was also blinking aside tears. Whether they were for the music, the long-desired playing of it, or the passing of time and of life, she couldn't tell.

It was only with the last notes of the Polonaise that the pair gave way to elation, laughing like the two children in a secret garden that they still were, behind their arthritic joints and painful tendons. Tovey whirled round on his revolving piano stool three times for joy. 'You see what a splendid job Hindemith has made of it!' he said. 'You can trust every note.'

'It's not all Hindemith,' Jelly smiled. 'Some of the violin part is me. With a little, er, help. We've tried to make some... adjustments.'

'We?'

'The spirits and me.'

'What?' Tovey looked genuinely shocked. 'Are you serious?'

'They are incredible. They tell me everything, advise on everything.'

'And they are who?'

'Onkel Jo and Schumann, or their messengers, as we understand.'

'Oh Jelly, Jelly… ' He shook his head.

'But that's what happened – and you like what we've done. You just said so.'

Tovey leafed through the pages on his piano, apparently pondering her words. 'All right,' he said, finally. 'So, tomorrow we'll sit down and make sure you're happy with every last second of it.'

Jelly was quietly relieved: she knew she still needed his expertise in analysing and perfecting the details.

'This passage – it reminds me of something, I can't place it… ' She picked out the second theme of the first movement, the one that finally transforms into the Polonaise.

'Could it be this?' Tovey began to play another melody, one that she knew very well: the Brahms Violin Concerto, again the second theme of the first movement. The motif stood out: the same pattern, almost a twin to Schumann's. This time, though, it seemed to link the wide swoops of the melody rather than making a statement in its own right.

'You mean Brahms used Schumann's theme? When did Brahms write his concerto?'

'About 1878,' said Tovey. 'Twenty-two years after Schumann died.'

'So – would he have heard Schumann's, or looked at the manuscript?'

'It's perfectly possible, given Brahms's astonishing brain, that he retained the impression of that melody, having seen it only once. I wouldn't put it past him. Whether he viewed the manuscript again – well, who can say?'

'But you think it's deliberately done?'

'There's another possibility.' Tovey was in lecture mode, thinking aloud rather than engaging in conversation, a pattern into which he often fell. 'With Brahms, Schumann, Clara and Onkel Jo, it's often a matter of a tribute. Their music is stuffed full of ciphers and symbols that were private references to one another. Take Brahms's personal motto, F-A-F – *frei aber froh*, free but happy. That was based on Onkel Jo's own one, F-A-E, *frei aber einsam*, free but lonely. Onkel Jo must have spotted all the Schumanneries and Clara-isms in Brahms, and if we had three clear days, I'd show them to you and you'd never hear a note of it the same way again. But now, listen to what happens in the Brahms Violin Concerto immediately after that little Schumann theme appears for the first time.' He half-closed his eyes and played the extract by ear. 'It's the darkest, most inward-looking moment in the score, before all those strong rhythms banish it, and in comes the violin for the first time, Onkel Jo in full flood. Now that we have this context, I believe Brahms was thinking of Schumann when he wrote that, don't you?'

Jelly imagined she had lifted a lid and beneath it found an unsuspected universe of space and stars. Not that anything should surprise her now.

'You see how vital it is that this piece should be played and known,' Tovey said. 'It doesn't only tell us about itself; it tells us much about Schumann and perhaps even more about Brahms.'

He stood and stretched his hands, wincing slightly at the pain in his knuckles. 'Come along, Jelly, what about a little stroll before supper?'

Tovey's idea of a 'little stroll' involved striding across country at a good five miles an hour. The flat fields were slick with mud and Jelly, in borrowed galoshes, picked her way round puddles and stray clumps of barley, trying to keep up.

Around them lingered the quietness that always drew Tovey back to East Anglia. Here, in a slice of nature that seemed 90 per cent sky, he could listen to the music in his head without the intrusion of city sound-clutter. It was early evening and their shadows faded in and out, length and shape exaggerated.

'Do you know, Jelly, of a woman named Bettina von Arnim?'

'No? Who is she?'

'Back in the 1850s she nearly became Onkel Jo's mother-in-law. He was very much in love with her daughter, Gisela. He proposed, but was turned down and I don't believe he ever got over it.'

Jelly was astonished, never having heard this tale before. 'What became of the girl?'

'She was a fine writer of fairy tales and she married – much later – the son of Wilhelm Grimm, the younger of the Brothers Grimm. They were great literary types together. Then she had some nervous trouble, sadly, and eventually she died rather too young.'

'I'm sorry.' Jelly thought of Onkel Jo's habitual severity – where had it come from? Perhaps the blow of Gisela's rejection had given him part of his bitter edge. Tovey, with his giant paces, was pulling ahead, and she had to pause to free one of her boots from the mud.

'I always wonder what explains "nervous trouble" in intelligent, married women,' Tovey was musing. 'My theory is that they're simply bored to death. If society permitted them to develop real careers, I doubt this would happen so often.' He barely bothered to veil his emotions – his first wife, Margaret, had succumbed to a similar problem. 'Goodness knows it never happened to Clara Schumann,' he added. 'She was far too busy. And I know something of how your sister Hortense suffers, yet you and Adila, professional musicians, have never had a moment's "nervous affliction" in your lives, have you?'

'I'm sure people think we are a bit crazy, but that's different.' Jelly thought briefly of Adila's terror of trains and ferries and her recurrent stomach problems – but that was rational in the first case, and physical in the second… wasn't it?

'Now, about Gisela's mother. When Schumann was in the mental asylum at Endenich, it was almost impossible for anybody to visit him. Clara was barred by the doctors, for fear of upsetting him. Jo went, and so did Brahms, when they were told they might see him. But then they found they were allowed *literally* only to "see" him: to observe him, from a distance, not speak to him.

'Joachim at this point was about 22, in love with Gisela and spending what spare time he had paying court to her at her family home near Berlin. He'd have written to her, terribly distressed about Schumann. Therefore perhaps Bettina, the intellectual battleaxe, felt she should intervene for the sake of her daughter's supposed beloved.

'She was a woman of extraordinary character, charm and determination. She went all the way to Endenich and she talked the doctors round. Jo told me that Schumann's doctors were quite horrible: cold, obstructive and cruel. But it occurs to me that where Jo was concerned, it's possible they gave as good as they got. One's attitude makes such a difference. Bettina, though, could talk the proverbial hind legs off a donkey, and somehow, goodness knows how, she was permitted access to Schumann himself.'

'And?'

'She came back,' said Tovey, 'and relayed to her daughter, and thence to Jo, that she thought Schumann was perfectly well.'

'You are joking.'

'Apparently she personally judged him sane and rational. And my goodness, she was angry. Bettina was a firebrand when she got into her stride, and she declared that Schumann was cruelly buried alive in that asylum, and that all it should have taken to get him released was the determination of Clara herself.'

Jelly took a minute to absorb this. 'So, Clara...'

'... possibly didn't want him back.'

'But – ?'

'I know. It defies everything we know of their love and their devotion. On the other hand, one can perhaps understand it. She was in an impossible position; she was struggling with seven children and an international performing career. How could she also look after a husband who, even if Bettina thought him relatively well, would still have required much care and caused much anxiety? To say nothing of the gossip and the stigma. Clara may sometimes have seemed superhuman, but taking on that responsibility would be a step too far even for her, especially with small children in the house. His suffering was very real, remember – he'd already attempted suicide. It's possible that Bettina had just caught him on a particularly good day.'

'So…' Jelly followed Tovey across a wooden stile; he could take the fence in just three steps, while she was constricted by her straight skirt. He held out a hand to help her down.

'Bettina was afraid he would make another attempt on his own life, in the hospital. She thought that if driven to desperation, he might starve himself to death. We don't know if he did this or not. Clara, Brahms and Jo weren't able to visit him until the day before he died.'

'But did Clara say anything to Onkel Jo?'

'Clara would never have said a word against her husband – or against her own attitude to him. Even if she had, in some moment of weakness or despair, Jo would never have broken her confidence.'

'Donald, the messages – we've had some that seem to come from Schumann, or from messengers relaying his wishes, and some from Onkel Jo, too. But not a word about Clara, or Brahms. What do you think about that?'

'I don't think anything about *any* of your "messages".' Tovey paused in his tracks and mopped sweat from his temples with a handkerchief. 'And nor, I fear, will many other people. I do worry that you're allowing it to become too much of an obsession. Sooner or later you'll have to accustom yourself to the idea that these practices are not so widely accepted now, not in this age of dictatorships, mechanisation and Einstein. But if it's any comfort, Jelly, I don't think you're making it up.'

'*Making it up?* But every letter came through the glass! I

was never interested in the glass game before all this happened. I thought it was only a game – until, you see, there was a message from Sep and I ran away, I didn't know what to believe… But this is different. Why don't you join us for a session? Then you'd understand – you'd see it with your own eyes – and you'd… '

Jelly was so distressed at the idea that his doubt might spoil their friendship that she could scarcely get her words out.

'Hush, hush – it's all right, really it is. I trust you. I just want you to be aware of the wider implications. Come along, let's go back now and forget about it over the very nice dinner that Clara is making us, then get some sleep in this fresh country air. We can talk about your messages tomorrow. Sometimes things are clearer in the morning.'

They were rounding a corner of a barley field; Jelly spotted the slope of the house's russet roof and tiles, dappled with lichen. 'We'll smell dinner soon.' Tovey rubbed his hands, smiling, Jelly sensed, a little too hard.

They walked on, amid silence but for birdsong in the nearby oaks; Jelly, breathing the scent of damp fields, counted a blackbird, a lapwing and, far away, a lark.

Tovey stopped abruptly in his tracks. 'I forgot entirely why it was that I wanted to tell you about Bettina von Arnim! The concerto. The last movement.'

'The Polonaise?'

'Exactly. That Polonaise possibly signals the intervention of Bettina.' He picked a strand of barley and turned it into a baton, conducting as if the crop were orchestral players spread across the field before him, while he sang the theme. 'A polonaise, dignified, celebratory… '

'What's that got to do with Bettina?' Jelly pleaded.

Tovey broke off in mid hum. 'You know Chopin was exiled from Poland. He left just in time, shortly before the uprising of 1830, and missed his homeland for the rest of his life. He and Schumann were friendly and I'm sure he must have met Bettina, one way or another. She contrived to meet everyone, and he'd have been no exception. Poland was occupied, you see, by Russia, which won the war after the uprising, and freedom for Poland became a great *cause célèbre* in certain strata of mid-19th-century intellectual society. Demonstrations, pamphlets, marches, you name it. Bettina was very involved with freedom for Poland; you might call her an activist. She'd have discussed it with Schumann and with Jo. She bent everyone's ear on the topic at length, whether they were interested or not. The polonaise was a national dance, a symbol of Polish pride and resistance. You remember how Schumann called Chopin's mazurkas "cannons buried in flowers"?'

'And – you think this Schumann polonaise is perhaps… a rifle in a rosebush?'

Tovey laughed. 'You have to understand, Jelly, because not many people do these days, that that was how their intimate musical circle worked. As I said, it was full of tributes, analogies, musical ciphers, coded messages. So – and this is really the point, for you – when it came to the question of what to do with the concerto after Schumann died, long after Gisela had turned Jo down, to him the piece may have felt a little bit close to the bone. It might have brought the pain of rejection back to life. Of course, he may also have had *bona fide* musical reasons for putting it away. What do you find most difficult in it, Jelly?'

'The last movement is – well, not totally impossible, but – !'

'Exactly. It's a transcendent, dazzling, Polish-style statement. And it makes you wonder what he's doing. But which is more alarming? The idea that Schumann didn't know what he was doing? Or the notion that he knew *exactly* what he was doing, yet nobody understood?'

After dinner they went to the gramophone to sample the latest recordings he wanted to play her, and listened, late and long. Jelly was too overexcited to sleep and Clara observed her enthusiasm as indulgently as a grandmother might a toddler's. But to the strains of Artur Schnabel playing Beethoven, Tovey nodded off in his armchair.

Jelly could not enjoy the music as much without him. She watched him dozing, his thinning hair reflecting the lamplight, his chin dipping towards his chest. Once it would have been unthinkable for him to slumber through a note of music. The many years she had spent in his orbit, sitting at his feet, playing to his accompaniment or even avoiding his declaration of finer feelings, spun before her as he began to snore. Look after him, dear Lord, Jelly prayed. Such great men are even rarer than pure memories in this world.

On a cloudless morning, the flowers holding sunlight captive in their petals, Jelly wandered alone onto Tovey's lawn, listening to the clarity. A breeze stirred the columbines and lilacs so that they seemed to converse, their leaves offering consonants while the birds voiced the vowels. The garden was awake and singing.

The Schumann concerto was hers. She and Tovey had brought it back to life. Today they'd play it through again, work on its details and know it better still. High above, a skylark was singing: a lark ascending. Shielding her eyes from the sun, she could glimpse the bird, a dark flickering speck against silver-blue; the sight so distant, the song so bright. This was perfection: solitude and nature, the eternal forces of growth and light.

Let me always remember this, her mind whispered. Let this garden, this extraordinary morning, be my touchstone, no matter what lies ahead.

Chapter 14

On 23 September 1937, Alec, Adila and Jelly set out in the car for Erik's book launch at his Portland Place residence. Adila wore a blue suit that matched her eyes, with a string of diamonds at her throat; Jelly chose russet red, a rope of pearls and a new hat.

The build-up to the publication of *Horizons of Immortality* had been long and fraught while Erik struggled with his finalisation of the text and Adila checked and double-checked her transcripts and notes; and once the book had finally gone to print, the two of them busied themselves with more checking and double-checking, this time of the guest list for the party. All Jelly's energy, meanwhile, was devoted to perfecting the concerto. Less than three weeks remained until the concert, which would follow hot on the heels of Kulenkampff's German premiere. She might have learned *Tzigane* in three days, but she was younger then, with memory and bones altogether more supple; the Schumann, moreover, was three times as long and ten times as daunting.

Review copies of the book had been sent to the press. A reporter phoned Netherton Grove a few days before publication, wanting to ask Jelly some questions for an article. He introduced himself as Rollo Myers, a music specialist from *The Listener*. Jelly, pleased that he was interested in the tale of the Schumann concerto and the spirit messages, answered as best she could, then returned to her work on the tricky last movement. Her anxieties had eased, and in her home circles she had noticed some resurgence of hope, now that Neville Chamberlain was prime minister. He had brought in better conditions – holiday pay for many people who had never had such a thing before, and limited working hours for women and children. As chancellor when Jelly undertook her cathedral tour, he had added a government grant of a thousand pounds to her proceeds; remembering that, she was ready to place her faith in him. Perhaps he could be strong enough to negotiate with Germany and avoid the war that everyone feared if Hitler's ambitions went unchecked. 'He's a great, great man,' Erik enthused. 'His heart's in the right place,' was all Alec would say.

At the Swedish residence, the door under the portico stood open to the warm early evening. Alec and Adila walked ahead, arm in arm; Jelly tottered behind, her sore feet stuffed into her highest-heeled shoes. Alec, exhausted by constant travel between London and The Hague, where the League had had a complex year, was fighting a recurrent cough and slight fever; he paused in the entrance hall, while Adila pressed a hand to his forehead, tut-tutting with anxiety. 'I'll be fine, my dear,' he insisted. 'Let's go up.'

The drawing room beneath its Wedgwood mouldings was filling with guests, who gathered in groups to converse and browse through the new book. Swedish and British mingled, as always at 27 Portland Place: the official, the titled, the press and a smattering of artistic types hand-picked to offset them. To one side, near the windows, stood a table piled high with fresh copies, the paper so new that it still smelled of wood. 'It's real! It's out!' Adila pressed one to her heart.

'Of course it's *real*,' Alec sighed. 'Otherwise what have you been working on all these months?'

Jelly had read little of the book, beyond the extracts that Adila had foisted aloud on them all. The proofs had been strewn about Hurricane House, but she had been too busy working to take much notice.

'Jelly! Welcome, welcome, my dear.' Erik kissed her on both cheeks. 'As you know, you have most of a chapter.' Smiles waltzed about his jowls as guest after guest gushed congratulations and asked him to sign their copies. Ebba with her walking stick stood by his side, gracious and pallid, the corners of her mouth fixed upward as if by staples.

Around the room scents mingled – beeswax polish, passing

whiffs of Chanel and dill sauce from the canapés; photographers' flashbulbs turned the assembled guests into freeze-frame silhouettes, glasses poised at various heights. Jelly wasn't sure if the cameras were for the embassy or from the press. Normally a constant bright planet, she felt adrift today in an unfamiliar universe. She accepted a glass of wine, then retreated to the stairs with a copy of the book to see what Erik had written about her.

It was right at the end, entitled 'Retrospect'. He'd called her 'J d'A'. The messages were there – well, many of them. The book suggested that the first their little group knew of the spirits was the occasion on which 'two friends' – Jelly and Anna, evidently – had received the initial communication from Schumann or his representative, and that it was only after this that Adila discovered her gift as psychic 'sensitive'. Why would he say that, when he and Adila and half the people they knew had been playing the glass game at salons and parlours and after-dinner parties for decades, even if it had become less prevalent of late? To put the responsibility on to *her*, Jelly, when she was the most reluctant participant? Perhaps to push his friendship with Adila into the background? Then there came the story of Schott's involvement, though not of Ulli's, and the tale of how Erik himself had gone to Berlin and rooted out the manuscript after others had failed to find it. This account made the author of the book into a hero. She took a sip of wine. Her old friend George would have directed her to something stronger for this occasion.

'Sai, what are you doing?' Adila bustled over to her. 'Everyone is asking for you! Someone from *The Times* wants to see you, and there is a charming young man who says he is a pianist, and our friends from the Society for Psychical Research who – '

'Adi, give me a moment – I'll be in soon.' Jelly, experiencing a carousel of disquiet, waved her sister back into the party. She leaned against the wall, trying to stay calm.

In the drawing room the chatter quietened and the baron took the floor, reading out an extract of the book. Jelly had just read those same words. They were the last in the volume.

'"The actual purpose of sending these messages is not the widening of intellectual knowledge; rather it is an inspiration, an awakening to a life which carries within itself the solution of our most urgent problems… "' The messengers, declared the baron, wished to reach not a small elite, but a grand multitude of people: all those whose souls craved the answers they could find nowhere else.

Our most urgent problems? In the short months between Erik penning his book and publishing it, world events had been threatening to overtake them all. Everywhere she went, even backstage after her concerts, the preoccupation of all conversation had become the likelihood of war with Germany, Chamberlain notwithstanding. Alec thought it only a matter of time. The government was talking about building air-raid shelters. Yet in this tranquil green-gold evening, the city seemed ripe with vitality and contentment… How could that be? What would they do? Where could they go? What would happen to their friends in Mainz? What of Ulli? He was only 35; if there was a war, with conscription… And why did Erik think his spirit messages could help? No earlier generation had had any idea how to handle war. Why should the spirits of those generations hold the answers now?

'Jelly! You're still there!' Adila was marching towards her, trailing in her wake a young man who sported slicked-back hair, shiny shoes and a buff-coloured trenchcoat, which he had not bothered to hand to the cloakroom. 'Here she is,' Adila declared. 'This is my sister, Jelly d'Arányi.' She walked up to Jelly and gave her a kiss.

'Miss d'Arányi? Lionel Hartshaw from the *News of the World*.' The young man held out a hand, which Jelly, briefly paralysed on the stairs upon hearing the paper's name, reached up to take and shake. 'Nice to meet you. I wonder, do you have a moment?'

'Of course.' Jelly rose and waited.

The reporter pulled from his briefcase a notebook, a pencil and the latest issue of *The Listener*. This he spread out in front of Jelly. A photo. A headline: *FINDING A LOST SCHUMANN CONCERTO: A recent discovery based on 'spirit messages'*. Quotations from Erik's book. And a name, Rollo Myers. 'Oh yes – he phoned me... '

'Now, here's my question,' said Lionel Hartshaw, pencil poised. 'Why should we believe that *messages from the spirit world* justify your claim to this famous composer's violin concerto?'

Jelly hesitated. 'I beg your pardon?'

'Let me rephrase that, Miss d'Arányi: all this frankly sounds a bit like woolly spiritualist balderdash to me and I think to many others too. If you believe it, then *why* do you believe it?'

Jelly's throat tightened. 'This is from Baron Palmstierna's book. He was there. He saw it all happening.'

'But you are the lady who's come along saying that the Nazi chap mustn't play it first, the Jewish–American chap mustn't play it first, it's yours because *you got a message from Schumann saying so*? Excuse me, Miss d'Arányi, but this is 1937. People will think it's a fairly outrageous assertion.'

'But... it is *what happened*. It is true.' Jelly grabbed the magazine and pointed. 'And look. Mr Myers, who wrote this article, agrees. He himself says we are vouched for by people of "absolute integrity".'

'Well, he would, wouldn't he?' Hartshaw gave her a cheeky smile. He had a dimple in his left cheek. Under other circumstances, it might have been charming. But though the dimple indented, the eyes mocked her. 'Evidently he means Baron Palmstierna, so it still comes back to what you think of the baron's activities in the, er, paranormal. How d'you intend to prove it?'

'Prove? It's there, in the book, exactly as it happened.'

'All right.' The dimple deepened, the mockery with it. 'So,

GHOST VARIATIONS

the first so-called "message" came to you, didn't it? Not to Baron
Palmstierna and your sister?'

'That's right.'

'So, can anybody corroborate your story?' He leaned forward, speaking too loudly and slowly – the way a nanny might
talk to a toddler, or a colonial Englishman to a native abroad.
Perhaps he thought that because she was foreign, she couldn't
understand English. 'Was there anybody with you who can confirm that what you claim is true?'

Jelly was about to protest that her personal assistant was
there. But – supposing he phoned Anna? Supposing she wasn't
well enough for the shock of being quizzed by a slimy reporter?

'Name? Telephone?'

'A friend.' She maintained a semblance of calm. 'But I am
not giving you this person's name and number.'

'Oh, Miss d'Arányi – that is just too, too tantalising. Surely
you want your friend to let us know what really happened? It
wouldn't do you any harm.'

'Excuse me, Mr Hartshaw, but I think my sister is going to
play.'

'You look rather pale. Shall I fetch you another drink?'

'Thank you, but no.' She moved away.

'If you ask me,' came the sly voice behind her, 'it's an outrageous heap of lies. The pack of you ought to be locked up.'

In the drawing room the clinking of glasses had stilled.
Music. A violin. Jelly, teetering across the landing, saw a picture
framed by the doorway: her sister, radiant in blue, in the centre
of the room, violin cradled beneath her chin, bow caressing the
strings in a Bach Allemande. The room's wood and glass took
up the sound and polished it. Erik presided at the front, stance
proud, arms folded. Alec at first was nowhere to be seen; eventually Jelly located him on a window seat. Her brother-in-law was
listening to his wife's performance with head lowered, his face
turned away, muffling his coughs with his sleeve.

Hartshaw slithered past her into the throng, not caring who

214

he disturbed, sneering at all he saw. Jelly watched him. With luck, she'd never set eyes on him again.

Back at home, much later, trying to joke and laugh and be pleasantly tipsy together after the party, Jelly concealed her rattled nerves as best she could, until Alec switched on the radio for the BBC news bulletin.

'A long-lost violin concerto by the composer Robert Schumann has been unearthed in Berlin,' came the announcement. 'The work was consigned to a library by the composer's family and friends after his death. But now the famous violinist Miss Gelly d'Arányi claims to have located the concerto thanks to an intervention in a séance from the spirit of the composer, asking her to find and perform it. A new book by the Swedish minister, Baron Erik Palmstierna... '

'They should know by now,' Jelly muttered. '*Yelly*. Not *jelly*-and-ice cream.'

'It *wasn't* a séance,' Adila said. 'It was the glass. It's not the same thing at all.'

The telephone rang; Alec answered. It was Anna Robertson, who had heard the broadcast at her new home in Sussex and was concerned for Jelly's peace of mind.

'Darling,' Jelly said. 'I'm not dreaming, am I? You were there. You saw it too.'

'Of course I did.'

'But please – if any reporter calls you – I didn't tell them you were. I didn't. The journalist man – I won't call him a gentleman, because he is not; he is a rodent, a rat... '

'Jelly, what are you talking about?'

'He wanted to know someone who could back me up. But I wouldn't tell him your name or your phone number or anything. If anyone calls you, you know nothing, yes?'

'But I don't mind, if it would help you.'

'No, no! He must leave you in peace.'

'Jelly, listen, call me any time. You know I'd do anything for you.'

No sooner had she hung up than the phone rang again. Tovey, in Scotland, had also heard the broadcast. 'I'm worried about you, my dear,' he said.

'I'm fine.' Jelly knew her voice had started to waver. 'Absolutely fine.'

It was late by now, but next came a call from her sister Hortense.

'Sai, what on earth?' she demanded. 'What are you doing? That's Adi's department. I thought you were the sensible one.'

'No, Titi darling, the sensible one is *you*,' Jelly told her.

'What a time for Schumann to choose to get in touch with you. Couldn't he have tried before there were Nazis? It would have been so much easier... I wonder why he decided to do it now. Has he said?'

Jelly didn't need her sister's barbed words just then.

'Seriously,' Hortense added, 'if you need any help, Ralph has friends.'

Jelly's second brother-in-law was as well connected as anybody in the country. 'That's kind of you, but don't worry. I'm fine. Absolutely fine.'

The phone rang as soon as she put it down, time after time. Her sometime pianist, Ethel Hobday. Madge's sister, Jane. Norman Hartnell, in person. Everyone had heard the broadcast. Everyone was worried about Jelly. Perhaps that meant she needed to be worried too.

'They hardly mentioned Erik's book,' Adila grumbled.

'This is ridiculous.' Alec took charge, fighting his cough. 'It's nearly midnight. Some of us have to work tomorrow. I don't know about you, but I've had enough.' He pulled the telephone receiver off its stand and left it dangling by the cable, swinging like a pendulum. The light switches were next, one by one, in the music room, drawing room and dining room, turning the house stage by stage from gold to grey, charcoal to black. 'Come on, ladies. Time for bed.'

The sisters paused in the dark entrance hall; Jelly reached for Adila's hand, which closed warm and strong around hers. 'Adi… This is going to be bad, isn't it?'

'It will pass – and we will win, because we have the truth. Whatever happens, remember that, little sister.'

Before nine o'clock in the morning, the phone, reconnected, started to ring. Adrienne, at her new boarding school, was in tears in the headmistress's office. 'They won't shut up about it,' she howled to Adila. 'They won't leave me alone. They're teasing me about ghosts.'

'It's nothing to do with you!' Adila stormed. 'Let me speak to that blasted headmistress.'

Jelly retreated to her room, dizzy and nauseous, with no appetite for breakfast beyond half a cup of coffee. Brushing her teeth, she nearly threw up what she'd managed to swallow. She sat on the edge of the bath, trying to calm her breathing, vaguely remembering that today she had not heard Adila make any reference to an impending miracle.

Not that one could hide from a telephone, but at least she couldn't hear what the headmistress said to provoke Adila's lengthy outburst of fury. Adila, a tigress when her cub was threatened, could send the anger at the right target: those beastly schoolgirls who could neither mind their own business nor imagine what they'd feel were they in Adrienne's shoes, dealing with an apparently deranged aunt.

Next *The Times* rang. Adila slammed down the phone.

Jelly called one of the paper's critics, James Gambrell – whom she had visited when she was first trying to locate the concerto four years earlier. He claimed no recollection of the event, then finished the conversation in a hurry, saying he was just on his way out. A telegram arrived from George in Dublin, saying that she had booked a phone call; Jelly, overjoyed to hear her voice, talked to her for ages, going round and round in circles as she tried to explain who knew what, and when, and why, and wondering how she ought to weather this storm. 'It mightn't be easy,' said George, who was somewhat experienced at protecting artists with supernatural difficulties. 'But stay strong, Sai. I'm here. I'm with you.'

Tovey, who called next, provided some light relief. He had received a note from a lady who was eager to tell them she was psychically in touch with the spirit of a Tibetan lama. 'She says,' he added, 'that the broadcast of Schumann's Violin Concerto will set loose a wonderful flood of Thought Power across the earth.'

Jelly's feet seemed to have acquired a life independent from her legs. They wanted to run and keep running. She had to escape. She could go to Battersea Park, get out of the house and away from all this madness. But there people might recognise her. They used to say good morning, tip their hats, smile. Today things might be very different.

Yet another phone call – and Adila, as self-appointed watchdog, summoned her and this time wouldn't let her escape. 'It's Adrian Boult. You'd better talk to him yourself, Sai. It's not about the report. It's Germany, and Mehuhin.'

'Can I call him back?'

'Sai, speak to him *now*, and that's an order,' Adila thundered. 'He's a busy man and you need him more than he needs this.'

He was *Sir* Adrian Boult now; he had conducted the orchestra in Westminster Abbey for the coronation and since then been knighted.

'Don't worry, Jelly, there's nothing about how you found the concerto that I didn't know already,' came the familiar clipped voice from his BBC office. 'Now, regarding the concert – well, there's a little spot of bother. As you know, what the Germans have cooked up is that Herr Kulenkampff must play it first, Yehudi Menuhin will play it second, and you will go third with the British premiere. They've made it terribly official.

We mustn't blame Kulenkampff – he may be little more than their pawn. I'm afraid that negotiating with the Nazis is not my favourite pastime... but in short, they've shifted the date once more.'

It took a moment for Jelly to absorb the implications. She longed briefly for Thomas Beecham. Boult she adored; shy and formal though he seemed, she knew that exterior masked both a ferocious temper and a great heart. But Beecham took no nonsense from anybody. She and Myra both rather dreaded playing concertos with him – you never knew when you might get an actual rehearsal – but Beecham would have stood up to those thugs in Berlin. He'd have defied the lot. 'What? They've moved the concert *again*?'

'Precisely,' drawled Boult. 'To November. They say there are complications to do with Kulenkampff's preparation of the violin part, and whether that's true, I couldn't say. What's certain is that, just like last time, we have no choice but to move ours so that it's after theirs. Young Mr Menuhin, who's champing at the bit, is having all hell to deal with at Carnegie Hall because he also has to rearrange his concert for after Kulenkampff's... '

Jelly hesitated. The concerto's sheet music would not be on sale until the day of its premiere – so Menuhin must have a photostat like hers. From Schott's. Apparently he'd been taking a sabbatical until his 21st birthday; now it had passed. Perhaps he's burned out, Alec had suggested. No, Adila countered: he's regrouping. And practising, hard. The Schumann was to be his great international comeback, complete with the tale of its rediscovery – which, as reported thus far, contained not one word about a glass game, spirit messages, London, or the involvement of any violinist but the golden boy who pleaded so irresistibly with the Germans for permission to play it that they released it to him... Presumably the American reporters knew nothing of Germany's race laws, which made prompt nonsense of their words.

'Why is it Menuhin's all of a sudden?' she protested. 'He never did a scrap of work to have it released.'

'Never mind that, Jelly. We have to work with what we've got, as best we can. Therefore, please suggest a date after 26th November when you're free and we can play this poor imprisoned concerto at last. Oh, and by the way... I'm afraid that rearranging the live transmission may not be as simple as one might like.'

'Do you think you won't be able to broadcast it now?' It would be so much easier if the English would simply say what they mean.

'As you know, Jelly, we plan things months in advance, and the detail involved in a broadcast is so complex that... '

Jelly, on edge with nerves, didn't want to cry down the telephone to the BBC's head of music. 'Is it all the fuss about... the messages?'

'It's nothing to do with that,' he insisted. 'We'll try to broadcast it, we really will, but either we can play it in late November without a broadcast, or we can put it off for a few months, or... ' He tailed off.

She didn't believe him. Obviously people's scorn of 'spiritualism' was poisoning the BBC against her too.

'Perhaps the Germans want to derail us, stop us performing it altogether,' she considered. 'They won't like someone who has Jewish relations playing their precious Aryan piece... '

'I couldn't possibly comment. But incidentally... I'm told there is some interest in Jerusalem. Our broadcasting counterpart, the Chamber Orchestra of the Palestine Broadcasting Service, has heard about the concerto and is hoping to perform it.'

'Jerusalem?' Jelly reeled.

'Their leader, Sasha Parnes, would be the soloist. The Nazis are not going to like that, either, but the cat's out of the bag – this concerto will be public property the very second Schott is allowed to release the printed score. Neither they nor you can prevent that.'

'All the more reason, then, that we must be able to do something about this. We can't let them keep on stopping us.'

'Good luck with that,' Boult said.

Jelly didn't like sarcasm. 'Well, if you were me, what would *you* do?'

'Hmm… ' A silence while Boult mused. 'He knows you from your cathedral tour, so I suppose you *could* always write to the prime minister.'

Jelly sat at her bedroom table, thinking hard. To bother Chamberlain over the date of a concert would be madness – even though he was the one person whose word might hold sway in Germany. Still, Alec had confided that he was not convinced the national hopes invested in the prime minister were entirely justified. He had come home from work distressed by news from Nuremberg concerning the Nazis' largest rally so far, and meanwhile was dealing with Foreign Office issues further afield: in Palestine two British officials had been murdered, and in China, under invasion by Japan, the British ambassador had been wounded in an air raid and the aggressors refused to apologise. The legal aspects of all this landed plumb on Alec's desk.

One thing worried him more than all the rest. Something odd, he told them, was going on near Weimar, at Buchenwald: a new type of prison camp in which they thought the Nazis were holding individuals they considered 'enemies of the state'. Within select Foreign Office circles, several such camps were known to exist already, including one at Sachsenhausen, but now it seemed a much larger compound was being constructed. His colleagues were attempting to gather information, but he felt helpless in the face of such a thing; there was little anyone could do from London to prevent it. 'You're wearing yourself out,' Adila fussed. His cough had worsened into a lung infection.

And at a time like this, Jelly wanted to write to Neville Chamberlain about Schumann. She herself had to laugh.

'On the other hand,' said Tovey, 'you have to stand up for yourself, Jelly. Because, as you say, it is the time it is, and nobody else is going to do it for you.'

Jelly rolled a piece of paper into Anna's old typewriter and began to bash out with two forefingers a letter to the prime minister.

Chapter 15

The next morning Adila went to the newsagent and bought every paper she could find that was likely to cover *Horizons of Immortality* and its association with Jelly and Schumann. At the dining-room table, the pages spread around them like a field full of landmines – and the detonators let rip.

After 15 minutes, Jelly, shattered, shook her head. 'I can't look at another one. I can't.'

'It's nonsense, darling,' Adila declared, though Jelly had never seen her so flummoxed. 'What do they know? Nothing. They weren't there with us. They didn't see the glass. They can't prove what we say isn't true and they're not even trying to. They're writing out of their backsides.'

'I don't understand. How can they be so sure they're right when they don't know anything? They didn't even call and ask.'

'Darling, they *were never going to* believe us. They'd already made up their minds. Whatever we said, they'd have quoted us against ourselves, twisted things to make us look bad.'

'But I thought newspapers were about reporting what happens, not about rubbishing it because people are too narrow-minded to listen.'

Adila passed her a fresh handkerchief. 'They've got to fill those pages with something.'

'But the world's falling to pieces. Why pick on us?' She scoured the reports for any mention of Anna; mercifully, there was none. 'I can't stop it being true just because it doesn't suit them! We were there. We saw it. We experienced it. They weren't. They didn't. They know *nothing*.'

Jelly felt a pang of envy, glimpsing the closed bedroom door that protected Adila and Alec. She was accustomed to being alone, but last thing at night, exhausted and with her defences down, that weakness, a longing for love, might invade her. She refused to feel sorry for herself: she had chosen music over marriage, and, in the past, the dead over the living, so she must stand by her decision and manage without a human sanctuary. Her sister, though, could rely on an understanding husband with a sensible mind and a warm, embraceable body. Perhaps, thought Jelly, that was why Adila was so calm and strong: she was not facing this mess alone.

Just for a few minutes, she allowed herself to consider what might have happened if Ulli Schultheiss were in London – and not German, and not so much younger, and not an impossible target for her pathetic longing. That was a mistake; in the morning his image was still in her mind, with the remembered sound of the Schumann piece he'd played on their Bechstein, once, several years previously.

'For God's sake, just speak to him,' said Adila, when Jelly confessed her preoccupation. 'Book yourself an international call. It can't make things any worse.'

The Fräulein Kammerling who answered the phone in Mainz explained that Ulli was away, attending a premiere in Berlin. A softness in her voice told Jelly that she understood more than she was saying.

'May I give him a message, Fräulein d'Arányi?'

'Please don't worry – it's not important. Thank you for your help, Fräulein Kammerling.'

How kind she sounded. Jelly thought of the acid that ate through the newspaper columns, moulding every German to the same image, no more real than the derisory caricatures of herself written by people who'd never met her, never heard her play and never attended a glass-game session, let alone one with Adila. Why do people think they know things that they don't know, then crucify other people who do know those things – because they don't want to know, because they are afraid of truths that would dent their own preconceptions?

'I need to go out somewhere,' she told her sister. 'I need to make sure the world is still there.'

'Don't be alone. I can't go with you, I have to teach, but why not call Myra?'

In her new home in Hampstead Myra took a break from practising to feed Jelly strong tea plus biscuits on a willow-pattern plate. Jelly felt intimidated by her friend's impeccable modern surroundings. The lease on the Carlton Hill house had expired and with the fruits of her American success Myra had bought a house on Wildwood Road, opposite the Heath Extension. It wasn't much more than ten years old, though it was supposed to look Georgian. Compared to Hurricane House it felt square, tidy, peaceful and devoid of ghosts.

'Let's sit out on the terrace,' Myra suggested, leading the way through her skylit studio to the garden. 'It's so delightful here that it can be quite hard to concentrate on music.'

It was indeed a haven; Jelly let the sun warm her skin while she explained, as briefly as she could, some of the ongoing troubles.

Myra's cynicism was no more or less than she expected, though at least she was generous about it. 'My dear, if you unleash "spirit messages" as a sane reason for your actions, I'm afraid you have to anticipate that 95 per cent of the modern public will be poised to die laughing. I'm not saying it didn't happen. It's simply that that's how people are.'

'They're sniping at Erik and the book without even looking at it,' Jelly protested. 'And me and the concerto too.'

'You have to be tougher, Jelly.' Myra poured out leaf tea through a strainer. 'One day you'll look back on this and, I promise you, you'll laugh.'

Jelly sipped the tea, wishing she could believe her.

'The important thing is to focus on the music.' Myra insisted. 'Everything else is so much nonsense. I can see it's a mess, but you have to insulate yourself and concentrate on what matters, which is that you have to play this concerto to the very best of your considerable abilities. Make sure you know it inside out and backwards and standing on your head, then go in and play it like an angel. More than that, play it like a professional. And for goodness' sake, make sure you get enough rehearsal.' Myra had a justifiable bee in her bonnet about how little rehearsal London orchestras provided. 'It'll be the first time the orchestra's seen the piece, of course – and Schumann can be a real pest.'

Jelly nodded. After two nights with no more than an hour of sleep, she'd been practising to escape, playing the notes but unable to absorb herself in the music. Concentration was becoming almost impossible. 'It's so nice to have a discussion that feels *normal*.'

'Exactly. In your world of spirits, you mustn't forget the here and now. Have some biscuits, Jelly, and do try to relax. You're so tense. It can't be helping that arm trouble.'

The telephone rang. Jelly started so violently that her tea splashed onto her lap. A few moments later, the bespectacled figure of Myra's assistant, Anita, appeared at the French windows: 'Myra, I'm afraid it's a newspaper person… '

'Thank you, dear – I'll deal with it.' Myra strode off to the hall.

'Yes?' came her distant voice, while Jelly mopped up the spilled tea with a napkin. 'Yes, this is Myra Hess. Who's that? What is this about?'

No, Jelly pleaded silently. Not here, too.

'Have I spoken to *whom*?' Myra put on her crystalline schoolmistress voice. 'No, I have not.'

Jelly stilled, listening.

'I have no knowledge of spirit worlds,' said Myra. 'Frankly, I find our present world quite bothersome enough… Jelly d'Arányi? No, I have not spoken to Jelly d'Arányi… That's as may be, my dear fellow. But I do not know anything about this matter, and I cannot help you. Goodbye.'

'Myra, you're an angel,' said Jelly.

'Don't worry.' Myra, returning, patted her shoulder. 'Everything will be fine.'

Jelly thought of Anna coughing blood on the station stairs; of Tom, slipping from one world into the next; of Tovey – much younger – pacing through Oxfordshire with Onkel Jo. George, auburn hair scraped back, painting walls gold and black in the Yeatses' Oxford apartment. Bartók and Elgar, eating her up with their eyes while she played; all her years of concerts and premieres and fame and – how had it come to *this*? All that interested anybody was whether she believed she had been in touch with the spirit of Schumann – and if she did, it meant she was a liar, when she was not. Had everyone forgotten the cathedral tour? Had everyone forgotten *Tzigane*? Why must everything come down to this one bizarre incident?

'I must go home,' she said. 'I am so tired.'

There, another disappointment awaited her.

'Ulli telephoned,' said Adila. 'He says he will try again, but he's writing to you in any case.'

'I *missed* him?' Jelly despaired.

'He said I should tell you to concentrate on the music and don't worry about anything else.'

It was just the sort of message Tom would have left. Jelly could see in Adila's eyes that she had thought of that too.

Another sleepless night, more ringing of phones, more letters on the doormat. Adila opened and filtered them.

'Head cases.' She crumpled one and tossed it backwards over her shoulder. 'Either they poke fun at spirit messages, or they say they've had them too. There's not much in between.'

Jelly scoured the envelopes for any sign of Ulli's writing. Nothing. Were letters from Germany being delayed by censors, perhaps? At their end, or in Britain too?

'Let well alone,' said one postcard. 'Schumann's orchestral music is dubious at the best of times. Why drag another dull, dreadful piece out of a resting place to which its dedicatee was right to consign it?'

'My dear Miss d'Arányi, your invaluable work has allowed the triumph of the soul,' read another, signed by someone claiming a fancy title in an esoteric order. Jelly tossed it after the others.

'You see? It's fun, playing ball!' Adila encouraged her.

The next missive, unsigned and scribbled in block capitals, contained the words: '*Go back where you came from, Jewish whores.*'

'Adi, they know where we live,' Jelly pointed out, trying to bite back tears. She didn't want to reveal the images in her head: bricks, broken glass, cricket bats.

'They wouldn't dare,' said Adila, who must have sensed it all. 'Everything's been quieter since Cable Street.' The battle between the British Union of Fascists, their opponents and the police was nearly a year ago. That didn't change the hate-mail on their table.

'I hope you're right,' was all Jelly could say.

The second post brought a very different letter: this time, on headed paper from 10 Downing Street, signed by Neville Chamberlain. It declared that the Foreign Office would take up the case with Berlin; and that he hoped all would go well, since he, personally, was looking forward to hearing her play the concerto.

The prime minister was on her side, and he had taken the trouble to reply. Jelly was speechless with amazement.

Adila wouldn't quite meet her eye. 'Whether they can achieve anything, even if they do write…'

'So…' She felt deflated. 'Do you think he's fobbing us off?'

'Perhaps he is, perhaps he isn't – but it may not make much difference either way.'

'There has to be hope, if that's what he says… He's the prime minister! If I can't trust him, whom can I trust?'

Tovey. She trusted Tovey. In the study, she picked up the

telephone; hearing his voice in his Edinburgh office, she nearly burst into tears again.

'Listen,' he said, 'I can't do much, but I can do two things, if they'll help. First, don't write to the papers yourself. Let me do it. I think I can, if not exactly stop things, then at least introduce a note of rationality. All right?'

'Oh, Donald, *thank you...* '

'As for the postponement, look at this another way. Play the piece at the BBC if and when you can. But come and play it in Edinburgh too, with my orchestra at the university. There's nothing in the world I'd like better than to conduct it for you. Whatever else happens, we'll give this concerto the resurrection it deserves, together.'

'You angel! But Donald, all the fuss... '

'I've been on a little journey of my own, trying to understand,' Tovey said. 'I'm writing you a letter about it, before I write to *The Times*, because I haven't decided what I should say in print. Be totally honest: where do you think the messages come from?'

Jelly paused. 'I don't know,' she said. 'I don't think there's another *place* they come from. I mean, I don't think that there's a Valhalla where composers go to live after they die. I don't know what to believe, but what I do know is that this happened. This happened to me. And I don't see why it shouldn't have. Why shouldn't I believe that Schumann's spirit wanted to contact me?'

Tovey gave a gentle laugh. 'Never mind, my dear. You'll get my letter tomorrow. Then there'll be an official version. Honestly, I find it strange enough that people can communicate with one another by any means at all.'

The letter was on the mat in the morning. Pages and pages of it, some handwritten, some typed, then handwritten again. She marvelled at the time and effort that Tovey was putting into defending her.

Moreover, his words made sense, in an extraordinary way.

Reading them again and again, to make sure she had understood, it seemed he was telling her that human beings are all part of one another, and that an interchange between them involved not only ideas, but in some ways an actual transfer of part of their souls to each other: our inner selves can flow into the mind of everyone with whom we communicate, and theirs into ours, whether we know it or not. Therefore our existence is inseparable from everyone else's; and that interconnection makes us what and who we are. If so, then music must be the best and the most direct way to reach and feed a shared consciousness within us all.

Tovey's letter to *The Times* was altogether more pragmatic, though replete with his acerbic humour. Yet he left no room for doubt: he believed her. He – the most distinguished musicologist in Britain – was willing to stand and be counted, publicly declaring so in *The Times*, with no need to justify his statement. It was a lengthy letter, exploring the concerto from many angles, but he had saved the best for the end. Having declared his personal, deep knowledge of the people concerned, now and in bygone times, he closed with the words: 'I assert my positive conviction that the spirit of Schumann is inspiring Jelly d'Arányi's production of Schumann's posthumous Violin Concerto. The sense in which I make this assertion is my own private affair.'

While Jelly rejoiced over *The Times*, though, Adila's face had begun to darken over *The Listener*.

'There's a letter printed here from our cousin Elisabeth. She says she always knew about the concerto. She says there was never any mystery at all!'

Jelly's newly recovered equilibrium collapsed.

Elisabeth stated that the manuscript, which had been in her father's possession for some 50 years, had been given to the Prussian State Library by all six of Joachim's heirs and that many friends knew this – Eugenie Schumann and her sisters included. She remarked, too, that a movement of the concerto had been played at Schumann's birthplace in Zwickau by the violinist

Adolf Busch, who was a close friend of Tovey's and sometime mentor to Yehudi Menuhin. 'Strange that the spirits should have to take such a roundabout way to reveal what was not concealed,' Elisabeth wrote.

Alec peered into the dining room; the sisters both began to shout about this latest misery. 'What is she playing at?' Jelly expostulated. 'I went to see her and she said nothing of the sort! And what's all this about Adolf Busch? Wouldn't Donald have known and told us?'

'Jelly, get dressed,' Alec ordered. 'We're going to Oxford.'

'What? *Now?*'

'Yes, now, by the next train. The quicker you get ready, the quicker we'll be there. I'll send a telegram to Elisabeth and tell her we're on the way. Chop-chop, old girl.'

'I'm coming too.' Adila jumped to her feet.

'No, Adi, not you. If you come, there'll be an almighty rumpus about spirit messages and that isn't what we need. You may have plundered the broadsheets today, my dear, but you haven't seen the tabloids – and I promise you, you neither want to nor need to.'

Adila was so shocked at this rejection that, for once, she was lost for words.

Today Jelly could take little pleasure in the sights and sounds of Oxford – the bicycles purring over the cobbles, the waterbirds chattering on the riverbank. She dreaded confronting her cousin; Adila would have done it much better. 'It'll be fine,' Alec promised, shepherding her towards the Banbury Road – for Jelly was so disconnected from reality through exhaustion that, left alone, she would probably have wandered halfway to Newbury.

Elisabeth's face showed that Jelly was not alone in feeling insecure; the Joachim glare was unmistakable. The house felt too dark on a day that was bright; an autumnal chill was beginning to intrude. Jelly conceded that her cousin might feel as uncomfortable as she did herself, which made her task a fraction easier.

'Lisa, I saw your letter in *The Listener* and I need to know why you wrote it.' Jelly challenged her, after ritual acceptance of tea.

'I'm sick of all this talk about spirit messages.' Elisabeth gave a shrug. 'It has to stop. It's ludicrous.'

Alec caught Jelly's eye across the sofa, silently warning her to be sensible.

'But if you remembered it all, why on earth didn't you tell me when I came to see you four years ago?'

'Well, I didn't remember it *then*. Johannes reminded me about the business of the library a little later… '

'But you're suggesting in this letter that you knew all the time. This will make everyone think that you told us, and that we must have gone looking for the concerto because of that, but you didn't. Lisa, do you have the first idea of how stupid this makes me look, and my sister, and, for goodness' sake, the Swedish minister?'

'Baron Palmstierna? I thought you didn't like him.'

'He's my sister's closest friend, and probably the best-respected ambassador in the country. And he's the man who went to the library and found the actual manuscript.'

Alec gave a nod. 'Whatever you think of his spiritual leanings, Baron Palmstierna is a highly intelligent man and an internationally prominent diplomat. He's not a gullible idiot. And I'm very much afraid that you have suggested, by implication, that he is.'

'Oh, good heavens.' Elisabeth drummed her fingers. 'That was *never* the idea.'

'What about Adolf Busch?' Jelly asked. 'We once met his brother, Fritz, at Glyndebourne – he's the conductor there – and Donald Tovey knows them.'

'I'm not sure… I *think* he played it. I am sure I heard of him playing it. If you know his brother, perhaps you can ask him. Or your friend, *Sir* Donald. Obviously you're convinced you know more about it than I do.'

'Elisabeth, this isn't very helpful,' Alec said. 'You should see the heap of hate mail Jelly's been sent. It's quite terrifying. It started with that Rollo Myers article, of course, and that's what prompted you to write your letter. And you're right, of course: yes, the gossip is sickening and, yes, we need to stop it, so I think there is something you can do to help bring that about.'

'Let me get just this right, once and for all,' Elisabeth said. 'Before this, none of you had *any idea* the piece existed?'

'I certainly didn't. I went to see Tovey. He looked it up and found it was real.'

'And my father never told Adila about it?'

'She insists not,' said Alec.

'And now you're receiving threats and abuse because a report in a magazine has sensationalised the suppression of the concerto, and nobody can stomach that story about the spirits?'

'That is why exactly what you do or do not remember makes a world of difference, and why your letter has, I'm afraid, possibly done more harm than good,' Alec said, a smile gilding his words. 'Your cousin here has been suffering an irrational onslaught enough to drive the sanest person out of her mind. I think it could help if you were to write another letter.'

Jelly watched him, admiring. What it was to have a brother-in-law who was accustomed to functioning in diplomatic circles.

'Think of it as a gesture towards keeping a diffuse family flame alight,' Alec added. 'The problem actually is that the headline used the word "lost". The concerto was not lost, but embargoed. But the word "lost" takes up less space on a page when an editor is composing a headline and in general it makes a greater impact on the reader's mind. The shadings of truth tend to be of secondary concern in that context. Had this occurred to you?'

'Oh,' said Elisabeth. 'No. I didn't think of that.'

'You see how easily a misunderstanding can arise? We can't change what's already happened, but I believe in sorting these matters out sooner rather than later – or else they keep festering. If we can fix the problem *immediately*, that's the end of it.'

Elisabeth glanced at her father's portrait. Joachim had been one to fester, and when he finally let rip, the repercussions were often profound.

'Don't do as he would have. Lisa, please assist us by writing a clarifying letter and entrusting it to us today? We'll then consider how best to use it. What do you think?'

'If you really believe it will help… '

'And you? Do *you* believe it will help?'

'Perhaps. Why… yes. Yes, I believe that it may.'

'Where do you keep your letter paper, please?' Alec stood and waited for Elisabeth's directions. It was only when he had set a blank page in front of her and she, pen poised, was ready to start, that Jelly let herself smile at how skilfully Alec had led her cousin into doing his bidding while convincing her she was exercising her own free will.

The letter was finished; Elisabeth completed it with a signature and a flourish. The glare fixed Jelly between the eyebrows. 'Here. Publish it if you want to. I hope it helps.'

Jelly read it quickly. Elisabeth, addressing the letter to Jelly herself, wrote of her intention to clear up what she had felt was a misrepresentation in *The Listener*; and saying that the details of the concerto's fate had slipped her mind until she saw her brother in 1934. 'I never for a moment intended to throw any doubt on anything that you had said about the facts which led to the publication of the Schumann concerto. I know you too well to doubt your absolute truthfulness,' she had written.

Waiting for the train home, Alec gave Jelly a piece of paper of her own. 'I think you should write a covering letter.'

'What? Now?'

'There's method to the madness. You'll see.'

Jelly pored over the paper as the train bowled eastward, trying to explain the difference between claiming to have found, via spirit messages, a work that nobody knew existed, which she had not done, and finding and wishing to play a piece that she, personally, had not known about before, which was the reality of it. It should have been so simple, she mused, reading back her text. Why all the hysteria?

Once they'd disembarked at Paddington and were climbing into a cab, Alec ordered it not to Netherton Grove, but to Fleet Street.

'*The Times*,' he told her. 'This letter is going straight in, if I have anything to do with it.' He looked pale and tired and sounded short of breath, but his eyes were tender over his moustache. 'Are you all right?'

'Oh, Alec, you're a wonderful, wonderful brother. I don't know what I'd do without you.'

'Steady on, old girl.' Alec peeled her arms away from his neck. 'It's all for the sake of world peace… I can't make *that* a reality, but this is within my power. At least, I hope it is. Let's get it over with, Sai, before you do something impossible, like growing up. I wouldn't like to see that happen, not now.'

Jelly woke at 2am from a dream in which her wrists and ankles were enskeined in a web like a spider's, but many times bigger. The more she struggled, the harder the fine threads cut into her flesh. Eyes open into the night, barely able to make out the shapes of her table, wardrobes and music stand, she could still feel the pain. It was real. It was back again. Part of her longed to give way, to let the web – and presumably its outsized spider – finish her off so that the agony would be gone for good.

The physical pain, which she was convinced was an arthritic flare-up, did her practising no good. 'It's fine,' she said to her concerned sister, trying to hide her winces when she attempted to play. She didn't want Adila to know how frightened she was. That anxiety compounded the emotional muddle, which seemed to drag her lower with every article, every letter, and soon every glance of a stranger in the street. Elisabeth's new missive, and her own, were noted; but the 'spook-haters', as Alec called them, promptly decided they were a fiction devised to throw everyone off the scent of a conspiracy. These people remained convinced that Jelly was inventing the entire saga of the spirit messages in order to grab publicity, promote herself and take the concerto away from everyone else. Apparently this was so outrageous that it had to be of immense importance to the British public, even when they should be more concerned with whether Chamberlain could fend off the very real possibility of war. 'If we were not foreign, and middle-aged women, and partly Jewish,' Jelly mused, 'I wonder if they would still be so angry?'

'We're lucky,' her sister snapped. 'A few centuries ago they'd have had us burned at the stake.'

As Adila had pointed out at the beginning, they were never going to listen. The fact that a Schumann concerto had been lying embargoed in a library, unheard for over 80 years, was the real scandal. Why didn't people notice *that*?

Tovey, appealed to, agreed to telephone Adolf Busch and tracked him down to a hotel in the Netherlands. The violinist let off a tirade in Tovey's ear and declared he was going to write to Eugenie Schumann. She in turn promptly told Busch that she would write a substantial letter to *The Times* herself, making a plain statement to insist the concerto should not be played, and that furthermore she was consulting her lawyers. A few days after what should have been Jelly's performance, in its second potential incarnation, Busch was interviewed in a Dutch newspaper: he denied ever having performed the Schumann concerto, although he had apparently seen and assessed the music before deciding to let well alone. Then they'd asked Eugenie for her view, and printed the response: 'No. Never have I given my agreement to the publication of the Violin Concerto, the last work of my father.'

'She's determined to stop the performances,' Tovey told Jelly. 'Legal advice and all.'

'Would she win?' said Jelly, horrified.

'I doubt it. The German state, apparently, holds the copyright – or has decided it does – because the manuscript was in the State Library, and if those officials are intent upon doing something, there's no law on earth they'll allow to stop them. Anyway, I think they'll tactfully explain that the concerto would certainly be published after she is no longer with us, so ultimately it's out of her control.'

Busch had not played the concerto, so Elisabeth was wrong yet again. People were on edge, afraid, lashing out at anything within reach; really, the issue was Germany. Jelly remembered the bombing, the ceaseless fear, letters from Sep, his sister Maisie arriving in tears. Why should she be attacked when she was afraid too?

'Come and stay,' Anna said, by phone from Sussex.

'I can't. It's sweet of you, but I won't drag you into this insanity,' said Jelly.

By night she sometimes fell into a fitful doze that resembled a kind of trance. She seemed to see Sep far away, in a grave; she still knew his face, riven by wounds. Then she seemed to hear him laughing as he left, and she thought he was closer to his companions, those elite young Oxford officers, than he'd ever been to her, and that he preferred their company to that of a gauche little girl who wouldn't grow up even if she passed 20, or 30, or 40. And the dream merged into another, where he embraced her, then told her that he loved her and he would come back. That was the worst dream of all.

'Sai, it won't do!' Adila exploded, around 11am, when Jelly surfaced, pale and headachey. 'Snap out of it.'

It wasn't that she was nervous, but when the day finally arrived, assuming the Nazis could not stop the performance in

February, how could she stand up on the platform of the Queen's Hall and play one note, wondering whether the audience might laugh at her and perhaps throw things and...

'Don't be ridiculous.' Adila grabbed a coffee cup and filled it for her. 'Nobody throws tomatoes in the Queen's Hall. Nobody throws tomatoes in *England*. This is the 20th century!'

'I should cancel it.'

'Never! Come on, where is your gumption?'

The Listener reviewed *Horizons of Immortality* and the baron was not best pleased. 'It's good to have a review at all,' Adila reassured him, 'even if it's hot air that belongs in a different part of their anatomies.'

'Anyone would think there was nothing in this book except the Schumann concerto,' he grumbled. 'It's a few pages, right at the end.'

Reading the review – by one Harry Price, who apparently had a reputation for exposing fake spiritualists – Jelly was torn between righteous indignation and a suspicion that certain ideas of his could perhaps be worth noting. On the one hand, he declared, if the baron's book was to be believed, here was proof that the spirit survives the body's demise. But on the other, he suggested that a 'sensitive' could acquire information, forget it, then inadvertently reveal it in a trance or automatic writing. Scientists, he continued, would probably conclude that that was what had happened to the d'Arányis and friends.

'Oh no, my dear,' Erik said. 'Don't worry. The messages come from somewhere much, much deeper than any human mind.'

Chapter 16

The day of Georg Kulenkampff's premiere of the Schumann
Violin Concerto in Charlottenburg, Berlin, arrived: 26 November 1937. After an ample breakfast of toast, eggs and smoked
herring in a cavernous hotel dining room nearby, Ulli decided
to go for a walk.

As a student he had spent much time here, for this was the
district in which Berlin's nightlife had sprung up in the old days
and mesmerised the city's artistic community. The westernmost
end of the Ku'dam had boasted one of the best spots, opposite
the Kaiser Wilhelm Church, the Romanisches Café – he remembered seeing Bertolt Brecht in there once, and you might well
have found yourself admiring the flair of the cross-dressers, or
pretending not to notice activities suggestive of an illicit affair
or several, or eavesdropping upon some outrageous philosoph-
ical idea being promulgated at the next table. Even if Ulli, as a
pianist in training, considered himself not remotely part of such
a crowd, he had the underrated gift of being able to blend into
the background to observe everything without having to take
part. Nevertheless, he was a tall, fair, attractive youth, and sometimes he had been quite successful with the women there.

Now Berlin seemed quiet – too quiet – and he was certain
not only because of the chill east wind blowing in from Poland.
Circular pillars for advertising – often glorifying the wholesome
delights of the Reich and its achievements – offered the only jolt
of colour in this clouded November: bright-blocked, chunky-
lettered posters showing fast trains, jagged mountains, blonde
women, green fields, raised fists.

He wandered past the sprawling palace, searching for ghosts
of his old life. Other than the shape of the roofs, the angles at
which streets met and a few newspaper sellers and flower stalls
that were unchanged, little remained to suggest the lure the city

had held. The Romanisches Café had been raided and a riot staged there as long as a decade ago – the Nazi Party's thugs out to destroy the left-wingers' favourite haunt. All the life seemed to have been sucked out of the place. Now an air of numb obedience lingered around the figures making their way towards the opera house, many seeming determined to vanish into safe and inconspicuous anonymity.

The Deutsches Opernhaus, previously called the Städtische Oper, was a solid yet elegant building seemingly from a bygone era – even though 1912, if he thought about it, was not really that long gone. All the people he remembered from its administration had left or been thrown out. Ulli approached the front entrance under the façade's five giant windows, but soon noticed crowd barriers all around, traffic police directing cars away from the closed road and a red carpet that had been rolled from kerbside to central doorway, ready to welcome the Reich's leaders to this historic event.

Midday in a down-at-heel suburb of Berlin was not quite what Ulli had envisaged for the modern world premiere of the Schumann Violin Concerto. But Goebbels and the Reichsmusikkammer, together with the state's leisure-time organisation Kraft durch Freude (KdF) – Strength through Joy – had developed some novel aims. They wanted to take music out of its concert halls and bring it to the people, in accessible venues that would not intimidate them with their formality and where tickets would be affordable for the ordinary man on the Charlottenburg tram. These concerts took a different form from mainstream events: the programmes were shorter, they might be held anywhere from a sports stadium to a factory, at lunchtime or in the afternoon, and they might involve not only music but recitations, political speeches and, occasionally, audience participation. The Violin Concerto was to take wing as part of this series, and as the centrepiece of a KdF conference; hence the opera house.

Eleven thirty: half an hour to go before his beloved concerto was to reach the world's ears for the first time, and Ulli, fumbling to find his ticket and identity documents on the way in, halted in his tracks. Into this sizeable, usually welcoming foyer were filing not only audience members, but innumerable officials in uniform; two giant swastika flags decked the far wall, dominating the pale stone with scarlet, white and ebony. Barked instructions from security staff alarmed him; he tried not to show it. The personages of the Reich were on their way; everything else was subordinated to their security.

He kept his distance from the Streckers, who as the concerto's publishers were expected to be accorded due recognition at some point. Ulli refused to put himself through another encounter with Goebbels. For all he knew, that man would be having his every step watched. He remembered the face of the minister of propaganda looming at him over that outsize table and felt sweat erupting on his forehead. 'Nothing is ever "just a piece of music"… '

'Ach, Ulli,' his mother had said at Sunday lunch, 'you're not yourself.'

'I can't sleep.'

'You're very pale and you don't seem able to keep still for a minute. You must take care. You know you're all I have left.' She turned the thumbscrews of guilt, but of course it was true. Nothing had been the same since that meeting in Berlin, at which Ulli found himself on the edge of a ravine, staring into what might lie beneath.

Inside the auditorium he found his seat, glad to be near the back and not with his employers among the dignitaries. He could feel tension pervading the place as it filled: people sitting in silence or, if talking, chattering too hard, too fast or too quietly; fingers twitching across handbags or against sleeves, knuckles pallid, gazes darting up towards the largest box, which was festooned with the usual regalia, yet still empty and waiting.

And then *he* was there. He was to awaken the Schumann Violin Concerto with a personal kiss of approval. The audience – the congregation, perhaps, of this church of political art –

stood at once. Feet struck the floor. Arms swept upwards. Gathered voices rose like an aeroplane engine, and there in the box was a dark, flop-haired, moustachioed figure, arm outstretched in salute, gaze scouring the crowded theatre beneath. The cheering assaulted Ulli's eardrums. Having no choice, he stood too, and saw his own arm rise to match the angle of everyone else's, because it would look very obvious if it did not, and it occurred to him that he had never in his life seen or heard anything like this roar of heightened energy in one mass of people.

He noticed a woman in early middle age occupying the seat beside his. She had not risen to greet the Führer, but sat in her chair, immobile.

'Why aren't you standing?' someone behind her challenged.

'I have a bad knee,' said the woman over her shoulder. Then she stared straight ahead. Ulli noticed the man take a breath to fortify the accusation, but fortunately for his neighbour the proceedings now demanded silence.

The Führer sat, and the people followed suit. The conductor, Karl Böhm, strode to the podium. A crash of cymbals: Wagner, the grandest of the Führer's favourites, the strings galloping through shimmering triplets, the horns bouncing along in their pomp and grandeur. The Prelude to Act III of *Lohengrin*. In the opera, it would introduce a wedding scene after which everything goes horribly wrong, but so stirring was its mood that now the context was ignored.

Here it was an introduction, as it turned out, to Goethe's *Prometheus*; Friedrich Kayssler took the stage alone to recite. Ulli had not seen the actor, an imposing 60-something with an aquiline profile, since the days when the great man had been based at the Berlin Volksbühne – the 'people's theatre' – where he had taken over from Max Reinhardt as director back in 1918. Goethe's poem addressed Zeus as a self-appointed human deity, deriding the old gods. There was no mistaking the intent of these words in Hitler's presence.

And the Führer? How insignificant he would look if you

passed him in the street without his uniform and moustache. It was all one big show, a manufactured identity complete with music, pictures, camera angles and stage management – yet people swallowed it whole, inexplicable and irrational as that might be. Ulli's head felt hot, yet he shivered; perhaps anxiety, perhaps the smoked fish at breakfast. There seemed to be no air in the theatre. He closed his eyes and tried to breathe deeply.

Kayssler finished and bowed in gratitude to the crowd's applause. Robert Ley took his place – the head of the German Labour Front, the official state replacement for the banned trade unions, which ran the KdF. Fighting some worsening stomach cramps, Ulli let Ley's words wash over him, straining his ears beyond the man's slightly peculiar diction – was he drunk? – for any strand of music seeping out from backstage. But one more speech remained; this time, the figure Ulli prayed nightly that he might never need to see at close quarters again.

A blanket of silence smothered the theatre as Goebbels prepared to speak.

'Today,' the minister of propaganda intoned, 'thanks to the generosity of the Führer, Schumann has entered Valhalla!'

The concerto started at last, with a pulsing on the strings and a rush of sound. Not as much of a rush as Ulli would like; Böhm was not noted for sprightly tempi. This was portentous, stately, ceremonial; it squared with the Reich aesthetic, less so with the personality of the composer. Kulenkampff, waiting for his first entry, betrayed no emotion; when his opening phrase arrived, it sounded all in a day's work. Ulli tried to imagine how he must feel. Soloist in the first performance of a concerto on which hung so much expectation, playing to Hitler and Goebbels. Was this really the opportunity for which poor Jelly had longed?

He glanced at Hitler, in the dignitaries' box. The Führer seemed absorbed, his head and hands moving jerkily, as if, deep down, he had discovered a would-be conductor who was longing to get out, take control and make the music move just a little faster.

Ulli was wishing to high heaven he had not eaten the smoked herring.

The slow movement began. Schumann's violin solo seemed disconnected from the cello's counter-melody: drifting over the top, lost in his own world, or perhaps trapped there. Heads turned; people glanced at their companions to see if they, too, were puzzled. Was it meant to sound like this? Was Kulenkampff's timing wrong? Ulli, who had worked on every note of the piece, knew it was right. If Kulenkampff and Böhm, those most rational musicians, could not make sense of the concerto, how could anybody?

And yet... within this musical jungle lay a naked beauty so exposed that it seemed almost indecent. Schumann's soul might be damaged and suffering, but he still gave its entirety. Could it ever have been right to leave this music unheard?

And yet, and yet... there *was* madness here, a precipice lying ahead in the fog and snow; a spirit filled with love, but lost, unable to master itself. For the first time, Ulli began to wonder what happens when insanity is unleashed through art into the souls of others. What exactly did Joachim and Clara know about this piece that made them put it to sleep?

The transition sounded and the Polonaise emerged into the daylight. The Führer was smiling.

Ulli forced himself to listen to the detail. Kulenkampff's version was considerably altered, whereas Yehudi had eagerly declared that he wanted to play every note exactly as Schumann had written it, without even the hushed-up Hindemith adaptations. Kulenkampff, ignoring Schumann's funereal metronome mark, played it as a true polonaise; yet though his delivery was graceful and elegant, its triumph felt empty. Everything would be all right, it seemed to say, when Ulli knew full well that it would not: only a few months after creating the blazing conclusion, Schumann threw himself off the Düsseldorf bridge into the black Rhine.

Final chord. Kulenkampff, domed forehead shining with sweat, his bow aloft, gaze locked for an instant with Böhm's. The orchestra standing, tired, inscrutable. The Führer, on his feet. The whole audience rising to ape him. And applause. And... Ulli sensed their puzzlement. This was no triumph. That slow movement – exquisite, yet out of kilter; was this concerto after all an insane work for an insane land? What had they done, letting it out?

While he searched his own soul, wondering why this malign potential had never struck him before, or whether the idea was just a creation of his own mind, in which case perhaps he too was losing his senses, the concert moved on to a group of patriotic songs. Strength through joy. Everyone sang along. The volume was submerging him.

Ulli suddenly knew that his stomach was about to lose its battle. A chorus of tutting and shushing followed him; as he stepped across his neighbours, trying not to tread on anyone's toes, a woman with her hands plunged deep within a fur stole heaped a curse on him. 'Please excuse me – something I've eaten,' Ulli said. Glimpsing her face upturned towards the Führer, he spotted a gleam of tears, not of sorrow.

Were people so completely fooled? How could they be so stupid, so believing? Would they gulp down, dog-like, whatever was put in the feeding bowl in front of them because it was so easy?

Outside, the world whirling around his head, icy air punched him in the guts. He staggered away from the entrance and doubled up – just managing to remember that at least now he would not have to see his employers being presented to the leaders of the Reich and congratulated on their achievement in rediscovering a great German concerto by a true German artist.

'It can't last,' Willy Strecker said, two days later, safely back in Mainz. 'All these things come to an end.'

'But when?' said Ulli. 'And how?'

Willy shook his head. 'Don't start being heroic, Ulli. You've done your bit. And remember, you're playing by the rules now...'

Ulli had scarcely eaten since the Charlottenburg concert. He wasn't sure that even during the deprivations of his childhood he had felt real despair before. Some of the country's best composers had been banned or had gone into exile; the greatest one had been conscripted as a signature tune to a mad dictator; now, so had this unstable and heart-rending concerto. Many times in the past he and his friends had grumbled about politicians' lack of artistic awareness. Yet today they had some who knew the power of music too well and could use it for their own ends, and this was a great deal worse.

Every postal delivery was a source of terror lest it contain the call-up papers that could be the Reich's revenge on an employee who had made the mistake of championing Jewish musicians. One of his friends, a young historian who had openly challenged the government's racial policies, had been arrested; nobody knew where he had been taken, or whether he was still alive. And Ulli's own handwriting had appeared on the envelopes in which the great Aryan Schumann concerto had flown the country into the hands of Jelly d'Arányi and Yehudi Menuhin. If that were noted and traced... Ulli could no longer tell which of his fears were justified and which the products of his frazzled insomniac brain. Trying to pick up the telephone to call Jelly again, as he had promised to do, his hand shook and sweated, his head spun and he could not continue.

To leave the country and find sanctuary elsewhere; to give up the job he loved and gamble on the outcome. Was it braver to stay or to go?

'What are we going to do, Willy?'

'All we can do is wait. Wait for the cycle to turn, because it has to, eventually. Wait for it to end.'

'*Das Ende.*' Ulli quoted Wagner's Wotan. '*Das Ende…* '

And beyond the deep windows of the Schott's headquarters, beyond the pink cathedral, the conservatoire that had thrown out its Jews, and the swastikas fluttering like crows on the Rathaus, the autumn winds were gusting in from distant mountains, bringing with them the first hint of snow.

Chapter 17

'The Nazis' biggest propaganda party of the year,' Adila fumed. She was trying to tune in to German radio to hear Kulenkampff's performance, fighting the wireless's unreliable tuning and cursing in Hungarian, by far the best language for it. Across the Atlantic, they'd been informed, Yehudi Menuhin was not only listening but had a journalist with him to monitor his reactions.

Jelly imagined her beloved concerto ready to sound its marvels in Berlin; more imprisoned now, in front of a capacity crowd swelled by Nazi dignitaries, than it had ever been while cocooned in its safe, quiet file in the Prussian State Library. She didn't want to hear it at all. She escaped to the Green Room with some magazines to wait until it was over.

'Didn't you want to know what he's done with it?' Alec asked, astonished to find Jelly there a little later, lying on the chaise longue and leafing through the latest *Vogue*, circling dress designs she liked.

'Yes,' said Jelly, without flinching, 'but not yet. He'll record it, for sure. I'll hear it sometime – *after* I've played it.'

'You might be interested to hear,' Alec said gently, 'that Goebbels made a speech. Then Kulenkampff played the concerto. And now they're all singing rousing nationalistic songs together with their Führer.'

Jelly's magazine slid to the floor. 'What did Goebbels say?'

'The usual.' Alec picked up *Vogue* and placed its bright colours face down on the chaise longue. 'It's not your fault, you know. You could never have imagined this when it all began.'

Jelly, usually so swift to tears, could find none. She couldn't let the import of what had happened drill through her shell, or...

'There, there, old girl.' Alec patted her arm. 'I'll leave you in peace.'

She sat still, listening to his steps fading on the stairs. Her

Sleeping Beauty had been awakened by the wrong prince. Could the spirits not see into the future? Could they not have known, when they chose to speak through the glass game, that the first person on whose ear the concerto would fall might be Adolf Hitler?

'They don't tell us what will happen,' Adila affirmed that evening, 'only what *is*, with their wider perspective.' Erik had arrived after dinner; Jelly found them all in the music room, drinking coffee, the baron looking as shattered as Jelly felt. 'Even then, they're sometimes wrong. Several times this has happened.'

'Do you remember, they thought we should look in Weimar?'

'Yes, and one of them said, "My child, we do not know everything,"' said Erik.

'The spirits are only human,' said Adila.

'There's no reason why a spirit fallible in life shouldn't also be fallible after life,' Alec remarked, his eyes smiling above his moustache. 'They're the same people, one presumes... '

'Erik.' Jelly rounded on the baron. 'Why is there nothing from them now?'

'I wish I knew.' Erik's gaze, like Alec's, like Adila's, was full of sympathy – and more, perhaps fear or guilt.

'There's something you're not telling me. Adi, is it Ulli? Did he phone again?' Despite the message he had left, there had been no sound – and no letter. She felt distraught. Something must have happened to him, and in Germany that could mean anything.

'Sai... ' Alec got up and came over to Jelly to press both her shoulders. 'It's Yehudi. He's going to play the Schumann in London. Erik has just heard about it.'

The shock struck like a missile. 'Has Boult cancelled mine?'

'No, no, you will play it. But he will play it too. A little after you, with a different orchestra.'

'But – when? As soon as next season?'

'As soon as – oh, Sai. Three weeks after you.'

'Where?'

'In the Queen's Hall as well.'

As if they were simply ignoring her existence. As if the hall, the promoter, perhaps the audience, had all decided she didn't count. Let's indulge the silly little woman and her spirit messages and let her play it first. And afterwards we'll have the *real* premiere.

Everybody's darling Yehudi. First he played the Schumann with piano accompaniment at Carnegie Hall in New York; then a couple of weeks later with the St Louis Symphony Orchestra at their home venue. He was making the Schumann Concerto his comeback work, when it was supposed to be hers. With less than two months until her own performance – confirmed for 16 February 1938, nearly three months after the German airing – a chasm appeared in Jelly's mind, like a lightning bolt in a tree. In her bedroom mirror, her reflection stared at her with furrows in her forehead that she'd not noticed before, a line across the top of her nose that was definitely new. Her elbow fired bolts of pain along her arm. What would Ulli think if he saw her now? What would Elgar say, or Ravel, or Holst? Muses are not supposed to go grey, or to develop wrinkles, or to suffer from arthritis. Muses are young, beautiful and perfect.

Like Yehudi. An artistic photo in the press showed a youth almost too handsome for his own good: those long eyelashes shielded fine-shaped eyes and the high cheekbones supported the glow of youthful skin above his violin. *That* was a muse. And if one muse grew old and ill and crumbled, there'd always be another ready to slide into his, or her, place.

Erik rang their doorbell one Sunday lunchtime shortly before Christmas, when they were just back from Mass – arriving alone, unannounced and unexpected. Before Adila could quiz him, embracing her with one arm and Jelly with the other, he declared, 'I have some news for you. I've resigned. Soon I shall no longer be the Swedish minister.' Adrienne, home for the holidays, gasped aloud, then clapped a hand over her mouth.

'Come in. Eat. Tell us.' Adila manoeuvred him through the hall, into the dining room. Jelly spotted an unfamiliar quizzical expression in Adrienne's eyes. She was growing up and beginning to understand.

Over Adila's goulash, the Fachiris and Jelly bombarded him with questions, the two women less tactfully than Alec. What had happened? 'Many things,' he said, without meeting their gazes. What had prompted his decision? 'Many things.' What would he do now? 'Many things. Another book. More research. I don't know yet… Look, this is a difficult job at the best of times. I feel there's nothing more I can do, and when one feels there is nothing more one can do in one's job, it's time to leave.'

'Don't be so gloomy,' Adila pleaded. 'It's Christmas.'

'Adi, we'll do Christmas in a minute,' Alec promised. 'Erik, I can understand this very well and I don't blame you a bit. It's no time to be a diplomat if you're also an idealist. We all need to wake up. Germany's going to explode sooner or later, probably sooner. I just heard that they're saying they'll take children away from their parents if they're not being reared to be National Socialist enough.'

'And probably send them to my school,' Adrienne mumbled.

'The whole of Europe's going mad,' Erik said. 'Look at Spain – thousands of young men being killed over an insane ideology. As for Russia, God alone knows… '

'Still, Erik, in some ways you've picked an original moment to abandon government circles – now that your own party is in power,' Alec noted.

Erik had spent some years as a Swedish MP, but being a Social Democrat, only in opposition. 'My one concession to English irony,' he remarked.

'It's nothing to do with the book, is it?' Jelly asked. If she felt so unsettled by the accusations surrounding its publication, its author must feel far worse. Besides, she wondered silently what his government might think about his enduring credibility.

'I wouldn't resign for the sake of a few idiotic reviews.' The baron shrugged. If it had been anything more than a simple decision, he did not plan to say so. 'There's a great deal to do, Jelly,' he went on. 'I'm in touch with some multi-faith organisations and I'd love to help them. The clash of religions causes so much trouble, yet at heart they're all the same. We can build bridges if people can be made to understand, and that's what I'd like to do next.'

Nobody had asked what Ebba might make of all this, or where she was today.

'You'll have to leave the Residence, won't you?' Adila said. 'Will you go back to Sweden?' Jelly noticed that her fingers were laced tightly together around the base of her wineglass.

'We must hand on the house to the next man in the job. As for Sweden, I don't know yet. There'll be big changes, for sure.'

Adila excused herself to fetch the dessert, then vanished to the bathroom, pleading stomach pains.

Immediately after Christmas Jelly and Adila both had to set off for new UK tours. Once upon a time Anna Robertson would have gone along to keep Jelly company, but now Jelly travelled alone – and perhaps that was best. The distances were substantial, the cold intense; no good for a recovering consumptive. Hull, Nottingham, Sheffield, Bognor Regis. She battled with icy draughts on stage and strained her eyes against dim lighting. At least the audiences warmed her spirit: people who loved music, wanted to listen to what she could give them, and even came to thank her for it; people who didn't give a damn how she found the Schumann, as long as she would play it for them someday. On occasion, mercifully, they didn't know about the furore at all; then she enjoyed the relief of pretending it hadn't happened.

Yet often she was sure they knew, but weren't saying so,

and she'd wonder half the night what gossip there might be behind her back. She'd never worried about such things before. She'd been too busy enjoying herself and charming people. Now she felt worn out by slow trains and bumpy roads; and the drizzle and the wind were eating at her joints. She would excuse herself politely from well-intentioned post-concert dinners and go straight to bed in whatever hotel or bed and breakfast she'd been booked into, and she didn't mind if it was simple, because nobody had any money these days and she had to do her bit to help them get by. Sometimes she ate little after the concert except tinned cream of tomato soup and a ham sandwich, sitting on a sagging mattress, a solitary lightbulb dangling overhead.

One night, just before the new year, she opened a newspaper and found there the obituary of Ravel, who had died after undergoing brain surgery. His birdlike gaze was still alive in her mind: the way they'd laughed together at Kettner's back in the Twenties, the gusto with which he tucked his napkin into his collar to protect his elegant clothes, and the thrill of anticipation when she opened the parcel he'd sent and saw *Tzigane* for the first time. She cried herself to sleep.

At last, at the start of February, just two weeks before the concerto, she reached the end of the tour, on a Sunday afternoon in Eastbourne. She stayed with her old friends the Southerns, enjoying a rare good night's sleep, besides a respite from tinned tomato soup; in the morning she headed home, ready to gasp with relief at the sight of Victoria Station's blackened archways and the smell of lingering London fog.

On the front step, the wind worrying at her hat and rain bedraggling her old fur coat, she battled with case, dress carrier, violin, flowers and keys. The house was silent and empty. Adrienne had gone back to school; Alec was at work; and there was no dog now to bark a welcome. The latest maid had left them and Adila had not yet found someone new. A note on the hall table told her that Adila was spending the afternoon at Portland Place, where Erik, Ebba and their staff had begun to pack up their household effects.

Alone, Jelly pottered about, putting away her last unworn tour clothes and piling her concert dresses on a chair ready to take to the dry cleaner's. She arranged in a vase the bouquet that had been presented to her after the Eastbourne concert, then placed it on the music-room bookcase. She swallowed aspirin for her arm, made some tea and boiled an egg for lunch. She was fishing it out of the pot when the doorbell jangled upstairs.

The postman? A delivery? Adila home from the baron's, minus keys? Jelly hurried up the stairs and flung open the front door.

A stranger stood before her in an overcoat and trilby: a figure only a few inches taller than she was, but with a breadth resembling a sportsman. She registered beneath the hat's brim a triangle of a face and a gaze aflame behind rectangular spectacles.

'Miss Jelly d'Arányi?' A strange accent, one she did not recognise, overlaid with a ribbon-curl of American.

'Yes?' A reporter? No camera, no notebook. A fan? No flowers.

'My name is Moshe Menuhin. I am the father of Yehudi Menuhin.'

Jelly felt briefly winded. Why hadn't he contacted her first? How had he found out where she lived? 'My goodness! Mr Menuhin, how very nice to meet you.' She extended a hand, which he shook briefly, but with a grasp so strong that it made her wince.

'I'm not sure if you got my letter?'

Upstairs, two weeks' worth of post had piled up in her absence. 'I've actually just been away on tour, and I only got back about half an hour ago, so... ' Jelly gave him her brightest smile.

'I apologise for turning up basically unannounced, then, but

I'm only here a couple of days and the schedule is pretty tight, so I thought I'd take pot luck. Do you have a minute to talk, Miss d'Arányi?'

'Yes, of course, sorry, please come in.'

Moshe Menuhin stepped into the house. She led the way to the music room. Whatever could she give Yehudi Menuhin's father to eat? Adila must have some cake in the pantry. 'I've just made some tea. Will you have a cup?'

Moshe Menuhin gave a laugh that Jelly thought more sardonic than warm. 'How English you've become – all tea and excuses and apologies. And there I was, expecting you still to be Hungarian. I can hear the accent, though. It's a good one.'

'I'm sorry?' Goodness, how little she travelled abroad these days: nobody had addressed her in such a way in a long time. A national issue, probably. American informality and suchlike. Normally she liked candour. Today she wasn't so sure.

'Amazing place you've got here. I love the rugs. Persian, no?'

'Our father bought them for us when we were just girls, with some money an uncle left... '

Menuhin senior was casting about the music room, peering around – was he looking at the paintings to see if they were signed? Opening the piano to note its brand? Healthy curiosity, perhaps. 'Ah, a Bechstein. Interesting. A very nice make, not used enough these days.'

'Are you a musician too, Mr Menuhin?'

'Dear me, no, I can't read a note of music. I appreciate it, of course, but the talent belongs to my children. I have the dignity of a father and the duties of a valet!' He picked up the portrait of Sep that stood atop the Bechstein and turned it around in his hands. 'Nice sketch. What is this – John Singer Sargent? Whew – *very* nice sketch. Who's the gentleman?'

'A friend. A musician. He died at the Somme.'

'I see.' That gaze was prodding her with its spike again; this man was quick on the uptake. 'What kind of musician?'

'A composer and pianist, from Australia. He was also a rower – an Olympic champion… Let me get you some tea, Mr Menuhin? And a piece of my sister's finest fruit cake? Do have a seat, please…'

'Thank you.' Moshe planted himself in the armchair beside the piano.

Jelly flew downstairs to boil the kettle and locate the cake. She hadn't eaten since breakfast in Eastbourne – cornflakes with the Southerns – and now her egg stood untouched, tantalising her. She took the cut cake upstairs on the best silver tray, together with her mother's tea set, at least the two cups that remained unchipped.

'My compliments to the chef.' Moshe appeared to be enjoying the cake. 'I gather Mrs Fachiri isn't in?'

'She's out seeing friends. I'm glad you arrived after I came home, or there'd have been nobody here.'

'I waited.'

What? He'd been outside all that time, anticipating her return?

'Your very kind neighbour, Mrs Garrett, spotted me walking around your cul-de-sac about an hour ago and asked me in. I find the sense of community here encouraging. People take an interest in one another's lives.'

Mrs Garrett? Kind? Interested, no doubt… 'I'm touched that you feel I'm worth waiting for.' Jelly tried once more to don her charm cloak.

'Oh, nobody could be more so.' He was smiling, but not the smile she'd hoped for. He was playing along. Why? And he'd put Sep's picture back on the piano in such a position that it appeared the poor lad was staring at Jelly over Moshe's shoulder.

'Let me come straight to the point, Miss d'Arányi. I want to talk to you about Schumann.'

Jelly tried to deflect him. 'I understand Yehudi's New York performance was a great success. He is such a beautiful violinist,

Mr Menuhin, you must be proud of him – but how silly of me, I'm sure everyone says that... '

'Oh, they do, they do. Pride doesn't matter. My boy has worked hard and he's made sacrifices, as have I and his mother and sisters. There's no such thing as a miracle, even if we'd like to believe so. What did Edison say? One per cent inspiration and 99 per cent perspiration?'

Jelly nodded. 'He has enjoyed his sabbatical, I hope?'

'I hope so too. He only gave up 2 million dollars' worth of work for it.'

Jelly tried to calculate. How many concerts would he normally do per annum? Surely no more than 60 or 70? That meant... *how much* for each? If only her mental arithmetic were better; she needed a pencil and paper to work this one out. Whatever the answer, it was unimaginable compared to the provincial music societies that put her up in cheap boarding houses or organisers' homes and always, always apologised for being too impecunious to offer a better fee.

'Miss d'Arányi, first of all I should explain he has no idea I've come to see to you. As you know, he's playing the Schumann here with the London Philharmonic Orchestra a few weeks after your performance. I'm in town to sort out some logistics, en route to Paris, but passing through London made me think of you, and I began to wonder if you have the slightest idea what has been involved in planning the US premiere?'

'Well, of course I can imagine. I've had similar experiences myself.'

'His performance in London was to be the UK premiere, and would have been, if it weren't for you,' Moshe pointed out. 'And if it weren't for the Nazis, he would have given the world premiere. Instead, what do we have? A fine mess, Miss d'Arányi. A fine mess indeed. I understand, from my correspondence, that they were obliged to move the date of Georg Kulenkampff's performance because of interference from London.'

'From London?'

'From you. You were, I understand, so adamant that these delightful 'spirit messages' gave you the absolute authority to premiere the work that you attempted to trump the Nazis at their own game. One imagines they weren't too pleased to hear about your Ouija board.'

'But Mr Menuhin, if it hadn't been for the messages, nobody would have heard that the concerto existed.' Jelly pointed out. How on earth had he arrived at such an idea? Had someone written to somebody without her knowing?

'What a tide of cock-a-hoop baloney!' Moshe was on his feet and Jelly shrank back, for he seemed about to knock over the occasional table complete with his plate of cake and full cup of tea, and it was right beside the piano and her violin case.

'I've heard much in my lifetime that's outrageous and unfair, you know.' He began to pace the room. She sat transfixed, incredulous. 'I've lived in the Middle East and seen injustices that could turn your hair white in one day. I've lived in Jerusalem and seen British arrogance drive wedge after wedge between different peoples, never mind who suffers. I've lived in New York and San Francisco, scraping together the cash to feed, clothe and house my family. I've worked every minute that God sends, I've paid my dues and supported my son through efforts I could never have made in 2,000 years. And now, here it is: this beautiful concerto, come to light after years of suppression, and my boy will give it its best chance. But, oh no. Everything is scuppered, the dates are changed and changed again, I won't tell you how much the rescheduling has cost – and what's more, Yehudi has had to let people down, which he would *never* do, including the best concert hall in the US of A – and all because Miss Jelly d'Arányi says the Schumann concerto is hers *becausea Ouija board told her so*! When the concerto is listed in the encyclopaedias and the history books and always has been, and *anybody* could have found it if they'd looked!'

There was a silence while Jelly worked out how to reply to this diatribe.

'What are you asking me to do?' she ventured, finally.

'Obviously,' said Moshe, 'you should consider whether you wish to go ahead with that concert.'

Jelly kept still and met his gaze. 'Would you save a beloved friend's life only to see him taken prisoner? I know Yehudi will play it well, but that concerto is not home again until it is here with me.'

'I have no idea what you're talking about.'

'Then I'll put it plainly. I will not cancel my concert. I will never give up my Schumann.'

When Adila opened the front door, despondent after seeing the Palmstiernas' packing cases piled high in the library at Portland Place, all was quiet. Jelly's coat and hat were on the stand. Upstairs, her suitcase lay open on her bed. She must be home; she'd unpacked. She'd changed her shoes.

'Sai?'

Adila strode down to the kitchen. An egg – boiled – stood uneaten in a porcelain cup. The pantry door was open; the lid was off the cake tin and a chunk of cake had gone.

'Sai! Where are you? What's going on?'

She stumped back to the ground floor. Jelly wouldn't have gone out without her coat. The drawing room and dining room were deserted. In the Green Room, on the velvet chaise longue, she found nothing but an upturned book, which belonged to Alec.

Only the music room was left. Two cups sat abandoned on the coffee tables. The picture of Sep Kelly was in the wrong place. A figure in a brown skirt and fawn blouse lay prostrate on the rug.

Adila plummeted down beside her. 'Sai! Speak to me!'

'Adi?' Her voice was weak.

'You're alive! Darling, what happened? Did you faint?'

She half helped, half hauled her sister towards the sofa, where Jelly slumped with her head down over her knees.

'Menuhin,' Jelly muttered.

'Sai, you are raving. You think *Menuhin* was here?'

'Not Yehudi. His father. He sat just there.'

'What did he say to you, this man?'

'I'm not sure. I can't remember... When he'd gone I took some of my painkillers, the really strong ones. Several. They calm me down.'

Adila made for the telephone.

'Adi, I'm all right, I don't need a doctor.'

'What did he say to you?'

'I don't know... he wants me to give up my concert... he says I'm washed up, no good anymore and apparently it's all my fault – the scheduling, the Nazis, Schumann being – I don't know, Schumann being imprisoned by the devil... All because of something I said or did to try and save him and myself, and –'

'Hush, you're talking gibberish. When did he leave?'

'I don't know what happened until you came in.'

'Let's put you to bed and I call the doctor. Come, now.'

Jelly managed the stairs and crumpled onto her bed the moment Adila had flung her suitcase off the covers. It couldn't be clearer: she was finished. Tipped over, all washed up, fit for nothing but incarceration. Scenes flew behind her eyelids. Schumann, seeking oblivion in the Rhine, then buried alive in the asylum at Endenich; his concerto, passing from Robert to Clara to Jo and then, abandoned, into the library; and her old self, everybody's darling little Hungarian, now ailing and vilified in a world she could no longer recognise. She thought of the concerto, alone and on the fringes, with a last chance to prove its worth. And if that image was what had made her reach for the painkillers, she could no longer remember.

The doctor decided against sending Jelly to hospital. She

had not taken a serious overdose; most of the problem was simply that she was overwrought. She needed a good rest.

'I can't,' Jelly said. 'It's the Schumann on the 16th... And I'm meant to work with Myra this week.'

She closed her eyes. Never had she longed so much for silence; never had silence seemed so loud. The quieter her surroundings, the stronger the roar from the gathered forces within.

Adila placed something on the pillow by Jelly's right ear. Her free hand closed around it. Silk, buttons, wool. Odd shape, strangely familiar. A doll, one of Adi's, that she'd stitched clothes for as a little girl. Brought all the way from Budapest, long, long ago.

Chapter 18

Myra's concession to Jelly's crisis was to come to Chelsea to rehearse a few days later, which should give Jelly a chance to pull herself together. 'The show must go on,' Myra declared. 'Nothing like good hard work to take your mind off things. Are you feeling a little better about the Schumann?'

'I think the broadcast is going ahead, at least.' Jelly tried to stay positive.

'You couldn't have a finer orchestra or conductor, and I'm sure it will be an astonishing evening,' Myra encouraged. 'It's almost sold out, I hear.'

Jelly decided to sit down for their rehearsal. She needed to lower the music stand to the right level; it took her three goes because her right arm hurt so much when she tried to twist the keys.

'Did you perhaps fall on that elbow?' Myra asked. 'The time you hurt your back?'

'I don't think so.'

'And you still don't know what's wrong?'

'Not really. I'll do my best,' Jelly assured her. The bigger problem, which she did not want to explain, was that sometimes her arm hurt, sometimes it didn't, but even if it was working she still felt afraid that it might not; and the effect of that diminished confidence could be almost as bad as the physical pain. 'Sometimes I don't know where my brain stops and my body begins,' she admitted.

They were working on Beethoven's 'Kreutzer' Sonata. In the opening bars, the violin plays unaccompanied.

'Try again,' said Myra.

Jelly tried; then shook her head.

'Shouldn't you be seeing somebody about the arm?'

Jelly rubbed her elbow. 'Every doctor I see says something different.'

'Yes... well, if it's any comfort, I feel fairly awful myself.'

'You do?' She had rarely heard Myra admit discomfort. 'Whatever is the matter?'

'Down and out in London over Berlin. Every time I see a news report, I sink one more notch.'

'Do you think we'll have a war?'

'My fear is that we won't have one soon enough. Do you know, Sai, if I were still myself, but I'd been born in Germany instead of here, I'd have lost my citizenship. I wouldn't be permitted to vote. There'd be a J stamped on my identity card. I might be thrown in jail on some trumped-up charge, or they might force me to emigrate. The fact that I have a brain, or that I can play the piano, or that people like my concerts, or that I am a good citizen – none of that would count.'

'But none of that's happening to you,' said Jelly. 'You're not German, you're English.'

'I'm not *English* English, am I? I have a German name. People are noticing that today. They're suspicious. And I'm Jewish; they're noticing that too. I fear there would be plenty of support here for the Reich's racial policies.'

'They accuse me too, because I'm foreign and I have a strange accent and name. But you are of course English!' Jelly insisted.

'And supposing I wished to be both English and Jewish, as I always have been and as I feel I am?'

'But can't you choose, then, that you're English rather than Jewish?'

Myra exhaled, leaning forward against the piano. 'I think you're missing the point. Look, if this can happen in Germany, the most cultured country in Europe, then it can happen here as well. There are signs. You've seen them too.'

'Perhaps some, but... ' The local restaurant in which she had lunched with Ulli had redrawn its 'No foreign produce' sign:

it was now three times the size, written in black block capitals. 'It all adds up.'

'Yes indeed, and if this vile philosophy takes hold, or if Hitler invades and we can't repulse him, I don't think I wish to live to see that day.'

Jelly rushed to hug her. 'You mustn't say things like that! I don't see why you should ever say you're Jewish if you don't want to.'

'Jelly, sometimes I don't know if you're actually anti-Semitic or just impossibly naïve.' Myra extricated herself from Jelly's embrace.

'But I'm almost Jewish myself,' said Jelly, stung. 'I wanted to go to Berlin to find the manuscript and Donald wouldn't let me.'

'Tell me, are you still seeing that German boy?' Myra's expression was contemptuous.

'I was never *seeing* him... I've only ever met him a couple of times. And he is *not* a Nazi.'

'You're still in touch?'

'Only by letter, and sometimes we speak on the telephone, but... actually I don't know where he is. He was going to phone me, but he has not... '

'I don't know how you could even contemplate a relationship with a German now.'

Was she not hearing Myra properly, or was her pianist the one refusing to listen? Picking up her violin, Jelly pretended she wasn't smarting within. How could Myra ever think her anti-Semitic? And Ulli would never espouse this madness, would he?

'Let's play.' Myra opened her volume of Schubert on the first page of the Duo in A major. A few pages in she stopped. 'No, you're late! Listen to my *left* hand here. You need to be together with the bass line. You can't just drift about up there like a bumble bee.'

'Sorry,' said Jelly. 'Once more again.'

'*Listen*, Jelly. You've got ears. Use them!'

'My arm… '

'Oh, my dear, this isn't like you. Is your arm affecting your brain, or is it the other way around? I've never known anyone's playing to tumble down so quickly.'

Jelly's innards crumbled. She was sure Myra had no intention of hurting her. Indeed, her words were all too true.

Myra fetched a handkerchief for her. 'You *must* get the better of this. You can't give in. You're not the only person in the world with a sore arm or vultures in the press – it will all pass, you know… You don't need to panic. Breathe deeply.'

Jelly tried; it was harder than her friend seemed to think, especially since the Schumann performance was nearly upon her and her arm had to be better in time, and supposing it was not?

'It's all right,' Myra soothed her. 'I know it's difficult, but you need to get a grip. I do wonder why your sister and her friend insisted on pushing the "spirit messages" source forward to such a degree. That's what's really upset you, and surely there was no need. An unknown concerto by Schumann is quite big enough news by itself.'

'I wish I'd never heard of it. I wish Clara had burnt the manuscript while she could.'

'Don't let it get out of proportion. Remember, Sai, it's one piece. Of course we revere great music. Of course it's what we live for. But think how lucky you are, Jelly, and I too. Most single women with artistic careers are living on the margins of things. We are both unusually successful and unusually fortunate. So let's be clear: in the end, it's just a piece of music.'

A line from one of Ulli's letters came to Jelly. Nothing is ever 'just' a piece of music.

'In a way, it isn't,' she said. 'I know it sounds strange, but it feels like our last chance, the Schumann's and mine together. In a way, the concerto is me.'

Myra was quiet, shoulders bowed. Jelly could sense her

mix of concern and exasperation. Myra the woman was worried about her friend; but Myra the musician had work to do.

'Now, look,' said Myra. 'I'm going to go home and leave you to get some rest. That's what you need most. Call me when you feel better.'

She gathered up her music into its case and gave Jelly a kiss. Jelly, immobile, watched her reach up for her raincoat on the stand, fasten it, then disappear into the day. There came a brightening of light as the front door opened, and a darkening as it closed behind her.

Jelly was lying on the music-room sofa an hour later, drifting in and out of consciousness, when she heard Adila's step on the front stairs and the clink of a key in the lock. With Myra's departure, her panic had quietened; she wept, then slept. And in that space of her awakening, through the brief clarity of her mind, something began to take shape. Something prompted by Myra's words, reinforcing the review of Erik's book in *The Listener*: an understanding that she'd always rejected because she relied on nobody more than her sister.

Adila's certainty, her conviction – with Erik, of course – that the 'glass game' was all it seemed. Adila's pride as she told everyone they had been receiving messages from Schumann. Adila bringing over the crassest of journalists to meet her at the book launch, convinced that only good could come of it. She meant to help; she was so genuine and guileless that she could see no alternative agenda to her own, whether or not it bore any relation to empirical fact. Had Jelly perhaps depended too much on her for guidance, and trusted to excess her confidence on daily matters and glass-game messages alike? She could stay silent; it would be kinder. Yet if she only wondered and worried, nothing would be aired, resolved or changed.

'Myra's been and gone?' Adila surmised now, glancing at the open piano.

'I'm not playing well, so she went home.'

'Oh, what rubbish. She's in a bad mood. I'm sure it's nothing to do with you.'

Jelly tried to begin her question, and faltered.

'What's the matter?' Adila planted herself down beside Jelly.

'Adi… Erik's book review – '

'That bloody nonsense in *The Listener*?'

'He said these messages might come from our subconscious, from things we've forgotten we knew.'

'Rubbish. How would this reviewer man know? He wasn't there.'

'You were close to Onkel Jo. You lived in his house. Are you absolutely sure he never said anything to you about a Schumann violin concerto?'

'I told you, he never said a word.'

'But *are you sure*? Because perhaps he did, and you forgot.'

'The first message didn't come to me. It came to you.'

'But supposing you told me, when I was still a little girl, and I forgot too? People do forget. Even Donald forgets sometimes. Look at Elisabeth and the trouble we've had with *her* forgetting.'

'Yes, yes, of course people forget. But I would have remembered. I would.'

'Can you be certain? It's 30 years since he died.'

'You want me to remember now whether in 1907 I forgot something I didn't know I had to remember?'

'Can you be sure?' Jelly swung herself upright and made for the shelf where Alec kept the family Bible. She slid it out and, grasping it with both hands, extended it towards her sister. 'Adi, swear to me, hand on *this*, that there is no chance Onkel Jo ever told you anything about a Schumann concerto.'

The gold-embossed words HOLY BIBLE shone up at Adila. 'Jelly, are you insane?'

'Perhaps, but I need you to do this. Go on.'

'Darling… '

'You can't do it, can you?'

'It's more than 30 years ago.'

'You can't swear.'

'How can I? It's too long ago.'

'Oh, Adi... so, you *can't* be sure?'

Adila breathed. 'No, Sai. I can't be sure. I wish I could.'

Jelly lowered the book. 'Then how will we ever know if the messages were real?'

'Of course they were real. You saw them come through, with your own eyes.'

'But how will we ever know if they're from spirits, or from our subconscious, or some form of both, which is what Donald thinks, or if there's some completely different explanation... ?'

'You've read Erik's book. You know every word is true. I took down the messages and I interpreted them. What do you want me to do? Pretend I've not experienced anything because it suits the newspapers? Or – ' A glint of understanding crossed Adila's face. 'Is this really about you hating Erik?'

Jelly recoiled. 'I don't hate Erik. But I'm not sure how much I trust him.'

'What is this all about? Jealousy?'

This wasn't where she'd wanted this talk to go. Now that it had, she must see it through. 'Adi, what is it with Erik, really? Are you in love with him?'

Her sister kept her cool – as if, Jelly thought, she had worked out her response long ago for just such an eventuality. 'We are friends. Colleagues. We share this project; he depends on me for it. You of all people know what it's like when you work with someone who is on the same wavelength.'

'I think you're in love with him and you can't admit it. I think the whole project – the messages, the book, the concerto – it's so you could have something to do together, something to work on that was yours and his.'

Adila, her eyes wide, surveyed Jelly, then began to laugh. 'Oh, Sai... What do you want me to do? Give him up?'

'I don't know.'

Her sister stopped laughing and turned ferocious. 'Many things I don't know. I don't know where the messages come from. I don't know why I can channel them. I don't know why people scorn one's experience, when one has more experience than they have. But one thing I do know: *Erik is non-negotiable.*'

'Only people you love are that important,' Jelly said.

'And supposing I do love him? Supposing he loves me? What does that mean?'

'It means – ' Jelly felt her face flaming.

'The messengers have told us all we need to know about love. You know what they say? Love has nothing to do with sex. It's beyond that.'

'You ask them about this?'

'Yes, we do, and about true love, and about soulmates.'

'And Erik is your soulmate?'

'I have no idea,' Adila declared, her jaw set.

'But what about Ebba?'

'Ebba is going back to Sweden, alone.'

'She's leaving him?'

'Don't look so horrified. It's the right choice for them both and will make Erik freer to follow his research. Our research.'

'But Adi! *What about Alec?*'

'Oh Sai, you should get this, but you don't. You may be the world's greatest violinist, but in your heart you're a baby. What do you know of real love? Living as a couple for years, building a life together, raising a child? For you it's all about men lusting after you while you fix on your unattainable ideal. You can't get beyond that. There's nothing real about it, there never was, and there never will be.'

Her allies had been dropping away one by one – Anna and Tom by health and fate, and in a special form of anguish Jelly could sense Myra's spirit was now dividing from her own. But Adila?

'Perhaps I should move out,' said Jelly.

Adila's eyebrows lifted. Then she shrugged and said, 'Suit yourself.'

In the silence that followed, Jelly, as if deep underwater, swam to the stairs and found her way to her room.

She had depended on Adila and Alec for her very life. She had been living here as their guest – a family member and an essential part of the household, or so she'd hoped – for nearly a decade. Supposing, just supposing, the unthinkable were to happen? Supposing, no matter what high words Adila uttered, there really had been some kind of... well, what? A ménage-à-trois? Taking place under her nose, all this time, yet she had refused to see it? Now the entire precarious balance of it, assuming it existed, must change, with the Palmstiernas leaving London and Ebba going her own way. What could she do? Was it not better to control her own fate and act now?

Her suitcase still lay in the corner, where Adila had thrown it three days ago. She watched her hands reach into the wardrobe for her clothes, garment by garment, and fold them as if she were going on tour. But where could she go?

She put her remaining allies into a sieve and shook it to see who was left. Hortense had enough problems of her own and would only be exasperated, or worry about taking sides between her sisters. Tovey? His door would be open, but in Edinburgh, and she had rehearsals for the Schumann in London very soon. George was in Dublin. Ulli? In Nazi Germany, if he were still alive and free, and she could scarcely stand to think of the alternative. Anna –

Of course, Anna in Sussex. She darted into the study and tried the telephone. The ringing, insistent, unanswered, jarred her. She let it ring, praying silently for a welcome Scottish greeting.

Nothing. She could try again later, but when was later? Where would she be by 'later'?

Ten days until the concerto. If she couldn't go to Anna's, she could find a hotel for a few days, then perhaps some other friend's until the concert was over, and think again after that. It could wait. This was only life, which wasn't music and therefore didn't matter. Take the music away and what was she? A maiden aunt? A washed-up, middle-aged spinster, mourning a long-dead hoped-for fiancé who might not have married her even if he'd lived? Did she have to accept her lot – any more than the Schumann concerto had to accept the malign judgement of Onkel Jo? Rubbish!

Jelly threw open her window and took a long breath. She'd start again. She only saw herself as a maiden aunt because she lived as one here, in this house. If she were on her own, if she lived at the centre of her own life rather than the fringes of someone else's, she could be free but lonely, as Joachim's motto said, or free but happy, like Brahms. Either way, free to be herself.

She thought of Sep and recited to his memory. 'My name is Jelly d'Arányi. I am the only woman who has ever had my name. I am the only woman who shall ever live my life. And live it I have, and I do, and I shall.'

She still had some money in the bank. What's more, she was still a star. And just this once, she would go to where stars belonged. She would go to the Savoy.

Jelly was halfway down the stairs, suitcases, dress carrier and violin case arranged over shoulders, elbow and knuckles, when Adila thundered up from the kitchen, mouth open in horror. '*Jelly!* What are you doing? Have you gone crazy?'

'As I said,' Jelly laughed, 'I'm leaving.'

Chapter 19

The uniformed, very young porter placed Jelly's larger suitcase on a stand in a corner of the room. 'What's your name, dear?' she asked him.

'John, madam,' he mumbled. Shy, about 14, probably new in the job.

'Thank you for your help, John.' She gave him a tip – his ears reddened – then waited for him to close the door behind him before falling onto the bed, still in her damp coat and shoes. Chaos reigning within, she began to take stock of what she'd done.

Thank heavens the room was warm; back in the Twenties the Savoy had installed central heating, apparently powered by steam. A large, comfortable bed; a shining mirror over the mantelpiece; a wooden desk by the wall, bearing a writing set; brocade draperies patterned with white, cream and grey, all of it in up-to-the-minute *style moderne*, with contrasting grains in the wood panels and forms sleek enough to feel positively aerodynamic. Jelly pulled back the curtain: the view showed her the Thames, glinting back reflections of charcoal and tobacco-coloured clouds. The double-layer window proofed the room against sound and draughts. Funny that it wasn't terribly British to like such windows. In Hungary, if you didn't have them, you'd die of cold in midwinter. In Britain, somehow you were thought wimpish if you minded draughts, however bad they were for your bones.

Perhaps she should move abroad. Somewhere warm. Not Hungary, though. Italy? Ah, Italy. Mediterranean sun, olive trees, fresh basil, ultramarine sky. The land of Botticelli and Titian, warm and dry and healing. Was Mussolini as bad as Hitler? She had no idea. When the Schumann was over, perhaps she'd read up on the situation. Nothing could stop her living the life she chose, if she held to her vision strongly enough. Loneliness. Freedom. Free but happy.

Right now, she felt free but hungry. It was dinner time. The hotel offered round-the-clock room service; she could order whatever she liked. Yet it was quiet up here; too quiet. A busy restaurant might be cheery. Or would it depress her to be there on her own? Would anyone recognise her, and if so, how and why? Would there be praise for her playing, or whispers, pointing fingers and sniggers over spirit messages?

A long-ago voice whispered deep in her memory. She seemed to hear Onkel Jo's voice just as it had been, fresh, clear, a strong tenor that tried to hide the ebb and flow of his Hungarian accent under a brusque Germanicism, the Rs rolled in the throat. She closed her eyes, listened. '*Dear child, I am with you. I love you and I want you to be all right.*'

Can a spirit from earth, held in a living body, go out to meet one that has departed? How do you know what is real and what isn't? Perhaps imagination *is* real? Or perhaps she really, seriously needed some food. She hadn't eaten since breakfast, it had been a dreadful day, and it was getting late. Sometimes she forgot she needed to eat.

She changed into a serviceable long black dress with scooped-out back, threw a silk and lace wrap over it, brushed her hair, put on some powder and lipstick. If fingers were to point, at least she would look good. The drift of dance music on the piano led her in the right direction along the soft-carpeted corridors.

A woman alone in the Savoy restaurant, though, was not as welcome as she had hoped. After all, the waiters didn't know she was a famous musician. The *maître d'hôtel* tried to show her to a table near the door to the kitchens, tucked out of sight of most other diners. She'd have to eat her meal beside the constant coming-and-going of trays, the door opening and closing, the draughts and the shouting of orders, just because she was a woman without a male companion. 'I'm afraid we're rather full, madam,' the *maître d'* said by way of apology, 'and you do not actually have a reservation... '

'I could come back a little later, if the kitchen is still open?' Jelly gave her brightest smile.

'It is entirely up to madam. For how long is madam visiting England?'

'I've lived here for more than 20 years,' Jelly said, smile painted on. 'I'm a musician. I'm playing at the Queen's Hall next week.'

He gave a stiff little bow. 'Perhaps if madam would like to wait for a more comfortable place, I might suggest a cocktail in the American Bar or the lounge, and we will call you when your table is ready?'

'What an excellent thought. Thank you, sir!' Jelly, putting on her theatrical self, set her shoulders back, tilted her neck, flashed her smile, and watched the snobby man recoil slightly under the bolt of charisma. At least she hadn't lost that.

She didn't feel especially hungry any more, only a little dizzy, which wasn't so bad. Making her way into the lounge, where sofas and armchairs lazed under the chandeliers, with low-glowing candles dotted around the tables for evening, she noticed that the resident pianist was remarkably good. Space was less of a problem in here at this hour; she spotted a few older couples, two or three gaggles of businessmen in dinner suits, and in the far corner a silk-gowned group who looked as if they might be sisters. As a single woman, it would be easier to disappear into a generous armchair here than to sit on full view in the Art Deco American Bar. She took the initiative herself, rather than allowing the staff to choose a table for her: 'As close as possible to the piano. And a White Lady please? Thank you so much, that is *won*derful.'

The armchair seemed to fold itself around her, warm and smelling a little of musky pot-pourri; she sat, legs crossed, head leaning back, breathing deeply and listening to 'Smoke Gets in

Your Eyes', a song that usually made her cry. She wasn't going to cry this time. She had to stop her silly habit of bursting into tears at the slightest excuse. She had to grow up. Forty-four was a little late, but it was time, was it not?

The cocktail hit home. Bliss. You had to drink the Savoy's White Lady; the hotel's own barman had invented it, adding Cointreau to gin and lemon juice, and its citrus flowers of coolness and heat could bolster you in an instant. It would carry you back to all the times you'd tasted it before, and beyond that to every occasion when you'd been here in this lounge with Sep, with Tom, with Tovey; with Elgar; and with Bartók, who wanted fresh fruit with his tea instead of scones and was overjoyed to find bananas there, since he couldn't get them in Hungary. And you'd laughed and flirted and never thought of the future, and if now and then a whisper passed through your mind hinting that this life was too good, that the fairytale had to come to an end sometime, you'd ignore it as pessimism, or simply nuff and stonsense.

Her cocktail was finished; she ordered another. The pianist glanced across at her and she saw a flicker of recognition behind his spectacles. And then she knew him: of course, he'd played at the baron's party. She'd spoken to him at length. He'd told her about Germany and his family's persecution; he'd been praying that his wife and children could join him. That was several years ago. Now here he was, playing in the Savoy.

'Miss d'Arányi?' he said, his fingers still moving through the notes.

His name came back to her. 'Bernhard Rabinovich! How *are* you?'

Something in him had unfolded a little since last time. 'Very well, thank you. It's a privilege to play for you tonight.'

'I'm *so* happy to see you. And you're *here*! A wonderful job, congratulations.'

'Thank you, I've been lucky.'

'Tell me: your family... are they with you now?'

'*Gott sei dank*,' he smiled, 'they are. You are kind to ask.'

'How wonderful – and are they all right? Are *you* all right?'

'Sometimes,' he said, playing a flourish, 'I think there really is somebody up in heaven, taking care of us. Yes, they are well and we have been fortunate with the kindness of people we've met here.'

'It must have been incredible to see them when they arrived.'

'I met them from the boat train at Victoria.' Bernhard gave the warmest smile she had yet seen him venture. 'I think I shall remember that moment when I am dying. They came towards me through the steam, and I knelt and held my arms out to them. And I thought the children would not know me, so long it was we had been apart – but they ran to me... and we make a vow together: nothing will ever, ever separate us again.'

Jelly wiped a tear from her eye. 'No wonder you're playing so beautifully. Please, let me buy you a drink when you take a break?'

'Let me play something for you.' Bernhard finished the song with a flourish that floated from end to end of the keyboard, then launched without a break into a Brahms Hungarian Dance. Restless syncopation, long phrases in six bars rather than four, intermediary flourishes like flames flickering in a Gypsy fire by night. Jelly's feet wouldn't keep still.

Her arms were empty of the one thing she needed. 'Don't stop, I'm coming straight back,' she told Bernhard, leaving her shawl on her chair.

Her violin was under her bed upstairs. It wouldn't take long to fetch it; and she'd brought a sheaf of music, too, with piano parts, having no intention of going to Chelsea any time soon to pick up more. She grabbed the lot from her room and, on her way back down, ignored the curious glances of the boy who worked the lift and the waiter who controlled the lounge entrance. Switching on her performance self, she seemed to grow to match the size of the rest of the world.

'May I?' she said to Bernhard, by the piano. She opened her violin case; glancing around she noticed a few curious gazes from the businessmen over their drinks.

'An honour, Miss d'Arányi.' He seemed unfazed, playing with one hand, reaching with the other for the piano parts she offered him.

Jelly didn't need the music. She knew all the melodies as if they inhabited her body. Bernhard followed her easily and his sense of rhythm soon matched hers. She joined in the first Brahms dance; then another. Onkel Jo and the young Brahms had taken the Hungarian melodies from a hotel café band; now Jelly and her unexpected companion were giving them back.

Surprised heads were turning at the tables across the lounge; rustles of silk sounded as the group of sisters rose to move closer to the music. Others followed suit. Floorboards gave the gentlest of creaks as motion spread, rippling like a mystery signal through a shoal of fish. She heard her name conveyed in a half-whisper. A young man slipped out of the room and returned a few moments later with two companions. Jelly closed her eyes and played on. 'All right?' she asked Bernhard; but rarely had any pianist looked back at her with such joy.

She recognised people who'd been eating in the restaurant where the waiter had wanted to hide her away, coming in, drawing closer. Dinner jackets, a curl of cigar smoke, the shimmer of a handkerchief in a breast pocket. Sea-green silk, eau de nil, a bare shoulder. Mouths decked with lipstick, scarlet, floral, open in delight. February and the snow was gathering high above them, ready to fall, but in here Jelly could feel sweat gilding her nose.

'Could you open a window, please?' she asked the nearest person with a smile. Word went round. A window opened; then another. Theatregoers returning from the performance of Karel Čapek's *Power and Glory* next door glanced through, paused at the sight and sound of the musicians, then came in. Her message was changing as it spread through the room. The violinist wanted to open all the windows. The violinist wanted to open all the doors. Jelly d'Arányi, she of the cathedral concerts, the Pilgrimage of Compassion. She wanted to open the doors of the Savoy Hotel and let in the world.

'And so we will,' decreed the night manager.

The doors opened on to the Strand. A free concert by Jelly d'Arányi, happening now! Come in out of the snow. Warm yourself by the fire of her presence.

Jelly sidled towards her pianist.

'What's going on?' he said. More and more people were filing into the lounge, many in boots and overcoats, murmurs of surprise and wonderment rumbling among them.

'I don't know,' said Jelly, 'but I like it. Can you sight-read this Hubay?'

'I'll try.'

Jelly's old teacher, Jenő Hubay, took Gypsy songs and made them into concert arrangements, following in Brahms and Joachim's footsteps. *Hejre Kati* was more than a little bit suggestive, but the audience in the Savoy didn't need to know that. Jelly invited them all with the sweetness of her sound, then snapped into the fast section, and Bernhard at the piano laughed aloud as he played. For the length of this piece, they could all share the present and rediscover the zest for living that they'd lost, or forgotten, or put on hold. Rushes of cool air betrayed the door opening and reopening; dark figures milling towards them, closer than before as the room surged with listeners, and Jelly wanted to hug them all; she sent her embrace into her music and hoped they could hear it there. They whirled the piece to its end and she whisked her bow up into the air with a shout.

Applause crashed back at her, and she couldn't see the Savoy any more for the people inside it, some still with snowflakes melting on their lapels, hats cradled under their arms while they clapped. How many? Several hundred, surely? How had the Savoy accepted this? How on earth – ?

'Jelly, my dear,' came a familiar tone, and there, elbowing

his way forward, was Sir Adrian Boult himself. 'Whatever are you doing?'

'I could ask you the same thing, darling,' Jelly cried, pressing his hand. 'This is Sir Adrian Boult, the great conductor,' she shouted to the crowd. 'We perform together next week, at the Queen's Hall!'

'We will all be there to hear you,' came a reply from somewhere in the throng, and Jelly, remembering Erik reporting a spirit message of those very words before Westminster Abbey, laughed aloud.

'I was just having a quiet dinner with my wife, Ann,' Boult told her, 'when I heard a violin sound that seemed strangely familiar. I'd know your tone anywhere, Jelly. Now, I don't know what you're up to, playing here, my dear, but you're extremely pale. Have you eaten?'

'No,' Jelly beamed. 'I'm far too busy.'

'You can tell me all about it in a little while. Come and join us for dinner, I beg of you.'

Jelly bent to put the Bergonzi back into its case. As she straightened up, the room began to fill with odd, dancing grey dots. She had just enough consciousness left to wonder how they got there.

When she came round, she was in her bedroom and a first-aider from the St John's Ambulance Brigade was rubbing her right hand, which ached, but for once in a good way. Boult was pacing up and down near the window and the manager of the Savoy himself was beside the bed, asking her how she was feeling.

'She hasn't eaten,' Boult cut in. 'I am sure we can fix her with nothing more elaborate than a jolly good meal. Now, my wife is waiting downstairs in the restaurant…'

'Sir Adrian, leave it to me. I will arrange everything.' The manager took his leave and strode away.

Jelly tried to laugh, but she felt too dizzy to sit up.

'Your sister is coming, my dear,' Boult said. 'I've telephoned her.'

'Oh, but – Adrian, you don't understand.'

'I understand perfectly. They'll come, we'll all eat and they'll take you home.'

'*Nooo!* I'm here because I wish to be, I need to be independent… '

'Yes, yes, you may be. You may be, and do, and go, anywhere you wish. *But not until after we've played the Schumann.* All right? I refuse to see you go off the rails. You may want to, but I won't let it happen.'

'I'm not off the rails. I've never been so happy in my life!'

'That,' said Boult, 'is exactly what I mean.' He sat beside her and kept his voice low. 'Do you know how this begins to happen to musicians? They drink. They drink alone. Then they take too many of the wrong pills, the morphine, the barbiturates, and they lose the thread out of the labyrinth. Some never find it again. Now, as long as I have anything to do with it, this is not going to happen to you. If need be, I shall kidnap you myself. But the person best able to look after you is your sister, and you know that as well as I do.'

John, the red-eared little porter, came in carrying a china cup and saucer. 'Miss d'Arányi, madam, my auntie in 'ousekeeping says this'll sort you out good and proper. A nice cup of tea with some sugar in it, right?'

'Thank you, John. That's so kind.' Jelly propped herself up to sip it, and sure enough, no drink had ever tasted more delicious, not even the White Lady. After a minute, the sugar reached her bloodstream and the room's revolutions settled into quieter orbit.

'*Jelly!*'

Adila was there, in a rush of blue silk and black coat. She

swooped on Jelly and gathered her into her arms. Boult made a tactful retreat.

'You silly girl, where've you been?' she boomed. 'What are you doing here? We've been worrying ourselves into *the ground*!'

'I've been playing the violin in the lounge. They all loved it.'

'I bet they did. Now, listen. Why are you doing this?'

Jelly didn't know where to begin. She had underestimated her own sister – and Adila, as she should know by now, was not a woman one should ever underestimate. 'Schumann. It's the Schumann, and the messages… I needed so much to get away…'

Adila sat back, thinking, then bent close. 'Listen. We won't ever know what explains them. We'll never be sure. But we have two things: we have them, but more importantly, we have the concerto. If Kulenkampff has played it and Hindemith has arranged it and the Nazis have conscripted it and Menuhin has taken it and someone else has done it in Jerusalem and some idiots have thrown abuse at you over it, *so what?* Why should that matter? Before the messages, we didn't have the concerto. Now the world has it. And next week you're going to introduce it to Britain. *So there.*'

'Adi, you're incredible,' Jelly snuffled. 'I don't know what I'd do without you.'

'Sai, so are you. You are the blessed one, the goddess, the muse.'

'Oh, what rubbish, darling. Can you ever forgive me?'

'There's nothing to forgive. Come along, Sai, we're going to celebrate. Tidy yourself up and come down to the restaurant. Alec is there with the Boults, waiting for us. You're here, you're with us and we will never let you go. Later you're coming straight home and tomorrow you're going to practise that concerto knowing that it's going to go down in history, observed by all of this world and the next. Yes? Promise me?'

'Yes, Adi, I promise.'
'For me, Sai. Play it for me.'
'I already am,' said Jelly.

Ulli Schultheiss wondered if it was worth ironing his shirt. Normally he would not be seen in public without everything perfectly placed: collar, cufflinks, jacket. But now he had to be selective, and fast. Nobody knew his plan. Everything must fit in one briefcase, a largish one, but a briefcase nonetheless. One shirt. A change of underwear and socks. His belt was buckled on its tightest setting, since he'd lost so much weight that his trousers would fall down without it. His most comfortable shoes were on his feet, for he would take no others.

He had to move quickly, not only in case danger might be imminent, if someone had followed him, read his mind and intended to stop him leaving, but because if he delayed he might never go through with it. After work he'd bade the Streckers goodnight, the bust of Wagner too, as if this day were no different from any other. Friday was normally his evening with Willy and family; he'd made an excuse about needing to see his mother. It was true enough: he did need to see her, for he had no idea when he ever might again. But he wasn't going there tonight.

He spent an hour and a half cleaning and tidying his flat. He made sure that the books were in alphabetical order; that the sheet music was flat and organised among its dividers; that his Bechstein was closed and covered with a protective blanket. The piano nearly broke his heart. He thought of its voice silenced, its strings untuned; were he never to return, it might be discarded and broken into pieces. Perhaps someone would look after it, though, and save it, and one day he could have it rescued and shipped to... well, somewhere. With evening the electric light inside seemed harsh, the windows and beyond blacker than ever.

He sat down at the table to write to his mother.

Dearest Mutti,

If you are reading this, it means that I am far away and sending it from my destination.

I know how much my decision will hurt you. Please know that I am thinking of you with all my heart.

Aside from living with other people, we have to be able to live with ourselves. I have to feel I can do that. I have tried always to be a person of honour, as you taught me and as my father was. I don't want to disgrace his memory, or you, or my own conscience.

I feel I have recently let down someone who depended on me to help her, and in doing so, let down my own profession, which I can roughly describe, even if it sounds pretentious, as bringing music to people. I want to make amends of some kind to this lady, who has inadvertently changed my life. This is not what you may think, but it's no less crucial to me for that.

I need to recapture anything that remains of my own integrity. That's all we have in the end, the only thing that can steer us through, no matter what the world throws at us. When the tide turns, if we are still on this earth, I will come back to you.

Please grant me your blessing and your forgiveness.

He just had time for a quick sandwich before the train. He was smearing on the last of the butter when the telephone rang. He paused, heartbeat choking him. Would it look more suspicious to answer it, or not to? He picked up.

'*Nah, Ulli!*' His mother, after all.

Somehow he managed to feign normal conversation. She told him about her lunch with her sister, wondered what to cook for Sunday lunch, wanted to know if he would be there. 'I can't,' said Ulli. 'I have to go to Frankfurt.'

'When are you going?'

'Actually, now. My train is in one hour.'

'When are you back?'

'I don't know exactly.' That, too, was true.

'Phone me when you can, then,' said his mother.

'I will,' Ulli promised, trying not to think or feel or fear.

'All right, dear, 'til soon, then.' A click. Silence.

It was time to leave. No more words, no more consideration: only to act. Ulli stowed the letter in an inside pocket in his jacket, close to his heart. He pulled on his coat and hat, put away the last coffee cup, switched off all the lights. He locked up as he did every time he went away for a work trip. The Streckers would be shocked when he did not appear at the office, but he had to trust that inwardly they would respect his decision. Outside, he turned his back on the block and walked swiftly, head lowered against the cold wind, thinking vaguely about how much he would miss his bicycle.

En route to the station, he passed the conservatoire; he remembered watching Hans Gál and his family treading the same route five years earlier. All the Jewish staff members had gone now, heaven knew to where; watching them go, or recognising that they simply weren't there any more, he had never imagined that he, too, would someday bid his home farewell, possibly for a long time. It wasn't as if he had to leave, unlike them. But since facing down Goebbels' committee on behalf of Jelly, Ulli was a different man. He could not sleep, had been growing thin and gaunt, and felt petrified at the sight of every unopened letter and the ring of every telephone; and he had searched deep inside the forest paths of his own mind. To retreat, to keep invisible, that was not enough. To live under fascism would destroy him, perhaps send him as insane as Schumann had been. He had to stand by his conscience. That alone could lead him and let his theme transform, breaking free, out into the light, like Schumann's Polonaise.

In London, assuming he could get there – he was by no means certain he could – he must explore every contact he had. He'd phone Tovey first, and Jelly, with trepidation. She had no idea of his plan, since he had told no one. Perhaps she would not speak to him; he wouldn't blame her if she didn't. But even if nothing came of that, even if all his friends there rejected him outright, even if internment as an enemy alien might follow, he would still be able to hold up his head and declare his lessons learned, his fears conquered and his mind at peace with his higher self. He would have done the right thing.

Ulli stood on the station platform and listened for the screech and rattle of the arriving train.

Chapter 20

Backstage at the Queen's Hall, Jelly unzipped the dress carrier that held her Schumann gown by Edward Molyneux. From her working-woman self in white silk blouse and tweed skirt, she had to become once more Jelly d'Arányi, violin star, muse to Ravel, Bartók and sometimes Elgar, great-niece to Joseph Joachim and chosen one of the blessed spirits. Or something. Preparing for the culmination of the strangest five years of her life, her mind remained resolutely earthbound. The dress was divine: white and silver lamé, with capacious shoulder puffs.

Jelly shimmied into the gown, pushing her arms through layers of silk. Material slid like buttermilk over her hips and down towards her ankles. Her throat rose from the neckline, dark against the dress's shimmer, and her fingers, sore in the February chill – oh, these accursed British dressing rooms – found the zip and slid it upwards. She took the Bergonzi and tried a few passages. The puffs played her their signature tune, rustling along like the turning of a hundred pages.

She always took her violin to dress fittings. Except this one. Surely she knew by now what she needed from a concert dress? Evidently not. After all that fuss, she was at last to play the Schumann, in one hour's time, and her silly dress was going to make a noise?

A tap on the door and Adila was there, lauding her in baritone Hungarian. 'Sai! You look good enough to eat.'

'Adi, it's a disaster. Listen to this… Rustlerustlerustlerustle!'

'Nonsense, darling.' Adila grabbed her hands and rubbed them hard. 'Nobody will hear it.'

'I will. Adrian will. And the orchestra will, and they'll die laughing.'

'They won't. They're on your side, you know they are.' The rehearsal that morning had flown by without a hitch; musi-

cian after musician came up to Jelly to exclaim on the excitement
of playing an unknown piece by Schumann, the beauty of the
Andante, the stateliness of the Polonaise. It had gone too well for
a dress rehearsal, the music shining out into the empty hall while
Adrian, Jelly and the orchestra pulled together as strongly as if
steering a new ship into its maiden voyage. If it had gone badly,
she'd be happier now.

'Don't be superstitious,' Adila ordered. 'You'll be fine. Now,
let's get your make-up fixed and your hands warm.'

'Who's here?' Jelly let Adila help her with her stage look, as
Adila loved to do on important occasions.

'Everyone. Erik is proud as punch. He and Alec have been
at the champagne already. Adri's here, the school let her come
back specially and she's *so* thrilled. Ralph has brought Titi, and
they're actually coming to our place later.'

'Myra?'

'She has a concert of her own, but she rang to send you her
love.'

Jelly closed her eyes and let Adila brush a light-gold shadow
over their lids. 'George?'

'There's a telegram. She's travelling in France, but she's
sending you all her love too. Anna called to say she'll come if
there is no snow today. But I think in Sussex, there *is* snow... '

'The Joachims, perhaps?'

'If Elisabeth is here, she hasn't told me. Perhaps she *forgot*...
'

'Jelly, *I'm* here.' Tovey was in the doorway, leaning against
the frame and wiping a tear from the corner of his eye at the
sight of her.

'Donald!' Jelly jumped out of her chair and cascaded across
the room to him. He flushed nearly as purple as the Savoy porter.
'You found your tickets?' She had booked complimentary seats
for him.

'Yes, thank you, my dear, and I have a friend with me. I

think you may find many unexpected friends here tonight, visible and otherwise. See how far you've come? You've turned an old academic codger like me into a mystic believer and yourself into a heroine.'

'But I've made an almighty mess for everyone and they've all told me so.'

'Ah, but that's where you're wrong. You see tonight as an end, but it's a beginning. This concerto has come back to life because of you, whatever anyone says, and violinists are going to play it, love it and understand it better for generations to come. That's thanks to you. You've achieved something everyone wants. Call it, if you like, immortality.'

Jelly pondered his words for a moment. She had never looked for that, merely for a slightly longer lifespan on the concert platform; it was a strange idea, one that might mean little if Herr Hitler could not be restrained from his military ambitions for ever. Besides, she felt that just now she would trade any amount of immortality for one word from Ulli Schultheiss. It was several months since his last phone call. Today no card had arrived, no letter, no telegram. Willy Strecker had wired a message, but Ulli had not signed it. She let herself imagine, for an instant, another type of world, one in which a German man and a partly Jewish woman, older than he was, could meet unencumbered, laugh together, dance the tango, play Schumann, and goodness knows what else, without the English Channel, mad governments and prejudiced societies to stop them.

Instead, should she take all that unborn feeling and sink it in the sea? She chose: she would not. She couldn't mourn a formless love; she'd already mourned too many others. There could be another way to look at it: perhaps it didn't matter if people she loved weren't physically there. Presence, as Tovey suggested, exists in other forms.

And the messages? What was the truth? The subconscious, or Schumann's spirit? Jelly chose again: Schumann's spirit. On the same principle as Ulli's.

She opened her eyes and assessed her reflection, awareness glinting out of her dark irises. She had to be no more tonight than the active component of her violin. No extraneous emotion – and no rustling dress – must upset the flow from Schumann's mind to the audience's. A musician is the truest medium there is. She, her technique and the Bergonzi were his channel now from world to world.

She let her sister massage her hands, one at a time. In the hall the orchestra was warming up; some overture was opening the programme, she couldn't remember which. She tried to blot out all that was extraneous, all that was physical. The concerto existed in sound alone, nothing that could be seen, claimed and owned. Everyone wanted to pierce it with a pin and fix it to a velvet board, but it belonged to everybody and nobody. It was the sum total of all that had passed: imagined by Schumann, nurtured by Clara, fired up by Brahms, twisted by Onkel Jo, guarded by all those gatekeepers, meddled with by Goebbels and Hindemith and even perhaps Ulli. Yehudi, she knew, would play it perfectly – so perhaps she and he were allies after all, desiring the best for the work – and whenever it was played, it would be born anew.

'Miss d'Arányi, ten minutes, please.'

Adila stopped the gentle motion of hand to hand. 'All right now, Sai?'

'Wonderful, Adi. Yes, go and find your seat.' Perhaps Adila was rubbing some spell into her bones; the pain was receding, the blood warm and coursing.

'See you later.' Adila kissed her on both cheeks and went.

Alone, Jelly played quietly through the passagework in the Polonaise one last time. Her mind calmed with the motion of her fingers across the strings.

Her call to the stage came; she glided through the familiar corridors. The dress hissed, whispered and crackled; she'd have to live with it. From the wings she could see the orchestra on stage, the curved shore of the ocean of auditorium, a reef of shadowed heads and shoulders. She stood alone for a minute, lost in her thoughts. Many times she had waited on this spot without a breath of fear. How had she ever had such confidence? Her elbow still ached. Would anybody notice? She had to convince everyone that Schumann's state of mind had not affected his music, but now, too, that she was not battling the interlocked spirals of body and mind on her own account. She forced herself to set aside this cacophony of alarm and to begin, instead, to pray. *Dear God, and dear Virgin Mary, and dear Schumann: if you ever give me your blessing, let it be now.*

Adrian was beside her.

'Ready, Jelly?'

'Ready.'

He turned and motioned her onto the stage ahead of him. She crossed herself and stepped out into the light. The wave of applause drenched her like a baptism.

In less than half an hour, it was over. Thomas Hardy, Tom's favourite novelist, once wrote that experience is not as to duration, but as to intensity; the expression drifted into Jelly's mind while she shook Adrian Boult's hand, accepted the flowers that were brought to her, and swished her sweat-soaked dress, puffed sleeves and all, into a deep bow. Some of the audience were standing. She thought she could glimpse Anna at the side of the stalls, snow or none. She couldn't see Tovey, though imagined he'd be holding forth to Alec, or the friend he had brought, in an enthusiastic mini-lecture about why Schumann chose to finish the piece with a polonaise. Nor could she see Adila; she'd be clasping Alec's right hand with her left and Erik's left hand with her right. Jelly could scarcely see at all, so blurred was her vision with tears of relief.

It was done. Now she could begin to let go.

Jelly ushered the throngs of well-wishers and autograph hunters out of her dressing room so that she could change before they went home for the party, for which Adila had been cooking these past three days. Through a tiny window she glimpsed falling snowflakes, generous clumps of them, sliding down from heaven to bless the earth. Her blood was rushing through her so fast that she could scarcely feel her feet touching the ground inside their sensible winter boots.

The rustling dress was back in its carrier, the room cleared of her make-up, violin case and enough bouquets to fill a greenhouse. Even within the hall's corridors there lay a snow-hush, despite a Sibelius symphony blustering through from the distant stage, the music of winter.

At the artists' entrance she paused in the doorway, sniffing the ice in the air, looking for Alec's car. An eiderdown of snow sapped London's colour: a red bus seemed filtered to black and white, a sepia wash of clouded night sky hovered over the sooty façades, while dark silhouettes hustled along Upper Regent Street, anonymous against the whitening pavement. Around her, could she feel the spirits of those who had lived and died and been reborn tonight? In the end, that was all there was: music and consciousness, both eternal.

'Sai, quick! Out of the snow!' came Adila's cry, with the purring of the car engine.

Jelly looked back into the arc of the Queen's Hall entrance, empty but for the ghosts of her concerts. What did it matter if she had lost the world premiere? That was no longer the point. Now, whatever lay ahead, she was ready. No certainty could be greater than the one she had attained.

'I am the only person who has ever had my name. I am the only person who will ever live my life. And live it I have, and I do, and I shall. My name is Jelly d'Arányi and I know that love shall live for ever.'

She blew the Queen's Hall a kiss and took a step towards the car.

'Jelly, wait! It's me... '

She turned. Outlined in the night, a dark figure with hat and overcoat was moving round the curve of the hall towards her, arms outstretched.

Coda

On 1 September 1939, Hitler invaded Poland.

Also in 1939, another previously unknown work by Robert Schumann was finally released to the public. It was a set of solo piano variations on the theme that Brahms had adopted for his own Op. 23 Variations (as played to Jelly by Myra in Chapter 5). It became known as the *Geistervariationen* – Ghost Variations – because Schumann believed the melody had been dictated to him in his sleep by spirits. What Schumann, in his disturbed state of mind, seemed to have forgotten is that he had already written the germ of this melody himself, in the slow movement of his Violin Concerto. He was writing the variations when he made his suicide attempt in February 1854. The day after his rescue from the Rhine, he gave the manuscript to Clara. She preferred to leave it unpublished.

Alexander Fachiri died of pneumonia on 27 March 1939. Devastated, Adila sold the house in Netherton Grove. She and Jelly lived together in a succession of London flats, then moved to Ewelme, Oxfordshire, to escape the Blitz.

Jelly apparently suffered a nervous breakdown in 1939, following Alec's death and some negative reviews of her concerts. Her career flickered on through the 1940s, but her glory days were over. Later the two sisters emigrated to Italy and lived in Bellosguardo, Florence, for the rest of their lives. Adila died in 1962 and Jelly in 1966. Adrienne married an Italian and, like Adila, had one daughter.

Baron Erik Palmstierna went to live with Adila and Jelly. Among other books, he published two further volumes based on spirit messages received with Adila's help. He became chairman of the action committee of the World Congress of Faiths. He died in Adila and Jelly's Italian house in 1959. His daughter Margareta died in 1942, aged 37. Her granddaughter became a celebrated supermodel.

Sir Donald Francis Tovey died of a stroke on 10 July 1940.

His editions of Brahms's symphonies and Bach's *Well-Tempered Clavier*, among others, are still used widely today.

Myra Hess founded a series of daily lunchtime concerts in the National Gallery during World War II, which became legendary for boosting the spirits of Londoners in the Blitz. Jelly performed in several of them, but their duo appears to have foundered. Hess was made a DBE in 1941. She died at her Hampstead home in 1965.

Yehudi Menuhin became an iconic figure in the classical music world and beyond it. At the end of World War II he played to survivors of the Bergen-Belsen concentration camp; thereafter, performing music to people who were suffering, ill or disadvantaged became a lifelong preoccupation. This led him to found the organisation Live Music Now, and numerous other initiatives to assist the training of young musicians. After settling in Britain he took UK citizenship and was ultimately awarded the Order of Merit. He died in 1999.

Georg Kulenkampff left Germany in 1943 in protest at the regime. He died in 1948, aged 50.

Hans Gál moved to Edinburgh after Tovey invited him there to catalogue the university music library. He later became professor of music at the university.

W.B. Yeats died in January 1939 and his wife George in 1968.

Richard Strauss wrote some of his finest works after the end of World War II, when he was in his eighties, including *Metamorphosen* and the *Four Last Songs*.

The Queen's Hall was destroyed by a direct hit during the Blitz in 1941. The Charlottenburg Opera House was destroyed by Allied bombing.

Ulli Schultheiss is fictional, but his moral dilemma is very real. Had he indeed lived, his move to Britain would have seen him interned as an enemy alien, possibly in the Isle of Man, but he might well have joined his principled friends and colleagues in rebuilding British musical life after the war. If only Jelly could have had an Ulli in her life. Perhaps she did.

The Schumann Violin Concerto has overcome its difficult start to become a staple part of its instrument's repertoire – even though in the US, after Menuhin's premiere, it was not performed again for some 23 years. Today, though, some violinists speak of it as perhaps the most personal, exquisite and heartbreaking of all the great concertos.

Author's Note

I first read about the strange history that has become *Ghost Variations* when I was researching my third novel, *Hungarian Dances*. I had found a second-hand copy of *The Sisters d'Arányi* by Joseph Macleod, the sole biography of these remarkable women. A chapter entitled 'The Truth about the Schumann Concerto' contained the whole extraordinary saga.

Of course creating fiction out of real events and people is far from straightforward. I humbly beg forgiveness from 'my' characters' living relatives, should it be the case that I've put two and two together and made seven, and I hope this novel will be accepted in the spirit in which it is offered: the evocation of a vanished world and a tribute to its vibrant inhabitants and their artistry. I hope, too, that it may help to win fresh appreciation for them and for their recorded and written legacies.

It became clear to me, through talking to a number of people who knew Jelly and Adila, that the sisters believed 100 per cent in the 'spirit messages' they were receiving. That others were less convinced is unsurprising. Baron Erik Palmstierna's book, *Horizons of Immortality*, contains transcripts of the messages, as does *The Sisters d'Arányi*.

The hiatus between the arrival of the first 'message' and Jelly's efforts to start looking for the concerto is fictional: it is a chance to explore the conflict between her passion for giving charity concerts, and the pull of so-called 'psychical research', which must have been at odds with her Christian faith (and Adila's). The culmination of Jelly's love for simply bringing music to her audience is the scene at the Savoy – which, along with her fall-out with Adila, is also entirely fictional. The cathedral tour, though, is very much real: Jelly's first cathedral tour in 1933 raised £2,500, including a government grant of £1,000 (the equivalent of around £118,250 in 2016). She gave a further tour in 1934 and in summer 1938 performed a recital at St Paul's Cathedral in London.

Jelly never married. The account of her friendship with Sep

Kelly is based as far as possible on reality. The relationship with Tom Spring-Rice, however, is a matter of reading between the lines in *The Sisters d'Arányi*. The glass-game session with Anna Robertson that produced the first communication from 'Schumann' was inspired, according to Macleod, by the end of a love affair; with whom, we don't know. Tom Spring-Rice, Lord Monteagle, died in a Dublin nursing home in autumn 1934. Macleod makes it clear that Jelly was much affected by his death, mourned him deeply, and sustained a succession of illnesses and injuries at this time. The nature of Adila's friendship with Palmstierna is not documented.

I have it on good authority from Jelly's family that Moshe Menuhin did give Jelly harsh words about her involvement the Schumann concerto, though the precise details of where, when and how are not clear. He has been depicted to me, by those who knew him well, as a difficult, somewhat pugnacious character.

A few of the characters are purely fictional: Ulli Schultheiss, the critic James Gambrell, the pianist Bernhard Rabinovich, Lady Chiltington, Charles and Mary Southern, Fräulein Kammerling, Maria the maid and the journalist Lionel Hartshaw.

The letters from Sir Donald Francis Tovey, Elisabeth Joachim and Eugenie Schumann, plus the published articles mentioned in the novel, are all real (and the reviewer of Palmstierna's book, Harry Price, has been accorded his own TV film). Eugenie Schumann's extended letter was published in *The Times*. Letters to Jelly from Tom and obviously from Ulli are invented.

The meeting between the Streckers, Ulli Schultheiss, Peter Raabe and Goebbels is evidently invented, since Ulli is not real, but many of the arguments in it derive from the Streckers' correspondence about the concerto, outlined in an in-depth study by Ann-Katrin Heimer published in the journal of the Hindemith Institute in Frankfurt-am-Main in 2002. Willy Strecker attended Jelly's performance of the Mozart 'Adelaide' Concerto himself and subsequently helped to unearth the Schumann manuscript, and he did apparently organise a meeting with some powerful officials of the Reich to determine that Schott's, not Breitkopf, should publish the concerto and to argue that Jelly should be accorded the moral right to the first UK performance.

It is possible that a serious rift took place between Jelly and Myra Hess; in Hess's fullest biography by Marian McKenna, Jelly, the pianist's duo partner for some 20 years, is mentioned only once, in passing. Nevertheless, when Hess started work on her National Gallery concerts during the Blitz, she devoted so much time to their organisation that apparently friendships often fell by the wayside. Their break may be as simple as that. Asked what went wrong, Jelly reputedly said only: 'The war.' The wonderful recording of the pair playing the Schubert Piano Trio No. 1 in B flat with the cellist Felix Salmond and the Brahms Piano Trio No. 3, Op. 87, with Gaspar Cassadó remains the only surviving memorial to their musical partnership.

A recording of Adila Fachiri and Tovey playing Beethoven's Violin Sonata Op. 96 in G major is testament to the warmth, rigour and dedication of these two exceptional people. I doubt that my portrait of Tovey can begin to do justice to this towering musical mind, a man of complexity, great personal integrity and true 'heart'.

Even though Jelly lost the concerto's modern premiere to Kulenkampff, and some glory to Menuhin, and was even pipped to the post by the Jerusalem performance in January 1938, without her investigations it would have taken much longer for the work to re-emerge. It may not have been technically 'lost', but it still needed to be found. Along with the many magnificent pieces of music written for Jelly, its resurrection has helped to assure her immortality in the canon of great musicians of the 20th century.

Among the countless individuals I would like to thank are Jane Camilloni, John MacAuslan, Nigel Hess, Steven Isserlis, Lucy Cowan, John and David Gwilt, Rohan de Saram, Chris Latham, Peter and Chris Lockhart Smith and (posthumously) Margaret Lockhart Smith, Tully Potter, Sara Menguc, Fiona

Lindsay, Sally Groves and Bernhard Pfau of Schott Music, Katy Bell and the Orchestra of the Age of Enlightenment, the Hungarian Cultural Centre London, David Le Page, Viv McLean, Philippe Graffin, Sir András Schiff, and my patient family, including my brother Michael and my long-suffering husband Tom. Profound apologies to anyone I may inadvertently have omitted. My deepest thanks, too, to the excellent team at Unbound and to everyone who has pledged support for the book.

Jessica Duchen, London, 2016

Bibliography

These are a few of the principal books and articles on which I've drawn for *Ghost Variations*.

Nora Bickley (selector and translator), *Letters From and To Joseph Joachim*, Macmillan, 1914

Humphrey Burton, *Menuhin*, Faber & Faber, 2000

Juliet Gardiner, *The Thirties: An Intimate History*, Harper Press, 2010

Mary Grierson, *Donald Francis Tovey*, OUP, 1952

Ann-Katrin Heimer, '...*wie sie vom praktischen Standpunkt des Geigers aus notiert werden müsse...* ', Hindemiths Bearbeitung der Solostimme des Violinkonzerts von Robert Schumann, Hindemith-Jahrbuch, Annales Hindemith, 2002/XXXI

Erik Frederick Jensen, 'Buried alive: Schumann at Endenich 1', *Musical Times*, Vol. 139, No. 1861 (March 1998), pp. 10–18.

—, 'Buried alive: Schumann at Endenich 2', *Musical Times*, Vol. 139, No. 1862 (April 1998), pp. 14–23.

Denise Lassimonne and Howard Ferguson (eds.), *Myra Hess By Her Friends*, Hamish Hamilton, 1966

Erik Levi, *Music in the Third Reich*, Macmillan, 1994

Marian McKenna, *Myra Hess: A Portrait*, Hamish Hamilton, 1976

Joseph Macleod, *The Sisters d'Arányi*, George Allen & Unwin, 1969

Rollo Myers, 'Finding a Lost Schumann Concerto: A Recent Discovery based on "Spirit Messages"', *The Listener*, 22 September 1937

Roger Nichols, *Ravel Remembered*, Faber & Faber, 1987

Tony Palmer, *Menuhin: A Family Portrait*, Faber & Faber, 1991

Baron Erik Palmstierna, *Horizons of Immortality*, Constable Press, 1937

—, Widening Horizons, Psychic Book Club, 1940

Tully Potter, *Adolf Busch: The Life of an Honest Musician*, Toccata Press, 2010

Harry Price, 'Quest for Reality – *Horizons of Immortality* by Baron Erik Palmstierna' (book review), *The Listener*, 13 October 1937

Ann Saddlemyer, *Becoming George: The Life of Mrs W.B. Yeats*, OUP, 2002